Michael Arnold lives in Petersfield, Hampshire, with his wife and children. After childhood holidays spent visiting castles and battlefields, he developed a lifelong fascination with the Civil Wars. *Traitor's Blood*, his debut novel, is the first in a planned series of over ten books that will follow the fortunes of Captain Stryker through one of the most treacherous periods of British history. The next three titles – *Devil's Charge*, *Hunter's Rage* and *Assassin's Reign* – available in Hodder paperback.

PRAISE FOR *TRAITOR'S BLOOD*

'Captures the grittiness, as well as the doomed glamour, of the Royalist cause' Charles Spencer

'You can smell the gunpowder and hear the cannon fire . . . Arnold's passion for the period suffuses every page' Robyn Young, author of the *Brethren* trilogy

'A fast-moving, exciting novel . . . Forget Sharpe and enjoy the exploits of Captain Stryker in an earlier and dangerous period of history. Once hooked you will look forward to the next in this series' *Ryedale Gazette and Herald*

Also by Michael Arnold

Devil's Charge
Hunter's Rage
Assassin's Reign
Warlord's Gold
Marston Moor

TRAITOR'S BLOOD

MICHAEL ARNOLD

HODDER

First published in Great Britain in 2010 by John Murray (Publishers)
An Hachette UK Company

Hodder paperback edition 2014

9

Maps by Martin Collins

A CIP catalogue record for this title is available from the British Library

Paperback ISBN 978 1 848 54404 8
Ebook ISBN 978 1 848 54405 5

Printed and bound by Clays Ltd, St Ives plc

Hodder & Stoughton policy is to use papers that are natural, renewable
and recyclable products and made from wood grown in sustainable
forests. The logging and manufacturing processes are expected to
conform to the environmental regulations of the country of origin.

Hodder & Stoughton Ltd
338 Euston Road
London NW1 3BH

www.hodder.co.uk

To John, who always believed it would happen

Late 1642

Royalist territory

Parliamentarian territory

Disputed territory

Neutral territory

Inverness

Aberdeen

Perth

Edinburgh

Newcastle

Carlisle

York

Lincoln

Newark

Chester

Nottingham

Worcester

Edgehill

Colchester

Pembroke

Gloucester

Oxford

Bristol

Brentford

London

Taunton

Basing

Langrish

Portsmouth

Plymouth

N
W E
S

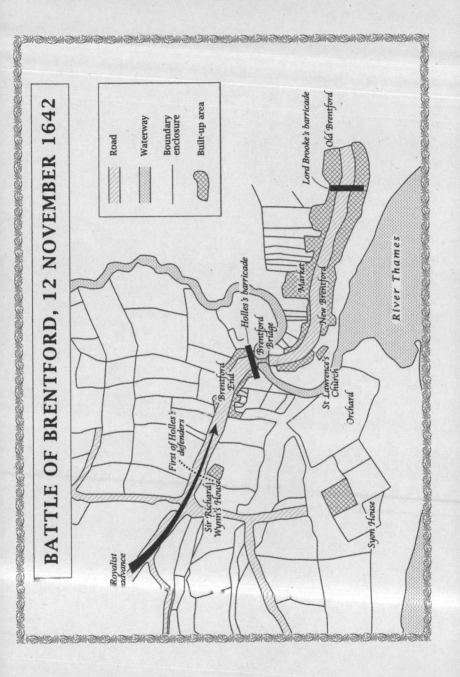

BATTLE OF BRENTFORD, 12 NOVEMBER 1642

Road

Waterway

Boundary enclosure

Built-up area

Royalist advance

First of Holles's defenders

Sir Richard Wynn's House

Brentford End

Brentford Bridge

Holles's barricade

St Lawrence's Church

Orchard

Syon House

New Brentford

Market

Lord Brooke's barricade

Old Brentford

River Thames

PROLOGUE

FEBRUARY 1642

Lisette Gaillard watched the skiff bob into view, waves buffeting its fragile hull. There were three men aboard, sailors who had come from a ship anchored out beyond the dangerous shallows. Three men to transport the most precious cargo imaginable.

'Girl!'

A man and a woman, both wrapped in long, fur-trimmed cloaks, stood behind her. It was the shorter of the pair that had spoken. His fine shoulder-length hair flowed loosely in the wind, and his pinched, shrewish face was white against the elements. His companion was hooded, with only her face exposed to the inclement weather.

'My horse.' The man's voice was querulous and pitched high.

Lisette looked past him, her gaze scanning the ridge beyond the beach where a crowd of mounted figures hovered, their dark forms spectral against the horizon's dying light. She raised a hand and a single rider kicked away from the group, leading a large, white charger behind his own horse down the steep dune.

'Jesu, but it's cold!' the man cursed through gritted teeth.

The woman dipped her chin, hunching against the wind's bite and pulling the cloak's warm ermine-fringed hood further down her brow. She stared at the swirling belts of sand around her feet, brought fleetingly to life by the salty breeze. At length, she looked up and rolled her eyes.

'No matter,' the man murmured quickly, catching her expression. 'Greater trials lie ahead.'

The woman set her lips in a stern line. 'They do, Husband. They should not. But they do.' She sketched the sign of the cross in the space between them. 'If God wills it.'

The man lifted a dainty hand to his chin, thin fingers worrying at the precisely trimmed russet beard. 'God wills such things?'

'Truly. England is a realm of heathens, Husband. Heathens and rebels. God placed you on His great earth to turn that tide. To crush rebellion and to lead the common man back to the true faith.' Her upper lip quivered. 'You did neither. Now you are punished. We,' she hissed, 'are punished.'

He turned abruptly to the sea. Lisette followed his gaze. Did he pray for the cold depths to lurch up and swallow him, she wondered? When he finally turned back, she saw that he kept his eyes fixed on the ivory buttons at the top of his wife's cloak, never summoning the courage to rise beyond the tip of her proud chin.

'I will redeem us, Hetty,' he said quietly.

She nodded. 'You must.'

The sailors were now wading in the shallows, dragging the bucking boat in their wake.

'Your Majesties,' Lisette said earnestly, 'we must depart.'

The queen did not look round. Henrietta Maria, Princess of France and Queen Consort of England, would leave when it pleased her and not a moment before.

The boat would wait. So would Lisette.

'Make haste to your kin,' King Charles said, 'and pray for your husband.'

'Pray, sir?' Henrietta Maria smiled fiercely. 'I shall do more than pray. I will petition my brother and Pope Urban. By the year's end you will have coin and men. Cannon. Horse.' She reached out long fingers to touch the king's cheek. 'My family, the church, they will not abandon you. Nor shall I.'

Charles glanced beyond his queen's shoulder, to where the sailors stood knee deep in the surf. 'I fear for you.'

'Do not, sir. Have strength. You are God's appointed. Chosen by Him and no other. Parliament's jackals cannot touch either of us. Be king, sir,' she said, softly now, pleading. 'For me, if for no other. Be king and lead your country. A monarch must command, my love. Others must follow.' Her mouth twisted, as though tasting rotten meat. 'Puritans. By God they would not thrive so in my brother's land. He crushes them beneath his heel before they would grow in number. Before they infest his kingdom as they infest yours.'

The queen's fingers tightened on Charles's arm. 'Do not fret. All is not lost. Gather your strength, Husband. Call your forces. Destroy the rebellion and prove, at last, that you are your people's rightful liege lord. I will make haste in my mission, sir. And I will return to your side, as God is my witness.'

They kissed, and Lisette marvelled at the tenderness they were unashamed to show.

3

'Come, Lisette,' the queen snapped, as she pulled away.

Lisette bowed and waved to the group that still waited on the ridge. At once a dozen riders, the queen's retinue and the royal children, began walking their mounts down the dusk-veiled beach towards them. At their head was a tall young man with broad shoulders and a perpetually amused gaze. 'Let us reach the safety of the ship before dark, Aunt Henrietta,' he said. His mouth twitched upwards. 'Damned if I am to swim to Holland!'

'Take my arm, Rupert,' the queen commanded. She waded without hesitation into the chilling surf. Lisette followed tentatively, gasping as the water licked up to her knees. In less than a minute the party was aboard the vessel, crammed on to low benches, and the sailors had pushed off.

Lisette Gaillard screwed her eyes shut as a stinging ribbon of spray leapt from one of the oars. She glanced across to her queen. She had not flinched.

As the skiff rode the first choppy breakers, the queen shrugged off Prince Rupert's restraining hands and stood, staggering slightly as her boots fought for purchase on the slick wood.

'Be king!' she cried back to the shore. King Charles raised a hand, then he leapt up on to his horse and urged the beast into a gallop. He headed towards the great cliffs that stood as sentinels, guarding this corner of England against sea-borne foe. Lisette guessed he would watch them until their ship had vanished on the horizon.

Long fingers fastened gently but firmly around Lisette's wrist.

'I am ready to do my duty. Are you ready to do yours?'

Lisette nodded. 'Yes, Majesty.'

Queen Henrietta Maria's eyes gleamed in the fading light. 'Find it. Return it to me. Our lives depend on your success.'

When Lisette Gaillard replied, her voice was a whisper on the winter wind. 'I will not fail you, Majesty.'

CHAPTER 1

It had snowed the previous night; not heavily, but enough to dust the fair-meadow so that its surface crunched beneath latchet shoes and bucket-top boots.

The captain stamped his feet to beat some life back into deadened toes. He squinted across a chaotic scene littered with the debris of torn flesh and shattered weaponry, toward the distant village of Kineton, its thatched roofs obscured by dense rows of pike thrust high above the enemy units. He tried to count the iron-clad heads that gleamed in the wan sun like grey pearls, but the ranks were too deep, the army too vast.

'Hot work!' A voice suddenly split the captain's thoughts like a warship's broadside. 'I said hot work, eh, Captain Stryker? Bloody chilly day, I grant you, but I'd wager Satan's goddamned britches it'll be scorching once the big guns cough!'

Lieutenant Colonel Sir Stanley Balham continued to bellow excitedly through his thin white whiskers as he drew his mare up alongside Stryker. The captain heaved himself up into his own saddle, the big sorrel-coloured beast twitching nervously beneath him, steam rising steadily from its flared nostrils into the cold evening air. 'I was just telling Butterworth that you and the lads have been up to your armpits already.'

'Aye, Sir Stanley, that we have,' Stryker replied, though he had no clue who Butterworth was. The lieutenant colonel's nose wrinkled as he studied Stryker's less than savoury appearance. The captain's buff-coat and breeches were shabby and daubed with crimson patches that hinted at the deaths of several men, while his long hair jutted from beneath the wide brim of a tattered hat in great sweat-darkened clumps.

'Nothing you ain't seen before though, I'd wager,' the older man said gruffly.

Stryker cast his gaze over the chaotic tableau stretching across the plain in front of them. 'I have seen plenty as you'd say were similar, sir, yes. But . . .' he paused.

'But?' the lieutenant colonel prompted. 'Go on, man, you may speak plain.'

'It is a rare and terrible thing to be facing one's own countrymen.' Stryker shrugged and looked back toward the battlefield. The push of pike he had been watching was dissolving in the deadly melee, and men were slaughtering one another in the packed ranks of bodies. It would be infernally hot in those ranks, and bloody. The air would stink of flesh and sweat and shit. Eventually it would turn sickly sweet. Blood and death. 'I never thought I'd live to fight an army of Englishmen.'

Perhaps not an army, needled a little voice from the back of his conscience, but he had certainly fought against Englishmen. Killed them even.

'Tragic.' Sir Stanley nodded gravely. 'But necessary, Stryker.'

'My men and I won't let His Majesty's cause fail,' muttered the captain.

7

The lieutenant colonel grinned. 'Capital, sir. Admire your courage, Captain, damn me, I do,'

Stryker nodded at the compliment, though he knew admiration for his particular talents would stretch only as far as those talents proved useful. A professional killer engendered more fear than respect in the upper echelons of society. He was dangerous, a man whose morals and appearance were considered more akin to those of common bandits plaguing Balham's estates than to a comrade-in-arms.

Worst of all, there was the scar; Stryker knew it would likely be turning Sir Stanley's stomach. The lieutenant colonel's careful approach on Stryker's right-hand side, in order to view the part of his face that remained intact, had not passed unnoticed.

Stryker watched Sir Stanley make the sign of the cross and wondered if he was asking God to smite the rebel horde or to protect him from another kind of demon closer at hand.

'Yes, sir, war is crucial!' Sir Stanley barked. He drew a wheezy breath and leant across to slap the younger man on the back, the leather glove making a dull thud against the captain's crusty buff-coat. 'Someone must stand beside our king in his time of tribulation. The rebellion must be stopped. Cut out like the festering canker you and I, good Christian men that we are, know it to be!'

'Praise God.' Stryker forced a smile as Balham hauled on his reins, urging his horse back down the lines.

'Praise God, Captain Stryker!' Sir Stanley called over his shoulder. 'And long live King Charles!'

*

Stryker twisted in his saddle to scan the escarpment that dominated the landscape behind them. His gaze rested upon a small group of figures, barely visible in the gathering dusk. 'What now?' he whispered, ignoring the twitching horse and creaking leather beneath him.

'What's that, Captain Stryker, sir?'

Stryker's body twisted back to face the massed ranks of humanity across the expanse of ground between Radway and Kineton. His one good eye, however, slid down to the man standing beside him. 'I was asking him what we should do now, Sergeant Skellen,' he clarified.

Skellen's uniform bore no demarcation of rank, but his bearing was confident. He was tall and lean, the owner of a dour leathery face and a deep voice that frequently dripped with sarcasm. His big, gloved hands wielded the vicious halberd, the only official token of his status, with an ease that denoted a man familiar with weapons and their deadly purpose.

The sergeant glanced up at Stryker to show he had his full attention, but was careful not to allow his dark eyes, sunk deep in their sockets, to meet the officer's gaze directly. 'Beg pardon, sir, but who?' he said in an accent common to the rough taverns of Portsmouth and Gosport.

'His Majesty, the King,' Stryker replied, with a jerk of his head to indicate the ridge behind them.

What should they do? The opposing armies had been locked in combat for the better part of the afternoon. Both sides had made gains, both conceded losses. It was now growing dark, and the snow had been trudged and pounded by hoof and foot into a blood-red slush during the battle.

'Aye,' said Skellen knowingly. 'Men won't stand for it, Mister Stryker.'

In an instant Stryker lurched down to lean over his sergeant, the muscles in his thighs protesting as they gripped the creaking saddle. 'They will stand for it, Skellen,' he growled dangerously, having to raise his voice above a fresh salvo of cannon fire that was being unleashed from the battery to his left.

The sergeant whipped his head back to face front. 'Aye, sir,' he grunted.

'They will stand for it as long as I bloody well tell them to, and I'll tear the goddamn throat out of anyone who so much as farts his dissent.'

Skellen clamped his mouth shut, fixing his gaze on the distant enemy formations. He knew that his captain was right. Yes, *his* men would stand – they'd follow him into the mouth of hell itself if he asked them – but the rest? The raw recruits and the farm-hands, only here under extreme duress? They would be away as soon as the dusk could cover an escape, dissolving into the night as if they'd never been here at all.

Edgehill itself was a ridge, a growth jutting out from otherwise low-lying land to form a long mound running north to south, seven hundred feet above sea level. It stood like a great barrier between the towns of Stratford-upon-Avon in the west and Banbury to the east.

Nestled snugly beneath this great escarpment – on the Stratford side – was the village of Radway, and running north-westwards from Radway was a wide plain. It was at the end of this fair-meadow that Kineton could be found, perched on the edge of the River Dene.

Stryker knew how different it would have appeared just two or three days earlier. The fair-meadow, punctuated by rough scrubland and flanked by ancient hedgerows, would have been a serene patch of unadulterated countryside. At its centre there was a ploughed field, which, though tough work at this time of year, would be subject to the toil of a farmer and his oxen.

But not today.

The battle had raged for much of the afternoon, ebbing and flowing like the great tides Stryker had seen dash the North Sea coast when he'd shipped out to the Low Countries thirteen years previously. It had begun with an hour-long cannonade, though the relentless pounding of infantry positions on both sides had had little effect.

As woeful as the Roundhead aim had been, Stryker had still heard the screams while iron balls skipped off the granite-hard earth and crashed through the Royalist ranks as if they were skittles. The wicked shot would cut a man in half. If it just took him at the knee, he was accounted fortunate.

Maddeningly, fewer of Parliament's troops went down under the Royalists' attack. Essex was either a clever man, or a lucky one, Stryker judged, for arranging his infantry behind the ploughed land in front of Kineton had been a crucial stroke. The Royalist cannon balls had, more often than not, sunk into the turned earth, nullifying the lethal ricochet that put paid to so many of the king's men.

'Which would you rather?' Stryker said, glancing down at Skellen. 'Fight a clever man or a lucky one?'

'Lucky, sir,' Skellen replied immediately. 'His luck'll run out. Now your clever cully makes his own luck. That's a man to be feared, sir.'

They were startled by a splatter of mud and snow, kicked up from the hooves of an incoming gelding. The rider, one of the colonel's aides-de-camp, wrenched on his reins, bringing his steed to a skidding halt.

'Captain Stryker, sir!' the aide shouted over the battle din, before Stryker could rebuke him for his impertinence. 'Compliments of Sir Edmund and you're to intercept yon blue-coated fellows,' he said, indicating an advancing pike formation. He evidently could not precisely identify the unit, though it was clear from their pro-Parliamentarian field chants that they were not friendly.

'He means us to advance?' Stryker asked urgently.

'I think not, Mister Stryker, sir. Think not. Rearguard action is all.'

'Rearguard?' Stryker was incredulous. 'We're retreating?'

'Not so, sir.' The aide shook his head vigorously as his mount fidgeted and whickered, thick clouds of steam billowing from its flaring nostrils. 'Ordered march back towards the hill.'

'We're damn well retreating!'

'The day is stalemate, Captain. His Majesty aims to remove himself from this place in an orderly manner and reconcile his forces. You are to keep', he continued before Stryker could reply, 'those damned Roundheads at bay while the main force withdraws. You'll have artillery support.'

Stryker acknowledged receipt of the order with a curt nod, and the aide wheeled his horse about in an ostentatious flurry of hooves and snow.

The men had stood idle for too long in this confounded weather anyway. Swinging out of his saddle with tremendous energy, Stryker thumped on to the frozen earth. A soldier materialized from somewhere and took his mount's reins without a word, leading the beast to safety behind the Royalist lines.

Stryker turned to his sergeant, who was standing like a statue a few paces behind him. 'You heard the man, Mister Skellen.'

'Indeed an' I did, sir,' Skellen replied briefly.

'We advance on my mark.'

'Sir.' Before he turned away, Skellen's gaze flickered momentarily to meet the single eye that stared back at him.

'Ready?' Stryker asked his old comrade-in-arms.

Skellen's look was sardonic. 'Yes, sir.' A tiny smile played across the captain's features, before vanishing back behind its usual saturnine mask. There was no one in the world he would rather have watching his back than Skellen.

The sergeant turned about and marched away towards the bristling ranks awaiting his order.

'Look lively, you mangy palliards!' Skellen yelled, as he took up his position to the left of the front rank. 'Eyes front! Shoulder pikes!' he cried, slamming his halberd, its fearsome blade dark with crusted blood, into the cold earth. 'We march on Mister Stryker's word an' no other!'

'Gives me the chills, that eye,' one of the new recruits murmured to his mate. 'From neck to nuts, as God's m' witness.'

'It should,' Skellen growled, startling the pikeman, who had not intended his comment to be overheard.

The pikeman swallowed hard. 'Beg pardon, Sergeant, but I ain't never seen a grey eye like that. Dark, but silver. A damned sparkin' anvil.'

Skellen nodded, his thin face splitting in grim relish. 'They say his mother was a she-wolf, Bicks.'

The pikeman, Walter Bicknell, was unable to stop his eyes swivelling over to where the captain now stood facing the company.

Skellen followed Bicknell's stare and chuckled. 'The flecks of silver only show when he smiles, which ain't often, or when he smells a kill, which he does this very moment.' The sergeant stepped away to cast deep-set eyes upon the rest of his men. 'Follow him, lads! Follow the good captain! Follow him and thank the good Lord above that he's on your side!'

The massed ranks straightened. Nearly one hundred pairs of eyes, made watery by the cold, blinked rapidly to regain focus. Lungs were hawked clear of gunpowder-spotted phlegm, shoulders were rolled and squared and the sixteen-foot lengths of ash hefted into the dank air. Pikes were damned unwieldy brutes, especially on a day like this, when a man's fingers were numbed to the marrow, but in these expert hands they rose in unison, dropped in unison, and nestled comfortably on to shoulders that had carried them for hundreds, in some cases thousands, of miles.

In front, a tall officer with one eye and a devilish grin drew his broad sword and showed them the way. And as one, they followed him.

The king had declared war on Parliament in August, but it had taken a full fortnight for the army to amass. Stryker had been summoned from his home in Hampshire, and hired to gather a company. It had not taken as long as he had feared, for the majority of his old comrades came swiftly back to answer the call. These were veterans, hard men who had seen war on a grand scale in Europe and lived to tell the tale. The king was glad of them, though many of His Majesty's more high-born officers had raised eyebrows at the rough-and-ready captain and his grizzled professionals. Stryker had swelled his ranks with lads from the shire whose eagerness partly compensated for their inexperience, and he had left Skellen to batter them into shape on the long march to the rendezvous point at Shrewsbury.

Some weeks later, the combined forces of the king had headed south, aiming directly for the capital. London was the key, the nest of vipers that writhed and schemed at the heart of this conflict. That was how Stryker's senior officers referred to the city, but Stryker had many good friends in the London Trained Bands, friends against whom he may soon have to fight. And fight he would, if it came to that.

The great mass of men, with its lingering train of baggage and hangers-on, had then marched south through Warwickshire. It had been made known that they would fall upon the Parliamentarian town of Warwick, striking a hammer-blow upon the rebel cause early in the hostilities. Stryker had had his doubts about launching an assault against such a well-fortified position. The possibility of a lengthy siege in the freezing weather was not enticing. He had fought in sieges before. He had camped through cold and sleet, blood and disease. He had watched as heavy ordnance had pulverized ancient fortifications and reduced another innocent population to famine and death. He had seen the rape and massacre of innocents when walls were finally breached. He was not inclined to repeat the experience, and certainly not on English soil.

He was pleased, therefore, that the order to bypass the well-garrisoned castle town had been received. Essex would be left to roam the Warwickshire countryside while King Charles would push south with the intention of taking Banbury. The town was another stronghold of Parliament, but it was considerably less fortified. The proposition had looked good to Stryker, and his spirits had lifted as they traversed the Wormleighton Hills that rose to the north and east of Edgehill. They would crush Banbury, leave Essex kicking his heels in the Cotswolds, and open the road to Oxford.

'Keep your bastard eyes forward, Powney, God rot your stinkin' hide!' Now Skellen's coarse battlefield tones penetrated the frosty afternoon air like a volley from a saker cannon.

Stryker glanced at the unfortunate Powney. He felt a brief pang of sympathy for the young pikeman as Skellen tore strips from him, but the sergeant was right. A lost footing now would throw out the man's stride and the effect would undulate back through the ranks causing chaos.

He forced his concentration back on the panorama of churned land stretching before him, littered with corpses of man and horse.

To his right the scattered debris of Prince Rupert's devastating charge lay like jetsam in tangled irregular clumps of flesh and blood. The grand pomp of cavalry-men had been reduced to carrion in but a few minutes.

The scene in the centre of the field was equally horrific.

It was as if a giant charnel house had disgorged its contents, dumping its macabre bounty on to the snow. Stryker was too far away to see the faces, and many were hidden behind the hedgerows that criss-crossed that middle ground, but he knew that each would be affecting its own sickening pose and expression. There would be those that grinned like demonic clowns and others that stared in shock, surprised by their own ends; some would be frozen like grotesque, terror-stricken statues. Each one would be like a ghoulish parody of the living. Here, though, there were fewer horses. It was the domain of man, where fathers and sons were impaled on long pikes, their bodies entwined with those pierced by shot or laid open by steel. Others had met their end by a hurtling cannon ball, though their bodies were broken and scattered, seeds tossed to the wind.

Stryker spat. The Banbury strategy had been a good one, but the enemy had discovered their plans and raced southwards to rescue the town.

In the end, it seemed to him that the two forces had stumbled into one another. Stryker had been at Edgecote the previous day when the council of war decided upon a course of action that would see Byron's brigade, some four thousand strong, push south to seize Banbury. Sir Edmund Mowbray's Regiment of Foot, Stryker's lads included, had been with that force, and they had fanned out to find billets for the night.

Stryker chose the little village of Cropredy, and though the night was unfathomably cold, the warm fires and even warmer sound of his comrades' banter and song had lifted everyone's spirits.

A staff officer, whose name now escaped Stryker,

though he would never forget that dog-tired voice, rode into their slumbering billet a little after four in the morning. The message was clear; the forces of Parliament were at hand. They had been spotted by a cavalry patrol out toward Kineton. A general muster was to be observed at Edgehill.

Stryker's company of pike and musket had begun the day in the centre of the king's lines, forming part of Byron's brigade. As the artillery bombardment crashed about them, an evil harbinger of the hostilities to come, the Royalist forces had been massed on the level ground in front of Radway. They had watched as Robert Devereux, Earl of Essex, formed his Roundheads across the plain from their own positions.

At around three o'clock the order to advance had been given by King Charles himself, and had been passed down from his vantage point on the ridge, seven hundred feet above sea level, through the chain of command and eventually to the officers on the plain. The brigade shouldered pikes and prepared for the march across the snow-dusted fields as the terrain sloped steadily down towards Kineton.

Stryker remembered the nervous excitement of the raw recruits in Byron's great brigade, like young destriers ready for the charge. As General Sir Jacob Astley paced in front of the line, resplendent in red and gold, the men fidgeted in their ranks, apprehension flooding every vein and tension stiffening joints. Some had prayed, whispering silent pleas to the Almighty, while others growled personal threats towards the Roundhead lines. Stryker remembered the youngster – barely in his teens – in the front rank as he had snivelled pathetically, teardrops tapping the taut skin of his white knuckles as he gripped his pike. Some men had laughed insanely to themselves; others spilled the contents of their stomachs, or bowels.

Like Stryker's lads, General Astley had worn only back and breast plates, having discarded the cumbersome tassets that would flap across his thighs. Stryker remembered the dark, wide-brimmed hat, adorned with a red ribbon and feather, as Sir Jacob made his way purposefully out in front of the great formation, holding his arm aloft.

'O Lord!' Astley shouted so that as many men as possible would hear. 'You know how busy I must be this day. If I forget thee, do not forget me.'

Stryker had not known whether to applaud this show of valour, his cynical eye casting around to see if the king or Prince Rupert were within earshot. But now, as he remembered how Astley had drawn his sword and pointed it like an arrow toward the massed enemy battalions, he could not help but feel admiration. Stryker had found himself drawing his own sword and, with Sir Jacob's rallying cry of 'March on, boys!' echoing in his ears, he had repeated the call.

Like some giant biblical behemoth, the entire Royalist front line had rumbled into motion.

In front of Kineton itself, the slope's downward gradient petered out, stalled, and began to rise steeply. On this rising ground were the waiting Parliamentarians and, in immediate response to the Royalist advance, thousands of their finest men had marched out.

Stryker remembered the close-up toil of the push of pike. His men had marched in their tertio headlong into the blue uniforms of Sir William Constable's regiment and levelled their wicked weapons, as the Parliamentarians levelled their own.

It was known as *the push*. Two bodies of infantry, each numbering in their thousands, pushing at the other, attempting to knock the other off balance, forcing the opposing tertio to fold and capitulate. Stryker often likened the manoeuvre to a pair of Greek wrestlers, shoving and grunting and sweating. But the classical allegory was abandoned in the field of battle. In this bout, the wrestlers were pointing sixteen-foot lengths of ash at one another, each topped with a wicked leaf-shaped blade. Amongst the grunts and oaths, the commands and the screams, another noise rang out rhythmically, constantly, in the background. The ostinato of battle. A thud, a squelch, and a loud sucking; blade impales man; blade twists in flesh; blade is jerked free to search for its next target.

Stryker knew that sound well. He had heard it countless times, on countless fields across Europe.

That first push of pike had ended inconclusively for Stryker and his men. They had been with Byron's brigade in the centre of the Royalist line and had smashed into the opposing tertio. He half expected the Roundheads to run at the sight of his hard veterans holding the centre of their particular battaile, but the enemy had been brave and had closed well, pushing and heaving forward with admirable resilience.

The ranks met one another, pushing as hard as was possible, then stalled. Pikes missed their marks, men were too closely packed to draw their swords, and the locked ranks screamed their frustrated enmity into the cold air. A melee was avoided as the Parliamentarian force eventually withdrew, maintaining an order that Stryker could only admire. The pikemen, including his own force, had removed themselves from the front line as musket companies took up the battle, pouring volley fire into the autumnal gloom.

Stryker had marched back toward Radway, finding a position of relative safety in order to see to the wounded. It was vexing that they were not in the main brigade, for a devastating Roundhead cavalry charge, led by the standard of Sir William Balfour, had swept into the shocked Royalist ranks like a wave. Stryker and his men could only look on in fury as horsemen burst into view like so many avenging angels. The call to *charge pike for horse* – angling the spiteful points upward in a bristling mass that would deter all but the most well-trained or crazed animal – was late and panicked, as the brigade braced for impact. Joined by Sir Philip Stapleton's heavily armoured cuirassiers, Balfour's cavalry charge hit home right across the Royalist centre.

Stryker had watched in horror as first Fielding's brigade, and then Byron's, broke and fled back toward Edgehill. Victorious cavalrymen whooped and cheered as they chased their now pitiful quarry across the fields like rabbits.

Almost an hour after that frustrating capitulation, Stryker and his pikemen now yearned to enter the fray once more.

Stryker strode out in front of his company. Once again, his men were bearing down on an opposing battaile, but the pace of the entire battle was slower. Firing a musket was hot work that dried a man's mouth and stung his eyes.

To level a pike, its weight pulling down from several feet away, was enough to have your hands burning and your forearms screaming for mercy. And all that was before combatants engaged in the melee, where swords were drawn and punches thrown.

The immediate enemy were, once again, a company of Constable's bluecoats. They were more numerous than his own unit, but Stryker could see weariness informing their every step. The light tunics were stained red with blood, the men themselves tardy in their formation, ragged and out of step. They had been sent forward by Essex in a last-ditch attempt to seize the day, but Stryker could tell from the rounded shoulders of the front rank that this was one fight too far for them.

'Ensign Burton,' Stryker called, without shifting his gaze from the oncoming enemy.

'Sir,' Burton said, appearing beside him, struggling to hold Stryker's company standard high.

'Look at those bastards, Ensign. They tire. They're scared. They've been battered and bruised all afternoon.'

'Aye, sir, but so have we,' replied the younger man.

'But your rebel pikeman doesn't need to know that, lad. How do we know they tire, Mister Burton?'

Burton considered this for a moment, and glanced up at his captain. 'Well, their pikes are low, sir,' he ventured.

Stryker grinned, the puckered skin that was once his eye socket creasing in its usual macabre fashion. 'Very good, Mister Burton. Their pikes are low. Their shoulders are down. Their step is all over the damned place. So what must we not do?'

'Any of that, sir?'

'Exactly. Pass the colour to Corporal Mookes and check

over the men, Ensign. Any man looking tired, dropping his shoulders, lowering his weapon, missing his step . . . I want that man on a charge. Do I make myself clear?'

'Sir!' Burton barked, handing the giant standard of red and white taffeta to the corporal before turning his attention to the block as it made its inexorable progress toward the enemy.

The young officer had puked his guts on to the reddened snow during the first push. This time he'd be too busy for that.

It was but a moment before the pike blocks met. Never a man to stand aside and watch his company do all the work, Stryker had cut down two musketeers as they hurriedly loaded their weapons to spew lead into the Royalist ranks. He heard the drummers shift their beat to indicate that pikes should be levelled, and he heard the thud as the front ranks lumbered into one another.

Eager to join his men and coordinate the push, Stryker began to move toward the mass of bodies as they heaved onward. Already the Parliamentarian force was reeling against the strength of his ferocious pikemen, and he felt a pang of pride. But before he had covered just a few paces, he was faced with a new threat. Two bluecoats had broken away from their unit and were approaching him in the chaos, one on either side, attempting to outflank him. The man to his right was of average build, but his eyes were fearful and wild, like a caged animal. He gripped a thin blade in his white-knuckled fist, holding it level with Stryker's face. The other was a gigantic beast, wielding half a broken pike. Unfortunately for Stryker, the half he held was the business end, its red blade glistening with menace.

Stryker was confident of besting a single opponent, but two were daunting, especially given his compromised vision. Deciding that all the courage was to be found in the bigger man, Stryker chose him as his first target.

The big man offered a peg-toothed grin and jabbed at the air between them with his half-pike. He was too far away from Stryker to do any harm yet, but he had made his intention abundantly clear.

Stryker lifted his sword, holding it high as if meaning to cleave the giant's head in two. As he had foreseen, the man braced himself to parry the blow, while his smaller companion, relieved he would not have to tackle the tall captain immediately, let his guard down a fraction. In a heartbeat Stryker had dropped to his knees and rolled sideways, finishing in front of the smaller enemy. He lunged like an adder striking its prey, and rammed his blade deep into the hapless man's groin. It would be swift, Stryker knew, for he had killed in this fashion many times before. He had been taught that this was how the Roman legionaries had fought, and it was easy to see why. A severed artery in the groin would see a man bleed out inside a minute.

Turning his attention to the bigger man, Stryker saw that he was already falling back. The ugly grin had dissolved into a worried scowl as the lightning-fast Cavalier sprang to his feet. The big Roundhead had been telling himself that this was an easy kill, that the Royalist officer was a rake and a wastrel, a one-eyed one at that, the foolish follower of a popish king and ripe for slaughter. And yet now, with every fluid, predatory movement Stryker made, capped by his well-practised countenance of pure, calm fury, he knew instinctively that the enemy's confidence would be trickling away. Stryker's clean-shaven face bore innumerable ancient scars, while the area that should have housed his left eye was nothing more than a mass of contorted flesh; disfigured and evil-looking. The giant would be staring with fear at that twisted socket, forcing himself to look into the good eye. Stryker, his silver gaze upon the Parliamentarian, looked into him – through him – so that the Roundhead would see his own death.

Stryker wanted to slash forward with his sword, but he knew the long pike would skewer him before he got close. *Hold. Hold. Let him make the first move.*

The big man lost his nerve. Swinging the length of wood like a club, he screamed with aggression, aiming the weapon squarely at the Royalist's head. But he saw the movement too late. His opponent had ducked beneath the blow, rolled through the bloody snow, and reappeared inches away like an acrobat. The world went black.

It took three attempts for Stryker to twist his blade free of the gigantic Parliamentarian's throat, but once it came away the blood flowed freely and the corpse crashed to the earth like a felled oak.

Stryker turned back to his own men. The push of pike had stalled. It was a crucial moment, where the engagement might break down into a melee, a close-quarters free-for-all where pikes were decommissioned and swords ruled.

When he reached the block, Stryker could see that his men were wavering. They had had the best of the opening exchanges, but their exhaustion was beginning to tell. The pikes at the centre of the push were vertical now, forced heavenward while the front ranks wrestled chest-to-chest, with no way of keeping the poles horizontal. It would be sheer hell at the centre. Daggers would be drawn, for there was no room for a longer blade in that stinking agonized crush. Men would stab at one another, or bite the faces of the enemy. They would stamp and kick, or butt like rutting rams. Anything to break the opponent.

On the far side of the chaotic mass, Stryker could see an officer in tawny uniform directing the Roundhead push. Sheathing his sword, Stryker stooped to retrieve a discarded pike from the rapidly freezing slush and made his way along the rear rank of his own troops, so that he was now at the bottom left-hand corner of the block. The opposing officer was on this side too, but was concentrating on the movements of his men. He did not notice Stryker until it was too late.

The officer died quickly. The pike passed through his unarmoured chest and burst out of his back in a shower of muscle and bone. Immediately, as Stryker had hoped, the Roundhead block began to lose impetus. Men looked unsure of themselves with no officer to command them. Their sergeants kept up their filthy bawling, but no level of verbal threat would match the peril of more than ninety enemy soldiers bearing down on them.

In moments the push had completely stalled and the melee ensued. Pikes were thrown down in panic and the bluecoats began to flee in the face of Stryker's men. Stryker allowed the melee to continue for several seconds, giving his men the chance to take out their fury upon a defeated enemy, but he soon gave the order to withhold. The Parliamentarians were racing back toward Kineton. Now was not the time to give chase.

'Mister Skellen,' Stryker said as his men regrouped,

'please take these scoundrels back to Sir Edmund. Tell him they've had enough for one day.'

'Dragoons, sir!' a musketeer called from one of the ranks to Stryker's right.

Ensign Burton limped across using the stump of a shattered halberd as a walking stick. 'Charge for horse?'

Stryker shook his head. 'No. Not now. They won't take us on, it gets too dark. And the bastards are not even in battle formation. They mean to hold the ground.' He turned to a barrel-chested drum-major. 'Sound the retreat.'

'If they want this godforsaken field they can have it,' he said wearily as the company performed an orderly retreat, in step and facing the enemy, to the sound of the drum's familiar call. 'Fall back.'

CHAPTER 2

Thunder rolled down from the craggy hills. A boy, playing with his younger sisters in the snow, squinted up at the sky. His mother, widowed the previous summer by the ague that had decimated this part of town, dashed out of their hovel to gather up her brood. As he was being ushered inside, her son was reminded of the hens they kept in the house; his mother too ran to and fro, clucking admonishingly, flapping her arms and scolding.

'Ma,' the boy began, but his mother cuffed him to silence. He clamped his mouth firmly shut, then watched as his mother stood briefly in the threshold, nose tilted slightly upwards like an animal sniffing the wind, then turned inside, slamming the door shut behind her.

The rumble grew in intensity as the widow joined her son and daughters at a low window. The boy could sense his mother's tension, and, as he peered across the street, he realized that other families too were similarly sheltered behind their walls, staring through rickety-shuttered windows out on to the road's frozen mud. And then the boy understood. Like his mother and his neighbours, he knew what caused the noise long before he saw it, for word of the impending arrival had long since reached them.

Horses. Oxen. Cannon. Carts. Men. An army.

He saw the horses first; the small group of cavalrymen that made up the column's vanguard. It was a disappointing sight. He had expected some pomp and ceremony. The great army of the King of England, marching into his little town! He had expected gallant knights cantering through the snow, waving bright banners and brandishing gleaming swords. He had imagined fearsome pikemen in gleaming armour, flanked by rows and rows of musketeers, rakish and dashing in their finery.

The horses seemed as listless as the grey afternoon. Their riders were tattered and unkempt, and their entrance brought no fanfare or cheering.

The boy looked on, kept close by his mother's vicelike grip, as the cavalry units petered out, replaced by a seemingly endless column of infantry. The first to pass their home were pikemen. No precise marching order here; simply a tired loping. Some of them did not even carry weapons.

In amongst the pikemen were units of musketeers, powder flasks swaying rhythmically from the bandoliers against their chests, blackened muskets pointed skyward from shoulders. Flanking the infantry were the drummers and, occasionally, fifes. But in this tired ensemble they neglected to strike up a tune, preferring simply to keep pace with their regiments.

Behind these men came a dozen carts, drawn by sullen oxen. These vehicles were packed full of men, some moaning as the great wheels bounced, rigid and unforgiving, along the road's frozen ruts.

'The wounded,' the widow whispered in her son's ear. 'God help 'em.'

Behind the carts came another team of oxen. This time, though, their burden was not human. These were the heavy guns, the great cannon that the citizens of Banbury had heard rumbling across the horizon three days earlier. The children watched in awe while the heavy iron pieces thundered past on bouncing wheels, traces and chains jangling in protest.

Behind the ordnance came other groups of pikemen and musketeers, a great ragged river winding away into the fields beyond the town.

'Come away, children,' the widow said after a while.

'But Ma—' the boy began to protest.

'No arguments,' she replied, finality in her tone. 'Come. It's rabbit stew tonight.'

Sir Edmund Mowbray's Regiment of Foot had been at the centre of that great marching column. As weary as the rest of the army, they had welcomed the chance to rest when the gates of Banbury opened.

There was no great enmity towards the king here, despite the fact that it had been a Parliamentarian town. Indeed, to the common folk, this war was not one in which they wished to take sides. But invading armies had a habit, on taking an enemy stronghold, of laying waste to its interior. Rumours of rape and pillage had been rife in the days since the battle, and the fearful inhabitants were staying indoors. They were taking no unnecessary chances.

Stryker's own company were in their usual marching position at the rear of Mowbray's regiment. The men were bruised and battered, but above all cold. The battle had not been a defeat, far from it. In fact, the Royalist leadership were losing no time in proclaiming a great victory. After all, the objective had been to secure the road to London, which they had done. Now the way was open for the king to take his capital and end this war, and Banbury was the first step to that end.

But for all the elation in the higher echelons, the soldiers were hungry and tired and numbed to the bone. As a result, the column trudged through this grey October evening looking for all the world like a defeated army.

Stryker was on foot. His stallion, Vos, walked at the company's rear, led by one of the wagon-master's men. Stryker gazed at the shadowy faces that peered fearfully from their windows, trying to catch the eye of some, revelling privately in the terrified expressions of those that met his scarred mask.

For a few terrible years his hideous appearance had pressed down upon him, slowly eating him alive. Every time a child cried as they looked into his face, he hated himself. Hated what he had become. Gradually he'd succeeded in shedding the burden. She had helped him do that. She had drawn that black bile from him like poison from a wound. She . . .

'Company . . . halt!' The cry of a sergeant further up the column cut into Stryker's thoughts, dragging him away from that faint, lovely, terrible memory. The call to halt echoed its way down the column's length.

An officer cantered down the line, repeating an order that became audible as he reached Mowbray's Foot. 'Column to stand down and find billets for the night.'

As the officer approached Stryker's company, he reined in beside the captain with a white-toothed grin. 'Alive then,' he said, in a voice that belied his cheery countenance. Stryker replied by turning his head away.

The officer wore a pristine costume of russet and gold, his chest encased with armoured plates that gleamed brightly, defying the drabness of the day. His hair was red, hanging in long tendrils about his shoulders. His beard was small and immaculately trimmed, its tip waxed into a sharp point that met the billowing material of a dazzling white ruff as it sprang up about his neck like the petals of a flower. The wide-brimmed hat, worn at a rakish angle, was a ruby red, the same colour as the sash that ran from shoulder to hip.

'Oh, come now, Captain Stryker, surely we can be civil,' the officer said, pushing an unruly strand of hair behind an ear, exposing the gold hoop that dangled from its lobe. Stryker was like stone. He sneered. 'Have it your way, but do not say I didn't attempt a modicum of cordiality.'

Stryker stared levelly up at where the man sat like a cockerel, perched on his glossy mount. 'You have no right to speak to me, Eli,' he growled. 'Leave now, while you can.'

'I am under orders from the king himself, *mon Capitaine*,' the officer replied in his haughty, mocking voice. 'So I'm afraid you're stuck with me.'

Stryker's right arm shot upwards. Before the mounted officer could react, he found an uncomfortable pressure needling his midriff.

Stryker's face was a mask of calm. 'Don't look down. Don't struggle,' he growled quietly, as Eli's face drained of colour. 'There is a dirk resting nicely against your gut. I would dearly love to spill your innards over those pretty britches.'

The horseman steeled himself, forcing his features into a defiant expression. 'You wouldn't,' he rasped. 'There are too many witnesses. There's a whole army here, you damned fool.'

Stryker narrowed his eye. For a moment neither man moved, then Sergeant Skellen's big hand fell upon his commander's shoulder.

'No,' said Stryker eventually, not taking his gaze from the mounted man. 'No, I wouldn't. But one day, you piece of horse shit. One day we will be alone, and that day will be one I will treasure. Now ride away, Eli. Now.'

Stryker retracted his arm in a swift movement that saw the blade back in its sheath without arousing attention from the soldiers around them. The rattled cavalryman kicked his steed's flanks, and galloped off down the line of infantry.

Skellen turned to Stryker.

Stryker sighed. 'An old acquaintance, Sergeant.'

Skellen looked dubious. 'I don't know him.'

The captain smiled sourly. 'We go a long way back. Further even than you and I.'

Skellen snorted. 'That *would* be a long way back, sir.' He had been at Stryker's side for more than half a decade. Marching and fighting, drinking and whoring. He knew the captain as well as any man. They were both just over thirty years old. Skellen knew that Stryker had been a soldier for nearly fifteen years. He knew that the captain was not a man to be disrespected.

Skellen screwed up his leathery brow. 'He looks too young to've known you so very long, sir.'

'Looks can be deceiving, Mister Skellen. Captain Eli Makepeace. An evil bastard, make no mistake. And he's not so young; he's the same age as me, give or take a year. But he was born to money, lots of it.'

33

'Hence the fancy attire.'

'Indeed. And his fucking arrogance.'

'A proper Cavalier, sir,' said Skellen, hawking up a wad of phlegm and depositing it in a great globule at his feet.

Stryker nodded. 'Cavalier, rake, wastrel, the lot. A pamphleteer's dream.'

'No wonder you didn't take to him, sir. Bit surprised you pulled a blade though, beggin' your pardon.'

Stryker sighed. 'We had a disagreement, Makepeace and I, many years ago. I could have guessed he'd be back with the army, but I didn't expect to see him on this day.'

'With the utmost respect, sir,' Skellen began, choosing his words carefully now, watching a familiar shadow pass across Stryker's features. 'But you've had quite a few disagreements over the years. It ain't my place to say so, sir, but you're not often bothered as to who it is you disagree with. Least of all brash little peacocks like that. With respect to the officer, like, sir.'

'The disagreement in question,' Stryker said, his expression still grim, 'left me with this.' He waved a dirty hand toward the mangled remnants of his face.

Skellen's stubble-darkened jaw dropped. 'Well I'll be buggered,' he whispered.

Nightfall was icy. Most of the regiments had decamped within Banbury, hiding behind the walls of houses, barns and taverns to keep themselves warm. But, despite the low temperature the sky was beautifully clear, and many units, mostly the hardened veterans, were happy to pitch up beyond the town. As darkness drew in, the white awnings of tents glowed like angels or ghosts against the orange beacons of a hundred fires. From Banbury's walls, it must have seemed as if the heavenly host had descended.

Stryker paced across the field he'd chosen for the company's temporary home. The frozen grass crunched rhythmically beneath his boots, and he tried to stop thinking of Eli Makepeace. He marvelled at how that sneering peacock was still, after all these years, able to crawl beneath his skin. That face, framed by the red hair and golden earrings, still needled him. Still inspired feelings of murder.

Meanwhile, he had his responsibilities. The situation was bleak. Two hastily recruited armies made up primarily of raw recruits had been forced out into weather that would freeze the balls off Satan himself, and made to stand firm in the face of musket fire and artillery. There was a smattering of professionals on either side, convinced, cajoled or bribed into whichever regiment they now found themselves, but they were too few to make a great deal of difference. No wonder, then, Stryker had to concede, that the two armies had staggered across the plain at Edgehill like a pair of drunken brawlers.

What concerned him, as it must have concerned anyone else unfortunate to be present at the battle, was just how evenly matched the two sides were. Who could win in a fight that was evidently to the death?

'It's fuckin' awful,' sneered a squat fellow with goggle eyes and a bulbous nose. As if to seal his point, he spat into the fire, the spittle writhing and bubbling as it landed on a glowing log.

'What is, Corporal?' a voice asked behind him.

The squat man scrambled to his feet and turned to

confront the man who had spoken, his body snapping rigidly to attention. He fixed his gaze on the crown of the newcomer's hat, careful not to meet the single eye that peered back at him. 'B-beg pardon, sir. Just agreeing with Samuels, here,' he stammered, indicating the man immediately to his right. Samuels, a skinny, feral-looking youth with a bandaged forearm, had also stood bolt upright. In fact all seven men huddled round the fire had followed suit.

'Agreeing?'

'Th-that yesterday was a bad show. For both sides, if truth be told, sir.'

Stryker liked this pikeman and his rough ways, but to be a figure of respect for one's men was important. 'They're not used to war here, Jimmy,' he said, nodding towards the flames. 'D'you mind?'

Jimmy smiled toothlessly. 'Course not, sir.'

With that, the men began to relax. He was a hard bastard, Captain Stryker, but a good sort of cove for all that. They had shared many a campfire with him over the years and knew he liked to chew the fat with them on occasion.

Stryker took his place, cross-legged, in the ring of men that huddled close to the fire's warmth. 'It's been so long since this country's seen land battles that men have forgotten how to fight,' he said, returning the gaze of each man in turn.

'There's a few who knows what they're about though, sir,' ventured the weasel-faced Samuels.

'Aye, there are,' the captain replied, offering the young man a wolfish grin. As the flames danced in the chill dusk, their tremulous radiance lit up Stryker's face, highlighting old scars and glittering in that all-seeing eye of his.

By Christ, the pikeman thought, he looked so much like a minion of Lucifer in that orange glow that Samuels could not help but shiver, despite the fire's heat. He had seen that terrible scar twist and convulse when the captain's ire was aroused. He had seen those powerful shoulders wield deadly weapons in a hundred different situations, and had witnessed the same outcome each time. Samuels, like all of his mates in the company, thought more of this man than any other in His Majesty's army. They had fought with him and killed with him. And they would always answer his call.

Stryker picked up a stick and began prodding the smouldering logs, sending sparks skywards in a manic rush. 'Trouble is,' he said to no one in particular, 'only those of us who've been in Europe have the experience. We are the ones who know what we're up against, Sammy. The rest are soft.'

His words drew a chorus of consenting grunts. Either force would have been cut to ribbons by the great martial machines they had fought against in mainland Europe.

'Still,' a voice came from opposite Stryker, beyond the flames, 'it wasn't all bad, was it?'

'How d'you mean, Sergeant?' asked another of the men.

Skellen sniffed, as he always did when he wished to show he did not appear to care about a subject. 'We've got the road, haven't we? That's what we wanted. That's what we got.'

Stryker nodded. Both sides had hoped for a crushing victory that would end this feud before it had really begun. Perhaps there was still a chance, given that the road to London had been opened if not by a victory, then by

Essex's failure to block the route south. They'd been ordered to Banbury, which had capitulated, and now Stryker, and evidently Skellen, fully expected the king to dash further south and secure Oxford. Then they could push on to the capital.

The fireside chatter soon turned to other things. The women they had left behind; the taverns they had frequented in former lives; the quality of beer on the Continent. Anything but the horrors of the battle. It had been a hard affair on that plain below Edgehill. Cold and bloody and brutal. The butcher's bill had reached Stryker as the column decamped in Banbury's houses and fields.

It was never easy reading, but this one was particularly difficult. Not that it was the worst Stryker had ever seen, but it was hard to stomach by its very nature. This was civil war, and every nameless man whose death was recorded on the bill's tally was from these islands. From the king's force five hundred lay dead, another fifteen hundred wounded. Stryker knew similar numbers would be tallied around Parliamentarian campfires at this very moment.

'Captain Stryker?' a voice from outside the circle broke into the group's friendly banter. 'Captain *I*. Stryker, if you please.'

Stryker stood slowly, the aches and pains of the last battle's exertions crying out against the unwelcome movement. 'I'm Stryker,' he said, turning to face the newcomer, whose form was gradually resolving in the darkness.

'Lieutenant Morris, sir,' the man said, offering his hand for Stryker to shake. He was a young man, barely out of his teens, but carried himself with an air of confidence that Stryker knew immediately was born of wealth and privilege. 'Compliments of Lord Saxby, sir, and what is the *I* for?'

'The *I*?' Stryker replied in a low, almost threatening voice.

'In your name, sir,' Morris went on, unconcerned by his superior's tone. 'What, may I ask, does it stand for?'

Around the campfire, the men tensed. None, not even Skellen, knew what Stryker's Christian name was, and it was common knowledge that to pry was dangerous.

'No, Lieutenant, you may not ask.'

Morris shrugged. 'Well, no matter. Lord John requests you attend him forthwith.'

'Forthwith? It's cold and late, man. Can I not at least see to my billet first?'

' 'Fraid not, sir.' The lieutenant flashed a sympathetic smile. 'He was quite insistent.'

Stryker gritted his teeth, the muscles in his jaw quivering in irritation. Eventually he sighed. 'Of course he bloody was.'

The room was opulent. A large fire roared in the impressive stone hearth, its light bathing everything in a tremulous glow. Bookcases lined the walls, shelves filled to breaking point with distinguished tomes, their spines crammed together like a regiment of pike. An enormously large chandelier hung glittering from the ceiling, while beneath it sat a vast table of oak, its surface invisible beneath scattered parchments. The owner of the room, and its clutter, was not in attendance.

Stryker had been ushered in by Lieutenant Morris, whom he had followed the short distance from the company's field of sheep shit, through one of the city gates, and into a quiet street of impressive houses, the hulking shadow of Banbury's Norman castle looming behind them.

Half the way up the street and past several Royalist patrols, they had reached a large merchant dwelling. Uttering a password to the surly musketeer on sentry duty, they were granted entry. As they walked down a long corridor, they had passed several doors and three more guards before reaching the present room. Once inside, Morris had beaten a hasty retreat while Stryker, alone, had been left to await the man who had summoned him.

Pleased to be sheltered from the bitter night, Stryker ambled across iron-cold flagstones and thick carpets to the great hearth. It was blistering in its intensity, too hot, but he held out his hands to welcome its energy. It was a satisfying feeling. He closed his eye.

Behind him, footsteps shuffled across the carpet.

Stryker spun on his heels, his hand moving instinctively to the sheathed sword at his waist.

The man froze where he stood, palms held up in supplication. 'Is a duel really necessary, Captain?' he said. 'This ruff is new, and the rug is Persian. We will never get the blood stains out and your dozen shillings a day won't be enough to replace it, I can assure you.'

Stryker shrugged. 'It is necessary when officers creep up on their men, Colonel.'

'You would speak to a superior officer in such a fashion, sir?'

'Only when it is deserved, my lord.'

Colonel Lord John Saxby's narrow face split into a broad grin. 'Good God, man, but you always were an insubordinate rogue!' He let out a great guffaw. 'It is good to see you, indeed it is. You look positively monstrous, as always.'

'Thank you, sir,' said Stryker, straight-faced.

Saxby brayed again. 'Sweet Christ on His cross, Stryker, you are a marvel. If I could have had odds on your demise, I'd have bet against you long ago. But here you are.'

Stryker reached out, shaking Saxby's proffered hand. 'Here I am, sir.'

'Here you are indeed. I heard you were in the thick of it.'

Stryker nodded. 'And I heard you were also, sir.'

The colonel's eyes glinted. 'I was. But where are my manners? Sit, Mister Stryker, sit.'

Colonel Lord John Saxby had been born into Dorset's landed elite. Yet as a second-born son, he was not entitled to his father's estate. With no inheritance, and no intention of playing second fiddle to a tedious, pious brother, he had joined the army in search of his own fortune. In the two decades that followed, he fought across Europe with the grand Protestant armies, perfecting his skills with sword and saddle. At some point during his military life, his elder brother had been careless enough to be thrown from his horse, making John sole heir to the family fortune. But by then he had fallen in love with his mistress – the army.

Having inherited his father's title and estates, Sir John was one of King Charles's most outspoken supporters and an invaluable asset to the Royalist cause. He was a close friend and confidant of Prince Rupert of the Rhine, and, it was said, had the ear of the king himself.

The friendship between Sir John and Stryker was an unlikely one. Stryker was well known, as feted and feared in England's great houses as he was in its lowly taverns. The Royalist elite wanted him as a leader of men, but that did not mean he was one of their own. Stryker knew he was the king's attack dog, a blunt instrument to be wielded in desperate times. If the Royalists should win the war, he would not be expecting an invitation to dine with the elite at Whitehall Palace.

Yet an invitation would most certainly come from Saxby House. Stryker and Saxby had met more than a decade ago, thrust together by war. The fiery struggle in the Low Countries had been hard and unforgiving, and a generation of young soldiers had been forged in its flames. These young men were now returning to England, some as Cavaliers, some as Roundheads, and their shared history bonded them in a way polite society never could.

The chair Stryker now occupied was an intricately carved affair. He leant back, pleased to feel its strength support his weary bones, as Saxby took his place opposite. The lord was of a similar height to Stryker, though of slimmer build. His eyes contained a clever, almost mocking glint in their brown depths, but not the arrogance that characterized the likes of Makepeace or Morris. His clothes were magnificent. The finest velvet cloth, cut by a genius, shone in the fire's soft light, complementing the sandy hair and neat beard. In all, he was in stark contrast to Stryker's battered appearance.

'Sir,' Stryker said after a while, 'I saw you follow the prince out on the right, sir. Quite extraordinary.'

Saxby grinned. 'Quite insane, actually, Captain. Not to be found in any treatise on warfare.'

'Why?' asked Stryker, as his superior began prodding at the glowing logs with a metal poker.

'Not His Majesty's decision, you understand. He knows, deep down, that he needs people like me, like Rupert, at his disposal. But my lord the Earl of Forth ain't too happy. Says the prince let us lose our heads. Led us off on a merry dance and to hell with the rest of you.'

'I saw you crush Ramsey's horse though, sir. It turned the day in our favour for sure.'

Saxby glanced up from the flames, his expression sheepish. 'But we didn't come back, d'you see? After we'd finished with Ramsey we sacked the Roundhead baggage. In the cold light of day, Captain, we should have turned back. Should have supported the foot. As it happens you held admirably. But Forth believes we'd have taken the field for certain if the prince's charge had been a tad more . . .' he turned his attention back to the fire and eventually said '. . . controlled.'

Stryker was at a loss to find a suitable response. The prince's charge had been one of the most impressive cavalry actions he had ever witnessed. But it had also been reckless and potentially fatal for the Royalist foot brigades left to defend themselves.

'I can see you agree, Captain,' said Saxby when Stryker failed to respond. 'Worry ye not. You were in the centre of that damned brawl. You were dodging pike and ball while we lined our saddle bags with plunder.' He paused to pick up a long pipe that lay on the stone hearth. It had already been packed with tobacco, and Saxby grimaced as he rummaged in the folds of his tunic for a length of match, which eventually appeared from a concealed pocket. 'Oh, don't mistake me, Captain,' he said, as he dangled the match over the roaring flames until its end began to glow. 'I ain't ashamed. We damn well routed Ramsey's lads and it saved us a deal of aggravation later in the day. But it don't require a genius to see now that our help was needed in the centre. For that I'm damnably sorry.'

'No matter.' Stryker shrugged as Saxby lit his pipe, smoke billowing around him in thick plumes. 'Taking the baggage train must have had some benefit, sir.'

Saxby's small white teeth and gleaming eyes shone through the smoke. 'Ah-ha! You always were a bright one, Mister Stryker. You are quite right. Some of the booty we took, it turns out, could be of profound significance to our worthy cause.'

Stryker raised his eyebrows, the web of scars puckering and creasing as he did so. 'Will you be so good as to make your meaning plain, sir?' he asked quietly.

CHAPTER 3

The large tent glowed orange with candlelight in the cold night.

Snatching off his hat in salute to the sentry at the tent's entrance, Saxby stooped through the opening, its grimy awning flapping in the bitter breeze. As Stryker followed, he was instantly plunged into a fog of pungent, bitter-sweet tobacco. It took several moments for his eye to cease watering as it strained against the gloom. At length he was able to force the shapes before him into focus through the thick fug.

Three men, members of the king's general staff, stood at a large circular table. Stryker, recognizing the expensive clothes and confident gazes, drew himself to attention, desperately searching for something to dispel the tension he felt. He was not easily intimidated, but this was eminent company. He looked again at the sturdy table and found himself wondering what a mighty endeavour it must have been to drag such a gigantic piece of furniture on campaign.

Saxby made an ostentatious bow and took a small step forward. 'Your Royal Highness,' he began smoothly. 'May I present Captain Stryker? Lately of Sir Edmund

Mowbray's Foot, though you'll doubtless have memory of him from days past.'

'Of course, John,' replied a man in the centre of the group. 'Of course.' There was a silver goblet at the edge of the table, and the speaker, a head taller than his companions, raised it in salute. 'Welcome, Stryker. It has been too long.'

Stryker remembered that curious accent well. Impeccable English, lifting almost imperceptibly at the beginning and end of each sentence. Impossible to pinpoint, a tribute to the speaker's pan-continental upbringing. This was an accent born in his native Bohemia, forged in The Hague, where he spent his childhood, and finished in England, where his restless and adventurous heart had found a home.

Prince Rupert, Count Palatine of the Rhine, Duke of Bavaria, was the king's nephew and General of Royalist Horse. Rupert was no more than twenty-three, yet he commanded more respect than any man Stryker had met. The ill-fated Westphalia campaign had been fought nearly five years ago, and Stryker remembered the dashing prince, a teenager then, had fought as fiercely and skilfully as a seasoned veteran.

Rupert broke away from his companions. He approached Stryker, bright eyes constantly alert, appraising him. Stryker wondered what sort of figure he himself cut before such an elegant member of royalty. Now, under Rupert's questioning stare, Stryker found himself wishing that he had followed Saxby's suggestion that he groom himself for the interview ahead. The general would be taking in the mutilated face, the long dark hair tied at the nape of the neck and falling in tousled clumps, fused together by sweat and gunpowder. He would be inspecting the bedraggled breeches and doublet, stained and frayed, and would doubtless have also noticed the blackened hands and scuffed boots.

Stryker shifted his weight from one foot to the other, unable to hide his discomfort, but the prince only smiled more broadly. 'How do you fare, Captain?' he said, as Stryker shook the proffered hand.

'Very well, Your Highness. Thank you.'

'Excellent. You were at our centre?'

'I was, Your Highness.'

'You may address me as *sir*, of course, Captain.'

Stryker dipped his head in acknowledgement. 'Sir. Yes, I was at the centre, sir.'

'Fires of hell, what?' The voice came from one of the men around the table. Stryker glanced beyond Prince Rupert to see a man of middle height, slim build and greying whiskers.

'Captain Stryker,' Saxby said, 'may I introduce you to Sir Jacob Astley?'

Sir Jacob Astley, Sergeant-Major-General of Foot, had led the king's troops at the centre of the battle.

Stryker dipped his head. 'Hellish, to be certain, Sir Jacob. I saw you lead out the lads. It was a tremendous effort, sir.'

Astley nodded, his obvious pride betrayed by the mere flicker of a smile. 'High praise indeed, Captain. Your reputation precedes you. I was in the Low Countries as well, do not forget.'

'As was I,' a third man interjected, and Stryker immediately recognized the booming voice with its Scots overtones. The big man strode forward, offering his hand,

47

which Stryker accepted warmly. 'Pleased to renew your acquaintance, Captain. It's been too long.'

'That it has, my lord.'

Patrick Ruthven, Earl of Forth and Captain-General of the king's forces, was seventy years old, but still cut the imposing figure Stryker had been introduced to a decade ago. A consummate professional soldier, the earl had fought countless campaigns, learning his trade from that champion of Protestantism, Gustavus Adolphus of Sweden. He had assumed command at Edgehill on the eve of the battle when Lord Lyndsey resigned his commission, and Stryker could not have been happier with the decision.

'I must say though, Captain, you're still an ugly-looking brute,' the earl chided.

'I am sorry to hear that, my lord,' Stryker replied solemnly. 'I thought I was improving.'

The earl grinned. 'Ah, Stryker, you always were an impudent fellow.'

'My lord.'

'Aye, well you're certainly a villain.' Ruthven turned to his fellow staff officers. 'This, gentlemen, is the best fighter I ever laid eyes upon. Should be burnt at the stake, if you ask me, for he becomes a veritable demon in a melee. And he has more campaign experience than all the soldiers in the king's army put together.'

'Then may I ask,' Astley now interjected, 'why he ain't on the staff, my lord?'

Before the earl could answer, Prince Rupert cleared his throat. Eyes swung immediately back in his direction. 'I can answer that, Sir Jacob. I will give you three reasons why Mister Stryker here is not on our staff, shall I? Firstly, he was asked and he declined.' The prince paused for effect as three shocked gazes came to rest on the uncomfortable captain. 'The blasted fellow won't be asked again. And for that matter, the last thing I require is another infantry plodder whispering villainy in my uncle's ear.' The prince glared at Stryker with those youthful, intense eyes, authority and steel united in their glare. Stryker attempted to fix his lone grey eye so that it met Rupert's with equal strength.

Just as the moment threatened to become uncomfortably tense, Rupert suddenly gave a great guffaw.

'Christ in His Heaven, Mister Stryker. I have missed you, 'pon my life I have!' Prince Rupert stepped forward to slap Stryker heartily on the shoulder. 'Saxby, here, warned me. I wondered if your manners had improved since the old days, but not a flicker!' He laughed again. 'Remarkable. I'd have most men whipped from here to Edinburgh for your brand of impertinence, but, by God, you ain't most men, and that's for certain.'

'Thank you, sir,' Stryker acknowledged.

'No. Thank *you*, sir,' the prince retorted. 'You're a man of action, and I have always liked that. I am a man of action too, Stryker, as you know. There ain't many kindred spirits to be found in these dark days,' he said, shooting a flat glance at the earl, 'so a true Brother of the Blade is always welcome at my table.'

Brother of the Blade. Stryker remembered the prince's old saying.

'Mister Stryker?' The Earl of Forth took the opportunity to cut in as Rupert went to stand behind his campaign table, the tall and powerful frame craning forward to inspect the giant map. 'Your assessment of the battle, if you'd care to indulge me.'

Stryker decided to opt for honesty. 'A stalemate, sir. Plain and simple. A pair of evenly matched sides fighting to a standstill.'

The earl nodded. 'A fair statement. And the cavalry action?'

Rupert glanced up from the map, his expression darkening. He and the earl had clearly been discussing that particular event in depth. Stryker's heart began to pound. Was he being tricked into insulting the prince? Or was the earl simply counting on an opinion from a professional soldier? Stryker took a deep intake of breath, and plumped for the latter. 'Brilliant, sir. One of the most impressive actions I've seen for years. And absolutely the most foolhardy.'

Astley and Saxby braced themselves as if awaiting a cannonade. The Earl of Forth looked smug. And Prince Rupert of the Rhine gave another shout of amusement. 'Jesu, but I should run you through. Really I should.'

His reaction cut the tension like a sabre slashing through silk. The men of the king's general staff broke into relaxed laughter.

'Beg pardon, sir,' Saxby said after a while. 'But the third reason?'

'Third?' the prince asked, regaining composure.

'You mentioned three reasons why my esteemed comrade here is not part of the general staff.'

'Ah, yes. So I did, indeed. Well, John, if you would be so kind, please tell us his damned name.'

'His name, sir?'

'Deuce it, John, but the man must have a Christian name. I refuse to believe he was named just *Stryker* by his mother. Nor do I believe you're not privy to this particular morsel of information.'

Saxby shrugged apologetically. 'I am afraid even I do not have it, Your Highness.'

'And there, gentlemen, is your third reason,' Rupert said. 'I knew this man during a time I would rather forget. He saved my life, and I am indebted to him. And yet not once did he deign to introduce himself properly, and I found it damned infuriating. When you've barely grown to man's estate, and a brutish officer is all that stands between you and Saint Peter, an officer's pig-headed refusal to give a name must be suffered with dignity. But I'll not have a man on the staff whose name I don't know. Good God, it won't do. *It will not do!*'

There was silence in the room, bar the sucking of several clay pipes. At length, the Earl of Forth raised his hand to gain the attention of the assembled group. 'Now, my friends, we must to business. John?' he said, addressing Saxby. 'What news of the road?'

Saxby frowned. 'Not a great deal, my lord, truth be told.' They all knew the road south, to London, was the key. The prize that must be seized in order to move on the capital. 'Patrols here, scouts there, spies everywhere. But no armies. No major force to block our progress.'

'Good,' said the earl quietly, deep in thought. 'Good.'

'Oxford next, eh?' the prince said, his spirits high. 'I would ride on London, as you all know. I'll ask my uncle for a force, not too many, mark, but a force enough to strike south effectively. We take London now, lance the boil while our needle is hot . . . and, gentlemen, we'll knock the stuffing out of 'em, mark my words.'

'Caution, Your Highness,' the earl said in his level tones. 'Let us secure our stronghold in Oxford before we make any rash moves.'

The younger man gritted his teeth in annoyance. 'Damn your caution, Patrick, we must strike now! Take London and leave Essex in our wake. He is weakened after the battle.'

'As are we,' the earl said levelly, long since used to cooling the young cavalryman's hot temper. 'You could ride on the capital and take it, certainly. But for how long? The main army is grievously harmed. We could not march to your support for some days. London is a vast swathe of humanity, much of which is set against your uncle, though he would not admit it. You would be spread too thin, I fear, and not able to hold it without us.'

'Then I would sack it. Sack Westminster. Teach those dogs a royal lesson.'

'And when you eventually withdraw, and withdraw you must, what will you have achieved? A sacking. You'll have wounded Parliament and its supporters, but not mortally. Simply enough to enrage them, and set them against us all the more fervently. It is not a sensible move. Valiant, surely, but not sensible.'

The prince made a gesture of exasperation, but chose not to argue his case further. He knew that to sack London would be to stir up a fearsome hornet's nest. The earl turned his attention back to Stryker. 'Captain Stryker. Has the colonel explained why you have been summoned here?'

Now to the nub of it, Stryker thought. 'In part, my lord.'

'Which part?'

Stryker recounted the conversation with Saxby. How he had described the cavalry's heroic sacking of the Roundhead baggage train. 'And I understand certain papers were captured, sir.'

The earl nodded. 'It was just a small leather satchel. Looked wretchedly unimportant, I can tell you. Remarkably fortunate the prince's men paid it a second's notice,' he said with a meaningful glance at Rupert. 'Within this bag was a mass of information about our movements. The combined efforts of a dozen spies in Essex's pay. Their network is prodigious.'

'Parliament has deep pockets, my lord.'

'Aye, it does, Captain. And deeper than even I had foreseen.' The Earl of Forth moved round to the far side of the gigantic campaign table and jabbed a meaty finger at a specific point on the map. 'Look here, Stryker. I believe you know it?'

Stryker moved to the table and leaned across to study the map. It was upside down from his position and his eyes quickly skimmed across the different shades of green that denoted the island's eclectic topography. Down through Scotland and the Pennines, across the Midlands, past the army's current position at Banbury, beyond London and down to the counties that hugged the south coast. And there his eyes rested upon the earl's hand and his home shire. He nodded. 'I grew up on Hampshire's border with Sussex, my lord. A place called Petersfield.'

The earl smiled. 'Aye, that's what we were counting on.'

'My lord?'

'When you mentioned the depth of the enemy's pockets, Captain, you were more right than you know. The papers we captured were indeed of great import to us, As a means to identify his damned spies,' The earl paced slowly around the table to face Stryker. 'Two in particular. The first is a certain Sir Randolph Moxcroft. You know who he is?'

53

Stryker thought for a moment. 'Yes, my lord. His estate is at Langrish, not far from Petersfield.'

The earl nodded slowly. 'Moxcroft is a spy, sir. Not just a spy, but a spy *master*. We know he controls a significant network across Hampshire and beyond, and the most damnable thing about it is that until now he has been one of His Majesty's most trusted, and vital, sources of information. He was *our* man.'

'Until now?'

The earl's face darkened. His brogue thickened slightly. 'The papers captured at Edgehill were in a familiar hand.' The Scots nobleman cut a sharp glance in the prince's direction. 'A hand all here know well.'

Stryker followed Ruthven's gaze and, for the first time since he had entered the tent, he saw Prince Rupert, the man he had shared a prison cell with all those years ago, looking self-conscious. Ashamed, even.

'The traitor is one of my men. A trusted confidant,' he cleared his throat awkwardly. 'A shock, to be certain. You recall my secretary, Blake? He wrote the papers. They mention Moxcroft explicitly. They even boast that Blake had turned him.'

Stryker's grey eye widened. 'Blake is a Roundhead?'

The prince was crestfallen. 'Aye, there is no doubt. He used his position with me to identify our chief spy in the south. With the promise of Westminster gold, he has convinced Moxcroft to turn his coat.'

The earl nodded. 'Blake said there was a complete dossier of Moxcroft's network. Names, locations, everything. He asks for funds to be made available, so that the rebels might purchase the information.'

Stryker chewed his lip. Men were changing allegiance

at an alarming rate, but for a key intelligence officer to throw in his lot with the enemy? That was hard to digest. It was equally shocking that Rupert's private secretary could be the catalyst for Moxcroft's defection. 'And Blake?'

The earl spoke, 'We have the dog in irons. He'll be hanged when all necessary information has been . . . extracted.'

Stryker felt a pang for the man. He would be undergoing unspeakable torture.

Rupert spoke now, concern and determination scouring deep lines into his handsome face. 'Now, Captain Stryker. We need you. You are to take Moxcroft, before he can do our cause further damage. Take him before this underhanded transaction is completed.'

Stryker had been waiting for an order since he had stepped into the tent. But he was astonished. 'Beg pardon, sir, but you wish me to travel to Hampshire to capture this spy?'

The Earl of Forth came to stand beside Prince Rupert. 'Blake turned Sir Randolph, lured him into selling his knowledge, and with it the lives of loyal men and women, to Essex. In return for his thirty pieces of silver Moxcroft will jeopardize our cause. Perhaps irreparably. Under the circumstances, I do not think "capture" is the *mot juste*, Captain.'

'You want him dead,' Stryker said.

Astley grinned wolfishly. 'That is the idea, Captain!'

The earl cast an iron glance at Sir Jacob. 'Actually, no,' he said, turning back to Stryker, 'Not dead. I want him alive, unfortunately. You can beat him to within an inch of his life if you wish, but make sure he finds his way back to me. You have heard of Lady Grace Parkes?'

Stryker nodded. The Parkes were an ancient family, tracing their roots back to the Conqueror.

'She is exceeding rich, Captain,' Ruthven went on. 'And much of that wealth currently swells the king's coffers.'

Stryker frowned. 'And Moxcroft?'

The earl grimaced sourly. 'Her cousin. A distant one, but I'd rather he were kept alive for the time being. Wouldn't want her suspecting we had a hand in his demise, now. Her good favour is crucial. So you will ride out of here with all haste, Captain. Reinforcements for the capture will be made available by Sir John Paulet at Basing House, so take yourself there *en route*. You'll have a letter with orders for him to relinquish as many men as you feel necessary.' Stretching out an arm, the earl rescued his pipe from the edge of the table. For a while all was silent as the assembled officers looked on, waiting while he reignited the pungent tobacco. He sucked on the pipe for half a dozen breaths before looking back up to meet Stryker's single eye.

Confident he had the earl's attention, Stryker spoke, careful to choose his words. 'You have reminded me of our precarious position, my lord. We mean to push for London, but the rebel is only hurt, not vanquished, so he will match our every step with powder and steel. More fighting will follow us like a bloody shadow at dusk, and, it stands to reason, you'll require people with my experience.'

'Now more than ever,' Ruthven agreed.

'So why, may I ask, does this mission fall to me?'

For the first time since Stryker had entered the tent, the Earl of Forth took his seat. It was a robust affair of polished wood, which creaked satisfyingly as he settled into its embrace. He leaned back. 'For your answer, I will defer to our General of Horse.' He glanced up at Rupert, who nodded briefly, before pacing toward the entrance to the tent.

'Will you walk a while with me, Captain?'

Rupert led the way. 'Here!' the prince snapped, as he pushed the awning aside. Stryker was startled as a large white dog raced from the tent as if its very life depended on following the prince.

'My dog, Boye,' Rupert said, ruffling the curly pelt.

The two men, with Boye at their heels, left the company in the tent and paced off into the vast encampment. It was rapidly becoming dark, but visibility was good amid the myriad white tents glowing bright between raging fires. Common soldiers were everywhere, repairing kit, cleaning muskets, honing blades. They parted like the Red Sea before the two men.

Rupert was so lofty that his head must have been six-and-a-half feet from the ground. He was a man at ease in his own skin. He strode confidently about his troops, knowing instinctively that they revered him, nodding here and there. This man – still barely a man, reflected Stryker, given his youth – exuded confidence. The troubles of his homeland had battered and weathered him until he seemed hewn from granite.

Eventually, Rupert spoke, but his tone was low, his manner subdued. 'Things are not as they were in the Low Countries, Captain. There, a man knew who he was. What he fought for. And, more to the point, what he fought against.'

'I know what I fight against, Your Highness. *You* know.'

'Aye, but you and I are a rare breed, Stryker. What of

57

the rest? The common folk? This is civil war. Neighbour against neighbour, father against son, brother against brother. The lines are blurred.' The younger man shook his head sadly. 'Men deceive. They betray. They turn their coats on the word of a preacher, or the whisper of a friend, or for a coin crossing their palm. Take these sorry villains.' He jerked his head towards a group of figures standing at the tree line on the camp's edge, some fifty paces away. 'They are to be shot.'

Stryker remained silent as they moved between and then beyond the dirty white tent awnings and out on to the open ground. As they drew closer to the group at the trees, he understood that a dozen of the men were soldiers, busily making muskets ready for action. Standing flush against the thick oak trunks were five others, in varying states of terror, hands bound at their backs.

'Taken at the battle?' he asked.

The prince shook his head. 'No, Captain. Taken after. They are ours. Two servants, a pair of cooks and this one, the one nearest us, is—'

'Captain Forde.'

Rupert regarded Stryker with keen eyes. 'Just so. You know him?'

'Of him. Distinguished himself at Kineton.'

'Thomas Forde is a traitor, sir. His heart is black as coke. He is named as a turncoat by Blake. Aye, Captain,' Rupert said. 'He is another of Blake's traitors. To my eternal shame.'

Stryker finally understood. For Prince Rupert of the Rhine, the situation had become a personal matter. Blake, one of the men most trusted by the prince, was Sir Randolph Moxcroft's Parliamentarian controller. Rupert had taken the betrayal as a personal slight, one for which he felt almost responsible.

'And that is the heart of the matter,' Rupert continued. 'Men like Captain Forde, here, fight like lions one moment, and would thrust a dirk deep between the king's shoulders the next. I cannot trust a single man, save my uncle, my brother Maurice, and, perhaps, one Captain Stryker . . .'

Stryker could not help but be startled by the compliment.

Rupert ignored the infantryman's raised brow. 'I am young, Captain, but until now I had never considered myself a fool. I trusted Blake with my life, and he was a goddamned rebel all along. Betraying us. Betraying *me*!' He sounded as astonished as he was angry. 'If my own secretary is a traitor, then who else? Astley? Lucas? Who? The earl thinks me mad. Says I should simply send word down to Paulet at Basing. Charge him with this mission. But I do not *know* the man. How could I trust him, given recent events? You were imprisoned with me after Vlotho, Stryker. We shared a cell. You saved my life. I hope – I pray – that I can trust *you*.'

'You can,' Stryker said simply.

'That was my hope. You would not be so swayed by politics or faith to turn your coat. You have sided with us, and your particular brand of loyalty will keep you with us.'

Stryker nodded.

'This issue must be resolved by my hand,' Rupert continued, 'as it was my man who betrayed us. Ruthven has agreed. As such, the course of action to be taken is my decision alone. And I cannot place my trust in more souls

59

than I could count on the fingers of my hand. You were my champion once before, and I ask you to be that champion again. Go to Hampshire. Get me that treacherous bastard.'

They reached the tree line. Forde had been bent forward, his spine curved, his head hanging like the bough of an ancient willow, but his hearing was clearly intact, for he straightened as the faintly Teutonic lilt of Rupert's voice reached him through the crisp air. It was easy to see he had been badly beaten, for one eye was glued shut with crusted blood, while his lips were cracked and oozing. Despite his sorry state, the prisoner managed a grin. 'Say your prayers,' Forde rasped through broken teeth. 'You have no hope. None. You are lost.'

Rupert sighed theatrically. 'I doubt that, Thomas, really I do.'

Forde's grin turned to a cackle that bordered on the hysterical. 'There is a storm coming. It will wash you clean away.'

'Fancy yourself Noah, do you?' the prince mocked.

Forde's good eye narrowed, flitting rapidly between Rupert and Stryker, but never settling. 'I am nothing but a servant of God. Our ark is Parliament. We will sail clear of this tribulation while the king and his Cavaliers are purged by the Lord's wrath.'

The prince nodded toward the assembled, and readied, musketeers. 'Well, there's only one place you're sailing today, Forde.'

Captain Forde lowered his head. 'If that is God's will.'

Rupert stepped forward, suddenly riled. 'It is *my* will, damn you!'

'It will see you burn in Hell's fires, Your Highness,' Forde replied, as he lifted his chin again, grunting with the effort, to meet the young general's stare.

Rupert shook his head. 'Jesu, but you Puritans are tiresome. Stone me, but you are.' He turned to the firing squad's commander, a burly, coarse-whiskered sergeant in his forties. 'Shoot the bugger.'

'A storm brews, sir!' Forde was shouting now, desperate to enrage the prince with his dying breath, as a dozen muskets were ranged upon him. 'Mark me, it brews!' He laughed, high-pitched and wild. Unsettling. 'Our pieces are in place! At the very heart of your army. They move even now to undermine you!'

'If you mean our dear friend Master Blake,' Rupert spoke over the sergeant's orders, 'you might care to know that he rots in a cell even now.' The prince turned away haughtily.

Forde's laughter died away, but to Stryker's surprise, his expression melted into a mask of calm. He smiled. 'Blake?' Forde shook his head as if attempting to rid it of bees. 'He is nothing. You know *nothing*.'

The world exploded in flame and smoke. Captain Thomas Forde's shattered body was lifted clean off its feet and sent crashing into the tree behind.

The silence that followed was shocking in its intensity.

As the thick cloud of gun smoke meandered into the dark sky, Rupert finally turned his back on the scene. 'Such men frighten me you know, Captain.'

Stryker looked up at him. 'They are zealots, sir. Nothing more.'

Rupert met his eye, concern tainting his handsome features. 'But imagine, Stryker. Just imagine what men like Forde, men with such conviction, would be able to achieve with a truly charismatic leader.'

'Forgive me, sir, but I'll wager you cannot name a man like that in the rebel ranks.'

Rupert shook his head. 'Not yet. But God help us all when they have him.'

CHAPTER 4

The man sat at the window, staring out at dark clouds pregnant with moisture. The road below was quiet, the creeping dusk having driven travellers from England's highways for the night. 'You tore my shirt,' he said matter-of-factly, not looking round.

'Do you really mind?' a gently accented voice responded from the recesses of the room.

The man smiled, fingering his collar's damaged fabric. 'No. I like my sport rough.' Lithe arms snaked around his neck and he lowered his nose to take in the intoxicating aroma of her skin. 'You are wondrous, Melisande.'

'I am French. We have more passion than you English.'

'I cannot disagree, my love.' He inhaled the scent of her skin again. 'You bewitch me,' he said with his out-breath. 'I am yours.' When a response did not come, the man twisted round to meet the girl's pale blue gaze. 'What is it?'

She freed her arms and paced further into the room. 'I am afraid, John.'

Colonel John Kesley rose from the chair, slipping his legs into breeches hurriedly discarded during their love-making. Still barefoot, he padded over to her. 'Why? Tell me.'

'I want to be with you, you know that. But you say we cannot be together – properly I mean – until this war is over. How will you ever overcome the king's forces, my love? How can you?'

Kesley reached out, placing comforting hands on his lover's slender shoulders. She was dressed like a man, boots, breeches and shirt, yet she still sent a wave of longing through him. 'How? We build an army,' he said. 'An irresistible fighting force. Professional and vast.'

'But *how*?' She punched his chest in frustration. 'Do not mock me, John, I beg you. Please, tell me how there is to be such an army. I fear for my life. For yours. You told me the king's cavalry are unbeatable. How can my lord Essex begin to challenge them?'

'He can pray,' Kesley said. It was his stock answer to a question she had asked half a dozen times.

This girl had beguiled him from the start with her skin like milk and cloud of golden hair. She had dazzled him with her delicate Gallic accent and gorgeous, sapphire eyes. As he watched her now, strutting away from him, he knew she was angry. He made a decision. 'And he can purchase.'

His lover turned, her eyes raking across him. 'Purchase?' she repeated the word. Kesley smiled slightly. 'Do you mock me still, John?'

Kesley held up a placating hand. 'Hold, my love. Hold.' She relented, and he stepped forward, spreading his arms wide in a gesture of honesty. 'I do not mock you. I speak plain, upon my honour.'

'How so?'

The colonel trod across the creaking boards to take a seat by the window. He gnawed on a fingernail. The

64

Frenchwoman had followed him, hooked upon his words, and he took her by the wrists, urging her down on to his lap. 'The enemy have wealth,' Kesley began slowly. 'They have gold and plate to sell, and with it they will swell their ranks. And yet they are bereft, for they lack the single most valuable object of all.'

'Which is?'

Kesley thought for a moment, considering his words. 'At the turning of the year, we saw that war approached. We put plans into action. One of those plans was to ensure that the king would not use his wealth to procure an army so powerful it would swallow us whole.' He paused, staring out towards the dark outline of the distant hills.

'Like that man in − where was it − Cambridge?' Melisande said. 'You told me of his daring capture of the university silver.'

Kesley nodded. 'Aye, precisely like that. We must lay our hands on as much of the king's riches as we can. But impressive as Captain Cromwell's success at Cambridge was, it was a mere drop in the ocean.'

'How do you mean, my love?'

Kesley stared at her, his eyes serious. 'A loyal agent managed to relieve the queen of her most precious possession.'

His lover looked at him, askance. 'The crown jewels?'

Kesley gave a bark of laughter. 'No, dear. This is a jewel so rare, so precious, that every other gem is like clay by comparison.'

The girl fixed her eyes on the soldier's handsome face, her jaw dropping slightly as she absorbed his words.

Kesley leaned back, satisfied with the effect of his revelation. 'A gem. A ruby. I have not seen it myself, for it is kept locked in a strongbox, but they say 'tis large as a goose egg.'

She gazed at him, studying his expression for a sign of amusement. 'I do not believe it. You still jest, John.'

'On the contrary. The gem is real, hidden for centuries in the bowels of Whitehall, they say. Knowledge of its existence was entrusted to just a handful of each reigning monarch's closest confidants.' He grinned, wide and triumphant. 'But, in these times, who is to be trusted? One of those confidants is our man. Parliament's man.'

His companion tried to speak, but a broad finger came to press against her lips. Kesley shook his head. 'I am sorry, my sweet. Even I do not know his identity.'

'And where is it kept, this ruby? Please tell me, John, I should love to know.' He frowned at her and she kissed him hungrily on the lips. 'You are so clever, my love. So clever and so strong.'

'I . . . I cannot,' Kesley said, licking his lips slowly. 'I would love to, for you would know just how close we are to changing the course of this war, but I must remain silent.'

Lisette Gaillard did not press him. Her heart soared, nevertheless. She had found it.

'So take heart,' Kesley was saying. 'And keep faith, for God has given us a great jewel. It is hard and cold and it gleams like the sun. And with it we will buy ourselves an army greater than King Charles could have imagined.'

Lisette leaned close. 'And you shall defeat the king?'

Kesley nodded. 'Oh yes, my love. As God is my witness. We shall defeat the king and, when the war is over, I will make you my bride.' When Lisette smiled, he bent low to kiss her tenderly. 'Now,' he said, turning towards the remainder of his kit, that was piled in a heap at the foot of the bed, 'I must beg your leave, Melisande. We have a consignment of muskets due tonight. Every single weapon aids our cause, does it not?'

Silence.

'Does it not?' he repeated, straightening up.

Lisette's knife was at his throat before he could turn, pressed uncomfortably at the Adam's apple, easing a bead of crimson from the skin.

'*Our* cause?' she said coldly. 'I hate your cause, sir.'

Kesley swallowed hard, wincing as his throat moved beneath the blade, and the blood escaped down his neck and bloomed like rose petals in the white linen of his torn collar. 'Forgive me, madam,' he whispered, the confidence drained from his voice. 'What is my offence?'

Lisette Gaillard's mouth twisted in disgust. 'The very sight of you offends me, sir.'

Kesley glanced down at the weapon, then at the arm that held it. She knew he was weighing up his chances of escape. But her knife was poised to kill. The grip was strong. The arm was steady.

'Who are you?'

'I am a viper, and I will bite you,' she said, her beautiful blue eyes narrowing.

'I . . . I do not—' Kesley stammered, panicking now, for he sensed no weakness. Only cruel triumph.

'I am vengeance.'

The wind bit like a whip, ice-cold breath stinging Lisette's eyes. She hunched lower, dipping her hooded head. It was barely light, but enough of the sun's weak rays pushed past the heavy clouds for her to be sure that day was breaking and the roads would finally be clear of the bandits that infested the darkest hours. It was still not safe. A woman travelling alone across land crawling with soldiers could not feel at ease. But Lisette was strong, and she had her purpose.

As she reached the stables and coaxed out the horse she had saddled in the inky depths of the night before, Lisette considered the danger she was facing. It was worth the risk.

The road was clear and the horse swift. Lisette hunkered down close to the beast's muscular neck, the acrid scent of sweat and hay that wafted from its chestnut mane making her think of the tavern again, and of that dark room where a man who prided himself on his virility had collapsed before her, bleating secrets in a vain attempt to save his throat being cut like a sheep's. She thought of the blood that pulsed warm from John Kesley's throat. She saw the life fade from his eyes. He was not the first man she had killed. The act was committed for her mistress and her God, and that was enough.

John Kesley had not died well, and that gave her no pleasure. However, she had needed the information more than she needed to salve her conscience. Lisette's knife had moved and he had given her what she needed.

She had time to make good her escape before they found Kesley's body. The hue and cry would come before long. Soldiers and common folk alike would be searching the countryside for her, but she would be further away than they could imagine. She was beyond their reach, moving ever southwards with spirits soaring as pounding hooves beat out their rhythm. She thanked the Lord for her good fortune. She would succeed. She had no choice.

—∽—

Stryker sat in the small tent as a choir of blackbirds heralded the breaking dawn outside. Carefully he inspected the nicks and chips that plagued the cutting edge of his sword, thumbing each one in turn, ruefully considering the battering Edgehill had given this perfect blade.

'Good God, man, I've never even furnished a woman with so much attention! Well, there was that Frenchy. What was her name, Stryker? Botheration! What was it? Françoise perhaps?'

Stryker looked up from his ministrations to see a beaming round red face through an opening in the tent flap. 'Claudette. As you know damned well, Forry. You were in love that time.'

The grin flattened out slightly. 'Ah, yes, Claudette. Porcelain skin, raven locks, and the most inviting pair of—'

'Forry,' Stryker interrupted. 'I'm sorry to tear you from such pleasant thoughts, but we have urgent business. You received my message?'

'Of course. And here I am.' In a blinding stream of morning light, Captain Lancelot Forrester, formerly of the London Trained Bands, lately aide-de-camp to General Gerrard, thrust back the awning and ducked into the cramped interior. He was a rotund fellow in his middle thirties, with thinning sandy hair and a ruddy complexion.

'I am forever in your debt, Forry.' Stryker said, consigning his sword back to its scabbard and thrusting booted legs out in front of him, the small stool on which he perched creaking its discontent.

Forrester was short and could stand upright in the tent.

He rubbed his back exaggeratedly, wincing as he did so. 'Ah, my poor spine. Hasn't given me this sort of trouble since I trod the boards at the Bear Tavern in Southwick. Remember, Stryker? The course of true love never did run smooth!'

'I remember it,' said Stryker, bracing himself. He was relieved that for once Forrester spared him a Shakespeare recital.

'Anyway, the battle gave my back a royal battering, and no mistake.'

Stryker's eyebrows rose. 'The battle? Did a lot of fighting, did you?'

'Oh come now, Stryker, my role was crucial. Crucial!'

'Your role as Gerrard's lapdog?'

Forrester's brow clouded. 'We aides perform a valuable service, as you bloody well know. You plodders wouldn't stand a chance if we weren't relaying orders. Jesu, Stryker—'

'A joke, Forry.' Stryker raised placating hands as he grinned mischievously. 'Just a joke. Here,' he said, indicating another wooden stool, 'have a seat.'

Forrester needed no further encouragement and dropped down on to the stool with an exaggerated sigh. 'So what's the rub?' he said brightly, once he had settled himself into a comfortable slouch.

'I have been ordered south, to Hampshire, in order to arrest a spy. You're coming with me.'

Forrester's eyes widened as he leant forward. 'I am?'

'Yes.'

Forrester frowned. 'Why?'

'I asked for you.'

'You *asked* for me?' Forrester looked like an incredulous

cherub. 'Damn it all, Stryker, but I have my duties with Gerrard now. You cannot simply thrust a sword in my hand and assume I'll follow you out of some misguided loyalty.'

Stryker smiled slightly. 'You used to.'

'Before I grew up, yes. I'm too old for charging over hill and dale on a mission. Moreover, Gerrard won't allow it. And Mowbray would have a thing or two to say about one of his captains up and leaving the field army.'

Stryker shook his head. 'This is Prince Rupert's mission. A mission sanctioned, I might add, by Ruthven. Mowbray had no choice in the matter.' He caught Forrester's eye. 'Nor does Gerrard.'

Forrester looked at him askance. 'You've already asked?'

'An hour ago. I cannot force you, Forry. I wouldn't. But the prince has granted my request to hand-pick my team. I'd like you with me.'

Forrester stared at his boots. 'I am not so . . . agile . . . as I once was, Stryker. You need speed, stealth. I have neither.'

Stryker grinned. 'You're certainly not the proposition you were a few years back.' He leaned forward. 'But I'd wager you can still handle a sword.'

'Yes, well, I know one end from the other,' Forrester said, the colour rising in his cheeks.

'And you have other qualities. Remember Father Johan? We would never have escaped that German patrol after Wittstock without him.'

Forrester smiled at the memory. 'Played the good father well, didn't I? My role as Friar Laurence at the Golden Goose stood me in good stead for the part.'

'That's what I need, Forry. I need brawn, but I need wits too.'

'The prince trusts you. But why would he trust me?' Forrester asked.

Stryker grinned ferociously. 'Because he knows I'll kill you if you betray me.'

'Good grief, Stryker, but you are an animal,' Forrester exclaimed. 'And who else will be gracing us with their presence on this foolhardy escapade? I presume that brute of a sergeant will be coming.'

'That brute of a sergeant, yes,' Stryker said. Skellen would rather like the description. 'And Ensign Burton.'

Forrester was taken aback. 'You think that callow youth will pull his weight?'

'He is green, of course,' Stryker admitted, 'but so were you and I once. And he did damned well at Kineton Fight.'

'So be it,' Forrester relented. 'When are we buggering off?'

Banbury stood at the junction of two ancient roads. To the west and south of the town was Salt Way, taking travellers from Droitwich in Worcestershire down to London and the south-east, while Banbury Lane began near Northampton before running through Banbury's High Street and on towards the Fosse Way at Stow-on-the-Wold. It was the latter road that Stryker's party took.

His men were assembled by mid-morning, and he had left them on the edge of a copse outside the town while he rode into Banbury for a final briefing with Saxby.

As he approached the town's triangular marketplace, an old woman darted from the shadows to block his progress.

'There now, Vos,' Stryker said soothingly, patting his startled horse's neck. 'Mind your carelessness, madam,' he called down, 'you might have been trampled.'

She ignored his rebuke, stepping nimbly past the beast's skittish hooves to stand at the saddle's side. 'Ribbon for your fancy lady, m' lordship?' she cawed, thrusting out a bony claw, a frayed piece of blue ribbon hanging limp in her grasp.

Stryker leant down and gripped her wrist, compelling her to take a rearward step so that Vos could move on. 'No.'

Instantly her face clouded in anger. 'Well ger'off with yer then!' she spat at his back. 'You ugly devil! Take your fuckin' soldiers with ya! Leave us! We don't want you 'ere!'

Stryker understood her. The war had been thrust upon her, and upon all the other civilians in the land. It was, in their view, a matter for the upper classes. A game of high stakes, but a game nonetheless. Men of all backgrounds would be forced to participate in the rich man's sport, like pawns on a chessboard, but it was about one type of aristocrat attempting to oust another. Most of the nation would prefer to keep their heads hung low, their eyes down and their mouths shut.

Stryker slowed Vos to a walk as a grubby barrow-boy skirted round the imposing stallion like a whippet. His rags, impregnated with a lifetime of grime, billowed about his skeletal frame as he drove the squeaking wheel over the frozen ruts of the road. 'Boy!' Stryker called. The squeaking ceased as the urchin's head flickered round in a jerking movement, as if he was prepared to be attacked at any second. Stryker's confident gaze met the boy's nervous eyes. He tossed him a coin. The movement made the youngster flinch, before his eager eye caught the glint of metal and a bony arm jerked out to pluck his prize from the air.

'Thank'ee, sir,' the boy called with a black-toothed grin, and he scampered away in haste.

CHAPTER 5

A blast of cold night air rushed through the open doorway, its tendrils whistling over mildewed straw and between chairs and tables. A dozen patrons hunched low over their pots, eager to keep close to the warming spiced ale. Most of the men ignored the intrusion, preferring to keep to themselves, though a smattering of growls greeted the newcomer when he was slow to close the door behind him. Two inebriated souls propping up the bar turned to stare bleary-eyed but threateningly at the man who had so gratingly disturbed their peace.

'B-back to your drinks,' the man in the doorway commanded.

After a moment's hesitation, the patrons returned to their pots.

'Cupshot arseholes,' the newcomer muttered as he finally shut the door and stepped on to the damp rushes. He scanned the room briefly and then paced purposefully to the far corner, where a man sat alone.

Captain Eli Makepeace looked up from his tankard and frowned. 'You are late.'

The big man's top lip wrinkled, but he spoke civilly. 'Sorry, sir. Had s-some tidying up to do.'

'Tidying?' Makepeace raised eyebrows. 'Judging from your appearance, I find that hard to believe. Were you *tidying* a whore, or *tidying* some unfortunate fellow into a ditch?' he enquired. 'Not sure I'd want to know anyway, Sergeant.'

Sergeant Malachi Bain was a giant. A hulking mass of muscle and malice enhanced by the savage-looking halberd he gripped with an easy confidence, as if the weapon were merely an extension of himself. Most sergeants carried the halberd as a sign of rank, but in Bain's powerful hands the short pole-arm was a lethal implement that would cleave a man in half with little effort. The great blade at its head was designed with three distinct and deadly features: a hook that could dismount a rider or throw an assailant off balance, an axe for hacking, and a long point for stabbing.

Bain propped the halberd against an adjacent wall, and as Makepeace watched him take up the chair opposite he marvelled, not for the first time, at how such a monster had come to be in his service.

'S-so what is it now?' Bain grunted, the myriad scars that ran across his face twitching in unison with each stammer. 'Sir,' he added.

'I see your manners are as elegant as ever, Malachi,' Makepeace said, taking a long swig of his ale and wiping his glistening moustache with the back of his hand.

'Who d'you want me t-to see?' the big man asked, scratching thick fingers across the grimy stubble of his right temple.

'No one. Not yet at least. Girl!' Makepeace hailed the young woman who bustled about the tavern dishing out and collecting ale pots. 'Two more,' he ordered when he had managed to catch her eye.

'So what is our b-b-b-business to be, Captain?' Bain kept his voice low.

Makepeace leaned forward, his voice dropping to little more than a whisper. 'Our master has made contact.'

Bain stared at the captain silently for a moment as the serving-girl placed two pots on the sticky table. 'And?' he said when the girl had hastened away.

'He has a task for us.'

Bain made no reply, but quaffed half his ale in a single breath.

Makepeace waited for Bain's concentration to return before he spoke further. 'At Kineton Fight, Rupert's boys sacked Essex's baggage train. They stumbled upon some interesting papers,' he said, leaning back to cool his own throat with a long draught of ale. He belched appreciatively.

Bain rubbed a meaty hand over his stubble. 'So what's on these papers?'

Makepeace's voice remained a whisper. 'The names of agents, Malachi. Spies. Traitors.'

'Like us, then,' Bain grunted.

'Quite so, my dear Sergeant Bain.' Makepeace smiled slightly. 'Fortunately, it did not mention either of us. Have you ever heard the name Blake?'

Bain's head shook slowly.

'Longshanks' personal secretary,' Makepeace elaborated. 'He was a spy for the Parliamentarians. He wrote to Essex, requesting greater remuneration for his clandestine work. That letter was in amongst the captured baggage.'

Bain almost spat his ale across the table. 'Bet that pleased the prince!'

'Voice down! Sergeant, have you no discretion?'

Makepeace hissed. 'They will cut Blake up or wring his neck, or both, I don't doubt.'

Bain took another gulp and sat forward. 'So what of him, anyway?'

Makepeace leaned closer too. 'Blake *also* mentions, in his letter, that he has come to an understanding with one Sir Randolph Moxcroft, who can be found in a place called Langrish. In Hampshire.'

'Hampshire?' Bain spat. 'The arsehole of England, if you ask me, sir.'

'Quite. Moxcroft is the biggest shit in it. He controls a spy ring for the king across the southern counties, but had struck a deal that would see him sell all the spies' names to Parliament. Blake's letter requested funds to secure the transaction.'

'So what the fuck has it to do with us? Long as our names aren't involved.'

For answer, Makepeace fished inside his doublet until the unmistakable chink of metal came from within its folds. Bain's eyes narrowed as a purse, heavy with coin, appeared, dropping on to the table in front of him.

Bain's hand snaked forward, quickly sweeping the purse from the table. As he lowered it on to his lap and loosened the string, his jaw dropped. 'Gold.'

Makepeace nodded. 'Angels and Unites. More than a year's wages there, Sergeant,' he whispered, as Bain hungrily inspected the bulging purse. 'Our master has assured me he will increase that tenfold if we succeed in our mission.'

Bain's hard gaze rose to meet that of Makepeace. 'He must want something b-big this time.'

'Now listen,' snapped Makepeace. 'He's learned that

the Royalists are sending a detachment south. They aim to take Moxcroft. You and I have to get there first. Rescue the bugger.'

Bain stared back at the captain, nonplussed. 'You're tellin' me that we have to ride all the w-way to the c-coast?' He shook his head. 'I hate bloody 'orses, sir.'

'I know,' Makepeace nodded, 'but you *can* ride when you so choose and you're bloody well *going* to so choose. We already lag behind, for the other detachment left this morning.'

'Why us?'

Makepeace leaned as close to Bain as possible, ignoring the fetid breath wafting from the sergeant's mouth. 'Because our master only had three senior agents posing as the king's loyal men. Forde is now executed, and Blake is captured.'

Bain grunted. 'Leaving you, sir.'

'Precisely. Resources are suddenly scarce. He has no one else left to call upon, not until the usual man from Parliament makes contact, but Christ knows when that might be. That is why he requires my services now more than ever. He will pay me well for this. And you, Malachi, and you.'

Bain chewed the inside of his lip as he studied the leather bag. 'You said they're a day ahead, sir. How can we b-beat 'em to Langrish?'

'I am informed they are due to pick up reinforcements at Basing.'

'That'll hold 'em up, right enough.'

'Indeed. So as long as we maintain our own speed, and we'll be travelling light and faster than them, we should reach Moxcroft first.'

'And we snatch him and sod off.'

Makepeace clicked his fingers. 'You have it, Sergeant. My orders are to convey Sir Randolph direct to the Commons. Mister Pym himself has a particular interest in the matter, for the names of all the king's southern spies will be crucial to his war effort. The Royalist arrest party won't even know we were there. All they'll find is an empty house.'

Bain thrust a wide finger into an even wider nostril and wiped the resulting gloopy tendril on his buff-coat. 'H-how do we know that ain't what *we'll* find, sir?'

Makepeace arched an eyebrow. 'Speak, Sergeant.'

'What's to say he'll be h-home when we come a-callin'?'

Makepeace sat forward eagerly. 'He is a recluse. Took a pistol ball in his back a few years ago and has hardly been able to walk since. The buggers come to him; farmers, yeomen, merchants. He just sits like a fat spider in the centre of the web. Unless he's already learnt the game is up, he'll be home. We'll put Sir Randolph in a nice comfortable cart and trundle up to the cap-ital like we're taking a sow to market.'

Bain stared at his ale pot, considering the plan. 'And then we simply stroll back into the regiments?'

'Aye,' Makepeace said confidently. 'Our master has provided legitimate documents to be delivered to Portsmouth. And we are charged with their delivery. That's the beauty of it, Sergeant. Our trip will be sanc-tioned by an officer in the highest ranks of the king's army!'

Bain, deep in thought, picked at his front teeth with a short dirk that appeared from somewhere up his sleeve. Half a dozen blackened stumps jutted from his raw gums.

'Fuckin' r-risky,' he said, ignoring his companion's disgusted wince.

'Aye, it is, but you'll be a rich man by the end of it.' A broad, predatory grin spread its way across the captain's features, giving him a demonic quality in the tavern's restless candlelight. 'Oh, and you'll have the satisfaction of fucking up the plans of the arrest party. And its commander.'

'Who?'

'Did I not mention he's an old friend?'

Bain stared back woodenly.

'In fact . . .' Makepeace paused. 'It is none other than Captain Stryker.'

For the first time, Bain returned his superior's expression of enthusiasm. 'You know what, sir? I fuckin' l-love Hampshire. Always 'ave.'

'You truly are ill-matched,' Lancelot Forrester laughed, as they broke camp on the second day.

The pike-thin Ensign Burton leaned forward to pat his chestnut gelding's broad neck. 'Pay him no heed, Bruce.' He spoke soothingly into the sharply pricked ear, then straightened up. 'Sixteen hands is perhaps a touch on the large side. But he was a gift from Father.'

They were headed south, but Stryker was making sure they avoided the major roads that bound England like arteries. Progress was painstaking as they picked their way through the hilly Oxfordshire terrain. Fields gave way to rocky climbs, which would suddenly dive into river-cut valleys. It was not safe to be isolated from the main army in this hotly contested region, and Stryker was acutely aware that just beyond the nearest hills there could be a restless enemy eager to fight.

'There's nothin' like the countryside,' droned Sergeant William Skellen, slowing his bay mare as they approached a crossroads.

They were four individuals in tawny buff-coats, muskets slung across their backs, with no obvious sign of rank to differentiate them. Stryker had insisted they be issued new kit; new swords, known as tucks to the men, sturdy bucket-top boots, well-sewn snapsacks and quality riding tack.

'You like the countryside, Sergeant Skellen?' asked Ensign Burton, drawing Bruce up beside the sinewy veteran.

'Of course, sir. Wet feet, cold bones, stench o' dung crawling up your nostrils. Love it.'

'You're a city boy, Will, I know,' Stryker said. 'But out here, you get to eat. You can fill your belly 'til you can't move.'

Skellen shrugged. 'I can do that in Portsmouth, sir, thank'ee. Or London, or Newbury or anywhere. That's the beauty of the city, see? Full of taphouses.'

'And wenches,' offered Forrester.

'Aye!' agreed Skellen. 'There's women in the country-side, but they're mostly a gaggle of gap-toothed rig-muttons.' This drew a chorus of jeers and laughter. 'But the city's full of occupyin' houses, ain't it, so the product has to be that much better, see? Why, I've seen some places where every girl in there's been nice as a nanny hen.'

'Well, your theory won't hold much longer, Sergeant. Well put as it was.'

'How so, Captain?' Burton asked.

'We're at war, Andrew,' Stryker said.

'With respect, sir,' Burton replied, 'Aren't we always at war? With the Dutch or the Scotch or the French?'

'And where do we fight these wars, Ensign? Where do the grand armies march? Up Ermine Street? Through Seven Dials? Across the Downs?' Stryker paused as the young officer thought for a moment. 'No,' he said eventually. 'They get on ships and take the fight to the Continent. And merry old England stays untroubled.'

''Cept for the taxes we all 'as to pay, sir,' offered Skellen.

'And what happens if the war slips into the year after, or the one after that?' asked Burton. 'I heard what happened in the Low Countries, sir.'

'It weren't just the towns neither,' continued Skellen. 'The peasants in the fields looked like ghosts, they were so wretched and skinny. I remember 'em clear as day. I should – it were me and my mates what took their food.'

'It was all of us,' agreed Stryker.

'Not to worry though, eh?' Captain Forrester spoke merrily. 'If the war drags on too long, young Burton,' he said with a wolfish grin on his round red face, 'we shall eat you.'

The wood had proved to be an excellent resting spot. A fire had been lit, which was a risk, but Stryker wagered that the mass of branches would shield them from the enemy.

Stryker slumped on to the mushy leaves of the forest floor and sighed with pleasure as the first flickers of life sprang up from the fire. He looked across to his companions as the whickering of horses behind them mingled with the men's chatter, the banging cooking tins and the sharpening of knives.

A stew of wild mushrooms and rabbit, shot by Skellen that morning, was soon cooked up.

As the men ate and talked and laughed, Stryker delved inside his coat and withdrew a folded piece of worn parchment. He followed the lines and contours of the land on the map spread before him. There was a long way to go, and he did not know what lay ahead. They could all be dead tomorrow. Damn Saxby. And damn the earl. And damn the prince, for that matter. A pox on the lot of them. They viewed him as a tool, a weapon to wield when they saw fit, and he was certain none would lose any sleep over the perils he and his men might face.

'Sorry to bother you, sir,' said Skellen. 'Just wondered 'pon our route for this afternoon and tomorrow.'

'More of the same,' replied Stryker. 'Push south, avoiding the larger towns. We cannot be invisible, so we'll aim to be fast. If we're accosted by our own side, I have the prince's letter.' He patted the side of his doublet where, sown into the inner lining, the parchment was concealed.

'And if we run into the enemy?' Skellen asked.

Forrester smiled. 'We ride like blazes in the opposite direction!'

By early evening they reached the brow of a low hill. As they crossed the crest, Forrester pointed to a community below. It was nothing but a little hamlet, wisps of smoke and ramshackle roofs marking its unassuming presence in the rolling countryside. They drew up their mounts to survey the scene, scouring building, tree and shrub for signs of enemy activity.

'Doesn't look too threatening, eh?' Forrester said as he moved alongside his friend.

84

On Stryker's order the company set off at a canter. They all knew their captain's mind; the village would make an ideal billet for the night.

It took another hour to reach the outskirts of the hamlet. The track they had followed had opened out into a clearing, presumably a place to graze livestock, beyond which a wide ring of gorse hedge barred their way, cutting left to right in front of them. As they searched for the hedgerow's limits, it became clear that the gorse was, in fact, a huge ring, encircling the village.

'A natural rampart,' Stryker said appreciatively. It was not a solid hedge, for there were plenty of gaps between the clumps of thorny foliage, but it remained a formidable defensive position.

'Wouldn't stop this,' Skellen replied, tapping his musket's wooden stock.

'Stop cavalry though,' Forrester said.

The first homes were erected on the far side of the hedge. As they entered the clearing the horsemen were tense and watchful. They could not prime matchlock muskets in the saddle, but their carbines were cocked, and swords were scraped in and out of scabbards in an effort to ensure they would not become stuck at a crucial moment.

With weapons trained on various points within the village, Stryker urged Vos into a trot and advanced beyond the first homes on to a small sliver of mud at the centre of the buildings, which he took to be the village green. No one came to greet him, and no shots rang out to fell him. He wrenched his body left and right, acutely aware of his blind left side, scanning doorways, pigsties and frozen water troughs for hostile activity. He felt a trickle of nervousness as he moved, the squelching of hooves unnaturally loud in the silence. He was confident of the men that covered his progress. Confident that an enemy would be put down in short order. But all it took was a single ball and Stryker's world would be over. At length a creaking sound broke the eerie still of the green. It was the complaint of rusty hinges.

Stryker wheeled Vos round, levelling his carbine in one smooth motion, ready to put a ball through any potential ambusher. The index finger of his right hand curled about the trigger. Most men closed their left eye when they took aim, but Stryker's lone right eye simply gazed down the short barrel like it was casually watching a bird take flight. And in front of that barrel, through the open doorway, came a man.

He was a tall fellow, dressed in plain brown breeches and a linen shirt. His neat beard and thinning hair were an iron grey. He approached Stryker slowly, hands raised in peace, though his bearing was one of authority.

Stryker saw the man was unarmed, and slowly lowered his weapon. 'Who are you?' he called.

The man, about ten paces away now, attempted a friendly smile, though his tension was evident. 'Thomas Archer,' he said. 'I am elder in this village.'

'Captain Stryker, Mowbray's Regiment of Foot, His Majesty's army.'

'God be praised,' said the elder.

———⚬———

It was barely a body. The limbs were twisted and the clothes were all gone. It was not a great deal more than a mound of decomposing flesh, abandoned in the sodden scrub at the road's edge.

86

'A man, that was.' Sergeant Malachi Bain had inspected the corpse with professional disinterestedness. 'Took a ball in his chest.'

Makepeace was standing with the horses some ten paces away, nose wrinkled in distaste. 'And they stripped him?'

Bain nodded. 'V-very thorough job.' He glanced up. 'Bandits, probably.'

'Perhaps. Perhaps not. Every man, woman and child we have passed has skulked away from us like we had the plague.' He jerked his chin toward the cadaver. 'That is why. This poor bugger might have been robbed by bandits, certainly, but he might equally have been attacked by troops.'

Eli Makepeace had been a soldier for a long time, and he could feel the fear on the roads, in the fields, and in the towns. Folk did not know friend from foe. They could not trust their own kin.

———❦———

'Oh, Lord God, I beseech you. Forgive us. We, your un-worthy subjects, sinners to a man, have betrayed you most heinously. We quarrel among ourselves. We lose sight of your true teachings. England has turned upon herself. She will tumble into the depths of hell. Do not let this happen, Lord God. Protect us from ourselves. Give our king the valour and fortitude to lead us—'

Father Benjamin Laney, kneeling before the altar of St Peter's church, was startled from his prayers by the echoing creak of the monstrous wooden door. The priest turned his head of scanty red hair and squinted towards the feature-less silhouette that stood like a carved statue in the elaborate nave. Gargoyles, saints and sinners writhed on cold walls as the candlelight, worried by the sudden rush of night air, breathed life into their carved expressions.

As the priest struggled to his feet in order to gain a better view of the newcomer, the great door swung shut, putting him in mind of the stone that protected Christ's tomb. A chill traced its way along Benjamin's spine, and it took every ounce of his faith not to turn and run.

The hooded figure moved. It paced forward along the nave with purpose, and Benjamin prayed again.

When the figure was no more than an arm's length away it stopped, and Father Benjamin frowned, for his nostrils were filled with a raw stench. The creature may have been a denizen of the netherworld, but its odour was decidedly earthly. It stank of leather, sweat and horse flesh.

'Good evening, Father.'

Father Benjamin's jaw dropped in surprise. The voice was a woman's.

'You startled me,' the father chided while they made their way to the back of the church.

'My apologies, Father.' Lisette said.

'No matter. I am glad to see you again, my child. I never tire of hearing your beautiful accent.'

'I have news.'

He glanced at her sharply. 'The queen?'

Lisette shook her head. 'The queen is well, Father. Raising funds abroad. She sends her regards.'

'God be praised,' the priest said. 'It is many a year since I followed an assignment for Her Majesty, but I am flattered she might think of me.' He studied Lisette's face. 'And yet here you are. The queen's favourite agent, and my old comrade. I imagine you have not made the journey to Petersfield in order to recant your Catholicism?'

Lisette smiled. 'No.'

'Then?'

'Something very important was stolen from the queen. Snatched by a traitor in the royal household. A strongbox. I was sent to England to recover it.'

When they reached the priest's private chambers at the far end of the church, Lisette described her final conversation with Kesley, omitting only the bloody ending. 'Old Winchester Hill. Where is it, Father?'

Father Benjamin wrinkled his nose as he considered the question. 'It's an old fortress. Very old. West of here.' The priest frowned. 'You sought this colonel . . . Kesley out?'

She nodded. 'Aye. Colonel John Kesley. He did not know what was in the box, only that its value to Parliament was mighty. His part in the theft was to find an appropriate place for the strongbox to be held while a buyer was found. I made him . . . he told me the cities were too dangerous to hold such a valuable item, and that the rebel high command had wanted it moved south, near Portsmouth, so that it could quickly be transferred to a ship and carried overseas.'

Benjamin shuddered. 'Please do not burden my conscience with the detail of your work. Against all probability, I will tell myself he spoke without duress.'

'As you wish, Father.' She regarded him with an expression of flint.

'The location he gave you was Old Winchester Hill.'

'Aye, buried there. At its summit.'

'And Kesley told you it lay in the downland near Petersfield,' the priest completed the thought. 'Yet you come to me, why?'

89

'You are the nearest of the queen's agents. And I know you are as committed to the Royalist cause as I am, even if you are a heretic.'

Father Benjamin held up a firm hand. 'Please, *mademoiselle* Lisette. Let us not debate theology tonight. We work for the same king.'

Lisette's upper lip wrinkled. 'No. I work for his queen. Henrietta Maria.'

Benjamin sighed. 'No matter. I will help you, Lisette, but not if I am to be blind. Tell me what bounty the strongbox holds.'

The Frenchwoman narrowed her eyes. 'I will tell you. But if you betray me, Father, I will slice off your balls and feed them to my horse.'

Benjamin swallowed hard. 'I do not doubt it.'

'It is a ruby. A wondrous thing the queen will sell to one of the great monarchs of Europe. She will buy an army for the king with it.'

Benjamin pursed his lips. 'What gem, no matter how wondrous, can be worth the price of an army?'

'I know not, nor do I care to ask questions,' Lisette replied. 'I have my orders, and I will fulfil them or die in the attempt.'

Benjamin turned away suddenly. 'Wait here a moment.'

Lisette thought of the strongbox as she watched Father Benjamin disappear into the antechamber at the rear of the small room. It did not contain only a ruby. The queen had spoken of other trinkets. A brooch, a small posy ring and an old letter were all kept within the locked walls of the box. None carried any particular monetary value, but they were all of sentimental worth to Henrietta. It seemed to Lisette that the queen wanted them back as much as she wanted the gem. It did not matter. She was charged with the box's safe return, and that was enough.

'Where are the others?' Father Benjamin was saying as he emerged from the antechamber clutching a tightly bound scroll. 'The queen would not have sent you alone.'

'Dead,' Lisette replied.

Father Benjamin's copper eyes widened. He swallowed hard and scratched at the wisps of hair covering his shining pate. 'You were discovered?'

'Be at ease, Father,' Lisette said, noticing his fingers tremble a touch. 'There was a brawl in a tavern overlooking the Thames. Before we could intervene, Jerome had been knifed in the guts.'

Lisette told the priest how she and her other companion, Cedric, had hauled the injured man to see the nearest chirurgeon. While there, as the sawbones had poked and prodded at the writhing Jerome's innards, they were approached by a soldier of the Westminster Trained Bands. He claimed to recognize the injured party; said he looked like one of the men who had guarded Whitehall Palace. One of the king's men.

'Jerome was skewered where he lay by that fucking militia bastard,' Lisette said simply.

Benjamin's mouth opened in horror, revealing small, yellowing teeth and long gums. 'And Cedric?' he managed to whisper. 'I worked with him myself when I was sent to spy on Buckingham. He was a good man, Lisette.'

She nodded. 'Aye. But being good does not keep you alive, Father. Cedric drew his blade in retaliation. Cut the Trained Band whoreson almost in two. But half a dozen of the soldier's friends appeared. Cedric did not stand a chance.'

'You escaped?'

'No. Not really. They simply let me be.' She shook her head at the memory.

Benjamin understood. 'They did not take you for one of Cedric's companions.'

'Praise God. I played the bystander. The frightened woman. The bastards believed me.'

And then she was alone. It might have been easier to have taken ship back to her mistress in one piece, but Lisette Gaillard loved her queen, and would not give up without a fight.

'I am sorry, my child,' Benjamin said.

Lisette noticed the scroll Father Benjamin had retrieved from his antechamber. 'What's that?'

She followed Father Benjamin to a small table at the room's centre, where the clergyman laid out the musty parchment. It was dark outside, and Lisette now noticed a flurry of snow shimmering in the moonlight as it fell, but the room's guttering candles proved equal to the task of illuminating the varying shades of the map that she now studied.

'My fair county, Lisette,' Benjamin said, casting his bespectacled gaze across the intricate lines and minute text that detailed the geography of Hampshire. 'We are here.' He jabbed a brittle-looking finger at the word *Petersfield*, scrawled in an almost illegible hand. Moving the finger down and to the left, he rested it at an unmarked point near the map's centre. 'And here is Old Winchester Hill. Perhaps ten miles to the south and west of here.'

Benjamin straightened up. 'But it is not a fort as you imagine, Lisette. It has ramparts, of course, but they are

dug into the chalk hillside. The legacy of an ancient city.'
He met Lisette's gaze levelly. 'You will travel there?'

'Of course.'

'The road is treacherous, my child. Especially during this blizzard. Wait until dawn, I urge you.'

Lisette considered his plea. 'Aye, I will. If I may rest here.'

'You need not ask.'

Father Benjamin rolled the parchment into a scroll once more and fastened it with a string tie. He held it out to Lisette. 'You will need this. The hill is up in the high downland. Not easy to find for someone unused to the area.'

Lisette stared back. 'That is why you are coming with me, Father.'

———m———

Stryker's eyes flickered open. He lay motionless for a moment, listening intently to the thunder that was shaking the new dawn.

It had rained during the night, and the men had been more than grateful for the room they now shared. Little more than a shed, leaning precariously against the gable-end of Archer's house, it was cramped and dirty, but a godsend compared with a night under the winter stars. Stryker turned to his side and saw that William Skellen was also awake, staring at the ceiling's damp timbers.

'Hear that, sir?' Skellen said. 'Strange. Sky was clear when I went out for a piss an hour ago.'

Stryker listened, more keenly this time, 'Shit.' He sat bolt upright, startling the others awake as he did so. For outside the world was shaking again – but this time with the rumble of hooves.

Burton was nearest the rickety door, and despite having just awoken from deep sleep, he was alert enough to scramble out into the grey light. He scanned the horizon with squinting eyes while the others got to their feet. 'Cavalry!' he called. 'They're on the hill to the north. Coming down at a rate.'

'Are they ours, sir?' barked Skellen.

'Can't tell, Sergeant. But I doubt it. Don't recognize the colour.'

'How many?' said Forrester, a sheen already adorning his red face.

'A score at least.'

As Burton spoke, another man raced from the house's main entrance to join them. It was Archer. 'I am sorry!' he cried, lungs gasping with his exertion, and with fear. 'Please believe me, Captain.'

'A trustworthy man?' Stryker spat as he and his companions hurriedly collected up their weapons. 'He was supposed to warn us, goddamn it!'

Archer was in a cold sweat, clearly fearing Stryker's wrath as much as the approaching cavalry. 'I beg forgiveness, sir. Marcus *is* trustworthy, upon my honour. He must have fallen asleep.'

Stryker fought to gain control of his temper. He had given the young farm-hand a shilling – more than a day's pay for one of his pikemen – and expected to be woken as soon as soldiers were spotted.

'I am mortified, sir, truly,' Archer was saying.

Stryker did not have time to discuss the situation. He shouldered Archer aside, making for the rear of the lean-to where the horses were tethered.

'*Jesu!*' he exclaimed, as he reached Vos, remembering in a flash of annoyance that the beast was not saddled.

94

Forrester turned to him. 'They'll be here before we tack up.'

Stryker nodded and glanced at the others. 'We have no choice. Put the horses in there,' he ordered, indicating the lean-to.

'There's no room,' Forrester argued. 'They'll kick each other to pieces!'

Stryker rounded on him, 'You have a better idea?'

Forrester did not.

Stryker led Vos to the shed's door, patting the stallion's neck as the muscular beast obediently disappeared into the gloom. The others followed suit, though it was indeed a tight squeeze.

'What now, sir?' Burton asked anxiously. 'We're trapped.'

'Have faith, Andrew,' Stryker replied, and turned to Thomas Archer. 'Time for you to make amends, Mister Archer.'

CHAPTER 6

The troop cantered into the centre of the village; they were led by an officer mounted on a large bay. The men wore thick yellow hide coats extending over the thigh, and pristine back and breast armour that shimmered like pearls in the dawn; each wore a steel helmet with three vertical face protectors attached to a hinged peak. Heavy single-edged swords swung at their sides, slapping against leather boots.

Beside the leading officer rode the cornet. He bore the blue and white standard high on its pole, yet it hung limp in the still air. Stryker, watching from one of the upper windows of Archer's home, did not recognize the symbols that marked the flag's owner, but he knew who they fought for well enough. 'Bollocks,' he whispered.

'Whose bollocks?' a familiar voice hissed beside him.

Stryker's hand instinctively went to his belt, grasping the hilt of his dagger, then relaxed. 'Jesu, Forry,' he said. 'I could have filleted you.'

Forrester displayed a mischievous grin. 'That's why I came to your right, old man. Didn't want to blind-side you, if you'll excuse the phrase. So, what are we facing?'

Stryker shook his head in exasperation, turning his attention back to the unwelcome cavalry. 'I don't know exactly, but they're not ours.'

'Do we take them?' Burton's voice came from somewhere to the rear. Stryker twisted round to see that Skellen had joined them as well. The order for them to stay in the back-rooms of the house had fallen on deaf ears.

'Take them?' Stryker stared. 'You'll make a fine officer, Andrew, but only if you learn when to display caution. They're harquebusiers. They're well trained. They ride well. They're superbly equipped. They're confident. No, we don't take them. We'd each get a shot off, and the remaining sixteen of them would ride us down like rabbits.'

'That's if they let us out,' Skellen added. 'They'd probably fire the house to save 'emselves the trouble.'

'Still,' Forrester said chirpily, offering a hand for Burton to shake. 'Admire your bravado, Ensign. Said like a young Captain Stryker.'

The cavalry halted on the village green. The tired steeds were clearly in need of rest and they walked listlessly about, foraging for the remnants of grass, their bloodied flanks heaving in unison.

The harquebusier captain remained in his saddle and surveyed the immediate area warily.

Thomas Archer, the tall village elder, appeared from his doorway, and the soldiers bristled in their saddles. Some reached to unsheathe lethal weapons that rested against the horses' muscular flanks. Archer raised submissive palms, as he had upon greeting Stryker. He called to the cavalrymen, though Stryker could not hear his words.

The troop held their ground until the man was within ten paces of the nearest horse. The captain's mount, responding to a gentle shake of its reins, lurched forward from the centre of the group. The fearsome stallion, bay hide glistening with sweat, halted a mere sword's length from the villager.

Stryker looked on, studying his adversary. 'Don't let me down again, damn you,' he whispered through clenched teeth.

The horse commander was young and his expensive attire betrayed an upbringing of privilege. He had dispensed with the buff-coat worn by his subordinates, preferring the comfort of a black woollen coat adorned with ornate gold trim. He wore body armour that had been enamelled black and studded with dozens of gilt rivets, crowned by a gleaming black helmet that he now removed to reveal a head of short blond hair. He had grown a beard and moustache, though the straggly facial hair only served to reinforce the impression that he had barely reached his twenties.

Stryker glanced at Forrester, handing him his musket. 'I have to hear what they're saying. Hold this, Forry.' His bandolier was to follow, eased carefully over his shoulders, and then the scabbard was unhooked from his belt. It was a painstaking and awkward process, but a necessary evil.

He crouched low, careful to keep below the windowsill, and crept to the rear of the room and then down the stairs, the creaking of each step seeming inordinately loud to his alert senses.

He quickly crossed the main reception room of Archer's modest home and secreted himself behind the small door through which the elder had passed. It was still ajar, a keen chill filling the room, and Stryker was able to squint through the crack where the door met its hinges. His lone eye flicked from left to right, taking in the green, the soldiers, their horses and Archer in one sweep.

'A loyal follower of God and Parliament. Like yourself,' the elder was saying nervously, nodding at the orange sash tied diagonally about the captain's torso. In this new war it was the only sign of a soldier's allegiance upon which common folk could rely. The Royalist cavalry had taken, more often than not, to wearing a blood-red sash.

'God, Parliament and King Charles, sir,' the captain retorted. 'For we fight to liberate our liege lord from the influences currently clouding his judgement.' He paused. 'Do we not?'

'Aye . . . we do,' the villager replied.

The officer, seemingly satisfied with Archer's display of loyalty, reached out to the left and handed his helmet to one of the two trumpeters that rode with the troop. He then swung his legs, clad in high leather boots, over the saddle and jumped on to the sticky mud.

'Captain Roger Tainton at your service,' he said, offering a gloved hand. The servile villager shook it enthusiastically, for he was relieved. Men on horseback, bristling with steel, were to be feared regardless of apparent allegiance.

'You are most welcome, Captain,' said the elder earnestly, 'but I fear we do not have sufficient feed for your mounts here in the village. There are stables out toward the church.' He pointed eastward, to a field beyond the gorse ring, at the far end of which stood a small chapel and some dilapidated outbuildings. 'Perhaps you might like to decamp there while I see to your victuals?'

Good, thought Stryker. Archer was following his instructions to the letter, drawing the Roundhead force away so that the Royalists could escape.

'Thank you,' replied Tainton curtly. 'But I shall take refreshment now.'

Roger Tainton was of noble blood. 'My father even had the ear of the king,' he said, 'before this . . . mess.' He waved a hand about in an attempt to describe the war that now raged. 'He now leads our men as colonel.'

They were seated in Thomas Archer's modest home. Tainton was in the best chair, while the elder and his wife were perched on a bench opposite. Between them was a sturdy, though rough-hewn table that was not truly flat. The meal was laid out in wooden bowls, which tilted precariously.

The bulk of the troop had cantered off toward the chapel and its adjacent stables, but, much to Stryker's vexation, Tainton had given responsibility for the men to a lieutenant, preferring to take his own victuals immediately. A pair of troopers had been stationed outside the house to guard their commander while the rest were away. Thus, Stryker and his three companions remained trapped in the house.

Stryker was now installed in a narrow, cool room, which served as the couple's pantry. It was adjacent to the kitchen, and provided a perfect place from which to eavesdrop.

The couple appeared to be listening intently to Tainton's words, though Stryker presumed this was more out of appeasement than fascination. Between mouthfuls of bread and meat their guest regaled them with stories of how the rebels would reap revenge upon God's papist enemies. 'And I shall play my own small part.'

'The pamphlets?' Archer said, remembering the

anti-Royalist parchments Tainton's men had nailed to the sides of some of the village buildings.

Tainton nodded. 'We must not let our enemies win the hearts and minds of the common folk. We have not yet secured this region. The king enjoys as much support in these shires as our own army. Therefore certain regiments have been dispatched to town and village alike to proclaim the rights of Parliament. Your village in particular, as you are in the path of any attack from the king. If he marches from Oxford, he will surely pass this way toward London. It is left to me to ensure that all men will rise up against his tyranny.'

'Amen,' Archer said stoically. 'I assure you, Captain, our village is steadfast in its support for Mister Pym and his Parliament. You can be certain of that.'

'That is good, sir. After all, I feel sure you would not wish me to compel you to offer support.'

'Compel, sir?'

'Aye,' Tainton's voice was low, his eyes narrow. 'If you are for the enemy, my friend, then you cannot continue here. I am authorized to facilitate your . . . *movement*,' he said, lacing the last word with a spine-chilling darkness.

Stryker knew what that meant, though he could scarcely imagine such a threat being carried out in England. He had seen the skeletal remains of towns and villages in the Netherlands and Germany. He'd heard the screams and smelled the charred flesh. The anguished wails of widows, lamenting the loss of their men, rang in his ears and twisted his guts. He'd seen the death throes of an entire family as they were hanged from the creaking bough of a tree. He remembered the youngest boy's thrashing legs, the urine dripping from his shoes to stain the earth, and could not help but think of the lad he had seen at Banbury.

Tainton brightened suddenly. 'But I have other duties also, of course. I must recruit new men to our ranks. Our strength must be irresistible when next we take to the field.'

'There will be further battle then?'

'Aye, sir, of that I am certain. No great advantage was gained at Kineton Fight, so we must regroup our army, bolster our faith and pray for one last reckoning. The papists are said to be already mustering their forces, just as we are.'

Thrusting the last piece of bread into his mouth, Tainton pushed the plate away from him with a satisfied grunt. When the bread was swallowed down, the captain's lips parted to speak again, but he was interrupted by a vigorous knocking at the door.

'My men,' the cavalry officer said. He fished in a pocket and withdrew an intricately woven square of linen. Calmly touching it to the corners of his mouth, he stood and, with a sharp nod to his hosts, paced from the room.

From his hiding place, Stryker could not hear the conversation, but the guard's words were spoken in undoubtedly urgent tones. Instinctively he knew the source of the man's animation and his heart sank.

Tainton paced back into the kitchen. 'There are horses in your house's annexe, Mister Archer.'

'They are mine, Captain.'

'You own four horses?' Tainton sneered incredulously. 'And four sets of tack?'

Archer took a step backward. One of his wife's hands moved to clasp his elbow. 'I . . . I do, sir.'

Stryker fished a dirk from his doublet. The Archers had taken them in. Fed them and given them respite. He felt obliged to defend them, even to the detriment of his own mission.

'And you keep your four horses in a small shed, when, in your own words, there is ample stabling at the chapel?'

Archer remained silent.

Tainton stepped forward. 'I believe you have lied to me, Mister Archer.'

'No, sir. Please!' Archer and his wife backed away further, recoiling from the captain's rising anger as though he breathed fire. 'We use them to draw carts to market.'

Tainton grinned wolfishly. 'Market? They do not sound like tuppence nags, sir. My trooper tells me they are fine beasts. Warhorses.'

Stryker tightened the grip on his blade and began to move.

'Sir? Sir!' the guard burst into the room, shattering the tense atmosphere.

Tainton turned. 'What is it now, man?'

'The enemy, sir. Cavalry. Up in the hills!'

'How many?' Tainton snapped.

'Can't tell exactly, sir, but it's quite a number. Threescore, p'rhaps.'

Tainton's jaw quivered. 'They head in this direction?'

The messenger nodded, and Tainton cursed, glancing back towards Archer. He was clearly tempted to linger long enough to continue the enquiry into the mysterious horses, but there was no time to lose. 'Run to the stables, Chaloner. Fetch the men and tell them to saddle up.'

*

The Parliamentarian troop streamed out of the village's southern entrance. They were significantly outnumbered but better equipped, and their heads were carried high, their backs straight as they cantered in tight formation. They had had little time to resaddle mounts and strap on the heavy back and breast plates that had been removed earlier in the day, but the danger posed by an approaching enemy of such obvious size and strength worked wonders in quickening a man's step and energizing weary bones. In short order the Roundhead cavalrymen were arranged in double file, a resplendent Captain Tainton leading the way beside his cornet. 'Follow me, my lads!' Tainton cried over his shoulder as he urged his excited horse on. 'Follow me!'

Stryker's small party had left their hiding places within Archer's house as soon as the rear rank of Tainton's column left the village. The Roundhead commander was a brave man, Stryker thought, or an insane one. A full troop of enemy cavalry was cantering down towards the village, threescore men bringing threescore blades, and he would ride out to meet them head to head. Stryker, too, had fought terrible battles against insurmountable odds, just because he wanted to. Now he watched as a younger version of himself kicked his steed into a gallop at the head of twenty metal-clad men, and knew just what that man would be feeling.

'But what if our boys get into trouble, sir?' asked Ensign Andrew Burton, as they ran to their mounts.

'Then they get into trouble,' Stryker replied. 'Our mission is too important to risk on a random skirmish.'

'Besides,' Skellen said, 'there's bloody loads of 'em. If our lads get their arses tanned by a couple o' dozen Roundheads, I'll eat me boots.'

Forrester reached the lean-to first and wrenched open the groaning door, peering into the gloom. When he turned back to Stryker, his face was drained of its usual colour. 'My kingdom for a horse.'

'Bastards,' Skellen grumbled as they crouched amid the village's gorse perimeter. 'Bloody bastards. I was beginning to like old Bess.'

Bess, the sergeant's brown mare, was at the rear of Tainton's column. She and the other horses had evidently been confiscated. Tainton clearly had not believed Archer's claim to ownership.

'We're getting them back,' Stryker had declared. 'We'll wait 'til they engage and isolate them.'

The four men were ensconced within the tangled claws of gorse, muskets and carbines primed, waiting for their chance.

'Sir,' Burton whispered sharply. 'What are they doing? They seem to be circling back.'

The men followed his gaze. Tainton's cavalry were assembled in the open ground between the hedge and the forest. Stryker had fully expected them to thunder through that flat area, past the trees, and up the track to smash into the head of the enemy formation. He was wrong: the Roundheads were doubling back on themselves. At least some of them were. Tainton had led his troop on to the churned clearing, but rather than taking them up the track, he was perched in his stirrups, calling to individual horsemen. As each received his orders, small groups were peeling away from the main force to gallop in different directions.

'They mean to ambush 'em,' Forrester said. 'Sneaky bugger.'

'Clever bugger,' said Stryker. 'He'll put some in the trees where the track opens on to the clearing. Some'll stay in the open to entice them in. And some,' he said with a dawning dread, 'will circle back this way.'

As if on cue, a group of three Roundhead cavalrymen urged their mounts towards the tangle of gorse that hemmed the village. They could not see Stryker's men yet, for the tendrils of the hedge were dense and dark, but they were heading for a gap in the thick brush and would spot the four men as soon as they had plunged through to the village side.

Stryker's group scrambled back towards the village, keeping as low as possible, and dived behind the nearest building. In moments, the three horsemen were through the gap. Mercifully, they had no intention of continuing into the village. They were, as Stryker had anticipated, to be stationed this side of the gorse in order to surprise the Royalist arrivals.

'Now what?' grunted Skellen.

'Now we wait,' Stryker said as the first of the Royalists whooped their excitement at spotting the Parliamentarian horsemen, Tainton's bait, milling in seemingly aimless fashion at the centre of the open ground. 'And we watch.'

The Royalist troops were impressive, but utterly chaotic. They were mostly recruits riding new mounts in shiny armour bought by proud parents. While there were always men like Stryker in any unit who brought coveted experience and professionalism to war, most soldiers were a bright shade of green. Skirmishes on horseback were all too often anarchic affairs, with formations collapsing amid swordplay of great enthusiasm and little finesse.

As a thin flurry of late October snow began to pepper

the hard land, a column of zealous youths burst from the ancient bridleway and into the clearing. Like their Roundhead counterparts, they were light cavalry: harquebusiers. They wore leather buff-coats with armour protecting the head, chest and bridle arm. Carried at each side and attached to belts crossing both shoulders were a broadsword and carbine. Emblazoned across all of this standard regalia was the bright-red sash of Royalist allegiance. They clearly intended to blood themselves on the handful of unfortunate Parliamentarians, whose horses fidgeted nervously at the sight of the oncoming tide of enemy troops. The Royalist captain had probably dreamt of this first encounter. Heroism. Valour. Risking all for king and country.

The young man was not the first – and certainly would not be the last – leader to be tricked by his enemy in the battlefield, but that knowledge would provide no comfort this day. As the first of his men fell on to the hard earth, small spheres of lead embedded in their flesh, Stryker could not help but feel sorry for the captain.

A moment later more pistols coughed, and a lead ball traced its way across the open land to puncture the lad's helmet, his skull and his brain. The Royalist leader slumped from his saddle. In all, a dozen hot carbine balls whistled across the clearing, like angry wasps, to pluck the flanking troopers from their mounts. Tainton had planned the ambush perfectly. He had known a pitched battle could not possibly have resulted in victory, so had staked his chances on an impetuous and inexperienced officer leading the enemy troop. For the gamble to pay off, he needed to introduce confusion into the Royalist ranks. He had selected a carbine volley to do the job. Traditional muskets were too long and unwieldy for mounted troops, so cavalry favoured the shorter carbines with barrels no longer than two and a half feet. The carbines were fired from all angles and, though notoriously inaccurate, and not generally deadly against plate armour, would still do a fine job of sending panic through the enemy ranks.

The plan had worked, and the Royalist commander had been taken down in that first volley. Now for the hammer blow.

'Charge!' Tainton screamed, as his horse emerged snorting and rearing from the depths of the copse. The image must have been terrifying to the startled, leaderless Royalists, who shied away from the snarling man in black. Then more Roundheads emerged to hack down at them with blade and venomous bloodlust. In disarray, the Royalists did not heed their remaining officers' commands, but attempted to scatter as more and more enemies came at them from out of thin air in a blaze of hooves, screams and steel.

'Look,' Forrester said, witnessing the unfolding chaos from the edge of the village, 'our friends are off, too.' As he spoke, the three cavalrymen hidden behind the gorse made their way through the narrow gap and on to the killing field.

'Unbelievable,' Will Skellen whispered as an immaculately clad Royalist was felled by a professional back-handed sword slash. The blade sliced the young man's face as if it were a strip of silk. Another, taken savagely just below the Adam's apple, writhed pitifully on the ground as iron-shod hooves pummelled the life from him.

Still the horsemen came. Scything. Slashing. Gaping

holes began to appear in the Royalist ranks. Wounded young men cried out for their mothers, others gurgled quietly, gasping through eviscerated lungs. Those that could flee, did so.

'Fuckin' unbelievable,' Skellen said again. 'Help me take off my boots. If I start now, I'll have 'em eaten by sundown.'

'They're running,' Burton said. 'But they still have the advantage.'

'In numbers only,' Stryker replied sourly.

'They're like a ship with no rudder!' Forrester exclaimed. 'There's no bugger steering them.'

Skellen snorted. 'Poor bastards just want to get out, sir.'

A light touch at Stryker's elbow captured his attention. It was Lancelot Forrester. 'I know we were only to recapture the horses, old man, but this bloody mess certainly wasn't meant to be in the play. Surely we could write our own third act now, wouldn't you say?'

It had become a rout. In a matter of minutes the grand, brave, reckless column of Royalist cavalry had been shattered by the Parliamentarian ambush like a rotten apple struck by a mallet. When Tainton's modest band of riders had emerged from their various positions to close with the enemy, it had seemed as though an entire regiment was falling upon the ill-fated Cavaliers. At least a dozen Royalists lay dead, hacked down by merciless steel, while the rest had scattered. Some rallied in small groups, valiantly attempting to stand their ground, while others made straight for the track from where they had come. That track, however, had immediately become a dangerous bottleneck, and those that tried to force their mounts through, rather than take their chances in the treacherous forest, received a savage beating.

The harquebusiers of Sir Edward Tainton's Regiment of Horse were exultant as they stabbed at those Royalists unfortunate enough to be at the rear of the fleeing troop. A young man, no more than sixteen, snatched off his helmet in order to increase his field of vision, desperately seeking an alternative escape route. He did not notice the blade scything diagonally from behind. He lurched forward under a searing blow to the back of his head. The pale blade crashed through hair, skin and bone, cleaving the crown clean off. A middle-aged comrade fought valiantly at his side, working his blade furiously as the mount wheeled and skittered beneath him, but there were too many blows to parry. He raised his weapon high, blocking a downward swing from his left, only to crumple forwards in a rush of agony as a low blade came at him from his exposed right, punching through armour and intestines with evil power.

Captain Roger Tainton remained in the centre of the clearing. He had removed his helmet, revealing blond locks now matted with sweat, and stood in his stirrups to direct proceedings as if he was conducting the royal musicians at Whitehall. The black enamelled armour gleamed in the autumn light as he surveyed the tiny battlefield. He had lost just two men in the skirmish.

As he shouted orders to his rampant troopers, pointing out quarry with a dripping sword, a strange crack, thud and cry somewhere to his rear made him twist his shoulders just in time to see the young cornet hit the frozen ground in a sickening crash. Before he could react, another shot rang out from the direction of the village and whistled past his head.

'Alarm! Alarm! Have a care!' he cried, realizing the danger his men were in as they manoeuvred their mounts across the exposed open ground. 'Take cover!' He replaced his helmet and slewed his horse around, kicking it into a gallop and making for the protection of the nearest copse.

More shots. Another man was plucked from his horse with a heavy sigh as the air was punched from his chest. Tainton bent low over his horse's mane as he followed his men into the trees. He drew up as soon as he was certain to be out of musket range. 'Where are they?' he growled, squinting across the open ground to the nearest buildings. 'Where the bloody hell are they, eh? By God, I'll cut these curs to pieces.' There was nothing to be seen but the occasional spark of musketry. No uniforms. No insignia. And certainly no faces. 'Move out, Murray. Draw 'em out, damn it.'

The nearest trooper nodded and nervously urged his mount out from the tree line. He had travelled no more than a few yards before a thick bough to his left splintered under the impact of a lead ball. It was clearly the limit of the shooter's range, for the damage was minimal as the ball bounced weakly to the ground, but the warning shot served its purpose. The trooper lost his nerve, backing away to regain cover.

'The bastards shoot well,' Tainton conceded. He scanned the buildings again. 'But there ain't many of 'em. Caught us on the hop, didn't they? A full company would've flayed us alive.'

Behind Tainton, a trooper reined in, sending gobbets

of mud and leaves in all directions. 'Enemy have gone, sir,' the man reported breathlessly. 'High-tailed it west.'

Tainton shrugged. 'No matter. We'll track 'em down. The game has changed somewhat.' He gritted his teeth. 'Lieutenant. Take half the men round to the right. Sweep beyond the village and come at them from the rear.'

'Sir.'

'No more than a handful's my guess, so we'll keep 'em sniping at us. You kill them all.'

'Yes sir.'

The lieutenant nodded gravely and swung his horse round, kicking it into a gallop. The nearest seven troopers followed in a blur of hoofbeats and mud.

'Rest of you,' Tainton ordered to the seven that remained at his side, 'take up your pistols. Give 'em fire. Let's keep those dogs facing this way, eh?'

At once the men rushed to obey. They dismounted, taking position behind the thickest trunks of the tree line. Each man had a brace of pistols wedged into holsters on either side in front of his saddle. They were shorter than the carbine, less accurate still, and fired smaller bullets, but would still provide ample cover for the lieutenant's attack. They knew that they were unlikely to hit a barn door at this range, but it was worth the effort for the distraction it would cause.

Tainton, on foot himself now, loaded his own pieces, pouring the powder down the thin muzzle with deliberate care. He edged up to an ancient tree, made stout by age, and peered out from behind its thick trunk. Another flash burst out from the side of the nearest building, sending a ball into the withering autumnal canopy above his head. The ground between the tree line and the enemy was littered with bodies. Mostly Royalist cavalrymen, admittedly, but now an extra pair of dead lay where they had fallen, musket-balls lodged deep within them. Joshua Blundell, the young cornet, lay in a twisted heap, his face a grotesque mask.

'Fucking peasants,' Tainton said to no one in particular. He'd torch this village when he had dealt with it. 'Make ready! Fire!'

'Counted no more 'an twenty shots, sir,' Skellen said, as he hurriedly reloaded the smoking long-arm.

Stryker nodded. Swinging open the musket's priming pan, he snatched a charge from his cartridge bag. He had a dozen wooden bandolier flasks hanging from his cross-belt, each holding enough black powder to fire off a shot, but it was a slow loading option and he preferred to leave them in reserve. He tore open the cartridge with his teeth, the ball dropping beneath his tongue, and poured some of its contents into the priming pan, filling it to the brim. With a deft flick of his right thumb, he snapped the pan shut and blew hard on the mechanism to clear any gunpowder residue. 'I counted eighteen,' he said. Up-ending the musket, Stryker tipped the cartridge so that the rest of its contents plummeted into the muzzle. Pursing his lips over the entrance to the barrel, he spat, and the small black ball tumbled from between his teeth and down to land on the bed of powder at the bottom of the dark shaft. The spent cartridge paper was promptly screwed into a ball and shoved unceremoniously into the barrel to provide wadding so that the powder and ball would not fall out. He unhooked his scouring stick from the underside of the gun and jammed it down the long shaft to flatten the wadding down. 'Which means, Ensign Burton?' he said, reconnecting the stick and wedging his slowly burning match into the teeth of the poised serpent.

'Which means,' Burton replied, as he prepared his own firearms, loading musket and carbine in succession, 'and assuming they have two pistols each, that wasn't their full quota. They've probably sent the rest to outflank us.'

'Good, Mister Burton. You're a quick study.' Stryker had held the match between the index and middle fingers of his left hand, careful that its smouldering end did not come into contact with cartridge or priming pan during the loading routine. Now he pushed the cord into the metallic serpent's jaws and blew on its glowing tip. 'So we'll expect company from the rear.'

'William!' Forrester barked. 'Get over there and cover our arses. You too, Ensign.' Forrester had indicated the buildings on the far side of the village green, and the men sprinted across the ground to take up positions facing the northern approaches to the village. 'Will two serve, do you think?'

'Two'll have to do, Forry,' Stryker nodded. 'You and I need to keep pointing at that bastard. Just make certain you have both guns to hand. Let's at least give them as much fire as we can muster.' He hefted his musket to a well-muscled shoulder and blew on the match's orange tip. It glowed just a few inches from his face, willing him to unleash its fury. He flicked open the pan and aligned the musket with the trees where a black-clad horseman waited. 'Come on,' he whispered. 'If you dare.'

Captain Roger Tainton's mount fidgeted beneath him, willing him to kick it into a charge, but Tainton knew better than that. He would love to rush this meagre band, cut them down like dogs, but they would get a volley off before the charge hammered home, and he would be damned if he'd risk getting killed for a gaggle of disaffected peasantry. No – he'd wait for the lieutenant to draw the enemy fire.

His horse skittered back as another musket cracked. 'Steady,' he said soothingly, patting the animal's broad neck, but immediately he knew something was amiss, for there was no splinter of bark at the tree line. He glanced at the nearest trooper. 'Was that shot at us?'

'No, sir,' was the reply he both feared and expected.

'Well, I dare say you'll see these turds move away in a moment. I am sure our men will do their duty.' But Tainton was not sure, for the occasional flash of tawny coat or the brim of a hat behind the walls opposite betrayed the continued presence of the enemy.

The cavalry troop waited beyond the trees for several minutes before clattering hooves signalled the return of two Roundheads. Their swords were still drawn, but not bloodied. The mounts' nostrils flared wildly, while their flanks were criss-crossed by rivulets of sweat.

Tainton's hand went to the pommel of his sword, his knuckles white. 'Where,' he said through gritted teeth, 'is the lieutenant?'

'Gone, sir,' was the breathless reply.

'Gone?' Tainton shouted. 'You mean killed?'

The trooper nodded meekly. 'Shot 'im straight off his saddle, sir.'

'God damn their eyes!' Tainton exploded. 'God damn them! How many are there, man? How many? What weaponry do they possess?' He gave a bark of rueful laughter. 'Who employs them? We don't even know who they are, for Christ's sake!'

The trooper shrugged. 'Well, they're not ours, sir.'

Tainton steeled himself, lest he strike his subordinate. 'Clearly. But are they regimentals? Are they bloody poachers? Are they bandits?'

No one answered.

'Well done, lads,' Stryker said as his two men returned unscathed.

'Sent 'em packing, eh?' Forrester grinned. 'My particular congratulations to you, Mister Burton. You're certainly proving your mettle.'

'Indeed,' Stryker continued. 'What happened, Ensign?'

Burton shrugged. 'There were eight of them, sir. We sent a shot each before they reached the village. Only hit one, I'm afraid to say, but he was the leader. The rest turned tail as soon as he went down.'

'Good work, Ensign,' Stryker said, gracing the proud young man with his scar-twisted grin. 'Always take out the man in charge.' He turned to Sergeant Skellen. 'Well done, Will.'

The fight had not gone the way Stryker had intended. He had planned to wait until the two cavalry troops were locked in mortal trial, each concentrating solely on the other, while he and his men quietly ambushed the men guarding their stolen horses. But events had overtaken them. The Royalists had been smashed so quickly that there had been no pitched battle, simply mad, blood-soaked carnage and a shockingly swift victory for Tainton. Stryker had elected to intervene. To help his fellow Royalists and perhaps force Tainton to abandon the captured mounts, but the blond-haired captain was not so easily spooked, and all Stryker had done was push them further away from his grasp.

He drew air into his lungs and bellowed, 'Leave the horses and we'll hold our fire!'

Tainton could not believe he had failed to make the connection. The horses. Warhorses! As the memory of those animals – large, well groomed and muscular – resonated in his mind, he came to a startling realization. These were no peasants. They were soldiers.

He turned to the nearest officer. 'They're after their bloody horses. That's what this is about.'

The officer glanced along the tree line to where the captured animals were corralled amid the cavalry mounts. 'But there are only four of them, sir.'

Tainton nodded. 'Impressive, eh? There may well be four, but perhaps there are more. The way they've conducted their fire gives us no clue. Can you tell me how many muskets we face?'

'No sir.'

'Precisely. And I have no muskets of my own.' He had the pistols and carbines that had done for the unsuspecting Royalist force, but this new, deadly opponent would scornfully ignore what little threat they posed. Tainton had horses, but they would be easily wounded or killed by the hidden snipers. He had the best plate armour money could buy, but a well-placed shot could find even the smallest chink. So he had a hard decision to make; should he charge the village and destroy the enemy, but suffer a number of certain losses, or ride into the hills? He could hardly bear to contemplate the latter option.

'Make for the bridleway,' he said after a time. 'Do not move into the clearing. They'll put a ball through you before you can blink. Just follow the line of the trees until you reach the bridleway and continue up the hill. We'll track the remnants of that Cavalier troop. Finish them off.'

Roger Tainton had made his decision. Routing a full troop of Cavaliers was one thing, but an unnecessary skirmish against what was probably no more than a handful of men would be viewed with utter disdain at Westminster.

As the men of Sir Edward Tainton's Regiment of Horse cantered from the forest and out on to the bridleway their commander stole one last glance down towards the village.

'What of our dead, sir?' ventured the man cantering to his left.

'Leave them,' Tainton said flatly.

CHAPTER 7

As night drew close, Stryker and his men set about burying the dead. A deep pit was carved from the open land beyond the community and the men spent a few awkward minutes staring down at the freshly back-filled tomb. It had been hard work, scraping at the frozen earth with brittle spades and numb fingers, and the men sweated as they bowed their heads in respect.

The parish chaplain had died of a late-summer ague a few weeks previously, and the assembly looked to the most senior officer to lead proceedings. Stryker had never been comfortable with spiritual matters, especially given the number of people he had sent to meet their Maker. However, after several pairs of eyes had swivelled up to stare at him expectantly, he reluctantly cleared his throat. 'God have mercy on their souls,' he murmured briefly. It was all he could think to say.

'*Omnia mors aequat*, eh what?' murmured Forrester.

'Sorry, Captain?' Skellen replied.

'Death. I said it's the great leveller. They hated one another, these fellows. Killed one another, or tried to. And now they're dead and gone and will lie side by side in this pit for eternity. We'll probably be joining them one fine day soon.'

Stryker shook his head. 'Enough. We have work to do.' He turned his back on the dark swell of soil and stalked back to the village.

The evening was spent making preparations for the march. And a march it would be, after the theft of their steeds. Weapons were sharpened, muskets cleaned and snapsacks crammed with provisions. Stryker had spent some time discussing Tainton's surprise arrival with Marcus Gammy, the farm-hand who had dozed on watch. The young man was now up on the high ground, keeping a keen gaze on the southern hills, having been given a black eye and the chance to truly earn his shilling.

Stryker fully expected to see a troop of avenging Parliamentarian horsemen explode from the night's depths, but the darkness remained still and peaceful. The men slept.

Stryker roused his company to action long before the first dawn rays appeared on the eastern horizon. Thomas Archer, the village elder, had scorned Stryker's insistence that the villagers should abandon the settlement. Tainton would not have been pleased to be forced to gallop into the hills by a band of faceless men with stout hearts and a good aim. He had been humbled. 'He'll be angry,' Stryker had said. 'He'll take his troop south and annihilate what's left of that hapless cavalry. And then he might turn around and come back for a taste of revenge.'

'If it is God's will for us to meet the good Captain Tainton again, then so be it,' Archer had said. 'But we shall not leave. Not for the likes of him.' He gave a small, bitter smile. 'Where would you have us go? We are loyal to our king, yet we cannot say the next village shares our beliefs. The country is dangerous, Captain. We do not know who to trust or where to run, my friend. We'll stay and take our chances.'

In the darkness just before dawn, Stryker's men had said their farewells and plunged into the forest's gloom, climbing the hill that would lead them south.

—ᵚ—

'Hold!'

The sentry stepped out on to the path and levelled a glinting pole-arm at the hooded figure's chest.

The newcomer's shadowed eyes fixed on the weapon, its curved head, made from an agricultural scythe, appearing all the more fearsome in the grey dawn. He did as he was told, raising his hands. 'Good-day to you, my son.'

The sentry's gaze dropped briefly to the hooded man's neck, where a small wooden crucifix dangled. 'You are a priest?' he asked dubiously.

Father Benjamin Laney slowly moved one of his open palms to the edge of the hood and pulled it down to his shoulders, smiling benignly. 'I am . . . Sergeant?'

The sentry nodded. 'Sergeant it is.' His eyes narrowed. 'What's your business up 'ere, Father? Ain't kindly weather to be out a-strolling the hills.'

'Father Ethelbert and I', Benjamin said with a quick glance to his companion who stood, silent and hooded, behind him, 'have come from the church of St John the Evangelist at West Meon.'

The sentry's eyes, small and black against his full sandy beard and stocky body, darted rapidly between the two figures. 'For what purpose?'

'Is it not obvious, my son? Your salvation. And that of your colleagues, naturally.'

The sergeant frowned. 'Salvation? We're God-fearin' folk to a man, Father.'

Benjamin nodded. 'Of course, of course. But do you observe your duty of daily worship?'

'Well . . . we . . .'

'I fear not, Sergeant.' Benjamin *knew* not, for he and Lisette had spent the entire previous day observing the comings and goings of the garrison.

Old Winchester Hill was an Iron Age fort. No stone and ordnance here, but deep ridges carved by hand into chalk slopes, forming imposing ramparts built to repel Celtic hordes and Roman legionaries. Even now, many centuries after its construction, the fort stood stark and proud atop the downlands.

The fortified hill formed a peninsula, jutting out from the southern tip of the range, challenging attackers that might come up from the coast. The land around Old Winchester Hill, its enduring ramparts and steep slopes, were cleared for livestock, but north of the peninsula, where it connected with the main range, the forest preserved its stranglehold. It was here, Lisette had surmised, that they might approach the fort undetected.

As soon as the blizzard had abated, they had ridden out from Petersfield on the Frenchwoman's piebald mare. The beast had whinnied and snorted its complaint against the cold snow that sloshed around its hooves in the sinister sunken bridleways west of the town, sepulchre-dark eyes twitching and nervous, but its footing had held. They had tethered the animal further down the slope, towards the village of West Meon, and had trudged up the hill on foot until they could see the stark ramparts. Keeping within the dense tangles of the forest, they had watched, a task made easier by the fort's original architects. The Celts had purged the crest in its entirety so that not a tree or shrub remained. That would change, since sharpened stakes were already being placed around the fort's perimeter, but at this moment Lisette and Benjamin thanked God that they could see a good deal of the flattened summit. Among the white dots of tent awnings, they counted a small force of cavalry, and perhaps a half-company of brown-coated infantry; watched frequent patrols come and go, and saw carts enter carrying what would probably be victuals or weaponry. But at no time had they seen any clergy. A permanent garrison almost always had a resident priest, especially in time of war. Regiments of the line would have a man of the cloth drawing a staff officer's pay. And yet here there was apparently none.

'You are building a permanent garrison atop this hill, Sergeant?' Benjamin was saying.

The sergeant nodded instinctively, before realizing his mistake. 'I am not allowed to discuss—' he began.

'Then you will require spiritual guidance. Prayers. Sermons. The soul of a soldier must be as full as his powder flask.'

Before the sentry could reply, Benjamin pressed on. 'We at St John the Evangelist have been expecting a summons from your commanding officer ever since you took position here.'

The sergeant grunted. 'He ain't 'ad time to arrange a priest.'

'Ah!' Benjamin twisted his head to glance at Lisette's

still form behind him. 'There you have it, Ethelbert!' He turned back to the sergeant. 'Then our trip into the hills has not been wasted. Lead on, kind sir. Ethelbert and I can begin work with you right away.'

The sentry's name was Sergeant Drake, and he quickly arranged for one of his subordinates to take up his post, so that he could take the visitors to camp. As Benjamin and Lisette followed him along the track that led towards the peninsula, they passed through the gap in the defences that served as Old Winchester Hill's entrance. They could see the scale of the refortification. Among the off-white tents there were piles of timber and cartloads of rubble, while a large cache of muskets, ammunition and blades was being built up in a tent near one of the burial mounds at the hill's centre.

'You mentioned your commander was absent, Sergeant?' Benjamin asked.

'Aye, the fort's commander, that is. He leads the cavalry troop. The infantry and engineers report directly to Sergeant-Major Hunter. Here he is now.'

Benjamin and Lisette followed Drake's beady gaze to where a tall, powerfully built man of middle age was stood in quiet conversation with a pair of musketeers. Hunter was well dressed, his coat and breeches of a fine quality. A voluminous orange sash engulfed his torso from left shoulder to right hip, and the hilt of his sword carried an ornate guard.

He turned to them and began to stride across the damp turf. 'Make your report, Sergeant Drake.'

Stryker set a relentless pace. He was angry about losing the horses. It was a foolish mistake, for which he and his men were now paying dear. And it hurt to have lost Vos, the horse that had been his companion through so many dangers.

'I took him off a Dutch lieutenant in a game of dice,' he explained to Burton as they trudged amid the boughs of a skeletal forest.

'Quite a prize, sir!'

'Only he didn't exactly win, Ensign,' Forrester said.

'Lost every throw,' Stryker nodded. 'Worst night of the campaign, that was. But the bugger tried to rob me afterwards.'

Burton gasped. 'You killed him, sir?'

'No. He was on our side, after all. But I made it clear that he'd been unwise. And then I took his mount for good measure.'

Burton swallowed. 'I see. I wondered at the name, I must admit. It is Dutch then?'

'Aye,' Stryker confirmed. 'It's their word for Fox. He was a fine horse. Mind you, right now any broken-down would suit me better than this.'

As they marched, the band of four kept away from the main roads wherever possible, preferring the camouflage afforded by weaving between ancient coppices and thick oaks.

At night, when the temperature plummeted and stars glittered across the clear black sky, great gouts of vapour spewed from between the soldiers' cracked lips. They shivered in their waxy buff-coats while they gnawed on dried bread and hard cheese, then curled into tight foetal positions in front of smouldering embers and dreamed fitfully of home and death and battle.

Occasionally they sighted a patrol, invariably mounted, cantering up a sunken bridleway or across the horizon at the summit of a distant hill, but there were always places to hide themselves until the danger had passed. The troops might well be of a Royalist persuasion, but in a land where spies and treachery were commonplace, would even their allies believe their story? They were almost as likely to be strung up from the nearest tree by their own side as by the enemy. Stryker had the prince's letter, of course, but their captor might prefer to hang them first and leave the questions for later.

Their path ran alongside the southern road to Winchester. They bypassed several villages in one afternoon, eventually resting in the woods outside of a place called Frilford Heath, where they sighted a cart drawn by two bony oxen. Taking a chance, Stryker stepped into the road to block the cart's path, and discovered its driver was headed for market with a large haul of apples. The men stuffed their snapsacks full. Stryker sunk his teeth in immediately, the sharp chalky tang of the fruit's juices cascading down his throat.

Presently the company reached the fields beyond Marcham. The land was relatively level and they could see a streak of silver that shimmered on the horizon beneath the dying sun. 'The Ock,' Ensign Burton said cheerfully.

'The what, sir?' asked Skellen.

'The River Ock, Sergeant. Beautiful place, this. I used to fish here when I was a stripling.'

'You're still a stripling,' Forrester said with a wry smile, causing a chorus of chuckles. 'We could have used you down at the Southwark Players. Why, you could have donned the dress and played Juliet like you were born to the role!'

Burton reddened, and Stryker reached across to jab at Forrester's tubby midriff with the butt of his musket, 'While you're more of the Falstaff type, eh, Forry?'

Burton chuckled. 'The huge hill of flesh,' the ensign added, igniting a glare from Forrester that had him hurrying to explain. 'Th-that is to say *Henry the Fifth*, I believe, sir.'

'Ensign, I am insulted! Wounded!'

Burton looked stricken.

'It is *Henry the Fourth*, of course! Part One, to be precise.'

All the men laughed. They bellowed into the evening air, happy to have something to be merry about.

'In my younger days, then,' Burton said after a time, returning to his original tale of the shimmering river. 'My father would take me to a little place further up stream, where the Ock meets the Thames.'

'Well, you're not fishing today, Mister Burton,' Stryker said seriously. 'You're finding a way to cross this bloody stream.'

As dusk settled, they reached the river. Stryker had intended to make the far bank before nightfall, but the light had faded too far and it was impossible to spot a ford in the gathering gloom. The four men scoured the bank for a moored boat, but none was visible in the thick of rushes that choked the shallows at the water's edge. Since no signs of civilization were evident, Stryker was comfortable enough to spend the night, at least its darkest hours, on the north side of the Ock. They would have to make do with the shelter provided by the drooping canopy of a weeping willow.

Skellen took first watch on picket duty. He could not cover all possible approaches, but patrolling the bank, east and then west, would provide some security. In two hours, the sergeant would be replaced by one of his comrades. After Stryker had completed last watch, grey stems of light would be prising open the eastern horizon, and they would move on again.

The men under the willow set a small fire to warm their numbed hands and feet. They sat around its welcome glow and talked into the night. As the trees on the far bank first became tall silhouettes and eventually vanished into complete darkness, all that could be heard was the trickle and gurgle of the river, bubbling below the droning murmur of their own voices. The rich, familiar smell of burning wood filled the men's nostrils making them nostalgic, so they spoke of past battles and lost loves. A number of small fish had been skewered on precisely wielded blades, and they sizzled over the embers as swords were rhythmically honed and musket barrels cleaned. The men checked their match cord and counted ammunition. Somewhere a scream echoed from deep in the darkness, causing the soldiers to lift their heads in alarm until Stryker identified the shrill bark of a fox.

'Vos,' Burton said. Stryker rewarded him with a brief nod of acknowledgement.

As they tucked into the piping hot fish, the men slouched back on the damp ground, propping tired bodies on elbows and feeling a measure of contentment wash over them. Between mouthfuls, Captain Forrester rifled in the recesses of his doublet, eventually brandishing a small bottle.

'Compliments of the good Mister Archer!' he announced. He glanced at Stryker. 'May I, sir?'

Stryker nodded. 'But try not to get insensible, Forry.'

Forrester looked mortified. 'I am not some jug-bitten copper-nose, Captain.' He raised the bottle to his lips. 'Begin thy health!'

'What is it, sir?' Burton asked as Forrester took a long draught.

'Perry. Fermented from Archer's pears.' He grinned. 'Strong stuff. If we're lucky Paulet'll go one better. He has deep pockets. Perhaps we'll be treated to sack or hypocras. Now that'd be a rare delight these days.'

'Paulet's a staunch fellow, by all accounts,' Burton remarked as he took the bottle.

'Loyal as any, I'd say,' Forrester said. 'Even if Prince Rupert *has* got the wind up. Lineage stretching back to Lord knows when and they've always remained loyal to the crown. His father supported the old king, bless his immortal soul.'

The old king was James. Men like Stryker and Forrester, in their teens during the accession of James's son Charles, barely remembered the previous monarch.

During the seventeen years since Charles took the crown they had spent their lives abroad, marching and fighting and killing, but even in the distant lands of Europe the looming discontent at home was known and discussed.

'Not been lucky, has he?' Forrester said.

'Paulet?'

'Charles. It's turned sour as a mouldy lemon. I'm amazed he's lasted as long as he has, if I'm honest.'

'Why, sir?' Burton asked politely.

Forrester settled into a more comfortable posture. 'Now mark, learn and inwardly digest, stripling. Charles dissolved Parliament back in '29. That's more than a decade ruling like he was a bloody Plantagenet. Even King John had to sign Magna Carta.'

Burton nodded. 'My father blames Laud and Strafford.'

'As do many,' Stryker said. He could not care a jot for Archbishop Laud and the Earl of Strafford, but many in the new Royalist army regarded them as heroes.

'Firebrands of Lucifer, my papa called them,' Burton continued, causing eyebrows to rise. 'Oh, he was a loyalist,' he clarified hurriedly. 'But he hated their excesses.'

'It wasn't just those venomous bastards, Andrew,' Forrester said, scratching his belly. 'The bloody Puritans were getting bumptious. Making a damned nuisance of themselves.'

King Charles, though publicly a fervent Protestant, was continually accused of harbouring Catholic sympathies. 'Just last autumn, it was. Seems like a lifetime now. The Irish revolted and His Majesty dithered.' Forrester said. 'Refused to condemn the rising. Not straight away. Not until he took the measure of public opinion.' Forrester stirred the fire with the toe of his boot. 'And by the time he eventually acted, the rumours of his sympathies toward Rome were spreading like syphilis. 'Course, it didn't help that good Queen Henrietta Maria's a raging Catholic.'

Even Burton knew what had happened after that. The real turning point had been this very year, when King Charles finally grew tired of the perpetual discord. He resolved upon a course of forthright action, culminating in the attempted arrest of five key members of the House of Commons on a charge of treason. But Charles had not understood the strength of the House's Puritan majority.

'I remember my father telling us of the Commons' refusal to present the five,' Burton said. 'And then we heard the apprentices were causing trouble. Inciting rebellion.' He shook his head, still astounded by the events. 'Next thing we hear, the king has fled London and armies are being assembled.'

And as the threat of war grew, men like Captain Stryker had been drawn back to England, commissioned into the new armies with promises of steady food and pay.

Stryker had needed the money, for sure, but his feelings for the country of his birth were conflicted. He would tell people that he left for the wars in Europe to make himself a name and a fortune, but in truth he had been running away. Escaping from an England where the past kept stabbing at him in his waking moments and, crueller still, invaded his dreams.

Stryker's father had been a wool merchant, working in the verdant chalk-hilled South Downs, where Hampshire met West Sussex. He was not high-born, but by the time his only son came bawling into the world, he had achieved status within his rural community.

He was a large man, in personality too, and the young boy revelled in being the charismatic merchant's son and heir. Stryker was prepared to take up his natural role in the family business, in the knowledge that his future was assured.

Everything changed after the merchant's wife died, suddenly, on an August day. She'd been shooing hens from beneath her feet, then fell dead from a weak heart. Stryker remembered the stench of his father after he had staggered home night after night from the local tavern. He would reek and shout, rage and punch and vomit, then snore. At the same time the family fortune was being steadily drunk away, the once blooming business left to crumble.

One Christmas Day Stryker's father was found bobbing beneath the ice of the millpond. There was no suspicion of foul play. The inevitable skinful had finished him off, a drunken sot tumbling down the slippery bank and to his death.

The teenage Stryker was left with nothing but a ramshackle house with some land attached, left fallow too long to be valuable, five chickens, a barrel of poor-quality ale and a small mountain of debt.

Stryker left. He sold the farm, ate the chickens, ignored the ale and turned his back on the debt. Packing only what he could carry, he walked to London and into a new life.

He had begun his new life as a thief. His quick wits and even quicker hands had lent themselves perfectly to the role of cutpurse. It had been enjoyable, exciting and often lucrative. But as the thrill waned and the need for bigger rewards gnawed away at him, he took ever greater risks. In the end, one man had been too much for him.

That man was Vincent Skaithlocke. He had ambled down the Strand one windy day without a care in the world, and the young Stryker had tracked him like a feral cat after a mouse, scenting riches in the portly man's gold-laced buff-coat and ermine-trimmed doublet. But the dandyish clothes were deceptive. As Stryker moved, Skaithlocke twisted away with the grace of a dancer, tripping his assailant, pinning him on the muddy road with a vicelike arm and a razor-sharp dirk. Stryker understood too late that this was a professional fighter.

Stryker remembered the pathetic threats spouted by his younger self with a brazenness only a guttersnipe could muster. The fat man had grinned. Indeed, the soldier bellowed to the skies like a lowing bullock, amused and impressed in equal measure by the callow urchin's bravado. And then Vincent Skaithlocke gave Stryker a shilling and asked him to join his company, bound for the Continent the following dawn.

The ship had taken him to foreign lands, foreign women and foreign wars. He had witnessed horrors beyond imagination as the powers of Europe tore each other apart, had revelled in the elation of victory and wallowed in the ignominy of defeat. But most importantly, he had discovered something of himself. Discovered that he was good in a fight – more than good – and the life of soldiering that began as a means to avoid the hangman's noose, fast became his career.

'Remember Praise-God Sykes?'

'Praise-God Sykes,' Stryker said, his eye staring off into the distance. 'I haven't thought on him for a long long time.'

'Beg pardon, sir,' said Burton. 'But who's Praise-God Sykes?'

'He was a corporal. A Puritan – and a vicious bastard who'd quote scripture at you while he beat you black and blue.' Stryker shook his head at the memory. 'Captain Forrester and I had the dubious pleasure of his company as junior officers.'

'Junior officers in a company of mercenaries,' Forrester added. 'This bugger was in charge of our training. And by God did we fear him! Worked though, didn't it?' The bottle had reached Forrester again, and he drained it,

133

letting out a hefty belch. 'Look at the state of your commanding officer. I wouldn't want to fight a bugger like him, would you? He's fit as a fiddle.'

'Unlike you,' Stryker said, a sly smile showing bright across his face in the fire's glow.

The alcohol had already given Forrester's cheeks a rosy hue, but he reddened further at the remark. 'It's true I've been resting on my laurels of late, but you know how it is with us men of the theatre. An impressive physique adds presence on the stage.'

'In his defence,' Stryker said to Burton, 'you watch him if we get into a scrap. He scares the wits out of me.'

Forrester dipped his head at the vote of confidence. 'Yes, well, Sykes's efforts weren't completely wasted. Now can we talk of something else?' He shot a wry glance at Burton. 'Do you know, for instance, how Captain Stryker here became such an ugly brute?'

'Careful, Forry,' Stryker said in a sharply warning tone. 'Don't let the drink rule your tongue.'

But Stryker's cautionary words were obviously too late, for Forrester had cast Burton a conspiratorial wink. 'Imagine those dark locks and intense gaze without the scars. He was quite the rakehell. Then he was careless enough to have half his face blown off.' He took another piece of fish and chewed it exaggeratedly, prolonging the story. 'He had a little help in that regard from a styptic little weasel named Eli Makepeace,' he said when his mouth was clear, 'who just happened to drug him senseless.'

Stryker sighed. Forrester was going to speak whether his commander liked it or not. 'While another bastard, though not so little, placed me next to a powder keg and set a fuse.'

'Ah yes,' Forrester nodded in sudden memory, 'a beast of a specimen. Malachi Bain, if I'm not mistaken. Never did a more sinful pair of punk-poxed weasels walk God's earth.'

Stryker twisted round to see that Skellen had returned. He stood suddenly. 'I'll take next watch. Get some rest, all of you.'

'He's a sensitive sod sometimes,' Forrester said quietly, as they watched their commander disappear into the night. 'Perhaps I overstepped the mark a little.' He glanced at the empty bottle in his hand. 'Never could hold me drink.'

Some miles to the north and west another fire glowed, though the smoke from these flames billowed up through the brick stack of a chimney. A thin face stared into the heat, the orange glow intensifying his red locks and neat beard. The face had mocking eyes and a hooked nose, a thin jutting chin and small, sharp teeth: at once both handsome and feral. Eli Rushworth Augustus Makepeace was deep in thought.

'Your throw,' a voice broke into his reverie and Makepeace turned to his right. He and Bain had taken shelter for the night in a small tavern. The tapster had stared with suspicion when Makepeace had entered, and with fear upon seeing Bain, but he served them their ale promptly and provided reasonable victuals.

'Eh?'

The man was stout, middle-aged and heavily pock-marked in the face. 'I said it's your throw, friend.'

'So it is,' Makepeace said, taking the dice. There were four players at the table. Makepeace and Bain had been joined by the fat man and a tall, reedy fellow named Climpet.

Makepeace shook the dice and sent them tumbling across the table's wooden surface. 'Fives again, gentlemen!' he exclaimed happily, gathering up his winnings. 'My lucky night!'

He collected the dice and passed them to Climpet as more coins were laid down. Climpet rolled.

'Fuck it all!' he shrieked in despair as the bone cubes rested with a 1 and a 3 on top.

'A shame, sir,' Makepeace said, reaching across to offer the dice to Bain.

Bain threw. Lost. Shrugged.

The fat fellow, Binkle, took his turn and was disappointed to see a 4 and a 6. 'I need more funds, gentlemen. Will you wait? I shall go to my rooms and be back instantly.'

The others agreed, and Binkle disappeared in the direction of the tavern's back staircase.

Climpet stood as well. 'Piss.'

Makepeace watched him leave, before glancing at his sergeant. 'You know, Bain, sometimes I wish I were more like you.'

Bain frowned, suspecting a veiled sarcasm in the captain's words. 'Come again, sir?'

'Seriously, Sergeant. You see something you want and you take it. You do what is required.'

Bain swallowed the meat. 'I've s-seen you kill to get something you wanted, sir.'

'Quite so,' Makepeace said impatiently, 'but only after thought and conscience and scruples have all had a merry old discussion in my noggin. But you, on the other hand, are not troubled by such spectres, are you?'

'No,' Bain said, taking a mouthful of his ale.

Makepeace smiled ruefully. 'I, on the other hand, tend

to think too much. My brother was like you in many ways. He took what he wanted to. In fact he took what I wanted too. What should have been mine.' He saw his sneering older brother Nehemiah, a tall, gap-toothed dolt who bullied him mercilessly. He saw Emily Moffat, the girl with long legs and golden hair and bouncing breasts, and he saw her laugh at his advances, before dancing off into the forest to spread her thighs for his brother.

'Money or w-women?'

'Both.' Makepeace sat back, propping himself up with his left hand, while his right fiddled with one of the golden hoops that hung from his earlobes. 'He and Stryker ruined my life between them.'

'Why didn't you just k-kill your brother?' Bain asked

'A good question, Malachi. I'd slaughter the self-righteous arsehole if he were here now. But of course he ain't.'

'Stryker is. Well not many miles hence.' Bain spat. 'I still owe that bastard.'

Makepeace nodded. He glanced up as Climpet and Binkle returned, forcing his features into a welcoming grin. 'Shall we resume? My throw, I think.'

Money was placed in a small pile at the table's centre.

'Fives!' Makepeace yelped in delight as the dice came to rest. 'The good Lord smiles upon my fortunes once again! Let me buy everyone refreshment.' He turned his head to catch the tapster's eye. 'Four ales, kind sir!'

The captain leaned forward, teeth gleaming from behind his broad grin, and made to collect the dice. As he lifted them from the table, he fumbled one of the pieces, dropping it once more. It bounced, once, twice, three times, before settling again.

Climpet's eyes narrowed. 'A five, Mister Makepeace.'

Makepeace's grin vanished. 'Coincidence, sir, I can assure you.'

'Then try again,' Binkle said.

Makepeace scowled suddenly. 'You question my honour, gentlemen? I am mortally insulted. Am I to be accused of foul play?'

Climpet spoke slowly. 'No, Mister Makepeace. I am simply asking you to throw again, as a matter of interest, that's all.'

Makepeace opened his mouth to remonstrate, but was surprised by the chubby hand of Binkle that grasped his sleeve. Binkle's pockmarked face was red with rage as he shook the dice free of Makepeace's grip.

Both pieces fell this time, followed by a third from the sleeve of the soldier's doublet. All eyes dropped to the table as the dice dropped, bounced, spun and rested. The first pair presenting 5s, the third showing a 3.

That was enough for Binkle, who thrust his chair back to clatter into the table behind. 'Damn your rotten hide, sir, but you are a cheat!' His face was bright red, his wobbling jowls seemingly on fire. A dagger was in his hand. 'No one cheats me!'

Makepeace rose to his feet. 'Now now, gentlemen. Do not be hasty!'

But before Makepeace could calm the situation, Bain lurched across the table. 'Oh, no you d-don't.' He thrust his balled fist into Binkle's pudgy stomach. The fat man released the blade and crumpled on to the stone floor, retching as he went.

Climpet's jaw dropped. He backed away from the table and drew a long sword from the scabbard at his slim waist.

138

But Bain's own blade was free now, and the massive sergeant cast the table aside so that there were no obstacles between him and his quarry.

Climpet darted forward, jabbing the sword's point at Bain's throat, but a deft and disdainful flick of the big man's wrist pushed the weapon aside with ease. And then Makepeace was beside his sergeant, blade in hand, and Climpet backed away, understanding that this was a fight he could not win.

The fire's heat was suddenly intense at his back, and he found he could go no further. He levelled his blade.

Makepeace stabbed him. Bain had feinted high and Makepeace had thrust low, and the razor-sharp tip of the captain's sword had plunged deep into Climpet's skinny midriff.

Climpet fell back into the fire, his clothes blazing sudden and bright.

With agonized screams ringing in their ears, Eli Makepeace and Malachi Bain ran from the building.

CHAPTER 8

L isette Gaillard woke in alarm.

'What is it?' a man's voice cut through the sound of her rapid breaths.

She sat bolt upright and looked across to where the outline of Father Benjamin Laney lay a few feet away. He had turned to look at her, propping his head up on an elbow.

'Nothing. A dream.'

She could see the priest's eyes narrow in the gloom, studying her. 'You must have suffered much in your short life, my child.'

Lisette gave a little snort of derision. 'We must get up. It is dawn.' She knew she would later regret the brusqueness of her tone, but, in the half-light of that newborn morning, she was still under the oppressive weight of her nightmare. The shrill cries of terrified children. The sickly sweet stench of charred flesh. The tears and blood. The laughter of men. Soldiers.

Father Benjamin heaved himself up, stretching to the low ceiling as his spine complained with a chorus of clicks. 'God be with us today.'

Yes, thought Lisette. God be with us.

*

Sergeant-Major Tobias Hunter was a pious man, a Parliamentarian for reasons of faith rather than politics.

He had been feeling bereft without the presence of a chaplain at the new fort. He viewed the sudden appearance of Benedict and Ethelbert as gifts from the Almighty, and was not inclined to query their presence more vigorously than some cursory questions regarding religion; questions Benjamin was able to answer with ease.

Lisette stayed a pace behind Benjamin, allowing the true priest to play a character close to his own. She kept utterly silent and watchful.

'We're down from Farnham,' Hunter had told them as they toured the fort's wide summit. 'Captain Wither holds the castle there.'

'You and your men have been detached for the purpose of raising this fort?' Benjamin ventured.

Hunter smiled coyly. 'I am afraid that is something I cannot discuss, Father.'

'I understand, Sergeant-Major,' Benjamin said, but added, 'She'll be a true beauty when complete, Praise the Lord. I look forward to praying with you and your men, sir. And shall I be praying with cavalrymen too?'

Hunter glanced at him sharply.

'Your Sergeant Drake told me the fort's commander was a horseman,' Father Benjamin said quickly.

Hunter nodded. 'Aye. I lead the infantry and engineers, but a troop of harquebusiers arrived a few weeks back. Their commander, Colonel Wild, holds temporary command while they are with us. I doubt he will be joining us. He has . . . *other* duties to perform.'

'But no harquebusiers are here now, I see,' Benjamin

said as Hunter gazed south toward the murky swathe of the Solent.

Hunter waved a large hand, protected from the elements by a soft, fringe-cuffed leather glove, towards the distant coast. 'No. They ride out to keep the land between here and Portsmouth safe.'

Benjamin spent the rest of the day ministering the troops. He prayed and worshipped and heard confession and preached God's word, raving against the king at every opportunity for good measure. Lisette remained close by, and kept watch over the largest of the burial mounds. The barrow, a stark hump amid the flat crest, lay toward the western end of the hill fort. It was here that the heaviest guard had been placed.

It did not seem a place of any significance. A small, filthy tent had been erected at its base. And that tent was where the guard stood, six strong, all armed with blade and musket.

So Lisette watched. She observed the guards change every two hours, replaced by equally formidable comrades. Never flinching, always vigilant, exceptionally well drilled. The cream of Hunter's men, it seemed.

When dusk threatened its approach, and Old Winchester Hill's ramparts began to cast gigantic shadows across her green slopes, Fathers Benedict and Ethelbert bade their farewells and set off to the north, in the direction of West Meon, and the church of St John the Evangelist.

This morning, having passed the cold night amongst the mouldy hay of a tumbledown forester's shed in the deepest recesses of the groaning wood, the pair were preparing to repeat the journey to Old Winchester Hill's bleak summit. This time, however, Lisette was determined not to leave empty-handed.

'You are quite certain?' Benjamin said while they tethered the mare to its gnarled trunk for the third day.

'No. But why else would they guard this bloody tent?'

Benjamin relented. 'You are probably right.'

'I am right. They would not put six men to guard a tent full of nothing. The only other items worth protecting like that are guns and powder. We saw where they kept these. What else could it be?'

'Unless Kesley deceived you.'

Lisette thought back to the colonel's wide eyes and whimpered pleas. 'He did not deceive me.'

They made their way along the track they had travelled twice before, the wet ground slippery beneath their feet as they wound their way up the hill.

'You remember what we agreed?' Lisette said as she fought to free a shoe from the sucking sludge.

Benjamin caught her eye. 'Do not think me a fool, my child.'

Lisette nodded. 'I do not.' She smiled briefly. 'Thank you, Father.'

The priest spoke as if gauging his words carefully. 'What was the dream?'

Lisette clenched her jaw. The realization that today might very well be her last dawned clear and bright in her mind. 'I dreamed about when I was seven. My father was a cavalry officer, sent south to fight the Huguenots. My mother and I went too. One morning my father's company was ambushed . . .' She paused.

'Go on,' Benjamin prompted gently.

'They destroyed the company. Completely. And then

they turned on the baggage train and the camp followers. Fired the wagons. Killed the people. Stole the animals.'

'But you escaped.'

'I was small. I hid. God protected me. I crouched and I watched them kill and I heard them laugh.' She fell silent.

Benjamin waited until finally she lifted her head, blue eyes burning bright and intense from the gloom of her hood. 'They raped her. My mother. Murdered her. All the while calling her a papist fucking whore.'

Father Benjamin said nothing.

'So now you know,' Lisette said, her voice barely a whisper.

Her companion nodded. 'I certainly understand why you hate us Protestants.'

She stared at him again, but this time the eyes were softer, some of the fire gone. 'Not all of you.'

'How did you come to serve the queen?'

'I was picked up – found – when the next column of my father's army marched through. They took me in. I followed the camp. I had nowhere else to go.' Lisette's memories flowed more easily now. At fourteen she had married Michel Gaillard, a cavalry captain, and at her request he had taught his bride how to wield a sword and a musket. Taught her how to fight and ride as well as any man.

'What happened to him?' Father Benjamin said.

'A fever. He left me with nothing but my skills. Of course, my face was fair. I caught the eye of one of King Louis's courtiers and found my way to the royal court in Paris. Henrietta was visiting her brother there when she saw me. She asked if I might be transferred to her service.'

Benjamin thought for a moment. 'Why you, if you do

144

not mind my asking? There must have been dozens of beautiful women at the palace.'

Lisette laughed. 'It was not for my beauty, Father. One of the palace guards thought he'd have me.'

'He failed?'

'He did. Rumours of how he received his injuries began to circulate. The whispers reached the queen's ear. She is a clever woman, Father. She felt I might be useful in a way her brawny ruffians could not be.'

'She was right.'

Lisette broke off. 'There it is,' she said, as the familiar Iron Age ramparts came into distant view between the myriad boughs and branches. 'Are you ready?'

—≈—

In the lingering morning mist the small company tracked the Ock eastwards for about an hour, eventually coming to a sharp bend in the river. They could not see beyond, for willows and bulrushes obscured their view, and so they approached with caution, nerves fraying, muskets primed. Skellen went first, cantering through the sodden grass at the water's edge, his weapon levelled in front of him. A musket was a heavy beast, but Skellen was a pike-man and could wield it without a flicker of discomfort. The remaining men followed a short distance behind, prepared to give covering fire, as Skellen's tall, loping frame evaporated into the mist. It was disconcerting, for Skellen's shape seemed to grow more ghostly with each step, but they could still see the orange glow of his match as it rose from the musket's serpent. Skellen would have the priming pan closed to prevent the weapon acciden-tally firing, but the pan could be clicked back in a fraction of a second to present black powder for the match to ignite.

All was still until a voice called out from the mist. 'Bugger all,' it said. The men unhooked their match-cords and went to meet the sergeant.

There was no enemy beyond the bend. No party of bloodthirsty rebels ready to shatter the morning peace with fire and lead. Instead, Skellen presented them with a narrow, rickety bridge. Their passage south.

'My pa sold a bullock up here once,' Skellen said as they made their way through the damp countryside. 'Yeah, in Harwell it was. Funny how things turn out. We lived at Newbury in them days, before we moved down to the docks, and we drove this bullock up here one year, me and Dad. Henry was his name.'

'Your father?' Burton asked.

'No, the bull, sir,' Skellen replied. 'It pissed with rain the whole bloody way. The road was like treacle. I lost a boot to it. Fortunately there were lots of taverns along the way. They do a fine Ould Hum in these parts. You can feel it in your toes from the first swig! Gets you bumpsy as a magistrate, I can tell you. Smooth as honey.'

'Wouldn't mind a drop myself,' Forrester said enthusiastically. 'Strong ale and a warm woman. What a heavenly mixture.'

'Not likely,' Stryker replied flatly. 'Especially after last night.'

Forrester coloured. 'Yes, well. I've apologized, haven't I?'

'Died of a fever in the end,' Skellen was saying.

'The bull?' asked Burton.

'No, Pa. Well, it was either fever or Ould Hum. He loved a drop, did Pa.'

As the day wore on they saw only lonesome drovers and farm-hands in the fields. No soldiers blocked their progress and spirits were high, since the men foresaw renewing provisions, especially ammunition, at Basing House. They had been well equipped on leaving the field army at Banbury, but the long journey south had drained their supplies alarmingly. Stryker had accepted the loss of a few musket-balls as trade for venison and rabbit. After all, the men had to eat. But the meeting with Roger Tainton's cavalry had taken a heavy and unexpected toll. Match-cord, powder and bullets had been expended against the Roundhead ranks, and Stryker wanted to restock the ammunition and refill the bandoliers. Most crucially of all, their allies at Basing would, God-willing, provide them with new horses.

At midday a flock of geese sailed on the wind overhead, wings flapping in unison with powerful grace. The men knew a first-class meal when they saw one. Skellen and Burton began to light match-cords as the birds were sighted in the distance, frantic to have the weapons loaded by the time they were in range, but Stryker was quick to curb their enthusiasm. 'No muskets,' he had growled harshly. 'You want to alert the whole shire?'

The matches were reluctantly snuffed into oblivion.

They gave Newbury a wide birth, preferring to stay a safe distance from the town's garrison. On passing Baughurst they reached a thin stream that provided fresh water to quench their collective thirst. The men dropped muskets and dipped flasks and mouths to the icy water that coursed across smooth grey pebbles, brown silt and shadowy stickleback.

Stryker alone did not stop to drink immediately. He

was gazing at a distant hedgerow. Beyond it the air was filled with small dark patches that rose and fell in a peculiar manner. He knew what they were: clumps of earth, tossed up by hooves. 'Into the trees!' he ordered suddenly, startling his three companions from their brief rest. 'The road's the other side of that hedge.' He pointed to where the earth was being churned. 'We'll have company ere long.'

Sure enough, as they gathered up their kit and scrambled across the sticky pasture to conceal themselves among the trees at the field's flanks, a group of horsemen rounded the hedgerow and came fully into view.

There were five men in leather buff-coats and tall bucket-tops. Their chests were encased in iron and, even from a distance, the two-foot-long barrels of their carbines were visible, hanging from baldrics that crossed over from each shoulder.

As Stryker followed his men towards safety, he heard a crack as one of the carbines was discharged. For a moment he held his breath, waiting for one of his comrades to fall – but no one even faltered. His first reaction was relief, but a shot had been fired. They must have been seen. He snatched a glance over his shoulder, trying to discern the allegiance of their aggressors. They did not have any clear insignia, though they were evidently light cavalry. Stryker's guts began to churn. A terrible thought had struck him: were these Tainton's harquebusiers?

Another carbine split the air. This time its missile whipped past the fleeing Royalists at head height and punched into the tree line beyond. 'Into the trees! Into the trees!' he repeated the order frantically, though it was almost unnecessary. The men knew not to face mounted cavalry on open ground and would get behind the widest bole they could find. In seconds they would be shouldering muskets and attempting to fight off the pursuers.

The four fugitives reached the cover of the broad trunks at more or less the same moment. They pressed bodies against the damp bark, hiding limbs from the sting of the little lead balls that rained on them mercilessly. Stryker peered out from the safety of the tree, to see the horsemen galloping at an impressive pace, swallowing up the space between them. The leading trooper kicked at his coal-black mount savagely, urging the beast on with gritted teeth and wild eyes. Stryker could see they understood the risk they were running. To charge four muskets was dangerous sport. But these riders were closing down the distance immediately. They knew that to give musketeers the time to load their firing pieces was to invite death. The horsemen would be in amongst the trees before priming pans were filled, and long before muskets were presented.

They knew their business, Stryker thought. But, then again, so did he. 'Shoulder arms!' he yelled, levelling his own weapon, aligning the dark barrel with the chest of the nearest horse.

'It's not loaded, sir!' Ensign Burton called from somewhere to his right.

'Just get the bloody thing up, Andrew. Make 'em think it is!'

Burton hurried to obey. The others followed suit.

And the harquebusiers stopped.

They stopped because they saw black holes at the end of black barrels that hovered at shoulder height among the green lichen and brown leaves. They stopped because they saw gun muzzles. And in those muzzles they saw death.

The five jerked hard on their reins, slewing their mounts to a muddy, churning, frantic halt. Stryker's men watched them as they pulled the muscular necks round, turning their backs on a tree line that had suddenly bristled with muskets, and kicked the beasts into a thunderous retreat.

Moments later they drew up again, hovering at the full range of a musket, safe in the knowledge that, though a ball might carry to them, its accuracy and power would not be a match for plate armour.

'Hold your aim,' Stryker ordered, as a single trooper broke away from the rest, letting his horse canter back toward the trees, stopping only when there were twenty paces between him and the musketeers.

'Lay down your arms,' the horseman called to the men behind the muzzles.

'No, thankee,' Stryker called back.

The cavalryman smiled and raised his sword. 'I salute your defiance, sir! But please step out from the trees.'

'I said no,' Stryker replied. 'In case you hadn't noticed, you have a number of muskets trained upon you. Don't throw away your lives for the sake of bravado.'

'Bravado?' The man laughed this time. 'I see a number of items pointed at me. But not guns. For they have no bullets.'

Stryker knew the horseman could not be certain. 'I can assure you they are loaded and made ready,' he called.

'You lie, sir,' the cavalry officer said dismissively. 'Why else did you not fire when you had the chance? We were well within range.'

'Then charge again, sir,' Stryker replied. 'You are most welcome to test your theory.'

Several tense moments passed as harquebusiers eyed infantrymen. Stryker's gamble seemed to have worked, since the risk of charging armed musketeers appeared not to be to the taste of the mounted troopers. At close range it would mean carnage.

'I am unwilling to risk my men on your goddamned muskets,' the cavalry officer said at last. He tugged at the black beast's reigns, turning its head back toward his four companions. The horse complied with a flare of its nostrils, sending a plume of vapour into the wintry air. The remaining troopers sheathed unbloodied swords and prepared to turn their own steeds away. 'But mark your back, rebel dog,' their leader called over his shoulder. 'Mark your back. We'll be watching for you.'

Stryker lowered his musket. 'Hold!' he shouted. The cavalrymen turned in surprise. 'You call me rebel?'

The leader of the horsemen nodded. 'Dog. Devil. Turd. You may choose the description that fits best, sir.'

Stryker ignored the insults. 'I'm no rebel.'

―᠁―

The third excursion along the narrow track to Old Winchester Hill would, Lisette and Benjamin hoped, finally bear the fruit of their carefully laid plans.

Lisette and Benjamin knew where the first sentry would be, and they parted company long before Sergeant Drake, or one of his comrades, could intercept them. They followed the trail from the north-west as it swept down toward the south and east, until they reached the place they had identified the previous day. A point beneath the dripping canopy where the fort-bound pathway splintered, forming a fork. Father Benjamin sketched the sign of the cross in the air. 'God be with you, my child.'

'And with you, Father,' Lisette said. She felt a pang of compassion and it surprised her. She smiled at the priest. 'Thank you for everything. Truly.'

Benjamin nodded and turned away, following the path that would take him to Old Winchester Hill and its defenders. Lisette pulled the hood as far across her head as it would reach, drew a long, lingering breath, and took the route where the path forked away. Their reconnaissance had discovered that this second path, a slender tributary of the main track, led directly south, plunging down the steep, wooded slopes to the valley below. It bypassed the barren peninsula altogether, emerging from the dense forest at the base of the fort's southern slope. That southern slope was where Lisette needed to be. And she was ready to kill any man who stood in her way.

'They're g-gaining!'

'I can see that, Sergeant! But thank you for your quick insight!'

Eli Makepeace and Malachi Bain had galloped from the tavern, leaving the ancient building to crackle and spit as the flames leapt from Climpet's blackened body to devour drapes and timbers. But they hadn't expected the band of vigilantes swiftly assembled to hunt them down.

It had been a shock to spy half a dozen horsemen on the road behind them, kicking heels into the flanks of exhausted mounts, whooping and calling to one another in predatory glee.

Makepeace had heard stories of the way common folk would sometimes react to the misdeeds of soldiers. To protect their smallholdings, possessions, food and women from the companies of armed men now roaming the countryside, local men had begun to form their own small forces. Armed with clubs and cudgels, these vigilantes were neither Royalist nor Parliamentarian. But they were willing to stand up against ravaging soldiers, regardless of which army they might be from. The fight, murder and subsequent fire at the tavern had, it seemed, drawn the attention of just such a band.

'We'll 'ave to f-fight the bastards!' Bain called above the thunder of his horse's hooves.

Makepeace kept his eyes fixed on the road ahead. 'There are too many! They would surround us! We need to get off this bloody road and split 'em up! There! Up ahead!'

Their main route south was bisected by the east–west road, and Makepeace knew that their only chance of survival would be to divide the chasing pack.

He kicked harder, urging his steed to greater speed. It began to pull away from the labouring beast that struggled beneath Bain's massive bulk. He twisted back to stare briefly at their pursuers and then at Bain. 'See the junction? We separate. You take the left road, I'll go right.'

'Then what?'

'Hopefully they'll split, leaving three each. As soon as they do, double back and kill 'em.'

As they reached the junction, Makepeace squeezed his thighs in a well-practised manoeuvre that told his horse to take the right-hand fork. Bain, lagging behind now, wrenched on his reins with the brute force of his powerful forearms, forcing his horse to slew to the left.

For a few moments they each cantered along their chosen routes, allowing the chasing pack to reach the junction, before wheeling round to face the main south road again.

'This way! This way!'

The cry could be heard several moments before the first of the clubmen rounded the corner, and Makepeace drew his sword. He also carried a brace of carbines, but the surprise appearance of the six horsemen and the subsequent frenzied chase had not afforded him time to load either.

The leader of the vigilantes was a grim-looking fellow of advancing age. The loose skin of red jowls jangled almost comically beneath his shock of white hair, but Makepeace was instantly wary, for the old man's twisted nose and broad shoulders betrayed the sort of hard existence that was unlikely to have spawned a weakling.

The white-haired man was immediately joined by two younger fellows. They were darker in complexion, but carried the leader's thick brow and sturdy build.

The three advanced, slowing to a canter now that their quarry had finally turned to face them. The odds were not good for the lone soldier, but, despite facing three blades, he was confident. After all, three was better than six. The others must have gone after Bain.

The sharp report of a pistol cracked the crisp air. The shot had not come from any of the men on this side of the southern road, but it threw Makepeace's confidence. He had not bargained on firearms.

Kicking his mount forward, he raised his tuck high,

challenging the trio of yokels to close with him. They duly obliged, and, as their own beasts surged forward, Makepeace caught the glint of light bouncing against the dark grey of pistol barrels. He kicked forward suddenly, compelling his horse to charge, clamping eyes tight shut as his body was jolted back by the animal's motion.

The clubmen fired. Three high-pitched coughs making his guts twist. But the aims were not true.

Slash. The old man went down, Makepeace's blade sliding along his opponent's own weapon, glancing up off the hilt and into the jowl-fringed jaw.

Makepeace galloped past while the body rocked back from the saddle, the wails of his victim's sons ringing as he wheeled his horse round for the next assault.

It came quickly and viciously. One of the sons, round-faced, with bushy black eyebrows and teeth that jutted from his mouth like tusks, came surging forward, swinging what looked like a partizan high above his head. As Makepeace engaged him, he wondered distractedly at the presence of such a weapon here, of all places, but almost laughed when he realized it was nothing more than a scythe.

The clubman's blow was heavy, but Makepeace knew how to counter such force with the correct stroke and an even balance. He parried the makeshift weapon, slewing round again for the next attack. This time the second son joined his brother, a meaty cudgel lofted in a huge fist.

'Well I say!' Makepeace cackled wildly. 'This one's an even uglier brute than his father and brother combined! My commiserations!'

The man screamed an obscenity at him and powered forward, spittle foaming at fat, purple lips. Makepeace let his body sway beyond the cudgel's short range, easily evading the blunt shaft, and lashed out with a venomous back-handed stroke. It did not penetrate the hide coat deep enough to kill, but the force was such that the cutting edge connected with flesh all the same, making the clubman cry out, arching his back against the fiery pain.

Makepeace did not stay long enough to carry out the killing stroke, for the second clubman was there again, swiping the air near the captain's head with the curved scythe. The weapon was unwieldy and, though fearsome to look at, required a great deal of skill to be made effective. Makepeace found little trouble in parrying the advances, yet he could not come close enough to ply a decisive stroke of his own, such was the length of the scythe.

Makepeace's horse stumbled. It did not threaten to throw him from the saddle, but the beast's rhythm had gone, its comfortable footing momentarily lost. Makepeace rounded the cudgel-bearer again and blocked the scythe, and as the animals passed one another to turn again like a group of medieval jousters, he glanced down to the horse's right flank. There it was. A patch of crimson against the beast's light-brown coat. Small and round, as if someone had ground a raspberry into the short, bristly hairs, it seemed innocuous, but Makepeace knew well that in a short time the horse's strength would fail and its balance would wane still further. One of the three clubmen had not been entirely ineffective when aiming his pistol.

Makepeace decided that the skirmish would need to be brought to an abrupt end.

He chose the spittle-faced man with the cudgel as his target. Closing quickly, while his steed still had the strength to carry the fight to the enemy, he stabbed forward with a series of short, sharp thrusts. The club-man dodged the blade admirably, avoiding all but one of the strokes, but the last caught him in the flesh of his shoulder. It was not deep, but the steel had penetrated nerves and muscle, and his hand jerked in involuntary spasm, releasing the cudgel meekly to bounce along the churned mud. A look of horror swept across the man's face, and he raised his arm to block the next attack.

Makepeace lowered his sword marginally and jammed it into the reeling clubman's midriff. It met with stiff resistance at first, the keen tip driving through the thick layers of the man's coat, but enough of the force remained to carry it beyond the tough hide and into the softness beyond.

The clubman screamed. Makepeace twisted the blade, feeling it slicing at his victim's guts, before wrenching it free. The wounded man pitched back as the weapon jerked loose. His frightened horse bolted, leaving the stricken clubman to flail haphazardly, bent backwards across its hindquarters, a spray of bright blood staining the air in his wake.

Makepeace turned to the man carrying the scythe. 'Your turn, lad.'

The clubman threw down his weapon, pulled savagely on his mount's reins, and galloped away. Eli Makepeace threw down his sword and laughed to the heavens with triumph and exhaustion.

CHAPTER 9

'S-skewered one,' Sergeant Malachi Bain said as he greeted Makepeace back at the junction, 'and the other two skulked off without a fight. Weren't up to much, were they, sir?'

'I don't know so much,' Makepeace said ruefully. He stood holding his own horse by its bridle. 'My goddamned mare's lame.'

Bain cocked his head to the side, studying the animal's wound. 'Pistol.'

'Of course it was a bloody pistol. They didn't have cannon, did they?'

Bain ignored him. 'Shoot her, sir.'

Makepeace nodded. 'It'll be damnably slow going for yours with two to carry though.' He turned away, muttering angrily as he unfastened the buckles and straps that attached the tack to his ailing horse.

He hefted the saddle on to his shoulder and staggered over to the dense tangle of thorns at the road's edge. 'Bloody Roundheads can reimburse me for this,' he said, before hurling the heavy leather seat over the hedge, followed by the bridle and reins.

'Throw me the saddlebag, sir,' Bain said. 'Hercules,

here, is strong. H-he'll manage.' Bain hooked the extra bag to his saddle, while the officer fiddled with his carbine's firing mechanism.

Makepeace strode up to the limping mare and shot it between the eyes. 'Now let's waste no more time.'

———◊———

The light-cavalry commander was Frederick Lawrence, recently promoted to the rank of major by his current master, Sir John Paulet, the Marquis of Winchester. He laughed aloud at Stryker's revelation, and jumped down from his expensive saddle. Feet squelching in the sodden, ice-crusted soil, Lawrence had stridden confidently over to the trees to offer Stryker his hand. He did not ask the small company to prove their allegiance, for he knew Stryker's name from countless Royalist despatches. He had naturally been shocked to find the group so far from home, but a glance at Prince Rupert's seal on Stryker's precious letter of introduction had been explanation enough.

'I am Sir John's bodyguard,' the major announced cheerfully, glancing around at Stryker and his men, who had squeezed on to the horses behind his own troopers. The group, now nine strong, made their way south to Basing House. It was a grand home, a palace in all but name, rising from the lush fields of north Hampshire. Paulet maintained a small but elite garrison within his walls, part of it, he now learned, being a cavalry force commanded by Major Lawrence. 'His attack dog, he calls me! Though I don't attack much at present. Our eastern flank, Sussex and Kent, is almost entirely for Parliament. There's fair support for our cause in Hampshire, but the buggers are spreading their pestilence further west all the time. We're on the defensive, Captain. Ever on the defensive.'

Frederick Lawrence was clean-shaven, big-nosed, thin-lipped and afflicted by an involuntary tick that made his eyelids flicker as he spoke. He might have been an exceptionally tall man – taller, even, than Prince Rupert – had it not been for his unusually hunched and rounded shoulders. His spindly frame curved forward midway up the spine, so that he stooped like a willow.

'Had to get this plate fashioned 'specially,' he said, wrapping knuckles against the polished steel at his chest. 'Damn this cursed hump. Set me back a mort, I don't mind telling you. Still, I'm mighty glad I could afford the trappings. Wouldn't have lasted a moment in the infantry! Besides, I like horses. They're loyal, they're fast, and they don't answer back.' He paused. 'Surprised you're out here on foot, if I'm honest, Captain Stryker.'

Stryker described the skirmish at Archer's village and the loss of their horses. Lawrence grimaced. 'My sympathies, sir. A good steed is hard to come by in times such as these. Stone me if they weren't all snaffled up by the armies in quick time.'

'Aye, that's right enough,' Stryker agreed. 'My own, Vos, was with me for many a year. Never found another like him.'

'Vos?' Lawrence considered the unusual name. 'He was red then?'

Stryker grinned. 'Aye, sir. Sorrell. Had a chestnut hide that shines red in the sun.' He was not a sentimental man, but Vos had been a constant since his Flanders days. He had galloped through gunfire and taken many a wound, even saving Stryker's life on occasion with his rapid hooves.

'He?' Lawrence said. 'Not a gelding, I'd wager.'

'No, sir.'

Lawrence's eyes twitched busily. 'Stallion's a grand beast if you can tame him. Not for the faint of heart. Ordinarily I'd advise against 'em for battle. Too blasted skittish. But if you win their trust there's no animal finer.' He leaned forward, stroking a gloved hand along his steed's auburn mane. 'Samson has his stones. I considered chopping them off when I purchased him, but I didn't want to douse your fire, did I, boy?' He straightened up. 'Yes indeed. Just don't get yourself a pale one, grey or white, or the like.'

'Why's that, sir?' Burton asked.

'Because you'll shine like a bloody beacon when the moon's out,' Stryker replied.

'You have it, Captain,' Lawrence agreed, nodding vigorously. 'Mark my words. A white horse'll get you killed quicker than dropping a match in a powder magazine!'

Lawrence had been on patrol when he'd bumped into Stryker's group. His orders were simple: scout for the enemy. If the opposing force was small, make all haste to engage them in battle. If, however, the force was too big to handle, and therefore a genuine threat to Basing, he was to retreat smartly and report to his superiors.

Sir John Paulet, Lawrence told them, was nervous. Not exactly frightened, for he was not a man to be easily cowed. 'But he knows the sons of rancid whores'll be at him soon if he ain't careful,' the major had said. Paulet was sending out as many patrols as he could muster without leaving the palace dangerously weakened.

'You're a fair trek from home, though, sir,' Forrester said.

'Perhaps for you plodders, but it's less than a couple of days in the saddle.'

Lawrence led the way, his helmet tethered to the bright leather saddle that had been polished to a keen shine by hours of contact with his rump. He held the reins in one hand, and ran the other through auburn hair that fell about his shoulders in tightly packed curls. A look of embarrassment crept across his face. 'I thought you the vanguard of some greater pack. When we galloped after you, you took flight. It settled the matter in my mind.'

'Well I'm just glad your carbines failed to catch any of my lads before we resolved the error,' Stryker said dryly.

'As am I, Captain. Your reputation precedes you. I'd have been a dead man. Still, no harm done, eh?' the major said, his mood brightening. 'And I'm devilish glad to make your acquaintance.'

'Reputation?'

Lawrence grinned, displaying an impressively complete set of small white teeth. 'Come now, Captain, don't be coy. Your service on the Continent is almost the stuff of legend. To those of us of a martial persuasion, anyway.'

Stryker nodded briefly at the compliment. 'Kind of you to say, Major.'

The cavalry officer eased himself straight suddenly, wincing as his spine protested. 'God punishes me for something,' he said with a long groan, before slouching again. 'And what of Kineton Fight?'

'We all four played our part,' Stryker said.

'Then I must congratulate you all, gentlemen,' Lawrence exclaimed.

'We were there to fight these hard-nosed Puritan arse-holes, sir,' Skellen growled. 'We did what we had to.'

The major turned to look at him. 'It may surprise you to learn, Sergeant,' Lawrence said, in an almost sheepish tone, 'that I am a reformer.'

'A Puritan?' Skellen replied, unable to hide his surprise and discomfort.

'Your words, not mine,' the major replied. 'I prefer reformer. And "Sir", for that matter, Sergeant, when you address me.'

'Perhaps you fight for the wrong side, sir?' Ensign Burton broke in.

Lawrence rounded on him, twisting rapidly in the saddle to thrust an accusatory finger toward the young man's chest. 'Curb your impertinence, boy,' he snarled, eyelids flickering maniacally, his former affability vanishing like a shadow at dusk, 'or I'll have it flogged from you.'

For a moment the assembled group froze, horses drawing to a standstill, the clang and jangle of horses and men and kit ceasing simultaneously. Burton's companions tensed, their hands falling instinctively to waiting sword hilts.

Stryker cleared his throat. 'Apologize, Andrew,' he said.

Burton seemed to shrink beneath his captain's stare. 'I . . . I'm sorry, Major Lawrence. My curiosity overcomes me at times and—'

'No,' Lawrence interrupted before the ensign could complete his stammering apology. 'You must forgive *me*.' When the muscles of his face had regained composure, Lawrence grinned in sudden return of his former cordiality. 'In these times one becomes defensive, too much so perhaps.'

The major turned to face the road again and, gathering up the limp reins, urged his horse onwards. The rest of the group followed suit.

'My sensibilities', Lawrence said once the animals had reached their requisite trotting pace, 'tend towards the Puritan persuasion, 'tis true. But Puritan does not equal rebel. You are all men of the world . . . well, most of you.' He glanced, mischievously this time, at Burton, the flicker in his eyelid perhaps a wink. 'So you must know that God has not chosen to daub this earth in black and white. There is no distinct camp into which a man should fall by dint of his faith. I am a minimalist in religion. I abhor the trappings and baubles of the Church, and I despise the excesses of the Papacy with every ounce of my being. But I am no Parliamentarian, nor one of those confounded dissenters, springing up from the dark like toadstools. My religious taste is for reform, yes, but my conscience dictates that I am foremost loyal to the Crown. If King Charles were to turn papist, I would pray for his immortal soul, but I would not take up arms against him.'

'There are many of your persuasion, Major,' replied Forrester. 'Fortunately for our side.'

Lawrence nodded. 'Aye, many. And the enemy's ranks are swollen with those who would gladly bow to their king should he acknowledge Parliament's place in the world. It is a matter of conscience, my friends. A man must think upon it. Plumb the depths of his soul. Choose his allegiance and be able to sleep sound at night.'

'My family are for the king in the main, sir,' Ensign Burton said with careful deference, 'though my cousin William took a commission with Balfour.'

Stryker frowned. 'We faced Balfour's cavalry at Edgehill. Was your cousin on the field?'

Burton shrugged. 'I don't know, sir, truth be told. Though I pray not.'

Lawrence blinked, and nodded sagely. 'Aye, it is a common tale. Families are split like wood on an axe. Brother fights brother. Father fights son. It is the end of things. The end of life in this land, even.'

Stryker pondered those words as he watched the ridges and furrows of the sucking road pass beneath him. How many times had he foreseen the end of his own life? They were beyond calculation. But there was one moment he would never forget. He did not remember much detail. He recalled the burning, searing flame and the blinding whiteness. He remembered vividly the laughter, the high, almost shrill chuckle of Eli Makepeace.

But Stryker had not died. His face might have been disfigured into a grotesque mask, his eye gone, but his life force remained. There were times, as the agony pulsed in his head, when he had yearned to die and prayed that God would grant him the sweet release of death. But then she was there. She had brought him – no, carried him – through to safety. Bandaging and cleaning and soothing. Loving. He did not die, because she would not allow it.

She had saved him, but she had not saved herself.

Stryker concentrated on the ground moving below him. But he still saw her face. Her hair and her eyes and her slender neck.

When she had died, the world ended for Stryker. He lived on, but all around him was ruins. That was why he no longer feared man nor beast, nor the devil himself.

*

165

They rode into a night obscured by gentle snowfall. The temperature dropped rapidly, turning the stagnant water in the road's furrows to brown ice. The horses found it difficult to pick their way between the treacherous pot-holes, especially while carrying two riders. When they came across a deserted tithe barn, Lawrence announced it was time to rest.

'I'm sorry, Major,' Stryker said, 'but I cannot afford further delay. With your leave, we'll forge on.'

Lawrence's face reddened and twitched as he jumped down from his mount. 'Hold your tongue, sir! The horses require rest. I hold seniority here, and I say that's the end of the discussion.'

Stryker gritted his teeth. 'You hold the rank, sir, but I am about the business of a prince.'

The mention of Prince Rupert calmed Lawrence's irritation immediately. 'An hour then. Enough for the animals to draw breath. What say you?'

Stryker nodded. 'Thank you, sir. I'm sorry to argue with you, but I am eager to make haste.'

'You'll find no argument from me,' replied the major. 'This road is haunted by as many Roundheads as Royalists. The sooner we're behind Basing's walls the better.'

─ ∾ ─

At midnight the fort was a blackish, ominous mass rising from the land amid a sky of an even deeper hue.

Along a narrow animal track skirting the fort's forested base, a figure moved, silent and watchful, its outline glinting momentarily. Progress was slow as it halted at every rustle from the bowels of the labyrinthine wood that swallowed the whole valley with looming

166

density, but no shouts of alarm split the night to turn wariness to alarm.

Lisette picked her way between ancient boughs and wizened branches, the grasping hands of a hundred skeletal giants. In twenty paces or so, her target would be reached. The point she had identified during the daylight hours where the southern slope was at its most steep. It would be difficult to scale, but the sharp angle rendered it near impossible for men on the hill's summit to see directly down on to the grassy incline. She could ascend the slope undetected.

'Mary, Mother of God,' Lisette whispered, and breached the tree line, taking her first steps on to the cleared earth. It was steep, even here at its lowest point, and she fell forward, wrenching herself up the springy turf with fingernails as well as feet.

Without the protection of the branches, Lisette felt exposed, her heart thundering against her ribcage and blood roaring in her ears. But she kept going, crawling, holding breath, tensing muscles, praying, praying, praying.

Above her, the outline of formidable Iron Age ramparts could be seen, gently lit by countless stars, but those earthworks were so high, they gave the impression of being man-made clouds in an otherwise clear sky.

'You must move in darkness,' Benjamin had said. 'Strike while the fort sleeps.'

Lisette had been trained in the use of diverse weapons by the French army, and she had the stealth and guile required by a spy, but she knew well that she lacked patience. She had first scorned Father Benjamin's words of counsel, reluctant to leave the fort once they were inside, but the priest had eventually convinced her. Of course, there would still be guards on the crest, patrolling the high perimeter, and the panoramic views afforded during daylight would render even the cleverest approach futile. A night-time assault was the only way.

The peninsula's single inland-facing side, while choked with woodland, was heavily guarded, and there was simply no chance of entering the fort unseen from this direction. The assault would have to come from the south, from the deep valley over which the fort loomed. In summer, an approach from here might have been safe, for the forest in that valley would be thick and verdant, but it was November, and the branches were bare. The merest flicker of movement would be spotted from the soaring ramparts. Moreover, Lisette had not been able to gauge the frequency and strength of the men on the hill's periphery. She needed an opportunity to watch them. To gauge what she faced.

'You need to draw them away, Father,' she had said.

Benjamin thought for a moment, rubbing his spectacles on the hem of his cloak. Eventually he nodded. 'A sermon for the whole garrison. Hunter told us the cavalry troop ride out every morning. We do not know if their captain would welcome my ministrations, but the sergeant-major will. We will wait until the cavalry are gone, leaving Hunter in charge. From what we have seen of him, he'll think a sermon important enough for everyone to hear.'

Once again, the priest had been right. Lisette had not witnessed Benjamin resume the part of Father Benedict, for she had been heading down into the valley while he led the sentries in worship, but she knew he must have succeeded, for her dawn dash through the wood to the hill's foot had not been impeded. By the time the patrols resumed, and, she fervently prayed, Benjamin was on his way back to the safety of Petersfield, Lisette was ensconced behind a thick tangle of scrub that would conceal her well but allow her to watch the hill. Sure enough, she spent the remainder of the day staring up at the high crest, watching patrols come and go, observing that a guard, three-strong, paced along the southernmost edge every ten minutes or so. After two hours there was a break of an extra ten minutes while the personnel changed. And that was the information she needed, for Lisette calculated that at midnight no guard would patrol the rampart for a full twenty minutes. Time enough for her to scale the slope.

Now, as Lisette pressed on towards a summit eerily illuminated by the clear night, she silently thanked the Holy Mother because the going was not as difficult as she had feared. It was steep, certainly, but dread and excitement energized her tired legs and sore hands, and she was able to keep up a reasonable pace. Gradually the angular shape of the rampart came into focus ahead, sharp against the natural irregularity of the hill.

Suddenly a grey blur raced across the grass a few feet away, and Lisette stumbled back, drawing a dirk from within the folds of her cloak, heart pounding loud and terrible in her head. The shape was gone in an instant, and she realized it had been a hare. Lisette sheathed the knife with shaking hands and a sick stomach, and swore viciously. She took a moment to steady her frayed nerves, breathing deeply, waiting for the prickly sweat on her brow to abate.

Lisette reached the first rampart, climbing over the jutting earthwork and rolling into the deep fissure beyond. She stayed on her back, looking up at the sparkling stars, listening for the sound of approaching soldiers. Nothing. Gradually she eased herself up and darted across the man-made ditch to the bottom of the next battlement. It was steeper than the first, and she found herself imagining the torrid hailstorm of spears and slingshots that would have greeted the Roman legionaries caught in this trench so many hundreds of years earlier.

Up the second ridge she went, scrabbling at the slick grass for purchase, propelling herself up to its sharp peak. She reached it quickly and silently, peering above the brow with care. The fort spread out before her. In the darkness she could discern cartloads of barrels and weaponry, and beyond them the row of mounds where kings of the past had been laid to rest. Beyond those mounds, to the north of the fort, she could see rows of pale smears, the tents of her enemy, and she prayed she would not stir them awake. She glanced left and right. No sentries here. The southern slope was virtually unprotected because an attack up the steep incline was so unlikely, and Lisette thanked God that her gamble was going to be justified. She still had a few minutes left before the regular three-man picket would reappear.

Lisette broke cover, holding her breath and dashing to the hill's artificially flattened crest. She reached the relative safety of the nearest wagon and pressed herself tight against it. The only sound was that of her teeth as they ground together. Edging out from beyond a broad wheel, Lisette studied the flat plain. Her eyes scanned from the right, taking in the tents again, and the far-off trees, sweeping to the left until they rested upon the western-most burial mound. The Great Barrow, Benjamin had called it. At its base, just as she remembered from the previous day's tour, a small tent sat grey and still. She thought back to the first time she had seen it. The way Sergeant-Major Hunter had skirted around it without explanation of its purpose. It was too small to be the billet of a soldier, and too heavily guarded to be a common storage area.

But now Lisette Gaillard's heart sank, for there, at its entrance, at first indistinct amid the gloom, but gradually gaining clarity as she studied the area with keen eyes, were two guards.

'God damn them,' she whispered. 'Or move them.'

'Well, if I don't I'll soil me fuckin' britches,' one of the soldiers was saying as he rose from a small stool.

His seated comrade sighed. 'Go then. Be quick, mind. They'll string you up if they catch you.'

The standing sentry spread his arms confidently as he strolled away. 'Don't fret, Billy. I'll be back to hold your hand in a moment.'

Lisette's heart seemed to smash its way into her mouth as she realized the man was headed toward her. She ducked down, scuttling under the cart on all fours. She clamped her mouth shut, forced the air to stay in her lungs, and kept every muscle rigid.

The soldier appeared at the rear of the cart. From her hiding place she could only see his legs, and she watched him shift his weight from one foot to the other as he unfastened the pewter buttons on the front of his breeches.

With a grunt, the soldier hauled the garment down past

his knees so that it bunched at his ankles, and crouched. He did not see Lisette at first, and his face was still twisted with the effort of answering the call of nature as Lisette drew her blade.

The soldier's face turned from strain to shock as his eye caught movement, but the dirk was already springing out from the black night. Its tip found his throat without hindrance and burrowed deep into flesh, stopping only when it met bone at the back of the man's neck. He rocked back, gargling quietly. Lisette knew she must move quickly, for the lone sentry might come looking for his mate, and, besides, the team of pickets would return to the southern ramparts at any moment, blocking her escape.

Erupting from beneath the wagon, Lisette broke into a sprint, covering the ground between her and the seated sentry in a few seconds. She was not laden with jangling armour or unwieldy weapons, and the soldier only registered her presence when she was too close to be easily intercepted. There was no time to draw his blade or shout a warning, and as he scrambled to his feet, she kicked him in the chest. The strike jarred all the way up Lisette's leg, and she realized that he was encased in plate metal. This man was clearly not one of Hunter's engineers, but a harquebusier. She recalled Sergeant-Major Hunter mentioning that the cavalry stationed at Old Winchester Hill were engaged on *other* duties.

The cavalryman did not fall, but he stumbled backwards, weighed down as he was by buff-coat, chest plate, gauntlet, helmet, cross-belts, sword and carbine. Lisette launched forward, closing the space between them before the soldier could unsheathe his sword. As he fought to free the weapon, she kicked him again, throwing him further off balance, and he slipped on the chalky ground. In a second he was down, struggling to find his feet, but she was on top of him. The trooper went limp as Lisette pricked his left eye with the point of her dirk. She felt his body relax beneath her, saw his tongue slide like a great slug across his bottom lip, and knew he was dead.

A sound carried across to her from the north. Lisette leapt off the stricken body and stared across the crest towards the tents of the main encampment. There was movement there too. She scampered to the Great Barrow and threw herself against the solid mound. The noise sounded again, but this time it was starker, more recognizable, and she knew it was the whicker of a horse. She raised the top half of her head above the brow of the mound, studying the distance for advancing cavalrymen. Again, she was surprised to see and hear nothing more, and she realized it was simply the contented sounds of the warhorses as they grazed among the trees on the far side of the hill.

Breathing more easily again, Lisette shrank back behind the Great Barrow and tracked its base to where the small tent stood. The corpse was at its entrance, still and silent, and she stepped over it, ducking as she reached the awning, and slithered into the gloom.

With no source of illumination, the blackness inside the tent was overbearing. She was on her knees, waving arms almost randomly around her, alert to the sounds of enemies outside. She could locate nothing. No treasures, no weapons, no victuals. But Lisette remembered Kesley's claim that he had overseen the burial of the stolen strong-box and, with renewed vigour, she dropped on to her belly and began to scrabble at the damp earth with desperate fingers. The grass was dense, so when her nails snaked across a patch of loose soil, Lisette's heart skipped excitedly. She hurriedly pulled at the turf, scooping it on to the grass at the tent's edges in great, frantic handfuls, and a hole gradually began to open up.

'Mother of God. Mother of God,' she whispered, wracked by desperation and elation. Eventually her fingers began to labour against a harder substance, and she realized she had gone beyond the soil and was now prising away chalk. She drew her dirk and jabbed it into the hole, breaking up the compacted rocks and scooping them out with her free hand.

Then the blade hit something hard, causing a dull thud to echo around the white awning. She worked frantically, scraping and digging and clawing at the chalky blanket until a regular shape began to emerge in the gloom. It was a rectangle, the width of her palm and the length of her forearm. She could feel already that it was made of wood, but bound by sturdy iron straps that ran widthways along what she now took to be the lid. It was a box.

Lisette scraped at the chalk edging, working the blade in long sweeps, tugging at the object every so often until, eventually, it came free. She returned the dirk to its place within her doublet and bumped forwards in a sitting position towards the flap, exiting the tent feet first, the strongbox cradled at her chest. She got to her feet, hurdled the first body, and darted between the carts where she knew the second would be. In a heartbeat she was at the ramparts, barely noticing the big flakes of snow that had started to fall all around her. She leapt over the high edge of the first rampart, scrambling down into the deep ditch beyond, and negotiated the second rampart almost immediately. Then she was careening down the southern slope, barely able to control her legs, yearning for the forest in the coke-dark valley to swallow her up.

'*There!*' A sudden cry arose from up on the ramparts.

Lisette risked a glance back. She saw three figures at the edge of the soaring crest. One pointed towards her. She felt her toe catch on a pothole in the steep turf, and she fell, rolling and bouncing and hurting, all the while grasping the prize to her breast. Then all was black.

When she awoke, Lisette thought hours might have passed, but it was still dark. The thought crossed her mind that she might be in the next life, embarking on her sentence in purgatory, but the ground was wet and cold, and her arms were still locked in a painful embrace with the wooden box. She realized that she must have knocked herself senseless for only moments, a minute at most. She eased herself up, standing gingerly as battered limbs protested, and found that her footing was steady and flat. Lisette discovered she had rolled all the way to the foot of the escarpment. Now there were voices behind and above her, carrying clearly. Her pursuers would be upon her soon.

The light from a lantern played up high, highlighting the straining faces of the three pickets as they negotiated the greasy descent.

'Bugger rolled all the way down,' one of the sentries was saying.

'Probably dead,' replied another hopefully.

The third gave a short snort. 'Let's make sure he's a dead 'un. Or at least that he ain't around to blab. I don't want a floggin', do you?'

Lisette guessed that these were the three charged with

patrolling the southern rampart. They were not interested in taking a thief, or avenging their comrades' deaths, but only that her presence had gone unnoticed by their superiors. Lisette turned into the forest, sprinting, leaping over branches and weaving between trunks, and prayed that the pickets did not know she had taken the box, or that she had killed the two soldiers. If that were the case, then they had merely returned to duty to see a figure fleeing down the slope, and were only concerned that they might be reprimanded for allowing the intruder to come so close to the fort. They would not chase her for long. And she had, at last, what she had been searching for. She had the treasure.

CHAPTER 10

The nine men and five horses left the tithe barn and emerged into a landscape of silver. It had not snowed heavily, but enough to sprinkle the fields and trees in powder, over which the lingering moonlight danced.

Stryker urged the horsemen to maintain the quickest pace possible, and by mid-morning the company reached Basing village. The snow had accompanied them in thin but stinging flurries, and the men were dejected and tired, but the approach to the magnificent estate would have lifted even the most jaded of spirits.

Stryker himself gazed with admiration as they rounded the final turn, emerging from the cover of the tall oaks that lined the River Loddon and on to the main road through Basing. He could see the Great Gate House encircled by formidable fortifications. And within those walls he knew there would be fires burning merrily in wide hearths, inviting men to thaw their frozen joints.

The village itself was nothing more than a cluster of small redbrick houses grouped between the river, fast flowing despite the prevailing chill, and the main road. But the ostentatious Tudor edifice that loomed over the humble village was like a giant from the book of Genesis.

Stryker had heard Basing was one of the largest houses in all Britain, and one of the most impressive.

Three harquebusiers emerged from the north gate and cantered to greet the newcomers.

'Welcome back, sir,' the lead trooper said with a curt nod to Lawrence.

The major returned the nod and removed his helmet. 'Thank you, Simpkins. I trust life has been quiet since our departure?'

'It has, sir.'

'Very good. My compliments to Sir John,' he said, turning to glance at Stryker, 'and we have guests. Captain Stryker and party. They're here upon important business. Please inform him of their arrival.'

Sir John Paulet, Lord St John, Earl of Wiltshire and fifth Marquis of Winchester, was not a happy man. He almost considered the rebellion a personal slight. Parliament, much of the south-east, swathes of the army and almost the entire mercantile class had bolstered the insurgence, watered its green shoots until they were great branches, and he and his fellow loyalists had found themselves powerless to hold back the tide. And now those malcontents had raised an army, holding the king's forces to a stalemate on a fair-meadow below a hitherto anonymous Warwickshire ridge. There was to be no way back. No return to the ways Paulet held so dear.

'I am at a loss, gentlemen, a loss.' He placed a bejewelled hand upon the ramparts of Basing House, fingers gripping tight as if deriving strength from the cold stone. Stryker and Forrester had joined the marquis for his daily constitutional walk around the great walls. 'Used to love to walk my property, bless me I did,' he continued, 'before the upheaval. Now it is more like a patrol. I take picket duty, God help me. Guarding me own house!'

The land about them might have been fraught with Puritan danger, but against the dull backdrop the marquis still stood out, like the parakeet Stryker had once seen in a Shoreham brothel. Paulet was resplendent in fine red doublet laced with gold trim. His stylish falling band collar, decorated with bobbin lace, fell elegantly over an expensive gorget.

As they stared down upon the village, Paulet studying every inch of the landscape, his lordship put Stryker in mind of the way soldiers study their breeches for lice. The marquis clearly thought it not unlikely that a Parliamentarian army would emerge upon the skyline at any moment. Beyond the small houses were clusters of tall oak and beyond that the great river, meandering westward, its banks a mass of bulrushes and stooped trees.

'But you've had no trouble thus far, sir?' Stryker asked as he followed Paulet's gaze. The little thatches seemed to be drowning in the thin mist that veiled the land.

'By the Lord's grace,' Paulet confirmed, 'and only by His grace. Our proximity to London troubles me greatly. We are a lamb beneath Pym's sharpened knife.'

Already, on arriving at the grand residence, Stryker had been treated to repeated tales of how the force at Basing might be of immeasurable value to the cause, if King Charles would but send extra bodies to man its walls and strengthen its patrols. 'I'm sure you'll have your troops before long, my lord.' Stryker said. 'And I doubt Parliament will detach a force of any significance while our army sits at its door.'

Paulet shook his head. 'Farnham has fallen, Stryker,' he said, his left eye twitching ever so slightly, 'and Portsmouth to the south. The rebels could reach us and be back to face the king in no time at all. London's no distance. So you see, Captain, for all your well-meant encouragement, if those troops don't hurry up, I'm ripe for the picking.'

Stryker remained silent. The marquis may have accepted Prince Rupert's order, set out in the letter Stryker carried, to supply reinforcements for the captain's mission, but he had not been gracious about it. At a time when he felt soldiers were most needed behind his walls, Paulet found himself compelled to give them up.

The house itself was set on a Norman earthwork that rose high above its immediate surroundings. It provided excellent views of the road, the River Loddon and Cowdray's Down to the north, and overlooked the hills to the south.

The Paulets had taken the old house, with its bailey and great walls, and extended the estate. To the east of the old buildings was the new house. This was larger and far more grandiose than the original residence, with massive fortified walls that enclosed a large garden. Wide bridges linked the two houses, making them effectively one large mansion. In recent months the marquis had refortified his position, building up the walls and guard-houses, and deepening the defensive ditches that surrounded the estate. He was as ready as he could be for Parliament. All he needed now was a big enough force to garrison the estate. He had a reasonable unit of musketeers, with fresh recruits levied from the surrounding settlements, and a smattering of decent cavalry, but it was a far cry from the formidable might upon which he had set his heart.

'Given half a chance,' Paulet said after a short time, his eyes fixed on the far horizon, 'we could cause a world of trouble for the enemy.' He turned to face the younger man. 'With more men, more horse, more cannon . . . this place would be a tick buried deep within Parliament's side, biting, drawing blood. Think on it, we could harass their supply lines, kill their patrols, and draw their forces from the front. And when the king finally launches his killing stroke . . .' He paused, slightly breathless.

Stryker nodded. 'This might be an excellent base for an offensive against the capital, my lord.'

'Just so, just so. But before that time, while the southeast remains in the balance, I should be, I *shall* be, taking the fight beyond these walls, cutting at the Roundheads as I can. I do not wish simply to hide.' Paulet leaned over the rampart to point at the road below. 'Well within range,' he said, brightening. 'The rebels will want to use that road.'

'And you'll be glad of it, sir.' Stryker finished the thought again. He imagined the carnage, the downpour of lead that would meet the men marching past, turning the dusty road into a killing ground.

'Of course, they will find other routes,' Paulet said, 'but with some decent cannon I might ensure they take the long way round.'

Stryker nodded. 'And those other routes aren't suitable for an army, if I recall, sir. They're barely more than ancient tracks.'

'And by the time they've widened them sufficiently, the war will be long finished,' Paulet said. 'So you see, gentlemen, I need more men, and more muskets, and more cannon. But for now I am lame. Impotent.' He sighed, and slapped his thigh. 'Enough. Let's have a bloody drink.'

Stryker's men were welcomed in fine fashion. Sir John had been curious to learn of the military and political developments in the aftermath of Edgehill. And he yearned to know every detail of the first great battle of this war. He had clapped at the tale of Prince Rupert's mad, inspirational charge, and shaken his head sadly when told of the loss of Sir Edmund Verney, the king's standard-bearer.

'He fought like a lion, I'd wager,' the marquis had said.

'They had to hack the very hand from his arm, sir,' Forrester had said truthfully. 'For he would not relinquish the colour. Even when he was dead.'

'Quite a man,' Paulet said wistfully. 'We should all wish to die so bravely.' He fixed Stryker with a hard stare. 'Now, sir, to business. You know I am hardly delighted by this order, but I shall of course respect the prince's wish. Will three men suffice?'

—⁂—

The barrack buildings were low, wooden rectangles. They were a recent addition to the great mansion, hastily erected to house the burgeoning ranks of Paulet's regiment. Inside they were sparsely equipped, containing no amenities but rows of straw pallets.

It was here that Stryker and his men awaited the arrival of their three new comrades. The delay might only be an hour, while Paulet's musketeers gathered their kit and saddled their mounts, but to be in a place away from the elements and be able to take some rest were luxuries now, and were to be appreciated as long as they might last. Young Burton aside, they had marched and fought through some of the most inhospitable lands on the Continent, and regularly bivouacked beneath stars, in tumbledown shacks or haystacks. They had slept on battlefields, their dreams penetrated by the moans of dying men. A dry room, with a solid roof, soft pallets and warm blankets, was comfortable indeed.

Stryker lay back, palms behind his head, staring at the beams above him and listening to the sounds of life in Basing House that reverberated around the great buildings. He had seen so much misery and pain in his life, had lost the one person he had truly loved, had killed more men than he cared to remember and even tortured a few of them. Now he was on a suicidal mission across countryside riddled with treachery and plagued by rebels. Yet here, in this isolated Royalist outpost, he found that he was as content as he could allow himself to be.

A heavy knock at the barrack-room door heralded the arrival of Paulet's reinforcements. Stryker and his companions rose from their pallets, and Skellen loped across the room, jerking at the handle to allow a stream of light to bathe the interior.

The three men on the far side of the door were musketeers, the most senior of whom was a stocky, ruddy-faced corporal with gunmetal grey hair and wire brush moustaches. He was a man of advancing years, but his powerful chest and shoulder muscles spoke of a tough campaigner.

'My apologies for our late arrival, sir,' the corporal said

in the nasal brogue of County Antrim. He patted a thick piece of wood that jutted from his belt like a cudgel. 'Couldn't find old Aggie. Wouldn't do to leave home without her, so it wouldn't.'

Stryker glanced to where the corporal's powerful and abundantly scarred paw had come to rest, and realized that the wood was the handle of a fearsome-looking hammer.

'Used to be a smith, sir,' the Ulsterman said in explanation, while he and his fellow musketeers stepped into the barrack-room, snatching off their montero caps in salute. 'But I found I was even better at fighting. Still carry old Aggie wi' me though, right enough.'

The corporal's name was Maurice O'Hanlon. He was a fervent Catholic and as passionate a Royalist as Paulet. He introduced his two men as Wendle Brunt and Jared Dance. Brunt hailed from the rough dockside slums of Plymouth. He was a thin man with deep-set, small eyes, giving him a slightly rodent-like appearance. Dance was younger than Brunt, probably in his early twenties, with a shaven head, evidently the result of a lice infestation, and big teeth split by large gaps.

'A bloody Irisher,' Skellen said under his breath, as he inspected the men. 'And a papist to boot.'

The corporal grinned, clearly not about to take offence. He flattened a hand to his chest in dramatic affront. 'These words are razors to my wounded heart, Sergeant.'

'*Titus Andronicus*!' Forrester blurted in delight.

O'Hanlon nodded. 'It is, sir.'

'Act one, scene one. Ah-ha! A kindred spirit in my midst at last!'

'I had the fortune to spend some time down in the

capital a while back,' O'Hanlon said. 'I'm no expert, sir, but I caught a fair few plays.'

'You were in London?' Stryker spoke dubiously. 'A dangerous place to visit, given the general slaughter of Protestants over in your homeland.'

The corporal grinned enigmatically. 'O'Neill's rebellion had nothin' to do wi' me, sir. I came to England for a woman. Married her, so I did. She was well worth the risk. We spent a glorious six months in each other's arms, before she was struck down wi' the plague.'

'I'm sorry to hear that, Corporal,' Stryker said.

'No matter, sir.' He sighed. 'Anyhow, I came south, joined the marquis's lads, and here I am. Ready and willing to cut down the Puritan horde like the spavined heretics they are!'

'Should I tell him we're Protestants?' Skellen said to Stryker. 'Or shall I leave that to you, sir?'

'The Lord will forgive you this once, Sergeant,' O'Hanlon said cheerfully, 'as long as you fight for good King Charles. We can't let the bloody Roundheads win in this heathen country, or they'll take their guns over the pond to play havoc with God's true chosen people.'

Skellen produced a scowl, without making it entirely convincing. 'He's got a big mouth, Captain. Why don't we ask for someone else?'

'Because you need me, Mister Skellen. The blessed men of Ireland have forgotten more about fightin' than you English bastards'll ever know,' Corporal O'Hanlon replied quickly.

Stryker began to laugh. He had a feeling O'Hanlon would prove useful.

*

It was early afternoon, and Stryker was keen to leave the comforts of Basing immediately. The men had been left to get their kit together, and would presently be at the stables to saddle new horses.

Stryker, alone now, stepped out of the barracks. He had pulled on boots and breeches, and strapped on his sword, but wore no other garments, for he had decided to bathe while the men were making ready for their impending departure.

The barrack buildings were on one side of Basing's large circular courtyard and on the other was a deep trough of water. Clutching his shirt in one hand, he made his way north across the courtyard that was little more than a filthy morass sucking relentlessly at his boots.

Stryker ignored the taunting whistles and leers as he passed a group of women heading in the opposite direction. His disfigured face, when not inspiring revulsion, often impressed women, perhaps marking him out as a heroic man of action, an impression his sinewy shoulders and slim waist did not dispel.

He peered over the edge of the trough, hoping the water would not be a solid block of ice. It was not – and he cupped his hands, plunged them into the painfully cold depths, and raised them to splash his face. It was shocking, agonizing and exhilarating in equal measure, and he repeated the process several times more until he was shivering, reasonably clean and fully alert. He hurriedly put on his white linen shirt, grimy as it was, to ward off the chill.

They needed to depart soon, but Stryker knew the men would not have the horses, arms and provisions ready for perhaps another hour, so he resolved to climb the high walls and take a look at the terrain they would soon negotiate.

Reaching the bridge-tower, Stryker passed the two guardsmen without hindrance and climbed the winding wooden staircase, eventually emerging into the chill breeze at the structure's summit.

The bridge-tower stood sentry over the eastern approaches. It rose above the main bridge that linked the two houses, and from its pinnacle Stryker could comfortably see down on to the new house. The mansion was unlike the original house in both size and appearance. It was of angular design, forming a great rectangular shape that was partitioned from north to south so that it contained two separate courtyards.

Stryker cast his eyes over the high walls that enclosed the entire estate. They were not, he considered, as impregnable as Paulet would like to believe. He had seen heavy ordnance make short work of even the thickest stone, and he wondered how long these particular ramparts would last under sustained bombardment. He did, however, note that all about the estate were huge defensive earthworks. These large, benign-looking ditches, carved deep into the hill, would make any assault hellishly difficult for even the best storming party. Stryker had both stormed and defended great man-killing trenches such as these and could well imagine the desperate defenders pouring cannon fire and musketry into a struggling mass of Roundheads caught at the bottom of those ditches. If Parliament's forces could punch holes in Paulet's walls with their artillery, then they would have to throw men at the breach, and the Royalists would use their own firearms to funnel those attackers into the earthworks, where they would be trapped like rats in a barrel. Perhaps Basing could withstand a siege after all.

After one last glance to the north, where the village was still, the river fast and the forest barren, Stryker turned and walked towards the steps leading down to the muddy courtyard. He took the stairs two at a time in an effort to keep his limbs warm, and on reaching ground level, started back to the barrack buildings.

He crossed the courtyard quickly, always careful not to become embroiled in the ground's thick slop, but his attention was drawn by the sounds of a commotion nearby, raised voices squawking in anger like argumentative rooks.

To his left there was a small crowd of men and women encircling an invisible figure at their centre, accusing, jostling. Stryker moved nearer. A distinctive, somehow familiar female voice rang high and loud above the others.

'*Ordure! Ordure!*'

It was strange, Stryker thought as he approached, to hear someone speaking French here. The French were not popular in the towns and cities of England. Parliament had been successful in using the queen's nationality against the king to foment mistrust and rebellion.

Stryker stood on his toes, craning his neck to identify the source of the fracas. 'Leave me, you bastard!' the woman shouted, this time in English. Stryker could not trust his ears, but the tone was clear and the accent was one he remembered well.

'Gi' me that, Froggy!' a fat man with no neck snarled, making a grab for a bundle of linen the woman was clutching tightly to her chest.

The woman dodged him, hooking the bundle under

188

one arm and producing a knife with the other. 'I'll cut you, son of whore. By God, I will do it!'

Stryker shouldered through the periphery of the crowd, knocking bodies left and right. And there she stood. He later realized that she scarcely required assistance, for a more capable hand never wielded a blade. His own sword was freed with viperous rapidity, but there was no call to use it. The crowd dispersed quickly when they saw the look in Stryker's eye.

All that remained were a tall, dark soldier and a petite, fair-haired woman. She slipped the dirk back within the folds of her cloak. Stryker's sword returned to its scabbard.

Eventually the woman blinked hard, her eyes round as moons and blue as the Mediterranean. 'Hello, *mon amour*,' she whispered.

'Hello, Lisette,' replied Stryker in a voice he found hard to keep steady.

The parade ground was a stretch of grass outside the high walls. Beyond the grass was a small copse, dense and tangled, and among its branches stood a man and a woman, still staring intensely at one another.

Lisette had followed Stryker's impulse, which was to drag her out through the high gate toward this secluded group of trees. He did not know why he had chosen this place, only that it was private and away from prying eyes and ears. They were close enough to hear the instructor's bellowed orders, but still some hundred paces away.

'Who are you?' Stryker finally said, his voice an unintentional whisper, as though the shock had squeezed his windpipe almost shut. He devoured his slender companion with his eye as she stood before him, taking in everything about her physical presence. The golden hair, bright beneath the late autumn canopy, the wide eyes, the small scar that marred her chin, the way her brow furrowed when she frowned or smiled. She must either be a figment of his imagination or a ghost. The real woman of flesh and blood had long since been laid to rest in his memory.

Lisette, still cradling the bundle of linen, studied Stryker. 'You look well,' she said after a time. He shook his head slowly and her face coloured. 'I am sorry.'

'Sorry?' repeated Stryker.

Lisette thought for a moment, struggling to pick words that might carry some semblance of worth. 'I hurt you, I know that. And, yes, I am sorry.'

Stryker made a strange noise in his throat. 'You died! You died, Lisette. One day I had you, we were happy, the next you were gone. Drowned. Lost at sea. They told me.' He shook his head, felt his eye prick, amazed now at how easy it had been to believe it.

Lisette touched his shoulder gently.

He shrugged off her fingertips with a jolt. 'I knew your work. Creeping in and out of corridors, whispering secrets, telling lies, committing murders. I shouldn't have been surprised at one further deception, no matter what the cost to me.'

Lisette frowned. 'We are neither of us saints, are we, sir?'

If a single person on this earth knew of Stryker's sins, it was Lisette Gaillard. 'But you were mine,' he said. 'I was yours. I did not know your duty would come before us,

Lisette. I did not suspect that.' He paused. 'I was broken when you left,' he said simply, the furious indignation now starting to slip away.

'Damn you, Captain,' Lisette suddenly snapped. 'You are a hard bastard. You always were. The scars healed well, I am sure, and I do not refer to your face.'

'Cast about!' the sergeant's voice echoed from beyond the copse. 'That's it, boys! The musket and match must stay in the left hand. Shove the stock on the ground on the outside of your left boot. Now place the charge!' With their muskets held in the cast-about position, the men poured the remaining charge from their flasks down their barrels. Once the charge was placed, each tapped the butt of the musket sharply on the frozen ground in order to compact the powder, then fished in their pockets and bags for a musket-ball to follow it.

The sergeant nodded his approval. 'Now place your wadding!' The men reached into their pouches to grasp small pieces of wadding. They crammed what they retrieved into their barrels, too busy to notice the pair of figures in the dense brush.

'Ram your wadding!' Still in the cast-about position, the recruits removed a scouring stick from the housing beneath their guns, pushing it down the barrel until the wadding was compressed against the top of the charge and its smooth projectile. The sergeant marched forward a few paces to confront one of the recruits. 'Don't hold the end of the stick, you puke brained bastard!' he bawled. 'If the bloody gun goes off now, it'll punch a hole straight through your palm!'

*

Lisette's reflexes were not fast enough to avoid Stryker's arm as it lashed forward. He slapped her cheek, sending her thumping on to the leafy soil, her heavy burden spinning away into a patch of soaking bracken. The tall soldier leapt forward, straddling her slim torso, pinioning her wrists with hands like iron claws.

'God damn you, Lisette!' he snarled, his grey eye gleaming silver in the weak light. 'Go back to hell!'

Lisette spat in his face. His grip loosened momentarily and she wrenched an arm free to rake her fingernails down Stryker's cheek. He cursed, letting the other arm go, and she thrust it low, grasping and twisting at his groin so that he scrambled back to his feet. She was up now as well, closing with Stryker as he retreated, and all he could do was swat away her fists as she targeted the sides of his head with buffeting punches. He took a pace backwards, and another, until the backs of his knees met with a broad log. Having nowhere left to retreat, Stryker leaned into the blows, ducking low, seizing Lisette around her waist. She swore as he hoisted her into the air, and he opened his mouth to command her to stop, but no words passed his lips, only a gush of warm air as the breath cannoned from his lungs. She had thrust her knee into his crotch, hammering pain into the very core of his guts, and she laughed in triumph as he dropped her to the floor.

Stryker collapsed over the log, his back slapping on to the mouldering earth. Lisette was no ghost. This was the same battling, snarling, wicked, gorgeous firebrand he had once loved, and, though he hated her, he wanted to laugh and dance and sing under the murky autumn sky, for she had been returned to him.

*

'Return to port,' the sergeant ordered. The musketeers levelled their weapons, achieving the port position. The sergeant filled his lungs, ready for the final, all-important orders. 'Musketeers! Prepare to give fire!' His little eyes momentarily shifted to the tangled branches some hundred paces to his side, for he thought he had seen a flicker of movement, but it had vanished as quickly as it had come, and he wondered if his eyes deceived him.

'Blow upon your coals!' Each man shifted his match into their spare right hand and blew upon it to ensure that it burned bright. 'Cock your match!' the sergeant brayed. In response, the men placed their respective cords between the jaws of each serpent. 'If any man's cord faces the wrong way I'll have 'em flogged from here to London!' The threat was unnecessary, for every man had fixed his match so that the glowing tip faced him. They all pulled upon their triggers, compelling the serpents to sweep in an arc so that the match touched the closed priming pan, ensuring the cord would not overreach its target.

'Present upon your piece!' the sergeant called. The men shifted their left foot forward and raised their weapons so that butts met with right shoulders.

'Secure your scouring stick!' Each man gripped the barrel of his musket with his left hand and could feel the ramrod connected to its underside. 'It ain't a big job, lads, but should you fire the stick accidentally you shall have the devil of a job reloadin'. And you'll be a dead 'un in no time. Open your pan!'

With their right hand, the recruits flicked open priming pans. 'Good! Good!' the sergeant bellowed over the clicking of the mechanisms. He paused to draw a hurricane into his lungs. 'Give fire!'

As if with one mind, the musketeers snatched on their triggers. Thirty serpents slashed back, sending thirty burning match cords on to thirty open pans. The charges ignited the priming powder, which, in turn, ignited the main charges that nestled deep within the barrels.

In the copse, Stryker felt pressure on his stomach, and he opened his lone eye to see Lisette kneeling above him, thighs either side of his midriff. He raised a hand to block the expected attack, but none came. Instead he felt the softness of her cheek against his calloused palm, and the light dimmed as her face lowered to his. He was vaguely aware of long tendrils of blonde hair tickling the sides of his head, and then the warmth of her lips was upon his own. Stryker tried to sit up, to take her in his arms, but she thrust her palms into his chest, forcing him back down, never taking her mouth from his. He resigned himself to her, letting his hands slide down to her backside, digging thick fingers into her rump, grinding her groin down upon his, revelling in the heat emanating through the fabric of their breeches. Mouths were still locked messily, lips and tongues writhing, continuing the duel their bodies had just fought. Teeth clinked, sweat mingled, groans echoed.

Stryker rolled her over, scrabbling to unfasten her breeches, but Lisette was just as hungry, just as ravenous, and she pushed him away, forcing him to stand so that she might tear furiously at his clothes, revealing him even before he had revealed her. When they were near naked, Lisette leapt into Stryker's arms, hooking her hands around his neck, clamping thighs at his waist, letting him take her weight as he had done so many times before.

She wriggled her hips slightly, desperate to guide him into her, Stryker rammed her up against the nearest trunk, moist bark sliding roughly against her back, and they took each other in unrestrained, animal frenzy.

Out in the clearing, as if nature itself responded to their passion, came the thunderous sound of hell erupting.

Much later, when the musketeers had marched away and the lovers lay side by side among the leaves, Stryker felt hollow. Lisette, staring glassy eyed at the gnarled branches above, repeated her explanations over and over, telling him again how she had been sent to Spain on a mission so covert that it called for a severing of all her ties in England.

'You still had a choice,' Stryker said when she had finished.

'You would have had me tell my mistress that I chose an English soldier over her?'

'I would have had you tell your mistress you chose to shove the assignment up her arse.'

Lisette laughed daintily. 'I believe you would. And that is exactly why I could not tell you. Do you understand me?'

'You're right,' he said after a time. 'I would not have let you go. And had you defied me, I'd have followed you to the ends of the earth.'

Lisette sat up, fastening the shirt she had been too busy to remove. 'I did – do – love you, Stryker. In my fashion.'

He sat up too. 'And your own fashion means you enjoy me when it serves your purpose? Cast me aside when your mistress calls? Is that the way of it?'

She did not answer as she stood, padding almost silently

over soil churned dark by their frantic movement to retrieve boots and breeches that had been flung haphazardly into the scrub.

'Why are you here now, Lisette?' Stryker said, as he watched Lisette dress. She did not answer, but began kicking at a pile of fallen leaves and twigs until a solid thump sounded against her boot. She stooped to retrieve the package. The swathes of linen had come away, revealing the wood.

'What's in that box?' Stryker asked.

She smiled enigmatically. 'You might think about donning your britches, sir, before asking further questions. The day is cold.' She reached out, drawing soft fingertips along his forehead and down the left side of his face, tracing the swirls and undulations of the scar she had once tended with poultices.

When she turned to walk away, plunging into the trees, Stryker scrambled to his feet, hurriedly dressing. 'Wait!' he called after her, hopping awkwardly in the wake of her rapidly disappearing form as he struggled to cram on his left boot. 'Wait, Lisette!'

By the time he had scrambled into the clearing, she was gone.

CHAPTER 11

'What do you want?'
The woman was old, wizened. She peered through the small hole in the door, presenting a sharp nose and suspicious eyes to the newcomers.

'Want?' Captain Eli Makepeace asked. 'We must see your master urgently, madam. It is a matter of life and death.'

The woman sniffed. 'They all say that. Wait there.' She slid the shutter closed.

Makepeace stepped back from the threshold and craned his neck to look up at Langrish House. It was an imposing, three-storied structure of beige stone and huge rectangular windows. In the gathering dusk it cast sinister shadows, long and jagged.

'Sh-shall I knock down the door, sir?' said Bain, standing a pace or two behind the captain.

Makepeace turned, looking up at him. 'Have patience, Sergeant. Old Moxcroft will open up once he hears our tale. No need to ply your skills yet.'

'And what tale's that, cully?' The speaker was a very short, wide, snout-nosed man in his middle forties, wielding an ancient-looking fowling piece. He and his half-dozen mates had appeared from the side of the house, all bearing muskets, poised and ready.

Makepeace glanced from one hostile face to the next. 'Easy now, gentlemen. Let's not be too hasty on those triggers.'

'Soldiers ain't welcome 'ere,' the barrel-bodied leader said. 'Cavalier, most like, by the sound o' that slick tongue.'

'Foppish arse'ole,' a young man, wet-lipped and jagged-toothed, put in.

'You are for Parliament?' Makepeace said.

'Not neither,' the leader replied. 'We're for our kin only.'

Makepeace thought back to the clubmen they had enraged further north. 'A fair stance, friend, and no mistake. I am no Cavalier, and I mean you and your village no harm. I carry a message for Sir Randolph. I must speak with him.'

'Shoot 'im, Marrow!' another of the men growled. 'Don't matter if he's Cavalier or a piss-lickin' Puritan. He's a soldier and there'll be more on their way. Always are. They'll want feedin' and clothin' and Christ knows what else.'

The short man, Marrow, stepped forward with clear intent.

'Hold, Jem!' a new voice suddenly echoed from somewhere behind the group. 'We said hold, you stubborn toad!'

'You must forgive Mister Marrow, Captain.'

They were in a small room at the rear of Langrish House. The walls were crammed full of scrolls, shelf upon shelf of them, vellum splashing the chamber in creams and ochres. The owner of the house was seated before a wide-topped desk, strewn chaotically with papers and open tomes. He leant back in his chair, making a steeple of long, bony fingers at his chin.

Makepeace was seated opposite. 'No harm done, Sir Randolph.'

Moxcroft dipped his head in what might have been apology. 'He and his sons are useful to us. We feed them a morsel or two, they keep an eye on our estate.'

'Fuckin' clubmen again,' a voice murmured from the doorway.

Makepeace twisted round to look at Bain. 'Hold your bloody tongue, Sergeant.'

'It is fine, Captain, really,' Moxcroft said smoothly. 'We admire a man unafraid to speak his mind.'

Makepeace wrinkled his nose. Bain stood a little straighter.

'And we're glad of his presence,' Moxcroft continued.

'*We?*' Makepeace asked.

Moxcroft rolled his eyes witheringly. '*We* are Sir Randolph Moxcroft.' He ignored Makepeace's bafflement. 'Jem and his lads don't . . . *appreciate* . . . our situation, naturally, so it is wise to guard the door. We maintain the pretence of a peace-loving merchant, and they consider us worth protecting. We would not like them overhearing us now.'

'Well, I apologize for Sergeant Bain all the same,' Makepeace replied. 'We had a small altercation with some clubmen a few days back, and it has left him irritable. He's no gentleman when he's irritable.'

Makepeace found Sir Randolph Moxcroft disconcerting.

He had expected a frightened rabbit, but Sir Randolph Moxcroft was entirely at odds with this preconception. An easy, flowing confidence marked every languid movement of his long arms, while his eyes, small and translucent, roamed with the lazy alertness of a reptile. The spy was indeed crippled, as Makepeace had been informed, but the limitations of his immobile legs were counterbalanced by a wicker chair, ingeniously adjusted to include axle and wheels.

'Sir Randolph, I must urge you to treat what I have to say with the utmost urgency,' Makepeace said. 'A godless villain named Stryker comes for you even now. You must leave at the earliest opportunity, with us as your protectors. Your new Parliamentarian masters are waiting in London to give you safe harbour.'

'Indeed,' said Moxcroft impassively. 'This is grave news.'

'I was half expecting Stryker to have reached you by now, such was our unfortunate delay in reaching your house. But it seems luck is still with us. Let us not try it longer.'

Moxcroft's eyes, the palest blue Makepeace had ever seen, settled on a point somewhere over his shoulder. 'How were we discovered?'

'Papers – written in Blake's hand – taken at Kineton Fight. They allude to the agreement he brokered with you.'

The long fingers rubbed at Moxcroft's pointed chin. 'And our good friend Blake?'

'Dead. Or soon will be. Forde was shot before we left Banbury. Our shared master is not inclined to lose your knowledge as well.'

Moxcroft nodded. 'Then we must leave without delay.' He glanced around the room. 'Allow us a short while to gather our things.'

'Take as little as possible, sir,' Makepeace urged. 'We must leave with all haste.'

A sudden rap at the door made both men look up. Bain spun round, alert and ready for a fight, but, as he inched the door open, dirk at the ready, only the drooped face of Ruth, the maid-of-all-work, peered through from the corridor beyond.

Moxcroft leaned to one side so that he could see past the captain. 'What is it?'

She bowed, casting eyes at the floorboards. 'Beggin' your pardon, Sir Randolph, but Jem Marrow's spotted more men. They're riding down the track from Bordean.'

'How many?' Eli Makepeace snapped, his heart suddenly racing. 'How *many*?'

'Seven. He reckons they look like soldiers, Jem does.'

———— ◊ ————

'Why here?' Father Benjamin asked Lisette as she joined him on the high ramparts.

'So that we are not overheard, of course. Walls have ears, Father, except perhaps ones that touch the clouds.'

The pair had reprised their parts of Benedict and Ethelbert to gain access to the walls, the pious guards eager for them to pray blessings upon Basing House and its defenders.

'You succeeded then?' Benjamin said earnestly, hope sharpening his tone.

'What makes you think so?'

He spread his palms. 'If you had not, you would be dead.'

The priest studied the elfin face, partially concealed within the cowl of her long, dark cloak, and he saw her azure eyes brighten in triumph.

'Bless you, Lisette.' He paused. 'Well? What is it like?'

'I have not seen it. The box is locked.'

'Of course, of course. I was simply curious. Where is it now?'

Lisette rapped her knuckles against her right thigh. The sound was like the knock on a wooden door.

Benjamin seemed surprised. 'You can walk with this weighty object at your leg?'

She nodded. 'Yes, it is not heavy. I have it fastened with twine. Besides, I was carrying it in my arms, concealed in cloth, and a thieving bastard thought he could take it off me, just because I was a foreigner and anything I had should be his. I am not taking the risk again.'

The priest's jaw dropped. 'You fought him off?'

'Aye. Barely.' But Lisette had not fought him off. She thought of the man with one eye and a lethal broadsword, and of how his very appearance had scattered the crowd like sparrows before a hawk. The man who would never know how close she had come to abandoning her queen and her God, simply to be with him. She forced her mind back to the priest. 'What have you discovered?'

While Lisette had been scaling the high rampart of Old Winchester Hill, Father Benjamin had ridden north to meet a Royalist agent in a chapel near the Thames, a man who would have word of England's shipping lanes. They had agreed to meet at Basing to exchange their news. 'There is a ship bound for the Netherlands in a week's time.'

'From where?'

Benjamin winced. 'London.'

The Frenchwoman looked as though she might attack. 'London? Tell me you jest, Father!'

He shook his head, placing a calming hand on her elbow. 'It is the only such ship making the journey. The ports are in turmoil, and the weather does not help matters. I cannot guarantee when the next crossing might be. London is your only route out of England. At least this side of Advent.'

Lisette ground her teeth together. 'It is the heart of the rebellion. The whoreson Puritans will have sentries on every street corner.'

Benjamin's expression was serious. 'Aye. And that is why you cannot enter the capital by land. I have arranged for a barge to take you to the coast. You will make rendezvous at Richmond. They are less likely to accost you if you travel by river.'

'I suppose.'

'The captain of the barge is called Horace Crumb. He conveys wool to the Port of London. If you can be concealed within that consignment, you will be put on the ship without hindrance.'

Lisette blew out her cheeks. '*Merde.*'

The priest remained silent. He knew enough French to agree with her.

※

The track was steep and the horses nervous, gingerly picking their way through the slick and sticky mud.

'Fuck it!' Skellen rasped, fighting to regain control of his mount as its hooves slipped.

'Steady, Will,' Captain Stryker, out in front, called back to his sergeant.

The seven men had galloped across the sapping terrain like a small herd of deer, weaving in and out of trees, over fallen branches, across man-made ditches and water-worn furrows. They had reached the hamlet perched high on Bordean Hill and funnelled on to the track that would take them down to a place called Langrish.

'The final act, eh lads?' Captain Forrester shouted.

It had nearly meant their deaths more than once, but Stryker had successfully brought them to this place, so far from home, and now they would complete their mission.

The men were all infantry by trade, but today, having replenished and improved their uniforms at Paulet's cavernous stores, they looked more like a group of light cavalry. Buff-coated torsos were crossed by two belts, from which hung a sword on one side and a carbine on the other. High bucket-top boots poked through stirrups, while saddlebags slapped the animals' flanks, heavy with spare clothing, gun oil, dry match, food, water, knives, spoons, sewing kit and tinderbox. They had also relieved Basing of ammunition, wadding and prickers. In short, they bristled.

'How much further?' panted the portly man, mounted to Stryker's left.

'Struggling, Forry?' Stryker said, noting his fellow officer's crimson cheeks and dripping brow. 'But your horse is doing all the work!'

'We', Captain Lancelot Forrester replied, patting his bouncing stomach, 'have seen better days.'

'*Julius Caesar*, sir?' Ensign Burton chirped in from somewhere to the rear.

'Give me strength!' Forrester barked, casting his eyes heavenward. '*Timon of Athens*, you ill-educated youth. Act four, scene two, as any fool knows. What are they teaching children these days?'

The group reached the foot of the hill, emerging from the random tangles of the trees, and passed the first of the village's buildings, the church of St John. Stryker slowed his mount, scanning the surrounding hamlet quickly, dragging a faint image of the place from distant memory.

He pointed south. 'That way.'

'Can't see much, sir,' Sergeant William Skellen said flatly.

'Where the road bends.' Stryker said. 'The house is just beyond those trees.'

He kicked his horse into a gallop, the beast responding enthusiastically now that they were on flat ground, and the others followed. As they rounded the road's curve, a building gradually began to resolve from the high canopy of leaves.

Stryker had led his men as far south as the high, escarpment-fringed plateau that cut through the land between Petersfield and Alresford. There they had briefly rested their horses at the White Horse inn, suffering the locals' suspicious stares and threatening glances, before covering the final distance.

Now, as dusk rapidly crept toward them, they cantered into the cleared land of the house's estate. The area around Langrish was a mass of small hillocks, the land undulating like furrows in a ploughed field. They reached the top of one such rise, the gardens sloping away from them down towards the house, which stood in a miniature valley. Stryker led the way, trotting down toward the building.

Langrish House had been grand once. But now, as the bitter November wind whistled through untilled fields, Stryker saw that the manor was not as well kept as it might have been. He recalled Prince Rupert's description of Moxcroft. He knew that the crippled spy could not work his own land, and presumed there had once been a considerable workforce of servants and groundsmen here. They would likely have fled the approaching tide of danger or joined the burgeoning ranks themselves, and now no one was left to care for the estate.

The company reached a cluster of bare trees that stood just a few paces out from the gable end of the house, their branches straining toward the sky like giant claws. A wave of Stryker's hand signalled for the men to dismount, and they jumped down, grass streaking them to their knees with moisture. Stryker turned to meet the eye of each of his companions.

'Right,' he said. 'We'll take him and go. Kill anyone who gets in the way.' Making for the front of the house, he turned back suddenly. 'Prime your muskets.'

Stryker glanced down at his own weapon, checked the pan remained covered, and pulled on the well-oiled trigger. It slipped back easily under the pressure and the glowing match arced down to touch the metal. Satisfied that all was well, he strode to the sturdy-looking door and hammered a fist against it.

There was no response. Stryker repeated the action, but to no avail. He looked round and caught the eye of Corporal O'Hanlon. The grey brows were raised in expectation. Stryker jerked his chin toward the side of the building. 'Off with you, Corporal. Find someone to let us in. There must be a servant around the place.'

But when the Ulsterman returned, he shook his head. 'Sorry sir. Not a soul about. Rear door's locked tight too.'

Stryker's jaw quivered in irritation. 'If he wants to make it difficult for us, we'll return the favour.' He looked to the gap-toothed musketeer who had joined them with O'Hanlon, and jerked his thumb at the stout wooden front door. 'Mister Dance. Let's have this bugger down, if you please.'

Dance grinned and flicked open the cover of his musket's priming pan, exposing the charge to the burning match that hovered ominously above it. He took a step forward, levelled his weapon and launched a massive kick at the big wooden door. There was a satisfying crack on the opposite side and Dance knew he had inflicted damage, so he kicked again, and a third time.

Jared Dance was still grinning as he hit the ground.

The shot had come from the gloom beyond the door. As the lock had broken and the door swung wildly inwards an almighty crack rang out, followed by a plume of thick, black smoke that filled the doorway. One moment Musketeer Jared Dance was battering a door, the next he was on the ground, staring at the weak sun, a clean hole ripped in his windpipe. A pool of blood raced out from beneath Dance's head, widening with every second and simmering under fine droplets of rain, the sticky liquid pumping rapidly from the large exit wound.

If time slowed in that first moment, it accelerated the next. As Dance's body twitched on the now crimson flag stones, the remaining six men instinctively ducked and scattered. Voices could be heard from inside the houses, speaking loud and rapidly.

'Soldiers!' Skellen hissed as he ran. 'Fuckin' soldiers!'

'To me!' Stryker ordered.

In front of the house, immediately opposite the gaping doorway, a wall rose out of the grass. It had once been part of the boundary to a kitchen garden. Originally dour walls of red brick, reaching no higher than a man's waist, would have enclosed a series of ornate flower-beds. Only one of those walls was left, the rest having fallen to ruin, but it would suffice. Instinctively the retreating men scrambled towards the brickwork, diving behind the protective barrier.

When all six were flattened against the impromptu barricade, Stryker raised his head slightly to peer over the top layer of ornamental bricks. He half expected to see a troop of Roundheads burst forth from the manor to complete the ambush, but no punitive force appeared. Stryker rapidly calculated. Attack, retreat, or dig in. If they were to attack, to pour fire upon Langrish House and take steel and death to the men who had put a ball into one of his own, he knew the defenders would probably pick his company off singly as they made for the door. However, if he led a full-scale retreat, the nearest cover was the tree line and that was too far behind them to reach and still live.

He turned to the others. 'We're staying here.'

'Staying?' Forrester was the first to respond, and voicing the surprise of the rest. 'I've heard more than one voice from that blasted house, old man. We can't very well charge 'em.'

'No, we can't. We're digging in. They'll be at the windows, with guns trained on us. If we make a run for it, or go for the horses, they'll like as not fire lead into our arses.'

The crumbling mortar between the bricks splintered violently at their backs as a pair of musket-balls thumped home. The men flinched as the wall vibrated behind them. Another shot thundered in, followed by a whistling sound as a ball displaced the air above their heads. Stryker caught his sergeant's eye and jerked his head towards the house.

'Musketeer Brunt,' Skellen said, acknowledging his officer's unspoken order. 'Give the bastards something to think upon.'

With a flick of his thumb, Wendle Brunt unmasked his priming pan and raised his musket. He sucked in a breath, gritted his teeth and stood, swivelling round on his toes as he did so. In a single, swift movement the musket was at his shoulder, the barrel trained on one of the building's upper windows, and the trigger pulled back. Brunt did not see his missile's final resting place, the cloud of acrid smoke obscuring his vision, but the others peering past the protection of the wall saw glass break and a dark silhouette fall back. The shot seemed to have the desired effect, for the sporadic fire from the house ceased. Brunt ducked down again, rummaging in his bag for the next cartridge.

'Right,' Stryker said. 'That'll do it.'

'Now what?' Forrester said.

'More of the same. Now they've been warned off, they'll stay back from the doors and windows. And we can take our time getting inside.'

Sure enough, the defenders were more reticent, only infrequently venturing near the windows to let off a shot. Stryker's men replied in equal measure with ragged shots – volley fire would not do, for it would leave all six barrels empty at once – while their captain considered his next move.

Stryker's back was flush against the wall. He scanned the surrounding area, searching for something, anything they could use to their advantage. A well-aimed ball clipped the top edge of the wall, skittering off the brickwork and missing Stryker by inches. He reloaded his own musket almost automatically, and stood, took aim. And fired.

'We're fairly pinned, sir,' Ensign Burton said in an attempt to sound casual.

Stryker threw a frown at his protégé. 'Thank you, Andrew. I am aware of it.' He peered back over the wall. If the commander of the men inside the house was worth his salt, he would know that Stryker's men, crammed in such a small space, would become increasingly choked by their own smoke. They would not be able to see well enough through the black pall to train their weapons on targets with the accuracy they had achieved in their opening sally.

Just then Stryker had his epiphany. 'Jared,' he said, raising his voice over the gunfire so that his men could hear. 'We need Musketeer Dance.'

'I'm afraid you'll have to elaborate, Captain,' Forrester panted, sending a shot toward another of the upper windows before ducking down to avoid a deluge of stone fragments as a ball struck the mortar near his position. By the time he had finished the sentence he was already beginning the laborious process of reloading his own weapon.

'Hold your fire!' Stryker ordered. He paused as the last of the men already taking aim ignited their charges, and then continued, able to lower his voice now as the deafening coughs of gunfire died away. 'Listen well. We need to get inside. We can't go through the front door for obvious reasons.'

'The upper windows are covered too, sir,' Ensign Burton said, unable to banish the tremor from his voice.

Stryker nodded. 'But the ground floor seems in the main unoccupied. They're in the main entrance in case we make a charge at the door. They have men up high, firing down upon us, but likely none in the ground floor rooms.'

Stryker could see a tinge of uneasiness in the faces of his men. His face also darkened, but with menace. 'Would anyone like to comment?' he said. His voice was soft. No one replied. 'Good. Volley fire,' he continued, ignoring the stares of dismay. 'One complete volley. Use your carbines as well. You three aim at the doorway.' He indicated O'Hanlon, Skellen and Brunt. 'We three'll go for the upper floor. I want them ducking right back, gentlemen. I want them dizzy as virgin lads in their first bawdy-house. We'll only buy a few seconds, but that'll be enough.'

The men prepared to break cover. Those that had loaded and primed muskets awaited the order. Those who had vented their musket's fury in the last moments before the lull quickly went about the familiar routine.

'On my mark,' Stryker said, casting his gaze over the men at his side. They were all crouched low, facing away from the house and toward the hills, backs pressed tight against the barricade. He paused while they pulled gently on triggers, testing the length of match, ensuring the serpent would definitely lower the saltpetre-soaked cord on to the pan when the time came. As soon as each man was satisfied that his weapon would fire true, they swept back pan covers in a series of clicks, and braced themselves for action.

Opening his own priming pan, Stryker balanced his long musket in one hand, his carbine in the other, sucked in a lungful of acrid air, and stood up.

Eli Makepeace was not surprised to see Stryker appear on Bordean Hill, but he was damned if he would resign himself and his valuable quarry to capture and death. There was not the time to make a clear break, and besides he could hardly leave Sir Randolph behind, for the spy was the very reason he had travelled here. To abort the mission now would be to incur the wrath of his master, the only man Makepeace feared more than Stryker himself.

So the turncoat captain would stand and fight. Sir Randolph had a private militia of sorts in the form of Jem Marrow and his six sons. They were no more than local ruffians, of course, but they were all strapping lads, well muscled from a life of toil on the surrounding farms, and they all knew how to use their weapons. They might prove Makepeace's salvation. They would have to be made to try.

The first throw of the dice had seen one of the Royalist weasels put down in a welter of blood and bone, but Stryker had gone to ground behind a low wall in Moxcroft's garden from where Makepeace, Bain and their half-dozen clubmen were having untold difficulty in extracting them.

'Keep at them, men!' Makepeace shouted down the corridor that ran between the bedchambers of the upper floor. 'Keep them there! They ain't got a prayer! They ain't—' His shouts of encouragement were cut short when, for the first time this deadly evening, a full volley thundered from the enemy position to smash into stone, glass and, for one unlucky clubman, skull and brain. Even Makepeace and Bain ducked down, the noise of the volley shaking the very foundations of the house.

'B-bigger 'n I expected, sir,' Bain growled as he pressed his powerful form into the floorboards.

'Aye, they're using carbines, judging by the sound.'

'What the fuck was that for?' Bain grunted as he regained his composure. 'The bastards haven't got a shot between 'em now, sir.'

Makepeace, drawing himself to his feet, frowned as his sergeant's words sunk in. 'God, man, you're right.' He thought for a moment. 'Stryker may be a devil, but he's no fool.'

For a heartbeat captain and sergeant stared at one another, considering the implications of a full volley, before both broke into a frantic scramble for the window. They peered out to where they expected to espy the enemy, but the low, pockmarked wall, shrouded as it was in swirling black smoke, revealed nothing. Not a single head peered over the top to take a view of the defenders. No movement could be seen at its edges.

Then, downstairs, a window shattered.

CHAPTER 12

The volley had been more effective than Stryker dared hope. Twelve firearms had sparked simultaneously to send deadly packages smashing into the house's exterior wall. The noise, smoke and flying lead put the defenders momentarily on to the back foot, and that was all he wanted. It gave Stryker and his men time to break cover, vault the pockmarked ornamental wall and burst forth from the cloud of powder smoke that had hitherto obscured the defenders' aim.

They covered the score of paces between the barricade and the building without drawing attention. Stryker knew that the men in the upstairs rooms would already be recovering composure and position. They would be eyeing up the black smoke as it wafted around the little wall, looking for signs of an enemy frantically reloading their long firing pieces.

They moved fast. To the left of the house's main entrance the wall stretched unbroken for several yards until a large, rectangular window punctuated the fastness. Behind this window they could see an empty room, silent and inviting. Stryker and his men were already gathered between the main door and the window. They pressed themselves up against the wall, hoping to reveal nothing to the defenders that had been stationed in that entrance. Beside them, his blood having darkened to a vast crimson lake on the cold stone, the form of Jared Dance was still staring up at the clouds.

Stryker nodded to Will Skellen who, passing his musket to O'Hanlon, bent low and placed big, gnarled hands on the nearest of Dance's ankles. The dead weight was difficult to shift, but eventually the sergeant had turned the body so that its boots pointed toward him. He dragged the body off the flagstones, leaving a trail of bloody slime, and on to the grass at their feet.

While the men battered at the window, shattering the shards of glass with the butts of their muskets, Stryker bent low, prizing the still-primed long-arm from Dance's already stiffening fingers. All that was left was for them to hurdle the stone sill and enter the house.

As the glass shattered in a piercing crash, Makepeace's first thought was that one of the ancient chandeliers had fallen from the high ceiling. A second later he knew that Stryker's men had somehow got into the house.

'God damn him!' Makepeace cursed as he led the defenders down the grand staircase. 'Damn that devilish fucker!'

At the foot of the stairs he saw Moxcroft, still impressively calm, though his face was slick with perspiration. 'Where is he, Sir Randolph? Which room?'

Moxcroft propelled the large wheels of his chair with one bony hand, and pointed the way with the other. 'The drawing room, we believe, Captain.'

'Then he's t-trapped, sir,' Bain said confidently as he

joined the officer on the ground floor. 'The men in the entrance hall will keep 'em hemmed in that room. They've no way out. And not an armed musket between 'em. We'll cut the bastards up p-properly this time. Thought you said Stryker was no fool, sir!'

The first of the Marrow boys to reach the room was equally confident. He knew the attackers had spent their ammunition in that final volley and he fully intended to fire into that packed room to kill his second man of the day. Raising his musket, Dick Marrow bounded across the threshold.

The second armed man was just three paces behind his elder brother, eager to share the glory and prepared to follow up the initial shot. Tommy Marrow watched Dick sprint the last few paces, bloodlust roaring through his veins, and heard the older man's primitive scream as he burst into the room. He had glanced down at his own weapon, shifting the priming pan open, ready to add his fire, so he only heard, not saw, the vicious cough of a musket firing in an enclosed space.

His brother's body came back at speed through the open doorway, feet several inches above the ground as if he had been catapulted. The corpse clattered on to the tiles in a bloody mess, a ragged hole carved deep into its chest.

Tommy slid to a frantic halt, his horrified gaze locked upon the body.

'Draw your swords, lads,' Stryker ordered, thanking God for Jared Dance's discarded musket. As the musketeer's lifeless body had hit the ground, the match had jolted free of his weapon's firing mechanism. Stryker had taken a risk on the weapon, for a significant amount of powder had been knocked free of the pan, but sure enough the charge had sparked true.

Stryker examined the room. It was small, square and sparsely furnished with a large table and four chairs pushed against the wall beneath the window. An idea occurred to him. 'Maurice! Wendle! Get that table up!'

'Sir!' The pair of soldiers laid down their arms and grasped opposing ends of the tabletop.

Stryker pointed to the hole in the wall where the glass had been. 'There. Get it up against the window.'

'With respect, sir, but won't it block our escape route?' Ensign Burton said urgently.

'It'll stop the fuckers shooting at our backs,' Skellen growled, 'beggin' your pardon, Mister Burton, sir,' he added respectfully.

'We won't require an escape route,' Stryker said. 'We're going in, not out.'

The main entrance of Langrish House led to a substantial hallway laid with large, terracotta tiles. Immediately in front was the grand staircase, plunging down from the upper floor, while to the right a long corridor swept away, serving half a dozen rooms of untold size and purpose. On this day, however, the main visible activity was concentrated to the left, on either side of a smoke-shrouded doorway.

To Eli Makepeace, standing in the entrance hall, the doorway took on the manner of the gates to hell. Black-flecked smoke roiled between the beams of the wooden frame, as if mocking them with the prospect of imminent death. Makepeace could make out a tangle of shattered ribs among the crimson gore of the chest of the late Dick Marrow who lay in the hallway.

Makepeace had underestimated Stryker. He knew he still had four of the six Marrow brothers, plus himself, Jem and Bain, to fight against Stryker's six. But he was beginning to doubt that his opponent was merely mortal. The attackers were supposed to be unarmed. Now they were inside the house, bearing weapons they must have somehow concealed until this point. Makepeace decided they should split into two groups, circle round the invaders, and lay siege until they surrendered or died. Fond though he was of his own skin, he frankly preferred the latter option.

The thick-set Jem came trotting into the hallway from the direction of the gardens. He was red-faced, furious and grief-stricken at the loss of his sons, and now thought only of revenge. 'They've barricaded themselves in, Captain.'

'Barricaded?' Makepeace said sceptically. 'How?'

'Looks to be a tabletop. Pushed up to the window. It's flush against the stone. We can't fire round.'

Makepeace's heart sank.

'Finish this, Mister Marrow. They're trapped in their own little prison. Make sure it stays that way. Make sure it becomes their fuckin' tomb.'

'How exactly do we break out of this shite-hole, sir?'

'Draw their fire,' Stryker replied calmly to O'Hanlon's question. He moved rapidly across the room, pressing his back against the wall, and risked a peek around the edge of the open doorway. Immediately he recoiled as a brace of musket balls flew through the air where his head had been, burrowing tunnels in the opposite wall. 'There are only five of them,' he said. 'Two 've just shot at me, which leaves three who have still got their dicks up for us.' He nodded towards the chairs that had been tucked beneath the table. 'Let's see what they make of those, eh?'

'Cry havoc, and let slip the dogs of war!' Forrester snarled.

'Sir? *Henry IV, Part I*?' replied Burton.

Forrester sighed. 'Fuck it, Ensign. Let's just have at 'em.'

Jem Marrow was not a soldier, but a clubman, armed only for the protection of his village. Yet now, for reasons he did not begin to understand, a band of determined fighters had brought fear and violence to his rural home. And two of his children were dead.

Jem and his remaining sons were out in the hallway, three still bearing loaded weapons trained upon the open door, ready to eviscerate the enemy with fire and lead in vengeance for the brothers they had lost. When an exquisitely crafted chair, oak sprig motif visible on the high-back, flew from the depths of the drawing room, they let rip, their small volley finding nothing but splintering wood.

'Out! Out! Out!' screamed Stryker as soon as the trio of firing pieces had been discharged. It was exactly as he had hoped. The Royalists had flung the chairs through the open doorway, and their enemies had reacted to the movement with their trigger fingers before they fully understood what it was they were aiming at. Their rash response was even more amateurish than he had expected.

The six Royalists discarded their empty muskets and flooded into the entrance hall, where their bewildered enemies stood slack-jawed and wide-eyed. The first man fell before he had a chance to move. Stryker, leading from the front, punched the guard of his sword into the man's terror-stricken face. It severed lips and shattered teeth, turning his mouth into a gory mass. The wounded man's head snapped back, but he was strong and his feet kept their balance, rigid like stalagmites, so Stryker kicked him in the chest, felling the body and piercing the chest with the tip of his blade.

There were no shots now, only the sound of steel upon steel. A second defender fell in a heap of blood and torn flesh. The Royalists appeared comfortably superior now that fighting was at such close range.

To Stryker's left William Skellen's teeth were bared in a wolfish, predatory mask, as he battered a man down with the edge of his blade. His opponent parried the first blow with his own sword, but did not possess the strength or will to raise it for the Portsmouth man's reverse sweep. The sergeant scythed low, cutting deep into the defender's midriff, and his opponent went down with a pitiful moan.

Moments after the first mad dash from the drawing room, there were only two defenders left.

'Careful there!' Sir Randolph Moxcroft snapped. Bain, pushing the wheelchair at an incredible pace, had nearly sent the spy crashing into a tall vase. 'You are here to rescue us, not kill us!' Small eyes darted up to the man running at his side. 'By He who is above, Captain

Makepeace, this is hardly the plan of rescue for which we might have hoped!'

Makepeace and Bain had been at the rear of the hall-way, as far from the drawing room as possible. This was ostensibly to protect Sir Randolph, though Makepeace had not truly trusted the Marrow boys, and was waiting to see how they faired against Stryker's men before he would commit his own skin to the fray. As Jem's fearsome-looking but idiotic offspring had let fly their knuckle-headed volley, Makepeace realized that to stand and fight would be suicide.

And now the three of them were racing along one of the house's long passageways, making for a small store-room at the rear of the building.

'We'll never get away, Captain,' Moxcroft said urgently. 'If they're the men you claim, Jem and his lads won't last a moment.'

'Will he fight?'

'Jem? Aye, he will. He's lost Dick and Nathan. They'll all fight now.'

'Good. That buys us time, at least.'

Moxcroft looked up at him. 'Time for what?'

'Time for this.'

They had reached the storeroom. As Bain drew the wheeled chair to a halt, Makepeace handed Sir Randolph his sword and carbine. Bain did the same. 'Lock us in here.' Makepeace indicated the storeroom. 'They'll search the house. When they find you, they'll discover you have prisoners.'

Moxcroft looked mildly amused, his oily half-smile reappearing. 'So you wish us to pretend that we have you under lock and key?'

Makepeace nodded. 'You have it, Sir Randolph.'

'I can see that this might help you absolve yourself of any wrongdoing.' Moxcroft raised thin eyebrows. 'But how might that aid ourselves? They are here for us, after all.'

Makepeace stooped, bringing his face close to that of the spy. 'Precisely! They cannot kill you, Sir Randolph, for their orders were to bring you back to Prince Rupert alive. I, on the other hand, am likely to be strung up from the nearest branch.'

In the entrance hall Stryker saw Ensign Burton locked in a violent embrace with a thickset pig-nosed fellow. The man was shorter than Burton by a full head, but he seemed proficient with his long sword and the obscenities he screamed, though unintelligible, spelled out his intentions.

Stryker turned to his men. 'Scatter. Check all the rooms. Skellen?'

'Sir!'

'Get outside and make sure no one's made a run for it.'

The men did as they were told. Stryker went to assist his ensign, but found the way blocked by the only other member of the enemy left standing.

Stryker stepped forward and faced up to the blade-wielding soldier. He was tall, taller still than Stryker, and slashed the space between them in an impressive flourish. It was only when the tall man lunged again, and they closed together for Stryker to block the heavy stroke, that the captain noticed the close resemblance between his immediate enemy and the broad man flailing wildly at Ensign Burton.

Stryker shoved the tall man backwards, but as soon as the defender regained his balance he lurched forward again in a sudden lunge that caught Stryker by surprise. The outstretched sword darted toward Stryker's belly, its wicked point plunging into its target's buff-coat, finding resistance immediately. Stryker leapt back, stumbling on a prone body, and barely managed to keep his footing. His enemy's grin grew broader, all yellow teeth and wide eyes.

Stryker was in pain, for the tip of the blade had found flesh. He was thankful for the excellent padding afforded by his coat, since the worst of the lunge's force had been absorbed within the tough hide. The lanky defender was closing with him now, waving the tuck from side to side and keeping his knees bent in readiness to launch a killing stroke.

Stryker knew his own reactions were becoming dull, blunted by the pulsating pain. Suddenly, sheathing his sword, he dropped to one knee and scooped up a discarded musket, presenting it at chest height in imitation of the *port* position. The solid wooden butt pointed skywards, preparing to receive and parry the next blow when it came.

When the defender made his move, it was a low, hard thrust. The tuck again met with resistance in the area already weeping a deal of blood, a dark, almost black stain blooming on Stryker's coat, but this time Stryker's jolt backwards just saved him from feeling the metal enter his flesh. Now the defender was off balance, for he had had to straddle the corpse to reach Stryker. He was desperately trying to bring his trailing leg over to Stryker's side of the body.

Stryker thrust his arms forward, throwing the heavy musket so that it ploughed into the man's upper body with all the force the captain could muster. His opponent raised his sword, but the musket crashed through his defence, the butt end forcefully meeting the side of his head.

Stryker was advancing as soon as the musket had left his grip. In one smooth motion, the fingers of his right hand closed around the hilt of his sword, the steel hissing its way out of the scabbard.

The dazed man stabbed at Stryker again, this time aiming high, hoping to catch the throat. Stryker side-stepped the thrust with ease.

The balance had tipped back in his favour, and Stryker was focussed on killing his prey. A flick of Stryker's wrist saw the tuck leave its owner's white-knuckled grip and clatter to the bloodstained tiles several feet away. The defender's expression of disbelief was frozen as the gleaming sword sliced deftly across his protruding Adam's apple.

Stryker was past the tall man before he had even hit the ground. He was making for the foot of the wide staircase, to where Ensign Burton's duel had staggered. Burton's stocky adversary was spitting oaths of vengeance. Burton had held his ground thus far, for the pair were now circling like rutting stags. Burton stood tall, wafting his tuck from side to side in front of the man's flat nose, while his opponent had sunk into a low crouch, holding his heavy blade level with the youth's chest.

The shorter man pounced like a great cat, launching himself upwards at Burton. The ensign had time enough to brace himself for the impact, and his sword took the full force of the incoming blade. A clang of metal upon metal rang out like a church bell and Burton was forced back. The broad man let his weapon drop to a few inches above the ground and lashed it at Burton's legs in a vicious swipe. The singing edge missed Burton's ankles by a hair's breadth, and the ensign was forced to retreat again, this time ascending the first few steps up the staircase.

Jem Marrow would not go down without a fight and, by God and all His Saints, he'd take of a few of the bastards with him. He had seen his beloved sons cut to ribbons, losing their lives in the wake of a counterattack led by a Cyclopean monstrosity in soldier's uniform. But before Marrow would go to meet his maker, he would dispatch as many of these demons as the Lord would allow, starting with the callow youth before him.

Marrow had just placed a booted foot on the bottom step of the staircase, preparing himself for another attack, when something thudded into the back of his leg, just above the knee. His leg crumpled and he found himself kneeling on the second step. At first it felt as though he had been punched, but when he attempted to straighten the limb he found it would not respond. When the pain arrived, it coursed up and down the leg, stabbing into his buttock and gnawing at his toes. He tried again to stand, but the agony washed over him again, sending a wave of nausea to his guts. He twisted around, peering down over his right shoulder. And there, lodged as firmly as an arrow in a tree trunk, was a dagger, its handle long and plain, sticky with his pulsing blood.

*

If the stocky defender had made any further progress up the staircase, Burton was quite prepared to turn tail and escape. His enemy might not have been blessed with the finesse of Stryker or Forrester, but Burton recognized a visceral fury in those small, anguish-filled eyes that terrified his very soul.

But when the short man fell, it gave Burton the advantage he needed. He jumped the couple of stairs that separated them and launched a thunderous kick to the swinelike face. There was a tremendous, sickening crunch, the sound of crushing bone. As the sword went skittering and his enemy crashed on to his back amid bloody tiles and bodies, Ensign Burton leapt down to finish the job. The stricken defender saw him coming and tried to sit up, but Burton was moving too fast, and he was above the injured enemy in a heartbeat, plunging his tuck deep into the broad exposed throat.

Burton drove in the steel with all his might, forcing it through skin and muscle and spine until it burst out the other side like a needle through a muslin sack. The tuck struck the tiles beneath the man's head and its tip snapped, but such was its force that the tile shattered and the next inch of the blade embedded itself in the ground beneath.

Stryker surveyed the carnage for a few moments. Twisted bodies were strewn around the entrance hall, a pall of black smoke roiled against the high ceiling and the familiar, stomach-turning stench of death was all around. Burton slumped to his knees, the shock of the action turning his limbs to jelly.

Forrester and Brunt appeared at the top of the staircase. 'Not a peep up here, sir,' the officer rasped, his chest labouring.

'Nor here, sir,' another voice came from the ground floor, and Stryker twisted to see Sergeant Skellen emerge from the front door. 'Gardens are bloody empty.'

From the depths of a long, dark corridor there came the clamour of voices. Stryker's men tensed, preparing themselves for another battle, but a familiar face appeared.

'Find anything, Corporal?' Stryker said.

O'Hanlon smiled broadly. 'That I did, sir. That I did.'

Another figure emerged beside the Ulsterman. Plainly clothed, and clearly unarmed, with foxy and handsome features. He had long red hair that fell about his shoulders like a mane, a neat red beard, waxed to an impressively sharp point, and golden hoops dangling from each ear.

'Hello, *mon Capitaine*,' said Eli Makepeace.

—m—

Lisette Gaillard might have chosen her queen before her lover, but it had been a closer contest than she would ever admit to Stryker.

Now their paths had split again, for Stryker had continued south while Lisette's mission took her north, and yet she was thinking of him as she rode against the spitting rain and spiteful breeze. Lisette had believed, when she left him that June day, that she was hard enough, staunch enough in her beliefs, to walk away without remorse. Now their frantic coupling in the copse had awoken emotions and memories she thought she had under control.

After she and Father Benjamin had passed below Basing's impressive gatehouse, crossing the bridge over the River Lodden and plunging into the shadows cast by tangled trees across the northern road, her companion

227

had prayed with her. It had been a strange experience, for the priest was a High Anglican and Lisette a Roman Catholic, but she had come to trust the kindly clergyman as much as Queen Henrietta clearly did. When they parted for the last time, she had leaned across from her saddle and kissed him tenderly on his cheek.

'Dawn, Lisette,' Father Benjamin had whispered hurriedly, fighting to regain composure. 'Crumb is a loyal man,' he added, seeing the look of misgiving in the Frenchwoman's eyes.

'You really trust him?' she asked dubiously.

Benjamin shook his head. 'I have learned to trust no one. But he professes to be the king's man. Besides, I have paid him well.'

'Dawn, then.'

He nodded. 'He will be waiting at his barge, the *Cormorant*. Speak the message and you will be allowed aboard.'

And that had been the last word spoken between them. Benjamin Laney would return to his parish, while Lisette would take the strongbox to The Hague and, she imagined with a pleasant pang of encouragement, a delighted queen. It felt strange, wrong somehow, to be taking the precious ruby to England's capital, for it was there that its theft had originally been engineered, and there where the rebellion's heart beat strongest. But it was her only foreseeable route to the Continent. Her only way.

⁓

Eli Makepeace grinned like a shark. 'I never thought I'd say this. But you are nothing short of manna from heaven, Captain.'

They were in Sir Randolph Moxcroft's small, scroll-laden chamber at the rear of Langrish House. Night had fallen fast, but the walls and scrolls, furniture and faces glowed bright amid phalanxes of candles.

After the skirmish the men had cleaned their blades and checked through the effects of the dead. Stryker turned a blind eye to this practice, so common among soldiers. After all, what use did a dead man have for material things? Once pockets had been searched and the few coins, musket-balls, knives or cartridges salvaged, they had lined the bodies in a row, shoulder to shoulder, on the grass near to the front path where Jared Dance had fallen. Eight in all: Dance, Marrow and his six sons.

Stryker's response when he saw the grinning face of Eli Makepeace had been to surge across the entrance hall, leaping over prone bodies and discarded weaponry, and add one more corpse to the butcher's bill. But Lancelot Forrester had stopped Stryker in his tracks.

'This is neither the time nor the place for murder,' Forrester had argued breathlessly. Stryker understood. Even amid so much death and destruction, he could not allow his men to see an execution in cold blood. 'They've acquitted themselves with skill and valour my friend. Now let them see that these men died for the nobler cause, rather not to satisfy a thirst for blood.' Forrester had doused Stryker's fire, like many times before, and the blood-spattered captain was able to master himself.

Makepeace, Bain and Moxcroft were summarily taken into custody, until they could be interrogated, and the business of burying the dead was completed in quiet solemnity.

The survivors had also needed time to see to their own injuries. These were stab wounds and sword slashes in the main, though Brunt had broken his nose under the weight of a musket stock, and O'Hanlon required a bandage to the head where a ball had grazed his left temple. Stryker's stomach, while painful, was no more than a flesh wound. This was soon closed up, somewhat haphazardly, by Sergeant Skellen's crude stitching.

'Good as new, sir,' Skellen said as he wrapped a dressing tightly around his captain's stomach to keep the wound compressed.

Two hours later Stryker and his officers, Forrester and Burton, stood before a large table of thick, dark wood. On the opposite side, perched on a massive chair reminiscent of a throne, sat Captain Eli Makepeace. Behind Makepeace, face grim and arms bulging, like a Nubian slave of the Roman Empire, stood the gigantic form of Malachi Bain.

Skellen and O'Hanlon were guarding the front and rear of the building respectively. Stryker was not inclined to take chances.

'I've no fancy for your rhetoric, Makepeace,' Stryker said. 'Just tell me what the bloody hell you're doing here.'

Makepeace explained that he had been sent with despatches bound for Portsmouth. The crucial harbour city had fallen to Parliament in September, and the king was desperate for local support in order to mount an insurrection against the new governor, Sir William Lewis.

'We', he glanced back at Bain, 'set out on a desperate race to the coast. The despatches were bound for a fellow named Gideon Harding, an influential merchant in the town. Our people there inform us that he has some considerable influence over his associates in the mercantile class. And, it is whispered, holds a candle for the king's cause. The despatches promised him great rewards if he might stir up ill-feeling toward Lewis and his nest of traitors.'

The mission, he explained, had led him from the throng of humanity at Banbury all the way down through the bleak autumn landscape of middle England, eventually stalling in this forgotten corner of east Hampshire. 'A perilous journey, for certain,' Makepeace said. 'But a more crucial one was never undertook.' He sucked at his pipe, drawing in a lungful of fragrant smoke before letting it slip through parted lips in measured tendrils that snaked up across his face. 'We dodged Roundhead patrols at every turn, placing our lives in the hands of the Almighty, praising His name with each passing day.' A sorrowful expression crossed his face, and he went on to explain that they had successfully reached the outskirts of Petersfield but were ambushed by a Parliamentarian cavalry patrol. 'We stood and fought,' he said wistfully, 'each of us sending a brace of men to the afterlife before we were taken. We might have made good our escape, had my brave steed not taken a shot.'

'And you were brought here, sir?' Forrester asked dubiously.

Makepeace winced, a painful memory it seemed. 'Moxcroft is a *traitor*,' he spat the word with venom, 'as you apparently know. The house is well built, with thick walls and strong locks. The bastard lets them house prisoners here when the Petersfield gaol is full. We were to be transferred back into town for hanging ere long.'

'Hanging?' echoed a shocked Burton.

'Aye, lad,' Makepeace said gravely. He glanced at Stryker. 'You and your men found us before the wicked fellow could . . .', he drummed lightly on the table, '. . . consign us to our fate.'

'But the men we fought weren't trained soldiers,' Stryker said.

'Local militia,' Makepeace said. 'Loyal to Moxcroft. His own private army.'

'A mightily impressive tale, sir.' Ensign Burton was clearly in awe of the man seated before him.

'Impressive?' Makepeace replied. 'No, young man. I did my duty the only way I knew how, sir. As an officer, I was entrusted with the most crucial of documents, and charged to guard them with my life.'

'And yet you failed to deliver them,' Stryker said bluntly.

Makepeace's brow creased. He looked away. 'And for that I am ashamed,' he said, speaking to the ranks of vellum rather than the men before him. 'I am. When we were taken by these Puritanical whoresons, I was wracked with guilt and distress.' He allowed himself a sad smile.

Stryker gazed at the flame-haired officer, his face unreadable. 'What is it I've sometimes heard you say, Forry? There's daggers in men's smiles. Isn't that from *Mac*—'

'Blast your black soul, Stryker!' Makepeace shouted. 'But you're a devilish cur. Read the bloody letters yourself, if you cannot believe the word of a gentleman!'

Stryker leant forward, taking a thin pile of parchment from the table. He began to leaf through them, occasionally glancing up at Makepeace.

232

'You see?' Makepeace continued. 'They're all there. They carry the king's own seal, for Christ's sake! Sergeant Bain and I have been through hell itself these past days. We have ridden hard, day and night, upon a mission of the greatest import. We were taken by a patrol and our lives nearly forfeit. And I would not lightly revisit the depths of despair to which I sank during our hateful incarceration within these walls. It has been no less than torture, sir. Your own corporal found us with that bastard spy's pistols pointed at our heads. He was preparing to murder us before you could come to our aid. And this is how you insult me? By branding me with insinuations and mistrust? It will not do, sir!' The suffused face of Makepeace sagged and he slumped back into the chair like a marionette with its strings cut. 'You can ask the bugger yourself, if you don't believe me.'

Stryker regarded Makepeace for a long time, the simmering hatred he felt for this man a match to the priming pan of his fury. Without another word, he stalked the few paces to the table and leaned across its polished surface, taking the startled Makepeace by his collar. Makepeace could do nothing but allow himself to be hauled up from his seat, until the table's edge pushed painfully into his lap and his upper body was suspended in Stryker's iron grip.

Bain would have defended his officer, but Burton had drawn his blade. The bald-headed sergeant sneered, but he was unarmed.

Nose to nose now, Stryker and Makepeace regarded one another with a loathing that seemed to engulf the room. 'It won't do?' Stryker said, his voice low, dripping with threat. 'It won't do, eh? I'll show you what fucking won't do.'

Stryker heaved on Makepeace's collar, twisting him over in a movement so fast that his victim was lying flat against the tabletop before any of the other men could react. From somewhere Stryker had conjured a blade. It was not a long weapon, like the dirk he kept at his waist, or the one in his boot, but a wicked little implement no longer than his index finger. At once the knife was hovering above Makepeace's throat.

'Good God, man!' Forrester was calling from somewhere behind him. 'Have you run mad?'

Stryker paid no heed. 'I'm going to kill you, Eli. I'm going to slit your throat and let you bleed out like a dung-smeared pig.'

Makepeace stared into Stryker's single grey eye. He had seen that flash of quicksilver before and knew that Stryker wanted his blood. He struggled, bucking against the infantry commander's lean body, which was all muscle and sinew. The knife broke his skin.

Stryker grinned fiercely in the knowledge that Eli Makepeace had been afraid. He withdrew the knife, leaving a small bead of blood to well up from where the steel had pierced the skin. It rolled down Makepeace's neck and collected in a blossoming red stain on his shirt collar. As quickly as the blade had appeared, it vanished about Stryker's person.

Makepeace exhaled with relief, but his assailant did not relax the vicelike grip. 'You are playing us false, Eli,' Stryker said. 'I know it.' He was less confident about this than he sounded, for he had seen the royal seal on those despatches, but he still hoped to catch Makepeace in an act of treachery.

'You are mistaken, sir!' Makepeace managed to yelp as Stryker finally released him.

'Hold your tongue,' Forrester snapped.

'What is to become of us?' Sir Randolph Moxcroft said as his wheeled chair was pushed into the midst of the officers. Makepeace and Bain had been moved to the adjacent room, under Wendle Brunt's watchful eye and loaded musket.

'We'll take you back to our lines,' Stryker replied. 'What happens then is not my decision.' He thought for a moment, not wishing to talk with the traitor, but unable to leave one question unanswered. 'Why did you do it, Sir Randolph?'

Moxcroft's thin lips drew back in a wan smile. 'We suppose we should not protest our innocence, seeing as you have already mentioned some correspondence regarding ourselves and Mister Blake.'

'Indeed.'

The spy nodded. 'Our trade is trade, so to speak. We're a merchant. Wool, wine, grain, anything that can turn one a decent profit.'

'And in turning that profit you have built up an extensive network of people who could be extremely useful at a time like this,' Stryker said.

The thin man's glassy eyes flitted disconcertingly between each of his captors. 'People that have, over time, become informants, yes. We've been feeding information back to Whitehall for years. Of course, in times of peace it did nothing more than supplement our income.'

'But now,' Forrester said, 'your news is vital. You must have become very well paid as a result.'

'Not exactly.' Moxcroft took a deep swig from a cup of water, the only concession to comfort Stryker had allowed. 'The king's staff paid more, certainly, but not what we are worth. Not nearly enough. In the king's arrogance, he viewed our loyalty as a foregone conclusion.'

'But it wasn't,' Stryker said.

Moxcroft tilted his head back in a squeaking laugh, the pale skin of his face seemingly stretched to breaking point. 'The divine right. Have you ever heard such delusion of grandeur? King Charles uses it as a stick with which he beats his subjects. To demand their loyalty or take their money, or force them into ill-conceived wars.'

Stryker thought about what Prince Rupert had told him. 'You made your feelings known?'

Moxcroft nodded. 'We did. In one of our dispatches. In fact, we told them not to be so damned conceited, and that we were worth a good deal more to them than they were hitherto willing to admit.'

'And that was when Blake made contact.'

'Aye. The good Secretary Blake. He turned rebel for reasons of conscience. More fool him.' Moxcroft waved a slim hand daintily, as if to brush Blake's death into insignificance.

'As the prince's secretary, he would receive your despatches, filter them, pass on any relevant information. He must have sensed your disquiet. That you were ripe for turning.'

'Aye, one supposes. Though we admit we did not take much turning, as you put it. Oh, do not mistake us, Captain. We share the ideals of the reformers no more than we share the belief that Charles was chosen by God. But Blake explained that Parliament would value us far, *far* more than the king ever did.'

Stryker had no desire to prolong this conversation. He decided instead to verify Makepeace's story.

'Tell me about Makepeace and Bain, and how they come to be here?'

Sir Randolph's brow rose inquiringly. 'Ah! Those were their names? We did wonder, but their lips were tightly sealed. Some men will do anything for their foolish honour.'

Stryker glanced at Captain Forrester, before returning his eye to Moxcroft. 'What were they doing here?'

'Petersfield gaol is small. We have often been paid to hold prisoners here. Currently Parliament has ascendancy, so we take theirs. If the king swept through here tomorrow, we would hold Roundheads, for a price.'

'Not likely,' Forrester cut in. 'Tomorrow you're coming with us.'

CHAPTER 13

The soldier waited in the shadows, watching while a night patrol of musketeers trudged by. His stomach turned over when they halted some ten paces away, the corporal in command seemingly disturbed by some flicker of movement or unusual sound. The soldier held his breath, preferring burning lungs to capture.

Just as he thought his chest might explode, the soldier heard the corporal give an order, and the patrol surged into movement again. With unsteady breaths he silently invoked his Saviour.

The soldier crept out of the shadows and on to the road, keeping a hand on his scabbard so that its jangling would not betray his presence. The moon was full and bright, illuminating the town of Reading, and he scuttled quickly towards the building described in the message.

'Knock three times, wait three seconds, knock three times more' had been the instruction, and the soldier rapped gently on the stout wooden door. As he counted silently, he listened for sounds from within the building, but none came. Perhaps no one was here after all. He completed the second set of knocks.

The soldier jumped violently as the door swung open. He was ushered in by a scrawny-looking lad in his mid-teens.

'If you keep me waiting again, Lieutenant, I shan't be as forgiving,' said a hooded figure as the soldier entered a dingy room at the building's rear.

They were in a small house, left empty when its Parliamentarian owners fled the town in the face of King Charles's arrival. The soldier bowed, offering a hurried apology. The hooded man's voice had been low, quiet, but its measured timbre did not conceal the threat of his displeasure.

The soldier straightened up, staring hard at the shadow of deepest black that hid the cloaked man's face, but, as ever, he could not discern a single feature.

The figure stirred, making the soldier flinch violently, though he had only shifted position in his chair. 'Tiffin?'

'Aye, sir,' the soldier murmured nervously. 'Lieutenant James Tiffin.'

'You had no difficulty in crossing our lines covertly, I hope?'

Tiffin shook his head. 'No, sir.'

'Good,' the figure said. 'I would not wish you to be subject to any unwanted interest.'

'Sir.'

The figure shifted in his seat. 'Well? You carry word from London?'

'Aye, sir,' Tiffin replied. 'There . . . there . . .' He could not force the words past his dry lips, such was his dread at the reaction they might garner. He did not know the identity of this man, but that had not prevented the rumours reaching his ears. Rumours of the things this man was capable of. Terrible things.

'Speak.'

Tiffin took a deep, steadying breath. 'There has been no word from Captain Makepeace.' The silence that followed was agonizing. Tiffin cleared his throat nervously. 'They wish me to . . . remind you of the price of failure, sir. To remind you that you have promised to deliver Sir Randolph to them. His knowledge is worth a great deal.'

'I am aware of that, Lieutenant. Quite aware.'

'Do you have a message for them?'

'Message?' the hooded man said, his voice carrying huskily on an out-breath. 'You might remind them that it was I who dealt with Moxcroft in the first place, who made his co-operation a possibility. The fools here believe they have cleared their house by dispatching Blake, but he was nothing. You may tell Pym, with my compliments, that his patience will be rewarded. My man will deliver the spy. I have promised it; it will be done.' He added under his breath: 'Captain Makepeace knows better than to disappoint me.'

His head jerked upward slightly. Instinctively Tiffin turned, and was jostled out of the way by another man, who made straight for the master's chair, leaning close to the tar-black hood.

Lieutenant Tiffin waited while the men conferred. They whispered, but he could hear that their voices were strained, anxious. He caught only two words. One was *Winchester*. The other sounded like *ladder*? Or was it *letter*?

The lieutenant was anxious to leave before the sun rose. 'Sir?'

The agitated whispers ceased and the men looked up.

'You are dismissed, Lieutenant!' the hooded man snarled suddenly. 'Tell Pym that Moxcroft will be brought to them, his knowledge protected.'

'Thank you, sir,' Tiffin said, backing away.

'Get out!'

—ᴡ—

They departed beneath a dawn of slate-grey skies.

Stryker's duty was to make all haste towards the king's lines. But where were those lines? Stryker had been warned that the Royalist forces would make their next move quickly, pushing south and east towards London. They would pass through Oxford and then on to Reading, the town where Rupert had ordered Moxcroft to be taken.

But since their progress had been significantly slowed, the army might by now be further advanced than Stryker was anticipating. He decided to make for Reading, regardless of any other possibility, in the hope that intelligence would reach his ever-growing company along the way.

There were nine of them in the party; eight soldiers were on horseback, while Moxcroft was slumped with little dignity in the back of a small cart. Sir Randolph grumbled intermittently as it rocked and jolted across the cloying, chalky mud, but Stryker ignored his complaints. A pair of skinny geldings that had been taken – along with the cart – from Moxcroft's stables drew the vehicle admirably, though it was arduous toil for their spindly legs and they staggered across the treacherous terrain.

The group was exhausted and chatter was scarce. Even Forrester had little to say. Makepeace, now riding Jared

Dance's horse, was insouciant enough in his manner, though it was obvious that most in the party shared Stryker's distrust. Sergeant Skellen, in particular, was hostile in his demeanour. Nevertheless, Stryker had ordered that no one harm the flame-haired captain. Moreover, the imposing figure of Malachi Bain was constantly at Makepeace's shoulder, a powerful deterrent to anyone who considered turning thought to action.

The countryside was deserted. Folk were not abroad in the foul weather and only by late evening on that first day did they come across another living soul, a lone shepherd labouring in a long smock heavy with rain. The shepherd kept his eyes latched firmly upon the soil at his feet.

Forrester asked him why there were no soldiers on the roads. He murmured in reply, 'They's mostly gone from here, sir. Took the London road.'

'London,' Forrester had said thoughtfully as they set forth once again. 'Significant, wouldn't you say?'

'We won't be making for Reading then, sir?' Burton asked as they gathered around a small fire. The company had taken shelter for the night within a tithe barn's high walls of slippery stone. The soldiers sat around the flames in a wide ring, enjoying the shelter's protection as rain came down like shot on the towering roof. Even Makepeace and Bain took their places, keeping silent as they ate.

Stryker tore at a piece of rabbit and wiped the juices away from a chin that had not seen the edge of a blade for some days. 'We'll keep our present course, Ensign.'

Burton looked at him quizzically. 'But if the king's marched on London, sir, surely our lads will be well clear of Reading by now.'

'*If* he's marched. I am ordered to make for Reading,

and until I'm presented with evidence more solid than local hearsay, Reading is where we'll go.' Stryker stood and went to where his buff-coat was hanging. They had propped their muskets and swords against the nearest wall, and various items of clothing were draped from them in the vain hope of drying. 'Of course, we must also trust', he said as he felt the buff-coat between thumb and forefinger, frowning at the obvious discovery of a still damp garment, 'that His Majesty has not already found more trouble than he'd foreseen and taken the high road back to Oxford.'

'Pray God we'll find him sitting pretty at Whitehall,' Forrester added.

Stryker nodded.

Burton was delighted. 'You mean to say the war may be ended, sir?'

Stryker leaned forward to stab another piece of sizzling rabbit flesh with his knife. The carcass bubbled on a makeshift spit over their small fire. They had shot three such animals during the day, and the hearty food was as welcome as the fire's warmth. 'Aye, it might. In London at least, though it'll take time to crush the resistance else-where. The capital is not the only place where the enemy has set down roots, though it's the heartland.'

A low sound came from the rear wall. Soft, effete, like a child's giggle. The men twisted round to where their prisoner sat. Moxcroft was not bound, for his lifeless legs rendered it impossible to make any bid for freedom. Stryker had not wanted the traitor anywhere near his men, and would not allow him to share the fire, but he had been afforded shelter from the elements. After all, he was to be delivered alive.

'You have something to say?' Stryker growled.

The soft laughter abated, though Moxcroft's smirk stayed wide and smug. 'Why on earth they would entrust any kind of task to men of such ignorance is beyond us.'

Stryker fought back his anger. 'Speak your mind, before I run you through, Moxcroft.'

Moxcroft's eyes seemed to take on a feline sparkle against the flames. 'You believe Charles will have found the courage to attack London? Forgive our laughter, Captain, but we find the very notion highly amusing. The king, in his *divine* wisdom, has decided upon a more cautious advance.'

Stryker frowned. 'What makes you so certain?'

Moxcroft smiled enigmatically, enjoying his power. 'One of our men made contact only yesterday. Not long before you . . . arrived.'

It irked Stryker to show interest in Moxcroft's information, but he yearned for news of the war, even if its source might be playing free with the truth. 'What of this cautious advance?' he asked impatiently.

'Oh, he moves upon the city, sir, that is most true. His very own Teutonic knight gallops ahead of the vanguard.'

'Prince Rupert.'

'*Prince*?' Moxcroft sneered. 'He is a homeless, landless foreigner, playing at soldier in a country not his own. No wonder the rebels hate him. We are told he has already taken Abingdon, Aylesbury and Maidenhead. How much destruction will that boy cause in the king's name? You love the talismanic Cavalier, we can tell. But he does you more harm than good.'

Forrester looked to Stryker. 'If Rupert leads the vanguard, the king cannot be far behind.'

'Far behind?' Moxcroft cut in again. 'You really are a naive gaggle of ruffians. The king has not a single decisive bone in his diminutive body. When last we heard, he was insisting upon bringing the entire royal army to Parliament's door. Meanwhile, Essex strolls back to London unopposed. He will put cannon on the Thames and rouse the Trained Bands from their homes. They will be as tough as rawhide when Charles finally attacks.'

'I was at Banbury,' Stryker said. 'The prince pushed for an immediate offensive.'

'Then you are a fool for believing he holds more influence than the cowardly nay-sayers in his uncle's employ.'

'Christ's blood!' Stryker hissed.

'Don't believe a word that passes the bastard's lips, sir,' Skellen said. 'The man's a fuckin' rebel.'

'But we are not, my slow-witted sergeant,' Moxcroft said, shaking his head in condescension. 'We are neither Royalist nor Parliamentarian. Simply a businessman. We care not a groat who wins this war.'

They set off at first light. The mood of the party had lifted with a break in the hitherto constant rainfall, and they trotted along the abysmal roads to the tune of Wendle Brunt's whistling.

They travelled on through the Hampshire countryside and into Berkshire, along churned roads and across sodden fields. At noon they arrived at a stream, and enjoyed a short rest. The men sat at the grassy bank, watching the clear water pour frantically over smoothed pebbles, exposed tree roots and tiny, darting fish.

The shallow stab wound Stryker had taken at Langrish House had cracked open with the strain of the journey and was leaking blood through to his shirt. Hoping that some cool water would ease the wound, he paced a reasonable distance upstream. Eventually he rounded a bend and walked down the sloping bank to the water's edge.

He removed the layers of clothing delicately, wincing as the movements occasionally needled the injury, and stooped to cup the icy liquid. As he splashed it on to his stomach, the immediate chill had its desired effect. And he remembered the way Lisette Gaillard had once bathed his wounds.

After they told him Lisette had died, things had seemed simple. His grieving had distilled small certainties in his mind. Kill or be killed. Live life as you wish. Fight for money and avoid politics. But now she had returned to life. Now he knew she had chosen to leave him, had even staged her own death so that he would not search for her.

As Lisette lay in his arms at Basing, after their mad love-making, he had been transported back to The Hague, to his infatuation with the little blonde Norman girl with the eyes of a doe and the spirit of a wolf. But she had chosen her duty again. He had no idea why she had been at Basing House, or why she had left him so abruptly, but he knew that the explanation would lead back to the French wife of King Charles. Lisette Gaillard, Stryker told himself, was a cold-blooded agent of the Crown. She was incapable of true love, and he must put her from his mind for ever.

Further along the riverbank, two men had led their horses down to the trickling current to drink.

'I am surprised by my own theatrical talent, Bain.'

Makepeace was triumphant. The forged despatches to

the fictional Gideon Harding had loaded the dice squarely in his favour. Corporal O'Hanlon was a short distance away, evidence of Stryker's reluctance to grant Makepeace and Bain complete freedom, but they had avoided a lynching at Langrish House.

'Had them eating right from my palm, didn't I? It is quite exhilarating, lying through your teeth.'

Bain did not share the captain's elation. Yes, they had technically been granted their freedom, but the atmosphere of suspicion was thick.

'So what the fuck do we do now?' Bain said.

Makepeace scowled. 'Watch your damned tongue. I'm still your superior.'

The corner of Bain's mouth twitched. 'Superior? I followed you 'cause you p-promised me r-riches. I could squeal to Stryker now if I wanted.'

'And he'll run you through as soon as he's finished with me,' Makepeace hissed. 'You'll still get your reward. We'll see this through and complete our mission. Moxcroft honoured his side of the bargain, didn't he?'

'Thought he'd betray us.'

Makepeace scoffed. 'Think upon it. He betrayed the Royalists for wealth. Money is his God. It seemed logical that he would aid us for the same reason.'

Eli Makepeace had promised Moxcroft gold. Not from his own purse, but from Parliament's. Some time ago his master had mentioned that a great gem had been obtained, one that would be sold to increase the rebellion's wealth a hundredfold. It was a slice of this wealth that Makepeace had been promised, and it was that same wealth Makepeace had used to persuade Sir Randolph to play the role of gaoler and save their skins.

247

'W-what now?' Bain asked again as he glanced back at O'Hanlon, ensuring the corporal was not within earshot. 'Make a run for it?'

'No, Sergeant, we cannot leave now. Even if we made an escape, they'd track us easily. Ride us down.'

Bain shrugged. 'We'll be quicker, sir.'

'Would you bet against that damned fiend? I, for one, would not.'

'But he's wounded, sir. They were patching his gut earlier. Besides, they've got to draw that b-bloody wagon.'

'You'd run without Moxcroft?' Makepeace turned away to stare across at the far bank. 'Not I. We must use stealth, our wits. We still have a job to complete. Otherwise we won't get paid. Anyway, our master will be no more forgiving than Stryker. He will have us swinging from the nearest tree, if we fail. Or do worse, if he cannot.' For a moment he was silent, glancing up to meet Bain's dull stare. 'No, Sergeant. Our immediate future must lie with the good captain and his men. We will stick with them. They'll watch the spy like bloody hawks for now, and us for that matter, but at some point they'll relax, take their eye off him. We'll wait.'

'We continue,' Stryker said as night drew steadily in.

'No rest?' Makepeace asked. 'I'm exhausted!'

'Stop your whining, Captain,' Stryker growled. 'I must take our guest to Prince Rupert. You rested at the stream. I saw you dozing. You can ride through the night with the rest of us.'

'But it's bloody dark, Captain,' Makepeace said. 'There are brigands on the road and the horses will break a leg if they cannot see true ground from a fox-hole.'

Stryker sneered. 'Eight soldiers should fear common bandits?'

Makepeace kept silent.

'Besides,' Forrester put in, 'the road hereabouts is good. We're out of the fields now, so the horses should fair well enough. And the moon's nice and full. Visibility ain't at all bad.'

They rode on, following a bridleway that skirted the village of Shinfield, taking them through a coppiced forest of hazel, oak and ash. When they came to an old stone barn, Stryker ordered the company to stop for a short while in order to stretch backs and shake life back into numbed bodies.

The wagon was drawn up flush against the side of the barn, and the animals were led inside to be tethered below the high beams. A little way beyond the structure was a rickety wattle fence, probably the remains of a livestock enclosure, and the men propped their muskets against it while they took on water and gnawed at hunks of dried bread, chattering and telling stories. Stryker threw some bread and a flask to Moxcroft. The prisoner, his pasty skin luminous beneath the bright moon, was slumped in the corner of the wagon. He caught the food and began to nibble at its hard edge, keeping his face averted from the soldiers.

Stryker strolled over to the fence and rested his elbows on its ridge, hearing the satisfying creak as it took his weight. He would deliver Moxcroft to Reading, and though there might well be a reward for his efforts, nothing would be more welcome than to return to his comrades in Sir Edmund Mowbray's Regiment of Foot. He looked forward to sharing a brandy and a pipeful of choice tobacco with the other officers. He closed his single eyelid, imagining those luxuries, tasting the fiery liquid and smelling the fragrant smoke, letting his senses fantasize for a moment.

Then his eye snapped open. He had heard the terrible, unmistakable rumble of cavalry.

CHAPTER 14

They came out of the darkness like demons, a torrent of men and horses, blades, screams and bullets. Stryker knew that night engagements were harrowing. You could not see your enemy, only the glint of his steel in the moon-shimmer and the flash of orange when guns burst forth like a dragon's breath, sending puffs of blue smoke skyward. But tonight was worse. They'd been taken almost unawares.

Two-dozen orange tongues of fire sent his men ducking low, praying the wattle fence was not rotten or compromised by woodworm.

Stryker had been tempted to order the company into the confines of the stone barn as soon as the thunder of the horses' hooves came to his ears. But, though the barn's walls were thick and sturdy, providing ample protection against steel or fire, there was but one door. One exit – or entrance. A retreat to the barn would provide protection at first, but would also mean they'd be surrounded in short order, trapped like rats in a barrel.

In fact, Stryker's options were almost non-existent. Knowing they could never hope to outrun a swarm of fast cavalry, Stryker held the men at the only defensible position he could see.

The wattle fence might once have formed part of a shelter for goats or pigs, but now it might be a life-saver for Stryker and his beleaguered force. Its knitted lengths of hazel were old and brittle, but the original workmanship had been of a high standard, and the fence was densely woven. Stryker had expected the first volley to obliterate their makeshift defence, but the fence held firm and that, coupled with the high-pitched cracks coming from night-veiled assailants, made him realize that it was not musket fire that poured down on them like a plague, but carbine and pistol. He could imagine the men on horseback aiming wildly in the direction of their foe, with no hope of a deliberate hit but every assurance of instilling panic within the enemy ranks.

Stryker knew that they could not hold their position for long. The ragged volley of short-arm pieces had failed to penetrate the barricade, but the enemy's main strength was based not on firepower but on horses. The thrum of hooves was drawing louder and closer. It was not a full troop by any means, but the detachment was large enough that it could simply circle round the wattle fence and chop down the small band with ease. The problem for Stryker was that his men would be equally vulnerable if they broke cover and made a run for it.

He thought of Moxcroft, and twisted back to see if the wagon had been struck. It had, for a couple of small marks shone bright in the dark timbers of its side, but it did not look as though the small carbine balls had found a way through, and he was satisfied that his precious cargo was alive – for now at least. Moxcroft would have to lie low and pray while Stryker's men fought it out.

Stryker cast his gaze left and right at the men hurriedly loading their muskets. 'Spread out!' he screamed. 'Into the trees!'

It was clear that an all-out retreat would see swords slashing at their backs, so on Stryker's order the men fanned out, each dimly sighting the nearest thicket of coppiced stems and moving quickly to get behind its shelter. It offered woefully scant protection against cavalry, but it at least meant that they were not forced to face the vengeful blades in the open.

Stryker leapt over the fence and made for a likely tree. It was dark, but he could make out most of his group among the trunks around him. 'Keep your charge!' he screamed, casting his order into the dark all around, praying his men would hear amid the chaos. 'Do not waste it, d'you hear? Wait until they're upon you!'

A score of horsemen exploded from the surrounding trees. Breastplates, pots and blades gleamed, teeth flashed in terrible contorted grins, horses charged and reared with shrill, blood-freezing whinnies. It seemed, in that dark, lonely place, that Armageddon had come.

The cavalry weaved in and out of the broad shafts of oak and the thinner clusters of hazel, clumps of mud and leaves flying up from their collective wake.

The first man to fall was Wendle Brunt.

As an enemy horseman charged him down, he fired his musket, but the aim was not true and the ball flew harmlessly into the canopy beyond. He unsheathed his sword, but a carbine ball caught his sword arm with a sickening crack, shattering the elbow. Immediately his fingers lost their feeling and Brunt dropped the tuck, a look of horror sliding across his face. The tuck fell vertically, and a combination of sharp blade and wet ground meant that its point drove easily into the mud, presenting its hilt for Brunt's eager retrieval. He snatched up the weapon in his left hand and held it aloft, bracing himself for the impact of the oncoming cavalryman.

Brunt was a professional soldier, a veteran of countless campaigns and proficient with sword in hand, even against mounted troops. But the blade now pointed toward the Roundhead horseman was held in his weaker hand and wavered unsteadily as the musketeer, engulfed in agony as he was, dared his enemy to attack.

The cavalryman swept across the Royalist's side, slashing down at Brunt's head as his mount carried him past. Brunt sidestepped and parried the blow, deflecting it in a clang of steel and a spark of light. The cavalryman hauled on his reins, wheeling the horse around, sending a spray of leaf mulch into the air. He kicked at his beast's flanks, urging it back into the fray, and Brunt prepared himself again, but this time his defence was found wanting and he mistimed the parry. His blade met the cavalryman's downward sweep but connected in a place that could not fully absorb its force.

The sword capitulated at an awkward angle under the blow, forcing the hilt to break from his grip, prising his desperate fingers apart in a painful jolt. And as his own blade plummeted to earth, so his enemy's drove into his face. The slash had been aimed high, designed to take Brunt at the crown, but the slight deflection meant that it veered lower and cleaved a deep gash vertically through the centre of Brunt's nose, then on through his mouth and chin. Brunt recoiled in an explosion of blood, his jawbone glowing white in the moonlight, one hand clawing helplessly at his shattered face, the other hanging limp at his side. This time the cavalryman did not gallop past his opponent, but simply allowed his horse to close with the wounded soldier. In a heartbeat he was within range and battered down again. The sword met with the top of Brunt's head with a satisfying crack, his skull splitting open instantly. By the time Brunt's corpse had hit the ground, the horseman was already kicking his mount away in search of other prey.

Another Roundhead singled Stryker out. He did not know whether it was because he was the nearest of the panicked infantry or because he had been marked as the leader. It did not matter. Stryker, clutching the heavy musket in his left hand, drew his blade with the right, holding it high in readiness to receive the crushing downward blow.

At the last moment, as steel swung towards steel, Stryker fell to earth. The Roundhead pulled on his reins in an attempt to slew his horse round, assuming his opponent had slipped on the rain-beaded leaves, but his mount did not respond. Another frantic tug on the leather straps achieved nothing and a sickening knot formed in the pit of his stomach. He tried to free his bucket-tops from the stirrups, aware that the beast was falling, but they were stuck fast and he felt himself crumble with his mount.

Stryker was up on one knee, keeping himself beneath the scything arc of the oncoming cavalry sword, and he swept his own blade horizontally in a vicious backhanded blow to catch the horse's front-left ankle. The weapon had sung as it first cut air, then skin and bone and crunched through to find air once again. Stryker's blow was executed with such vicious finesse that the horse did not even break stride. As it planted the shortened limb where it expected the ground to be, the ragged stump plunged into the forest floor. In a shriek of agony the beast lost its footing, toppling forward to roll in a cacophonous crash along the damp soil. Its screaming rider disappeared in a gruesome tangle of limbs, leather, flesh and metal.

Stryker took the burning match from his mouth. It had been dangling there throughout his duel with the felled cavalryman and the glowing tip had burned his neck in several places, but until now he had barely noticed the marks that fizzed on his skin. He forced the cord into the teeth of his musket's serpent mechanism and took aim as the next trooper attempted to run him down. For a moment his eye roved beyond the trooper's buff-coated shoulder to focus upon a cavalryman further back among the trees. The rider wore dark armour and perched confidently upon a large bay horse with wild eyes and muscular shoulders. At first Stryker did not spare the man a second's thought, but then he remembered a black-clad officer with distinctive blond hair and expensive weapons. Roger Tainton.

The nearer trooper spurred his horse toward Stryker and his eye refocussed, taking aim along the five feet of musket barrel that stretched before him. When he squeezed the cold trigger, his vision was obscured by the familiar spark and cloud. The heavy thud of a body hitting the ground let him know that the shot had flown true.

As the powder smoke dissipated, twisting and writhing its way through the forest canopy, he caught a glimpse of gold rivets dancing in the gloom about forty paces away.

All around him deadly duels were raging. Cavalry-man beating down upon infantryman. In any other circumstance the men on foot would be cut down like the dummies used in cavalry drill. But the close-cropped trees did not allow enough space for the Parliamentarians to manoeuvre easily, while the men facing them were agile and well trained.

The surviving Royalists were getting their own shots off now. They had held firm with blade and ferocity against the first wave of the ambush, and now, as the cavalry broke off to regroup, they were able to follow Stryker's example and affix matches to the already loaded long-arms. Small explosions that announced the successful ignition of a priming pan cracked across the forest, echoing far into the night sky, and three Roundheads toppled from their saddles.

Stryker scanned the scene as best he could. Will Skellen was to his left and, though much of his vision on that side was impaired, he caught the occasional glimpse of the lanky sergeant jabbing his long blade up at a Parliamentarian who was doubtless regretting having chosen the experienced fighter for single combat.

Skellen disappeared from view suddenly and for a moment Stryker's heart was in his mouth, but a chilling shriek from the muscular horse told him that the sergeant had used the sword to stab around the palomino's fetlocks, toppling both man and beast.

Somewhere behind him Stryker could hear Corporal O'Hanlon. The tough Ulsterman was screaming obscenities at all and sundry, daring the Roundhead force to test him if they had the stomach for it. Three riders took up the challenge and kicked their mounts towards the muscular, blood-caked figure, and Stryker had an almost irresistible urge to take up position at O'Hanlon's shoulder and face the assault with him, but he was too far away to reach the musketeer in time. O'Hanlon was on his own.

Infantry could not defeat cavalry, especially when the unmounted soldiers were in such disarray. It was only a matter of time before Tainton's men overran them. They might have kept the Parliamentarians at a distance had they been formed in a block, able to muster closely packed volley fire, but even then there were probably not enough muskets to make a difference.

Stryker glanced down at his own gun. Ordinarily, he would keep holding it during battle, even when its charge was spent, for it made an effective club; but it was next to useless against a man high up on a horse. He discarded it, dumping it in a patch of rotting, brown bracken, and drew his sword again, backing away from his position, hoping to make it back to the cart to protect Moxcroft. He glanced back to check that the spy had not been harmed. Despite his doubts about them, he was relieved to see Captain Makepeace and Sergeant Bain standing beside the vehicle, swords drawn, ready to take on any cavalryman that might make a target of the prisoner.

A screamed challenge rang loud in Stryker's ears. He turned back to face the horseman who stood in his stirrups, his lavish black armour, riveted in gold, gleaming under the moon's illumination.

Tainton did not slow his horse, recognizing the danger of putting the beast within range of Stryker's blade. He spurred past the waiting Royalist, slashing down at the tall enemy, for-cing him to raise his own weapon in a desperate parry. The two blades met and Stryker staggered back under the weight of the blow, while Tainton wheeled his horse about to make a second pass. Again he came, standing high in the stirrups, hacking down at the Royalist with impressive power and practised accuracy. Stryker wanted to stoop, to strike low at the horse's fetlocks, but he did not rate his chances of delivering the blow while avoiding the Roundhead's blade. He chose to hold his ground, to seek and exploit a weakness; but the collision of steel had jarred his arm from fingers to shoulder and he knew he would not best this well-trained officer.

Tainton came again; charge, stand, hack, wheel. Stryker presented his blade, braced, parried, turned.

This time, though, as he turned, he saw the wagon in which Moxcroft had been carried. Makepeace remained in position, but was now bending low, carefully, never taking his eyes from the attackers. Bain was bowing too, repeating his companion's odd gesture.

And then Stryker understood.

Makepeace was not defending Moxcroft against the cavalry. Bain was not beating away Roundhead assailants in a gallant attempt to protect the company or keep the prisoner. For there was no one attacking them. With a lurching stomach, Stryker saw that neither man held his sword, and he realized that Makepeace and Bain were surrendering.

And then he knew all was lost. Stryker had started the skirmish with the odds stacked against him, but, just as his small company had begun to offer valiant resistance, two of his men had surrendered.

Tainton was wrenching his mount round again, kicking up clods of wet earth in a wide arc while he built up speed to smash through Stryker once and for all. He had thought of revenge every hour of every day since the retreat from Thomas Archer's village, where this raggle-taggle band of Royalists had seen him off with such humiliating ease. He had not known the identity of his conquerors at the time, only assuming they were professional soldiers by the quality of their fire and the condition of their mounts, but upon his return to the puny hamlet a few well-placed questions, made at the end of his carbine, had revealed the truth about the musketeers.

He had sought them out, tracking them through the countryside in search of retribution. But the trail had ended on the banks of the River Ock. It was several days before the questioning of every pilgrim, farm-hand and innkeeper he encountered had revealed anything significant. But significant it had been, for he had been willing to gamble a great deal that there were not two tall, dark one-eyed men roaming southern England, leading a band of heavily armed soldiers.

He kicked again, savagely raking his horse's flanks, demanding more speed, more power. He would aim the muscular steed directly at Stryker. Even if Stryker were able to parry the blade, he would be mown down by the horse's bulk.

Tainton raised his sword high, savouring the moment, drawing in a great breath, as if he could muster an extra ounce of power as he exhaled with the downward thrust.

Stryker gripped the hilt of his sword tighter as Tainton bore down upon him. The armour-encased Roundhead, blonde locks poking out beneath his helmet, was up in his stirrups, long cavalry sword held aloft, poised for the killing blow. Stryker braced himself. Perhaps he could duck beneath the stroke or dive clear of the thundering hooves. But there was no chance at all. He closed his eye, wondering where he would be going after his life was cut from him by this young officer's blade.

It was only when the hooves had passed by and the whinnying and snorting of Tainton's massive charger was behind him that he realized Tainton had withdrawn his weapon. It had been at the last moment certainly, for the sound of the blade had sliced across the top of Stryker's head at alarmingly close proximity.

Roger Tainton wheeled round, levelling his blade at Stryker's throat. 'Do you yield, sir? You have no chance of victory or escape.'

The very idea of surrender nauseated Stryker. But then he saw the body of Wendle Brunt. He had already lost at least one man in this fight and he had lost his prisoner, the very man they had made this journey to capture. Could he allow the rest of them now to die here in ignominy if he chose to fight on? He would not – could not – sacrifice what remained of his company for the sake of his pride.

Stryker thrust his sword into the ground in front of him. The blade, a glistening shade of crimson, was left to quiver in the earth.

He looked up at Tainton. The Parliamentarian was still standing, hovering above the ornate saddle, and he pointed his unbloodied sword at Stryker.

'You accept my invitation, sir?' Tainton called and Stryker heard the granite in his voice.

'Aye,' Stryker replied in a low voice. He nodded toward the length of red metal that still trembled before him. 'You have my sword, Captain.'

Tainton twisted in his saddle, surveying the panorama

of destruction that lay all about them. 'Hold!' he screamed above the continued clamour of the melee. 'Hold, I say!'

Gradually, the Parliamentarian troopers disengaged. Stryker scanned the carnage, locating his comrades within the jumble of men and horses. The battle, which had come on them so suddenly and catastrophically, was over.

'We lost Maurice,' said Skellen, cradling a deep gash to his left forearm. The Royalist company were being herded, at sword-point, into a line. They were to be bound and put on the cart.

Stryker was genuinely sorry to hear the news, for he had liked and respected the jovial and outspoken Ulsterman. He turned to meet his sergeant's stare. 'What happened?'

'Blade nicked him 'cross the temple,' Skellen replied. 'He fell back and the bastard swept low. Took him in the crotch. Bled out, poor bugger.' Skellen twisted round to glare at Makepeace, who stood at the end of the line with Sergeant Bain. 'We might have been all right yet if those fuckin' cowards hadn't dropped us in it.'

Bain loomed threateningly. 'You watch your p-pissin' tongue! Else I'll give you the same pretty face what I g-gave your captain.'

Stryker stood back in response to the sword waved at him by a Parliamentarian guard. He glared up at the vast man at Makepeace's shoulder. 'Make that little speech again, Bain, and I'll cut your balls off.'

Bain grinned broadly. 'When, *sir*? You're a prisoner.'

'Oh, I'm certain he'll find an opportune moment, Sergeant,' Lancelot Forrester said.

'Speaking of opportune moments,' Eli Makepeace cut in suddenly. 'Perhaps this is one.' He waited for the men in

the line to turn so he had their full attention. 'My surrender was not due to cowardice.' He stepped out of the line,
fishing a small fragment of parchment from the side of
his boot. As the guard moved to push him back into line,
he waved it under the man's nose theatrically. 'Fetch the
captain, would you?'

'Not bloody likely,' the cavalryman answered gruffly.

'I shan't offer this for you to read,' Makepeace replied,
'as I don't suppose you have your letters. But I assure you
Captain Tainton will wish to cast his eye over it straight
away.'

As Stryker lay in the cart, he was thankful for the hardy
constitution afforded him by God and by years of
campaigning abroad, for the cold seemed to permeate his
very bones now that his limbs were bound and inert.

He cast his eye around the mass of men and horses that
made their way east toward the metropolis. He felt sorry
for the next pilgrims to traverse this highway, for the large
company was carving up the road beneath with so many
shod hooves that nothing more than a ploughed field was
being left in their wake.

This was Tainton's full troop, probably numbering
around fifty, Stryker reckoned. They were well armoured,
with good, expensive, well-kept mounts that would put
most cavalry units to shame. Their helmets and breastplates glinted in the dawn's wan light, while their leader's
black armour left no doubt who was in command.

As he quietly observed his captors, assessing strengths
and searching for weaknesses, Stryker noticed an addi-
tional group of riderless horses led by the reins at the rear
of the column. At first he assumed they were the animals

taken in the Shinfield skirmish, but a quick count told him that there were four beasts too many.

And then he saw a large stallion, its rich chestnut coat shimmering red in the sun, and he realized with joy that Vos and the others were there, apparently unharmed.

With such a large force now assembled, Tainton had decided to travel in the open. It was not likely that a Royalist faction of similar or greater strength was abroad in this region. Besides, anything smaller than a main road would have been virtually impassable in this weather.

'Where do they take us, d'you think, sir?'

Ensign Burton was leaning against the opposite side of the cart. Propped to his right was Sergeant Skellen, while Captain Forrester sat next to Stryker. At the foot of the cart, furthest away from the pair of horses that drew it through the sucking mud, sat Sir Randolph Moxcroft. Tainton had not wished to transport him in the same vehicle as the prisoners, but the spy's disability prevented him taking to the saddle. To ensure his safety, Tainton had placed one of his cavalrymen next to Moxcroft. The man held a carbine in each hand, loaded and ready to curb any hint of insurrection.

Stryker's gaze met that of Burton. 'London, like as not.'

After the surrender, Stryker and his men might have been executed on the spot, but Stryker had guessed correctly that Tainton would not choose that path. They had been disarmed and were under constant guard, but no further deaths were sought.

As Stryker silently contemplated the human toll, a voice broke across his thoughts. 'London it is.'

Stryker twisted round to see that Roger Tainton had

reined in beside the cart, keeping pace with the labouring vehicle. 'Six dead. Two more will doubtless follow by dawn. Zounds, man, you've cost me dear. Again.'

'Glad to be of service, Captain.'

Up close, Stryker could see the sheer quality of Tainton's armour. The black plate was spotless and gleamed so brightly that Stryker could see his own face staring back at him. 'It's Milanese,' Tainton said, observing Stryker's interest. 'The best that sovereigns can buy.'

Stryker tore his gaze from the armour and stared up at Tainton's face. 'What do you want, Captain?'

'I wished merely to tell you that it has been an honour and an education to face you, Captain Stryker,' Tainton said seriously as he rode alongside, bobbing up and down beyond the wooden slats that formed the cart's flank. 'Though you've made me sweat a deal more than I'd have preferred.'

'Next time I'll make you die,' Stryker said.

Tainton's grin was radiant. 'That's the spirit, eh? I confess I was rather glad to have found you again, after you gave us such a hiding at that little Papist hole.'

Stryker thought of the village where his men had intervened in Tainton's rout of the Royalist cavalry. 'They're not Papists. They're just peasants. Common folk.'

'Popish sons of whores, Captain,' Tainton said, his tone suddenly sharp. 'I languished low after our first encounter, I am not afraid to admit. Been seeking to reacquaint my men with you ever since. Thought I'd lost you at one point, but fortunately a man of your . . . description . . . does not remain unnoticed for long.' He laughed. 'And to cap what has turned into a very fine night's work, we have the good Sir Randolph in our possession, thanks to Captain Makepeace. The man has a genius for deception.'

The parchment Makepeace had handed over to Captain Tainton had contained nothing but a blob of dried red wax and a simple piece of text. But that text had been an order from Robert Devereux, Earl of Essex, beseeching any God-fearing Parliamentarian to offer help and assistance to the parchment's bearer. The wax contained an imprint of the earl's personal seal. Tainton spent half an hour listening to Makepeace's story, shook him and Bain by the hand, and returned their horses.

Stryker had listened too. He had heard, with anger and astonishment, the story of Makepeace's journey to Langrish. His stomach had churned as Makepeace explained the 'despatches' bound for the fictional Gideon Harding. And he was convulsed with fury when Moxcroft had verified the whole sordid tale in a tone that dripped with relish.

'We'll see if he's clever enough to avoid my sword running through him,' Stryker said to Tainton in barely a whisper. 'And when I've dealt with him, then I'm coming after you.'

Tainton laughed again. He tilted back his head and brayed to the stars. 'I admire your courage, sir. It is truly inspiring!'

Stryker might have laughed at his own ridiculous bravado, had the situation not been so dire. He was the cuckold to Makepeace's treachery.

Tainton cocked his head to where Makepeace and Bain rode alongside his own men. 'Makepeace and his sergeant are good Parliamentarians, sir. Honest, pious men who have listened to their conscience, as you all should.

Captain Makepeace took a great risk in abandoning the king's flawed cause, and an even greater one in rescuing Sir Randolph. I only thank the Lord I had the magnanimity to offer quarter, and that you showed the good sense to accept. My men might have skewered him!'

'Nothing wrong with that. Skewering would improve 'im,' Skellen growled to himself.

Tainton grinned. 'Well, fortunately he was able to convince you of his loyalty to the crown. Clever fellow.'

'And now?' asked Stryker.

Tainton shrugged matter-of-factly. 'Now you're to be taken to Westminster. Moxcroft will transfer his knowledge to Parliament, while you and your men will be questioned. You'll inevitably swing, I'm sure, but not at my order, though the good Captain Makepeace is keen for me to pursue such a course.'

'I'm sure he is.'

'Perhaps a stay in the capital will clear your mind. Enlighten you.'

'You think I'll turn my coat?'

Tainton seemed to study his captive as he thought. 'Perhaps not. But you'll share information, I'm sure. Troop movements, regimental strengths and the like.'

'You're mistook, Captain.'

'No, sir. You are.' The cavalryman's eyes were grave. 'Every man talks, given the right persuasion. Not sure what your poison will be . . . blunt, sharp, hot, cold . . . but whichever it is, you will talk in the end.'

'And my men?'

'Your men shall be interrogated along with you. And I'm certain the execution of a man of your renown will be a tonic for public morale.' Tainton kicked, and his powerful mount surged forward. As he plunged along the road ahead, he called back, 'May I know your name, sir?'

'You have it.'

'No, Captain Stryker. Your *Christian* name!'

'No. It's just Stryker to you.'

'Makepeace warned me you'd say that!' Tainton called. His laughter lingered as he evaporated into the mass of men and horses.

CHAPTER 15

'Pray God the winter will be mild,' Lisette Gaillard said quietly.

The man she addressed was a short, morbidly fat fellow with sagging, wine-red eyelids and yellowish skin. He had been perched at the river's edge, cleaning the muck from his boots with a small blade, but hauled himself to his feet upon hearing her words.

The man waddled away down the bank, Lisette in pursuit. They strode past long and short vessels, those with high sides and those that seemed so shallow that they would not survive more than a brisk breeze. At length, the fat man stopped at the prow of a stout barge and turned to grin at Lisette. 'Come aboard.'

The *Cormorant* was a flat-bottomed transport barge that carried goods the length of the Thames, from the arable lands of Gloucestershire and Wiltshire to the towns of Surrey and Middlesex and to the North Sea beyond.

The fat man introduced himself as the *Cormorant*'s skipper, Horace Crumb. He apologized for the clandestine arrangement. 'I'm for the king, see?' Crumb said. 'But there's plenty here about, 'specially as you sail further east, what'll see your neck wrung for expressin' such.' He tapped his yellowing nose with a grubby finger. 'So we keeps things quiet.'

He started making busy with the ropes. 'Mind you, war's got its silver lining, same as everything,' he huffed. 'Industry, that's the key. The rebels are busy forging weapons and building armies. For that they need 'orses. Troops to carry, wagons to draw, messages to pass. You needs 'orses for all that, and more. And that's where I come in.'

Lisette had pushed her unflappable mare hard during the night, and as dawn cracked the dark sky she had arrived at Richmond. The wharf had been where Father Benjamin said it would be, and she had easily identified Crumb from the priest's detailed description.

'So you gather hay in the shires and sail it into London?' Lisette asked.

'Indeed. Or we shall in the summer months. We'll load up with hay and ship it in. At a good price, of course.'

'And until the hay season?'

'Wool, m' dear. There's always a need for wool on the Continent. Always.'

So Lisette Gaillard crawled between the great bales of wool and curled up. She would wait patiently for the barge to wend its way past Kew and Westminster, Lambeth and Greenwich, and she would pray. After reassurances that his men, five in all, valued their jobs too highly to betray him, Crumb had told her that the Dutch trading ship was anchored out towards Tilbury, so she prayed that their passage would be swift and that the ship would not have sailed by the time they reached it.

At first it seemed as though her prayers would be answered. They made reasonable progress northwards from Richmond, passing the great curve in the river that signalled their arrival near Hounslow. Crumb's men leapt from the barge's flanks with practised ease, landing with agile feet on the bank to moor the *Cormorant* so that she might take on more goods. From her hiding place, Lisette could hear the men calling to friends on the shore or other moored vessels.

As Crumb shuffled past, Lisette grabbed him by a fat ankle. 'You didn't say we would be stopping,' she hissed.

Crumb looked down. 'Patience, *mamzell*. We shall be away soon. But I must collect an extra shipment. Manure.'

She stared up at him. 'Manure?'

He nodded enthusiastically. 'Dung! There's gold in dung. We shall load a few sacks and be on our way.'

After an hour or so at rest, the barge drifted away from the bank and began to build up pace once more. She was completely full now, her flat hull packed tight with cargo, and Lisette's private thoughts were interrupted by the smell of dung and the merry singing of the *Cormorant*'s plump skipper. He had a strong and surprisingly melodic voice, and she began to let her mind wander with the infectious tune. Despite being curled amongst piles of dirty wool and stinking manure, Lisette felt her spirits begin to lift.

'Hold there!' A voice, sharp with authority, cut through the air, shattering the jaunty song.

Lisette could not see the approaching vessel, but she heard Crumb protesting that he was due to connect with a Dutch trader toward the coast, and that any delay would be fatal to his business.

It was to no avail.

'Corporal Grimes!' An authoritative voice barked the order. 'Take a dozen lads and board her immediately!'

*

Lieutenant Ross was in command of a small passenger ferry that had been commandeered by Parliament for the express purpose of searching London-bound vessels. He and his men had been empowered to stop, board and, if necessary, seize any suspicious river traffic. It was a nebulous remit, but then Ross's superiors did not know exactly what dangers might come via the Thames. The people of London were only too aware of the proximity of a large Royalist army, and they feared the possibility of ferryloads of musketeers sailing down the great river and into Westminster while Essex and his army marched west. They foresaw gunboats loaded with ordnance mooring at Southwark and pulverizing the rebel heartland, or troop upon troop of sabre-wielding Cavaliers unloading at one of the numerous wharfs and galloping through the city's streets, plundering and burning all in their path.

'We must all play our part in the defence of this great town,' Crumb said, but there was a tremor in his voice.

'Quite so,' Ross replied. 'And Parliament is leading the way. They raise more regiments daily.'

'Well, God bless Mister Pym!'

Ross nodded. 'London will be a veritable fortress, man. It'll be a hell of a thing to break us, should that time come.'

'And the Trained Bands have been mobilized, I'll be bound,' Crumb said.

'Of course, sir. Mobilized and itching for a fight.'

'How many does that add, Lieutenant Ross?'

Ross paused, presumably in thought. 'Seven or eight thousand, I believe.'

Crumb whistled. 'An impressive number, sir. Pray God

they'll stand shoulder to shoulder with the full regiments such as your own.'

'The London Bands are no common breed of scrappers,' Ross replied seriously. 'They are better drilled, better organized, more professionally led than any other militia. And a militiaman's sole loyalty is to his family. The London Bands will be defending their very homes if Charles attacks.'

'I feel safer already,' Crumb said.

Down below, Lisette was curled tight, cloak drawn over her body, breath held as still as blazing lungs could tolerate. Instinctively she moved a hand to where the strongbox was bound at her midriff, letting her fingertips brush the reassuring angles of the wood. Her mind ran with curses. Using the Thames to reach the coast was risky, but neither Lisette nor Father Benjamin had foreseen wholesale searches of vessels.

A pair of boots came startlingly close. Quality boots, clomping heavily across the flat timbers. Crumb and his men did not wear this kind of shoe. Lisette gritted her teeth, snaking a hand to a secret hook in the cloak where her trusty dirk rested.

'Nothing, sir!' the soldier called back to his commanding officer. 'Just wool and shit.'

'Then we'll bid you a good voyage,' the lieutenant called out. 'My apologies for waylaying you, sir, but we cannot allow the river to prove our Achilles heel.'

The soldier who had come so close to Lisette began to move away, and she almost sobbed with relief. But his pacing abruptly ceased. With a plummeting heart, she realized he was coming back.

'Wait, sir,' she heard the soldier say. 'I'm sorry sir, but there's one more sack down here I haven't checked.'

—∽—

Eli Makepeace was in ebullient mood. The master's promise of wealth and glory was now within touching distance.

Moxcroft was secure and Stryker detained, no doubt destined for torture and execution. Makepeace would be lauded as a hero of the new regime. Perhaps they would even be presented to John Pym himself?

Luck had smiled upon him. There had been the constant risk that Moxcroft would turn on Makepeace, and decide it was more advantageous to spill his guts to Stryker about the captain's real purpose at Langrish. But lured by the promise of riches, he had kept his word and his silence.

Until the Parliamentarian cavalry exploded from the depths of Shinfield forest, Makepeace had had no plan for escaping Stryker's party, let alone with Moxcroft in tow. Now the solution had been handed to him. Stryker was a reckless warrior, a cavalier in the classic mould, and, on any other day, might have been tempted to fight to the death, but Makepeace knew him to be conscientious enough not to waste his men's lives in a fruitless skirmish. As the icy wind whipped at ears and numbed noses, and the party was finally able to see the dark haze of the innumerable fires clouding the horizon of the metropolis, Eli Makepeace knew that his star was truly rising.

Rumours that Charles and his army had marched south and east to wrest London from Parliament's grip had been circling with every traveller they had encountered. Those rumours had been confirmed yesterday, the tenth day of November, when the troop had intercepted a messenger bound for Farnham Castle. The rider told them that the Royalists had indeed closed upon London and were now camped in the area around Windsor and Colnbrook. It was said that a delegation had ridden out from Parliament to talk of truce, but neither Tainton nor Makepeace expected much to come of such negotiations. Charles believed in his divine right to rule, and he would surely not deal squarely with low-born subjects now; subjects that had chased him from his capital with such humiliating impudence. No, the time to avoid further bloodshed had long since passed.

So there would be a reckoning, and soon. Makepeace did not welcome fighting another battle, but he recognized its inevitability. If it came to conflict, he would stay close to Bain. Some skins, Makepeace reflected, were too precious to be risked, and some were not.

He scratched himself. He could do with a bath, some good wine and a woman.

'Morden is behind us.' Roger Tainton's voice rang like a bell in Makepeace's ear as he reined in on his right. 'Only ten or so miles more to travel.'

'Praise the Lord, Captain,' Makepeace said, the pious rhetoric sliding easily off his tongue. He had promised the young officer a share of the glory in rescuing Moxcroft, if Tainton agreed to convey them to London. It irked Makepeace a little that another man would deliver the legendary Stryker for execution, but the pay-off was well worth it. He had made a powerful new ally.

As the front ranks of the troop rounded the road's gentle bend, they saw the halberd first, hovering above a deep hedge like some silver bird. Presently the soldiers themselves came into view.

There were eight, a half-dozen musketeers with mud-caked latchets and flat montero hats, led by a long-faced, feral-looking corporal and a squat, heavily bearded sergeant. The hook, axe and blade of the latter's pole-arm gleamed in the wintry sun, heralding the soldiers' purpose like a martial banner. The soldiers wore orange sashes about their waists and Makepeace breathed a private sigh of relief. They had reached the Parliamentarian lines.

Tainton spurred his horse forward. He cantered the last thirty or so paces between the troop and the small picket, followed by Makepeace and two other officers.

Tainton had donned his sash as the first of London's smoking columns had risen from the horizon and the sergeant stepped out from his small group to greet them. 'Good-day, sir,' he said, long teeth jutting crookedly between cracked lips.

Tainton nodded curtly. 'Captain Tainton, Sir Edward Tainton's Horse.'

The sergeant let his eyes – small, black and suspicious – wander beyond the mounted officer to where the long troop trotted round the muddy road's curve. 'Name's Howling, sir. Sergeant-at-Arms; Tower 'amlets Trained Band. Beg pardon, Captain, sir, but may I ask your purpose?'

Tainton shifted irritably in his saddle. 'We're bound for Westminster, Sergeant. I carry prisoners.' He indicated the cart with a rearward jerk of his head.

The sergeant scanned the cart's bounty with interest, black eyes lingering on the captives for a second, and he licked his lips with a fat, wet tongue. 'Hang 'em, I say. Hang 'em all.'

'Spare me your opinions, Sergeant,' Tainton barked.

Howling tore his baleful gaze away, meeting Tainton's once again. 'Sorry, sir, but I've orders that says you're not coming through 'ere.'

'Orders, you say?' Tainton asked, his tone level, though his brow had darkened.

The sergeant nodded and produced a wad of tightly folded parchment from within his doublet. 'King's at Windsor, sir. Peace talks, it is said.'

'Your point, Sergeant?' Tainton said, his voice sharpened by irritation. 'Come on man, spit it out!'

The soldier ambled up to Tainton's horse and handed the parchment to the officer. 'You'd better take a look, sir, for I do not have me letters. You're to be redirected though, sir, right enough.'

They left Sergeant Howling and his picket behind, and, as the road forked east and west, took the left-hand route that would lead them west of the capital. Tainton had yearned to canter into London's teeming streets resplendent in his fine armour and glorious after his capture of one of the Royalist army's most talismanic figures. But the orders had been clear. The instructions were for any Parliamentarian units the picket might encounter. All troops were to make haste to the fields between Chiswick and Brentford. Robert Devereux, Earl of Essex and commander of the Roundhead armies, was not inclined to leave the west of the city open to surprise attack. A vast Royalist force was camped on their doorstep and he was not about to grant it leave to simply stroll along the Thames unhindered. To that end, he had ordered any newly arriving units to divert towards the fields and villages that hugged the ancient river from the metropolis as far as Brentford. They could not raise a full army, for any such move might be misconstrued as an act of provocation and Parliament were anxious to pursue a peaceful solution after the bloodletting at Kineton. They had therefore elected to post units towards the city's western fringes, but nothing large enough to be construed as hostile intent.

Evening crept across the country and most of the cart's human cargo slept. It was not an easy slumber, for they felt every lump in the road as the vehicle tossed and jolted them, but it had been an exhausting time since they left Langrish House and all were weary.

Stryker did not sleep. He sat against the cart's raised side and watched. Watched the mounted troopers, his beleaguered men, Makepeace, Tainton, Bain and the countryside. Studying for weaknesses to exploit. But none presented itself. They would be carried to the Parliamentarian command and interrogated, probably tortured, and almost certainly executed.

Worse still; they had failed. *He* had failed. He had taken Sir Randolph Moxcroft at the behest of a prince and an earl, and then he had let the spy fall into the enemy's hands. Moxcroft was free to sell the names of all Royalist informants in the south to an eager and vengeful Parliament. And those informants would die slowly.

Stryker heard water. It was a heavy flow, a substantial river. He twisted his head to peer over the side of the cart, only to see a wide torrent below. It had to be the Thames, he surmised, for they had passed Richmond some time ago. He looked ahead to the end of the road. A mist was descending, and it coupled with the black shroud of night to obscure his view of the far-off lights. But lights there were. Many of them, glowing orange in the distant gloom, telltale signs of at least a dozen homesteads, with the promise of more beyond. He squinted into the darkness but could discern no further indication of where they might be. It was clearly a settlement of substance.

As the mist grew thicker, they reached the ferry crossing. Tainton marshalled his men well and they boarded the barges with little ceremony. Even the horses offered only token protest while they were ushered on to the wobbling vessels. They disappeared into the whiteness, the water splashing noisily at the ferry's flanks, and there was a moment when Stryker wildly considered escape. After all, if he jumped into the water his captors would never be able to pick him out in the mist's depths. But he was laden with heavy clothes. The visibility was so poor that he might never find his way up the slippery banks, and the water was so cold that it might end him long before his enemies could.

Tainton had had the foresight to send a rider ahead some time earlier, and the convoy was presented with a replacement cart upon arrival at the north bank.

'Where are we?' Stryker asked Tainton as the black-armoured captain cantered past, urging his troop to pick up the pace once again. The Thames swirled at their backs now, so he knew they must be heading north. The settlement he had seen earlier was now far closer, its lights burning brightly to his right.

'Syon House, sir,' Tainton barked. He pointed to his left. 'Well, the house can be found in that direction, though we'll not see it. We mean to cross its grounds and join the London Road at Brentford End.'

'And then?'

'Then we follow it westwards, away from the town, and find shelter at the home of Sir Richard Wynn.'

Stryker frowned. 'He is loyal to the Crown.'

'Indeed,' Tainton replied, his face splitting in a ghoulish, moonlit grin. 'But he is not at home.'

Stryker watched him surge away to retake his place at the column's head. The carbine-wielding soldier at the vehicle's far end eyed him lazily, before turning to watch the trees and fields trundle by.

Sir Richard Wynn was not home, his place as lord of the manor instead filled by one Lieutenant Colonel James Quarles.

'Gone to lick the king's arse!' Quarles said of the absent owner upon greeting Tainton outside the house's grand entrance.

'And Colonel Holles?'

'Gone to lick Devereux's arse, I don't doubt,' Quarles replied. 'So I find myself here, in charge of this fine body of men.'

The body of men turned out to be Denzil Holles's Regiment of Foot. Holles was a Member of Parliament and one of the rebellion's most staunch supporters, and had raised his regiment from the apprentices of London. Mostly young men of the butchery and dyer trades, they were a well-respected fighting force, for all they lacked in professionalism. They had made quite a name for themselves at Edgehill, where they had held firm amid the anarchy of those first moments after Prince Rupert's cavalry charge.

'He'll return in a day, maybe two,' Quarles had

explained. 'Until then, feel free to report directly to me. And that's an order.'

The cart and its prisoners were left outside the house, under heavy guard, while Tainton, Makepeace and Moxcroft – the latter perched upon a chair carried by two burly pikemen – were conducted inside.

'Please, sit,' James Quarles had said, indicating two of the three wooden chairs in the room that served as his temporary quarters. As well as the chairs, there was a large oak desk, a tall bookcase and an ornate, wall-mounted lantern clock, its weights providing a steady heartbeat. The captains sat and Sir Randolph was set down next to them. 'You see, gentlemen,' Quarles continued as he settled into the remaining chair, the one nearest the crackling fire, 'I am charged with defending this road. That is my concern. I require that you do not interfere with my one obsession. What do you require?'

Tainton and Makepeace glanced at one another. 'We must convey our charges to London. It is of the greatest import,' the latter replied.

Quarles smiled with his teeth. 'Then you may be on your way as soon as the peace is signed.' He was a handsome man, with a long face and strong jaw, but his features carried a hint of steel, a warning to any man tempted to provoke his ire.

'We understand, Colonel,' Moxcroft spoke now, his smooth voice full of its old confidence again, 'but our cause is of the utmost importance, we can assure you. John Pym himself will wish to speak with us.'

'By "us" you mean yourself only?'

'We do indeed.'

Quarles examined Moxcroft dubiously. The man before

him had a fragile physique. His pale complexion and languorous movements were at odds with Quarles's own powerful build and vigorous energy. At length realization dawned. 'You are a spy of some kind?'

Moxcroft nodded. 'Of some kind.'

Quarles looked away. The invocation of Pym's name had unsettled him. He rubbed his chin, his stubble scraping beneath calloused fingers. He met Tainton's gaze, happier to be addressing the kind of man he understood. 'And those vagabonds you hold?'

A crackle of musketry rippled into the cold night somewhere beyond the house. The drill-master's stentorian tones carried on the air, berating, commending or correcting his men. 'You have heard of a Captain Stryker?' Tainton asked.

Bushy black eyebrows shot up Quarles's high forehead. 'Aye! His reputation is impressive. You have him?'

'Indeed.' Tainton was unable to keep the pride from his voice. 'He had captured Sir Randolph, here. Then we captured *him*.'

'Then I commend you on both the rescue and the capture.' Quarles stretched out his long, booted legs and stared at the ceiling. Then he glanced back to the pair of officers sitting expectantly before him. 'But, while I understand you must take your party to London, and forgive me if I repeat myself, my priority is the road and, therefore, the defence of Brentford.' Tainton opened his mouth to speak but Quarles held up a big hand to silence him. 'I cannot spare you, now that you are here. Nor can I afford to spare anyone else to convey the prisoners and Sir Randolph to Westminster. There are rooms in this house that can be secured as well as any gaol, and enough armed men to guard them. You will remain here until the peace has been agreed, or until we have all perished in the attempt. I must depend on the former eventuality. So must you.'

'Lieutenant Colonel,' Moxcroft said calmly, 'We protest. Our knowledge is crucial to the rebel cause.'

Quarles stood to leave. 'I'm certain it is, sir. But if the peace talks falter and we are attacked, Brentford must be held. If it falls, there will be no rebel cause left.'

Outside, the prisoners on the cart were wide awake. It was a misty, peat-black night, but fires had been set all around Sir Richard Wynn's house and gardens, by which the red-coated men of Denzil Holles's Regiment of Foot warmed their hands and faces.

The orange glow of the fires gently illuminated the house. The building was an impressive pile, though not, Stryker suspected, a match for Syon House, the great stately home that stood on the north bank of the Thames. More of Holles's men would be there, staring into the blackness for signs of an enemy that was gathered only a few hours' march away.

'Sir Richard would not be enamoured to find them camped around his home,' Forrester said, staring up at the house, the vapour from his breath rising in a white puff above their heads. 'Still, it's as good a place as any to watch the road.'

'You've been here before, sir?' Burton asked.

'I have been past here many times,' Forrester replied. 'London is to the east, the main highway toward Windsor runs through Brentford old town and up past here.' They had travelled along the Great West Road for a short time after crossing the Thames. The house perched on the highway's southern edge. It was a perfect place to set pickets. 'If the talks fail and Charles chooses to attack, he'll have to come through here.'

'Why, sir?' Burton said. 'Could he not sail down the Thames, or swarm his army across country, rather than funnelling them down such a narrow road?'

'Aye, it's not impossible. But Parliament controls the river upstream and will have artillery pointed direct at the water. Our boats would be kindling inside an hour.'

Burton nodded. 'And a land assault?'

'It is winter,' Stryker took up the explanation. 'The fields are sodden and treacherous. No good for a large army on the march. And besides, they are not open. The land hereabouts is all turned to pasture. It is not a great expanse of fair-meadow like Kineton, but a patchwork of ditch and enclosure, else the livestock would be lost to the hills and the river.'

'You saw how we laboured along the main roads to Banbury, Ensign,' Forrester said. 'It was tough going, but we had no alternative, for it is an even slower march that must negotiate hedgerow after hedgerow. And if battle were joined while on that march, cavalry would be rendered next to useless, for they could muster only the weakest of charges.' He shook his head. 'No, Charles is confined to the road.'

Their conversation was interrupted by a musketeer from the house. He made his way across the flagstones that swept along the front of the building and on to the muddy path where the cart and its guards were stood. He was a youngster, with wispy red fluff for a beard, and he spoke briefly with one of his comrades, who in turn stepped forward.

'Right, lads,' he said, his head obscured by a cloud of vapour as he spoke. 'Orders from the colonel. Let's get this lot inside. Stick 'em in the cellar.'

'I hope there's sufficient wine for us down there,' Lancelot Forrester said as the rear of the cart was unbolted. 'A passable claret would go down rather nicely.' He addressed the company in general. 'I once played *King Lear* in a cellar. The stage floor caved in, all rotten you see, so they moved the whole production down with the barrels. By the final act there wasn't a sober man, woman or child in the house. Great fun. Now where was it?'

'Shut yer face!' the nearest of the red-coated guards snarled as he approached the cart. He was tall, reedy and blue from the cold. 'Out you get then, you popish arse'oles,' he sneered, a bubble of slime blooming at one of his nostrils.

The redcoat sidled up to the cart, peering from one face to the next, counting them off on his fingers. As he laid eyes on Stryker, he cocked his head to the side like a curious animal. 'Stone me, Ben!' he called to one of his colleagues. 'Ever seen an uglier bugger 'an this?'

Stryker head-butted him.

It wasn't a heavy blow, for Stryker had been craning upwards to reach the tall guard, but its speed and trajectory caught the musketeer flat-footed and unprepared. Stryker's forehead hammered into the Parliamentarian's mouth, turning purple lips red, smashing into the teeth beyond. As the lanky soldier crumpled to the frozen ground, whimpering like a puppy, his comrades surged forward. Blades were scraped clear of scabbards, muskets levelled.

'Hold! Hold I say!' Tainton had stalked from the house

on hearing the commotion and strode into the thick of the red-coated, angry throng. 'That man is my prisoner. As are the others. Harm them and you'll have me to deal with.'

'But look what 'e done, sir,' one of Holles's men remonstrated, pointing a grimy finger at his prone friend, who was fingering his mouth. 'We should 'ang 'im.'

Tainton rounded on the soldier. 'You'll do as I say, Corporal,' he snapped, his voice full of patrician authority. 'Retribution for this man's crimes will be fast on his heels, I can assure you, but not before I command it.' He glanced down at the crumpled form of the injured musketeer. 'Yon fellow got a little too close. That is the sum of it. Take it as a warning and hold him at arm's length. The captain is dangerous as an adder.' Tainton about-turned and strode back towards the house.

'What about the prisoners, sir?'

'God's teeth, Corporal, lock them up!' Tainton called angrily over his shoulder.

CHAPTER 16

Stryker and his men were herded into a cellar. Fetters removed, they were manhandled from the cart and prodded through the house's dark corridors until they reached a hatch in the floor at the rear of the building.

Sir Richard Wynn clearly took pride in his fine cellar of wines and various other intoxicants, the produce of the oast houses of Kent, the vineyards of Provence and beyond.

Descending the stone steps into the bowels of the house, Lancelot Forrester had reverently gazed upon the tightly stacked barrels and translucent amphorae that lined the damp walls. 'I' faith, but he knows how to take care of himself.'

'Surprised the butcher boys haven't had a proper pot-walk already,' Skellen said, his deep-set eyes sepulchral in the gloom. They had all reached the hard flagstones of the floor now and it was very dark, but the tall sergeant's wiry frame was outlined by the light that dribbled through the open hatch above them.

'The curse of abstinence,' Forrester replied sorrowfully. He was tracing the outer limits of the cellar, feeling his way around the barrels and clattering into the great glass jars. 'Denzil's lads are Puritans in the main, Sergeant. They wouldn't even know what to do with all this.'

'All the more for us then, sir,' Burton said, wincing slightly.

'Indeed, Ensign,' Forrester agreed enthusiastically. 'Despite the circumstances, I like this place and willingly could waste my time in it.' He raised his eyebrows enquiringly at Burton, but the latter didn't rise to the bait for once.

'Touch the drink and I'll kill you myself,' Stryker growled. 'I need you all sharp.'

'For what, beg' pardon, sir?' Burton asked, adding the courtesy hastily. 'If we're to die down here, or presently—'

'We're not going to die, Ensign,' Stryker said, but before he could continue a hollow patter of boots tapping down the stone stairs echoed around the room.

'I trust you are comfortable?' Roger Tainton asked. Makepeace was with him, his face split in a sharp-toothed foxy grin. The hulking form of Malachi Bain followed them through the hatch, lumbering slowly down into the dark depths.

The newcomers reached the cold stone floor and paced back and forth before their captives, reminding Stryker of a pack of wolves he had once seen in the forests after the Battle of Lutzen. The pack had eventually closed upon their hapless prey. He winced at the memory, for the prey had been a Bavarian aristocrat, and he had screamed and flailed and bled until finally vanishing amid a blur of frenzied jaws and matted pelts. It had been Stryker's blade that had opened the German's guts, sending the smell of a fresh wound drifting into the forest.

'I see you're still in league with this treacherous snake,' Forrester was saying to Tainton, jerking his head towards Makepeace.

'Come now, Lancelot,' Makepeace interjected. 'I am hardly treacherous. Only a loyal servant to God and His Parliament. Captain Tainton and I share similar goals.'

'Which are?'

'To reach London. I have Sir Randolph safe. Captain Tainton, here, has you four as prisoners.'

'Then why do we remain here?' Stryker asked.

'Sadly,' it was Tainton who replied, 'duty prevents us from escorting you to Westminster. At least for now. We are bound to Brentford until there is peace.'

'Then we have a long wait,' said Stryker.

When their captors had gone, the four Royalists searched the cellar once more, aided by narrow chinks of light that forced their way through the gaps at the sides of the hatch. But their efforts discovered nothing useful. It was a square room with a low ceiling and no features save the staircase. The barrels were pushed tight to one another but, after heaving them apart, it was clear that they hid nothing but the damp, slime-smeared walls. Neither a hole nor a weak point could be found in the solid structure.

It was a cold night, and the group stayed close to share their warmth. As they shivered they winced, wounds old and fresh complaining. Skellen had a gash on his forearm that remained livid and leaked blood through his dirty bandage, while Burton had suffered a number of knocks in the fight at Langrish and the forest ambush. Forrester had cuts along his knuckles and a long, angry stripe where a sword had sliced him above the ear. Stryker's own injuries still plagued him, throbbing uncontrollably when he shifted his position on the hard ground.

Above them, in the warmth of a small reception room, elegantly furnished and warmed by a substantial hearth, Eli Makepeace enjoyed a brandy. He leant back in his comfortable chair and took a brief sip. Grimacing pleasurably as the liquid burned his throat, he glanced up. 'We must remove ourselves, and our honoured guest, from this infernal place as soon as we are able.'

Bain had been holding out calloused palms towards the roaring flames, eager to absorb the heat. He looked down with a puzzled stare. 'What's so infernal about it? We've g-got the spy, T-Tainton's protecting us and we've reached the rebel lines. What more d'you want?'

Makepeace glowered. 'You will address me correctly, Sergeant!'

'Sir,' Bain added.

Makepeace took another sip, before meeting his sergeant's cold stare. 'What I want is to reach safety. You think that pompous prig Tainton has our best interests at heart? Of course he doesn't. You're right; we have succeeded in securing Moxcroft. But where are we? Bloody Brentford, that's where. The war's front fucking line!'

Bain frowned. 'But there's h-hundreds o' rebels 'ere, sir.'

Makepeace laughed mirthlessly. 'And when the king attacks, he'll hit these few hundred first. Brentford will be in the thick of that first assault. You wish to loiter for that?'

'But ain't they talkin' peace?'

'Peace? You think Charlie will make friends with Parliament after all that's happened? No, Sergeant. He couldn't, even if he wanted to. His scold of a wife and roaring bloody nephew wouldn't let him.'

'So you want to get Moxcroft out?' Bain said.

'Aye,' replied Makepeace, casting his eyes back to the flames. 'The sooner the better.'

'And what if Quarles refuses?'

'He ain't going to refuse, Mr Bain, because we won't bloody ask him.'

Bain scratched the scar at his temple and searched the floor and the ceiling with small, darting eyes. Eventually he looked at the captain. 'B-but we can't just walk out. On our own m-maybe; not with the spy. Not like he can move fast, is it?'

Makepeace sank the contents of his glass in one gulp. His free hand made a habitual play for the thick gold hoop that dangled from his ear. 'We cannot leave him. My master does not tolerate failure.' He glared at Bain. 'And your neck is as tender as mine, I fancy.'

At some point during the night, though they could not tell exactly when, the hatch was hauled open once more. The prisoners winced at the sudden illumination, shrinking away from the candlelight that poured from the floor above.

'You have a guest, gentlemen!' Captain Tainton's patrician bark echoed from the top of the stairs.

Stryker and his men looked up. Two of Tainton's troopers were climbing awkwardly down the stair, scabbards clanging noisily. Between them, held tight by the shoulders, was a third figure, short, far smaller than the guards, and dressed in a cloak of the deepest black. The man did not go willingly, leaning backwards against the soldiers as they propelled him into the makeshift cell, but their strength was too great to resist.

At the foot of the staircase, the guards released their captive, slinging him across the room to crash into the barrels at the room's edge.

Stryker's men stared as their new fellow-captive slumped to the ground. Burton went over and knelt next to the prone form.

The troopers were already moving up the stair when Tainton called back down the hatch, 'An awkward arrangement, granted. But one that cannot be helped. Still, while I'm a gentleman, my chivalry does not stretch to idolatrous French whores.'

The hatch dropped back into place. Silence followed. Stryker's eye strained against the gloom at the diminutive figure before him.

Ensign Burton drew back the figure's hood. A mass of blonde hair shone like a beacon in the diminished light. His jaw dropped. 'It's a woman, sir.'

As the brandy scoured Lisette Gaillard's throat, she was taken back to exquisite nights in warm taverns, imbibing spirits and singing songs. Then the image changed subtly, so that her drinking, dancing, singing companion was a tall Englishman with a lean, hard figure and a kind heart.

And then the warm tavern vanished, replaced by cold darkness. But the taste of brandy was still on her tongue and the tall Englishman was still staring down at her.

She sat up, head swooning uncontrollably. She rocked back again and felt strong hands catch her.

'Lie back.'

'Since when do I take orders from you, Captain?' she protested, forcing herself to sit again.

'She'll be fine,' said Stryker.

For the next few minutes Lisette steadied her swirling balance and gingerly dabbed fingertips at her damaged eye. 'Son of a whore hit me,' she said eventually.

'Tainton?'

She shook her head, wincing at the pain it stirred. 'Man at the river.'

'I think you need to explain, Lisette,' Stryker said.

Lisette Gaillard recounted the story of her journey from Basing House. 'I was due to take a barge from Richmond, bound for the coast,' she finished.

'Why?' Stryker asked.

'To meet a ship of course.'

'Why?'

'I cannot say. Only that I need to leave England quickly.' She peered round at the bemused stares. 'The bastard rebels were searching all boats on the Thames.'

'It stands to reason!' Forrester exclaimed. 'Our army's on its way to wrest back London. They're as nervous as kittens in a bear pit.'

'*I* did not know! Not that they would search so diligently, anyway.' She tentatively moved her jaw from side to side. 'They found me just a way down river. I think they'd have taken me to London for imprisonment, but they got an order to come here urgently.'

Stryker blew out his cheeks. 'You might have explained your way out of it. Said you were sleeping on the barge, perhaps.'

She looked about the room, her blue eyes furtive as she

considered a response. 'I was carrying a package,' Lisette said eventually. 'They took me for a spy.'

'A package for the queen?' asked Stryker.

She ignored the question. '*He* has taken it. The young one with black armour.'

'Look like the innocent flower, but be the serpent under 't.'

'Sir?'

Captain Lancelot Forrester was slumped in a dank corner with Burton and Skellen. He glanced across. 'The Scottish play again, Sergeant Skellen. Act one, scene five. Though the innocent flower in *our* midst may well conceal a blade, rather than a serpent.'

'Who is she, sir?' Burton asked.

'Lisette Gaillard,' Forrester said so that the Stryker and Lisette, sitting in the opposite corner, could not hear him. 'She was Stryker's woman once, a very long time ago. She supposedly died. Drowned in a wreck off Calais.'

'Oh,' was all Burton could think to say.

'Oh, indeed, Ensign,' Forrester said. 'She was – *is* – an agent of the Crown. Of Queen Henrietta. She and Stryker were kindred spirits, I suppose. Each as hard, clever and untrusting as the other.'

'An' she's a fine looker,' Skellen added.

'Undeniably, Sergeant. When he thought she'd died, it near destroyed him—'

Skellen gave a small snort. 'I first knew him around that time. He was a proper bastard.'

'Aye,' Forrester agreed. 'He was in a rare dark place. Christ only knows what went on between them at Basing, but it must have given him the shock of his life.'

*

294

'They are talking about me,' Lisette whispered in Stryker's ear.

Stryker stared toward the faint outlines of his three comrades. 'Do you blame them?'

'I suppose not.'

Lisette had sought him out in the dungeon's murkiness. Her big eyes, azure pools in the heavy gloom, played across his face, studying him. There was softness there. The first genuine hint since she had reappeared in Stryker's life.

'Where did you go, Lisette?' Stryker said after a time. 'When your ship was lost, I mean.'

Without reply, Lisette reached up to his face, fingers snaking through the short bristles of his chin and up past his cheek until they traced the contours of his formidable scar. She smiled as she traversed the rough skin, her fingers touching every furrow in turn. 'I remember every moment, you know,' she said. 'Every cry of anguish when I dressed your wound, every feverish murmur. In a way I am pleased you have this scar. It binds us.'

'Lisette—'

'Sweden,' she said, shivering suddenly. 'They sent me to Sweden. I do not recommend it. Bloody too cold.'

Stryker could see the dim light play across the whites of her eyes. His nostrils were full of her scent. It took all his strength not to lean forward and kiss her.

'And now?' he said, steadying himself. 'Why are you really here, Lisette? What package were you carrying?'

'I could not tell you before,' she said, glancing quickly at the men at the far end of the room. 'I should not tell you now, though I suppose I no longer have anything to lose.'

She told Stryker of her clandestine mission, of how she had been so close to escaping with her prize when the Thames patrol had captured her.

'You risk your life for a gem?'

'You speak with such conviction. Tell me, *mon amour*, why are you here? It must be something nobler, more crucial, I'm certain.' When he did not answer, she continued. 'Do not lecture me, Stryker. My mistress's orders are as absolute as any you follow.'

Stryker nodded. 'What was to become of this treasure?'

'The queen means to sell it. She is at The Hague, even now, raising funds for Charles's cause. That man would be *nothing* without her,' Lisette hissed. 'When she has the money, she will raise an army so powerful it will swat the Puritan sow-spawn like flies.' She had leaned close, such was her zeal, and Stryker felt her warm breath upon his face.

He opened his mouth to respond, but found his lips blocked by hers. Her tongue, hot and exhilarating, flickered out to touch his and a jolt of burning arousal ran through him.

He reached out, feeling for her waist beneath the thick cloak, pulling her toward him. 'You believe that?' he said, as their lips parted briefly.

'What?'

'That your mistress will forge a great army? No gem is worth that vast a sum.'

She frowned, her forehead puckering in the darkness. 'Of course. My mistress told me so.'

The fleecelike mists of the darkest hours refused to shift with the rise of the morning sun.

The Roundhead scouts had spotted red-sashed horse-men on the part of London Road that snaked away westward. Numerous hedged fields skirted that road, and sightings had also been made around those flanking enclosures. At first the Parliamentary pickets had reported back to Lieutenant Colonel Quarles, the senior officer at Brentford, that the king had sent out patrols, nothing more, for they were small groups, lightly armed, appearing for the briefest of moments before vanishing into the thick fog once again.

Slowly, though, the scouts began to count more figures within the white miasma. From a distance, they were like spirits, partly solid, partly transparent, always fleeting. It was impossible to tell how many of the ghostly apparitions they could see, for as soon as one resolved from the roiling, pallid shroud it would disappear, only to be replaced by another. But as day reached high noon, one thing was certain. This was no patrol. It was an army.

James Quarles, mounted and stretching upwards in his stirrups at the western fringe of Wynn's modest estate, stared in bewilderment at the figures that began to emerge from the mist.

'Cavalry, sir!' an aide said brightly.

'God damn it, but I know what they are, Benson!' Quarles snapped. He raised his spyglass to get a better look, though the horsemen were close enough to see with the naked eye. Harquebusiers materialized from the dense mist like harbingers of Satan. They rode bays and blacks and greys, piebalds and brindles. They had leather buff-coats, broadswords, open-fronted helmets, carbines, pistols and armour across chest and bridle arm. 'There is peace,' Quarles said to no one in particular. 'The king is at Windsor. He agreed a truce.'

'Then we are betrayed,' growled Timothy Neal, the regiment's bluff sergeant major.

For a moment Quarles just stared. He watched the Royalist cavalry gallop along the wide road, eating up the ground between them, seemingly transfixed by the sudden appearance of the enemy. Sergeant Major Neal cleared his throat with all the subtlety of a saker cannon. At last the face of his superior hardened into resolve.

'Fall back,' Quarles said quietly, as if he were weighing up the order in his own mind. Then, as the first – utterly impotent – pistol shots rang out from the oncoming cavalry, he wrenched on his own mount's reins and screamed at the red-coated infantry units that milled uncertainly, awaiting orders. 'Fall back! Make for the hedgerows!'

Further west, on the frozen expanse of Hounslow Heath, Patrick Ruthven, Earl of Forth, clothed in full battle regalia and mounted on a glistening black stallion, shouted words of encouragement as line after line of infantrymen filed past. 'On to London, my boys!' he called. Some offered a hearty '*huzzah*' while their officers doffed caps in salute to their Lord General.

'This is it,' Ruthven said to himself as his horse tore up a mouthful of frosty grass, crushing it between big teeth so that the froth at the sides of its mouth bubbled dark green. 'The final push. If we prevail here, the war will be over by Christmas Eve.'

The earl was confident. His force was strong, some twelve thousand men. They had left Colnbrook and

Windsor that morning and assembled on the mist-smothered heath, the king finally giving the order to take Brentford, the first step toward his capital. The first step on the road to smashing this rebellion once and for all. Prince Rupert had led the vanguard mustering at Hounslow, but Ruthven did not entirely trust the reckless General of Horse, given his wild charge at Edgehill, and had ridden up himself to take overall command.

Reluctant to commit his entire strength to an all-out assault on London, the earl had elected to split his army, sending a smaller force to purge the first real blockage on the road into London, and, in the process, establish a bridgehead for further eastward thrusts. To that end, infantry from the regiments of Sir Thomas Salusbury, Earl Rivers, Sir Edward Fitton, Lord Molyneux, Sir Gilbert Gerrard, Thomas Blagge, John Belasyse and Sir Thomas Lunsford had been mobilized and were now making haste to tackle the Parliamentarian defenders at Brentford. This division amounted to close on four thousand troops, enough to obliterate any opposition and clear the road for the remainder of the Royalist army.

Ruthven leaned slightly in his saddle so that he could reach a deep pouch at its side. He extracted a small silver flask, jerked out the stopper and put its well-worn rim to his lips. Taking a long draught, he sighed with pleasure as the fiery whisky cascaded down his parched throat.

He rammed the stopper back into the flask's thin neck and returned it to the saddle pouch. As he straightened up, he turned to a nearby aide. 'The Horse will have engaged by now.'

The aide nodded gravely. 'Aye, General. God willing.'

'Amen.' Ruthven had ordered elements from three regiments of cavalry to speed ahead of the infantry and shatter any Roundhead pickets they might find. He was taking no chances. That vanguard, formed from the regiments of Lord Grandison, Sir Thomas Aston and the Prince of Wales, was eight hundred strong. This was not the traditional fighting that veterans of the continental wars such as Ruthven had known. It was King Charles's final assault on London. He would break the rebels, awe them into surrender and return to Whitehall, where he belonged. It would not be a matter of giant field armies staring at one another across desolate fair-meadows, but of the Royalist force swarming into the capital's streets, overwhelming all resistance, forcing Parliament's supporters to evaporate or die. And in order to achieve that victory, the earl needed a hammer to smash a hole along London Road, a hole big enough for an entire army to march through. His cavalry would be that hammer.

He watched the last of the musketeer companies trudge past. They were straight-backed, confident and walked in swift, purposeful motion, and he felt a swell of pride. These were good troops. The earl offered a silent prayer that they would find little resistance at Brentford and even less beyond. The enemy had ample numbers to defend their heartland, but he prayed that they would lack the stomach for a real fight.

The final company to take their leave of Hounslow Heath and file on to London Road were the pikemen of Earl Rivers' Regiment of Foot. Ruthven watched them march by in their blue uniforms, black standard flying high. Good, he thought, let the rebels see these shadowy figures emerge from the mist like an army of demons. Let them piss their breeches and run home to spread panic and terror.

As he watched the pikes bob in the cold air, noting with some displeasure the slightly shortened shafts, victims of the soldiers' need for firewood, he thought of a certain captain in the pay of Sir Edmund Mowbray. Stryker had been gone for more than a fortnight, and no word had been heard from him since his departure from Basing House. He considered the possibility of Stryker's failure. It would be a damaging blow to lose such a respected – and feared – officer from the Royalist ranks. Mowbray would most certainly be unhappy. He had been most damnably uncomfortable with releasing Stryker in the first place.

'Boys are away, General,' came the bright voice of Colonel Lord John Saxby.

'Indeed,' Ruthven replied.

Saxby reined in beside the Royalist army's supreme commander. He flashed the most wolfish of grins. 'On to the capital, and damn the rebels, eh? They give me a pain, Gabriel's teeth, they do.'

Ruthven's mouth twitched slightly. 'On to the capital, John. We're taking His Majesty home.'

Saxby whooped and wrenched on his grey mount's reins. The beast reared and snorted and spurred away in an ostentatious truculent display that doubtless pleased its rider. The Earl of Forth smiled. Men like that would win this day for him.

Ruthven had ridden out from Windsor with the clear instruction that Brentford was to be taken as a prelude to the assault on the capital. He had decided to take his force straight up the main highway to London. The king wanted to make the grandest of entrances into his country's first city, and what better way than to follow the route he might have taken in times of peace? So they had reprovisioned the tertios of pike and musket at their Windsor billet and spent the morning massing on Hounslow Heath. From here they would launch the assault, which would take first Brentford and then Chiswick, and then devour Hammersmith until there was no more road, merely the metropolis itself.

As the earl urged his mount away from the great heath and on to the cold mud of London Road, he turned to the stern-faced colonel who rode at his side.

'Prince Rupert gives his word not to stray beyond Brentford. I do not wish him cut off from our infantry.' Rupert had wanted to lead a flying column of cavalry directly into London, bludgeoning and killing as he went, but the earl had sought his word that he would do no such thing. Ruthven grimaced. 'You know, Gentry, if the prince had held his dogs on a shorter leash at Kineton Fight, we'd be warming our bones before the great hearths of Whitehall Palace.' He sighed heavily. 'Instead, we find ourselves traipsing like peasants through freezing bloody countryside.' The earl had resolved never again to allow Rupert such a free rein.

'He will hold, m'lord,' Gentry replied.

'He'd better. I've a mind to—' The Earl of Forth finished his sentence, but his subordinate did not hear the words, for in the distance cannon fired.

It had begun.

Lieutenant Colonel James Quarles had not been expecting the attack that burst forth from heavy mists to the west of Brentford End, and his bowels had turned to water at the sight of the vengeful cavalry ploughing the earth in their wake into great flying clods. He fervently thanked God that the need to make provision for defence had not entirely escaped him.

'Reload if you please, Captain Bennett,' Quarles barked.

The fields surrounding Wynn's estate were a mixture of arable and pasture, and the farmers had enclosed each plot with dense hedgerows. Quarles had positioned his force in a great line, three ranks deep, behind a particularly high hedge that ran in front of the great house, either side of the highway. To reach the house, the Royalist cavalry would have to gallop down this road, funnelled into tight ranks by the hedgerow barriers on either side. On Quarles's order, his men poured fire and hell upon the hapless riders.

The artillery had been positioned behind that great hedge the day before. Quarles had hoped that the peace talks at Windsor would make this precaution unnecessary, but gut instinct made him place the midsized saker cannon, capable of shredding man, beast or stone, out of sight but ready for action.

Now, as the smoke drifted into the cold midday skies, the first Royalist horsemen lay in bloody tatters across London Road and their comrades were kicking their mounts into desperate retreat.

Captain William Bennett, the young officer charged with commanding the artillery teams, snapped crisp orders to his men and their soot-shrouded faces became grim masks as they fell into deadly routine. They would be ready for the next assault.

'Thank you, Mister Bennett!' Quarles called. He had

dismounted now, preferring to keep his head low behind the defensive hedge. He surveyed the scene, noting with satisfaction the twisted remains of the enemy dead now scattered across the road. They would hold this position until reinforcements arrived. The hedgerows were too broad, too high and too barbed for the cavalry to safely negotiate, and they would be cut to ribbons by cannon fire if they chose to make another attempt at using the road.

Quarles ordered three more of his captains, Povey, Lacey and Hurlock, to make small holes in the tightly meshed branches, through which muskets could be thrust. Moments later the hedge had been perforated in a hundred different places by slashing swords and sweeping halberds.

'Keep 'em back, lads!' Quarles bellowed. 'That's all I ask! Make the dogs too frightened to growl at us, eh?'

In the field beyond the hedge the foremost cavalrymen were summoning the courage to storm the road again, hoping to punch through the gap before the cannon could belch its devastating load into their flesh and armour. They stood in stirrups; calling to one another, whipping their comrades into frenzy, cursing the heathen rebels, beseeching God to intervene on their behalf.

When the first man fell, plucked from his saddle before the musket's report had even reached his ears, his compatriots wheeled around in alarm, looking for an impertinent musketeer who'd dared to venture brazenly into the open. But all they saw was the hedge, stretching left and right in front of them.

There were two more loud reports. A second man fell, and a third.

Too late, they saw the glinting musket barrels, scores of them, poking through the hedge, levelled at their ranks. The defenders had transformed the landscape into a tool of war. The hedge had become an organic parapet, complete with its own arrow slits.

The Cavaliers panicked and kicked at their horse's flanks as more musket-balls were unleashed by the hidden infantrymen. They hauled on reins, desperate to turn the heads of their mounts so that they could fall back beyond the range of the long-arms.

The men of Denzil Holles's Regiment of Foot cheered.

The morning light had never come for those huddled together in the dank cellar. Indeed, they would not have known dawn had broken at all, had it not been for the bucket of water brought down by a weary redcoat.

'And what are we supposed to do with that?' Forrester had asked, outraged.

The infantryman shrugged. 'Drink. Wash. Piss.' He dumped the bucket down on the cold stone, the liquid slopping haphazardly and darkening the floor.

When the guard had trudged back up the steps and slammed shut the hatch, they began to stretch cold, stiff limbs. Stryker took the water first, drawing a long draught of the liquid before passing it round. The water was bitter, granules of grit swirling manically within the bucket, but it was welcome nonetheless.

As they drank, another creak came from above. The hatch was violently wrenched free and they were bathed in dazzling light again. All eyes squinted up at the cellar's entrance, where footsteps now rattled down.

Captain Eli Makepeace was wearing an odd

expression. Behind him, Sergeant Malachi Bain thudded clumsily down, followed by four of Holles's redcoats, all brandishing primed muskets.

Like a flock of starlings instinctively turning from the threat of a diving falcon, all the captives except Stryker and Forrester stepped backwards into the room's depths, shuffling towards the far wall.

'When do we receive our victuals?' Forrester demanded. 'I'm bloody famished.'

Makepeace shot him a withering glance. 'By the look of you, Lancelot, you might benefit from a period of abstinence.' He grinned at Forrester. 'Still, it's probably too late for that.'

'Are we to be murdered, then?' Burton said in a voice that hardly hid his fear.

The turncoat grinned. 'I dearly hope so, young man. But that is not my decision, I am sorry to say. Sergeant Bain and I are here to bid you farewell. We leave this morning, bound for London. With Sir Randolph in our care. Don't want to be caught here when the king's lads come a-knocking, y'see.' He fixed Stryker with a triumphant stare. 'You may yet be vouchsafed to your regiment, Captain. But you will have failed in your mission. And I will have succeeded.'

Makepeace's eyes drifted beyond Stryker, fixing upon a face he had not expected to see. Gradually the corners of his mocking grin flattened out. 'You—'

'You!' Lisette was already moving as she echoed the word. 'You! Bastard! Bastard! Bastard!' She was pushing from the rear of the group to the front, making rapid progress to where Makepeace stood.

Makepeace backed away, scraping his sword clear of its

scabbard, while Bain advanced to put his great bulk between his master and Lisette.

'Why, if it ain't F-Froggy!' Bain growled, producing a dagger, bending low in preparation for her attack.

'Out of my way, you troll!' Lisette screamed, but she found herself stuck fast, her progress abruptly halted, like a fish hooked on a line.

Stryker had a good hold of Lisette's cloak, and he spun her to face him. 'What are you doing? They'll kill you!'

At that moment, the stone floor seemed to shake as a low boom sounded from far off. It was a dull sound, like distant thunder, and for a while everyone stared at one another. Burton pointed down to the ripples that were tracing their way across the surface of their water pail.

Stryker let Lisette go so that he could kneel and touch the floor, while others pressed palms against the moist walls. Sure enough, the tremors coursed through the room once again. 'Cannon,' Stryker said. 'The king is attacking at last.'

Sergeant Major Timothy Neal was a pious man. He attended church, he prayed as often as he could, and he'd named his first-born Josiah, a good biblical name. Yet now he cursed. He cursed loudly and violently. For the mist was beginning to clear, and the day was giving up its secrets. There, hovering on the far side of the hedge above the low cloud in tight, bristling ranks, were hundreds – no, thousands – of pikes. They could perhaps be kept at bay, but with the pikemen would be musketeers, and a hedge was no barrier to flying lead. The cavalry that threatened from the adjacent fields also carried firearms, but carbines were less powerful and had no accuracy at this range. They were easily held back, especially now that Tainton's troop had sped on to the field in small but swift sorties, harrying them with impressive skill and drawing their focus from Quarles's redcoats. But muskets – that was a much more fearsome proposition.

Neal was forty paces from his lieutenant colonel and ran along the thorny barrier to draw up next to him. 'Infantry, sir,' he said breathlessly.

'Seen 'em, Timothy,' Quarles replied. He was peering through one of the thicket's hastily cut holes and did not look up at his sergeant major. 'They'll have muskets.'

'They will, sir.'

'Then we cannot remain.'

'I fear not, sir.'

Quarles turned then, meeting Neal's gaze. 'Where the hell are my reinforcements, eh?' he demanded fiercely.

Neal shrugged helplessly.

'I sent for them an hour ago. Damn them, Timothy, but they've high-tailed it back to the old town, I'd wager. Heard the guns and fled.'

Neal spoke carefully. 'We are told of the peace accord, signed by the king's own hand, and ordered – upon pain of death, sir – to hold ourselves with all discipline when encountering the enemy.' He shrugged. 'We must commit no hostile acts, sir. Perhaps the men at Brentford believe they are honouring that command. They do not know we face this horde.'

'They can hear the damned guns, can't they?' Quarles snapped in frustration. His ire was cut off abruptly by the cough of a musket from the opposite end of the field. It was a lucky shot, and a Parliamentarian musketeer fell back soundlessly.

The men looked to Quarles for orders. He looked through the hedge. What he saw turned his insides to churned butter. The advancing Royalist infantry had emerged from London Road and were fanning out in wide ranks across the fields that spread to the west of Sir Richard Wynn's house. Three thousand at least; possibly four. Quarles's meagre detachment had no hope of holding the house. They could continue hiding behind the hedgerows, sniping at the oncoming swarm, but they would be overwhelmed in short order. When the cavalry rode in, cutting and slashing down at their backs, every one of them would be annihilated.

'Sir?' Captain Bennett, the young officer in charge of the saker crews, had approached the lieutenant colonel, eager for orders.

Quarles affected a jauntiness he did not feel. 'We make an orderly retreat, William. Orderly, mark me, no bloody running. We give 'em volley fire, keep the buggers at arm's length, and fall back to our lads at Brentford End. There's a bridge over the Brent. It's nicely barricaded. We'll get across and hold 'em there. They'll not—'

Captain William Bennett was no longer listening to his commanding officer, for a musket-ball had passed through his windpipe. It burst from the side of his neck in a great fountain of gore.

'Fall back on my order!' Quarles bellowed, as Bennett's body sank to its knees.

CHAPTER 17

Captain Roger Tainton sat in the former bedchamber that currently served as his quarters staring at the contents of a small wooden box.

He had been given the strongbox during the night. God's hand was clearly involved, for it had been pure chance that Tainton's men were on picket duty at that time. Roused from his sleep, the captain had been told of the capture of a Frenchwoman down at the river. Trooper Bowery had explained that the patrol needed to have her incarcerated quickly, for they were charged with sailing on towards Kingston-upon-Thames, and Wynn's was the nearest viable option. Tainton had agreed. And then Bowery had passed him the strongbox, which had been tied to the suspected spy by a length of twine.

The lock had not given a fraction until Tainton had taken a pistol and blasted the lid from its hinges. Now, as the battle raged outside, he found himself transfixed by what he had found inside.

Tainton lined up the objects on a small, polished table. There was a yellowing piece of parchment, folded several times into a tight square; a small brooch, edged in gold, with the ivory silhouette of a woman at its centre; and a posy ring, just a small, gold band, adorned with nothing more than a faint inscription.

Tainton picked the ring up between thumb and fore-finger, turning it so that he could read the words across its inner surface. 'None shall prevent the Lord's intent,' he whispered. 'Amen to that,' he breathed.

Setting the ring down, the cavalryman's eyes moved to the item he had saved until last.

'Why do I always 'ave to d-do the donkey work?' Sergeant Malachi Bain said unhappily as he hefted Sir Randolph Moxcroft on to a broad shoulder.

Makepeace nonchalantly smoothed down the front of his exquisite purple doublet and flicked specks of mud from the matching breeches. He had enjoyed his brief stay in Sir Richard Wynn's house and had raided the building's cavernous chests to furnish himself with new, beautiful clothes. 'Because, Malachi, you're the donkey,' he replied, the wide ruff, thick with frills, bobbing at his throat as he spoke.

'We're hardly enamoured of this arrangement, either,' Moxcroft snapped, wincing as Bain's muscular shoulder dug painfully into his midriff.

Makepeace glanced up at him. 'My apologies, Sir Randolph, but the current situation necessitates a swift and, I'm afraid, uncomfortable solution.'

As soon as the gunfire started, Makepeace's instinct had told him that to linger on the front line was tanta-mount to suicide. But even he had not anticipated the Royalist attack coming so soon.

Makepeace and Bain had run from the cellars. They ordered the hatch shut and barred, and, while Makepeace was locating their cart and saddling the horses, Bain went to fetch the spy.

'There are fucking thousands of them,' Makepeace breathlessly explained to Moxcroft as they emerged from the rear of the house. 'Wynn's will fall. Then the town itself. And then God only knows.'

'So one should escape?' Moxcroft asked, his confident demeanour shaken by the gunfire and by the panic on Makepeace's face.

Makepeace watched as Bain dropped the spy, rather unceremoniously, into the wagon. 'Quarles told us there's a bridge further east, between Brentford End and the new town. We'll cross the river there.'

'But they'll ride us down, Captain.'

Makepeace shook his head as he helped Bain bolt the vehicle's rear flap shut. 'If we stay this side of the Brent, yes. But the bridge is well defended. Once we're across, we'll have some time before the king's men break through.'

'What of Stryker?' Moxcroft said. 'Is he dead?'

'Tainton's problem now.'

Bain growled as he joined Makepeace at the front of the cart. 'That Puritan arse'ole won't deal with 'im p-properly.'

Makepeace flicked his wrists sharply so the reins slapped at the horses' spines, urging them into motion. But even as the cart surged forward, his mind was wandering, for he knew the sergeant was right. Tainton would undoubtedly be up to his neck in the fighting. And, when the rebels finally relinquished their hold on Sir Richard Wynn's house, would the cavalryman have time to gather his prisoners? There was a good chance that Stryker's company might yet go free.

'L-let me go back,' Bain said. 'I can't leave 'ere knowin' he's still alive. And that froggy b-bitch of his. She nearly stuck a blade in you once.'

'I had not forgotten, Malachi,' Makepeace snapped. He thought of Lisette Gaillard. The French whore had tried to murder him in the days following his maiming of Stryker. The provosts had stopped her, but the memory of her burning fury still frightened him. He made a decision. 'As you wish, Malachi.'

Bain turned to him. 'Eh?'

'Go back there. Rid the world of their interminable presence.'

Sergeant Bain grinned, wafts of foul breath drifting from behind rotten teeth. He leapt down from the wagon with impressive agility for such a big man.

'When it's done,' Makepeace called after him, 'meet us at the bridge.'

'Sir!' Bain shouted over his shoulder.

'And Malachi?'

Bain turned reluctantly.

Makepeace smiled. 'You might want to have some fun with the girl.'

Out in the grounds at the front of Sir Richard Wynn's house eight units of infantry sent as vanguard by the Earl of Forth vastly outnumbered Quarles's red-coated defenders, but the butchers and dyers of London were veterans of Edgehill and not an easy nut to crack.

The Parliamentarians were arrayed in their companies, pikemen forming bristling blocks at the regiment's centre, musket companies taking up the flanks. They would make a stand here, in front of the house, straddling the road.

Quarles was with one of the musket companies on the right flank. 'When the first of them come through the gap, feed the heathens fire and lead!' He was gratified to receive a cheer for that. 'When all arms are spent, fall back ten paces! Pikes to cover!'

It was a simple enough plan. They would fire their muskets into the ranks of the enemy and retreat, by increments, toward Brentford End and safety. It was true that the numbers were daunting, near four thousand Royalists bore down upon them, but it remained for those attackers to funnel, one company at a time, on to the road, for the enclosed fields were impenetrable. It was then, when they were at their weakest, that Quarles would hammer them. It was a difficult, bloody way to retreat, but to break cover and make a run for it would invite the Royalist cavalry to mow them down. That time might yet come, but he would be damned if he'd give the king's men an easy time in achieving it.

The first ranks of the enemy passed beyond the hedgerows, the head of a great snake winding its way toward London. Quarles recognized their colours immediately. 'Salusbury's chaps!' he bellowed so that as many of his men could hear as possible. 'Heard they cut and run at Kineton Fight! They'll run again, mark my words, boys! You must make 'em run!' He drew his sword, holding it aloft momentarily, before sweeping down his arm in a silver arc. 'Fire!'

The ruby was a thing of beauty. A perfect, shimmering sphere casting shafts of soft red light across the room in all directions to dance playfully along the walls.

Tainton held it in front of him, wondering at how it

had come to be in the girl's possession. She had stolen it, no doubt. But where had she found such a precious thing?

He gathered up the objects, depositing them in a small leather bag that he hung about his neck. He knew nothing about the ruby, except that it must be worth a great deal. If he could take it to London, the rebel cause would be aided by the money it would fetch.

The crackle of musketry was constant now. Tainton paced quickly through the house and out into the courtyard. There he found chaos, for the wounded were being carried back to the house for treatment, while aides scurried to and fro with orders.

Tainton caught one such man by the sleeve. 'What news?'

The aide shrugged him off, fear overcoming respect for the chain of command. 'Ordered retreat, sir. Back to the bridge. We're to keep fighting, though. Stall the buggers for as long as we can.'

Tainton understood. They were no chicken-hearts, the soldiers of Denzil Holles's Regiment of Foot. They had fought hard against the seemingly irresistible tide of Rupert's cavalry at Edgehill, and had held steadfast against his three regiments for the last hour, but while heavy cannon and dense hedgerows could limit a cavalry charge, it would not withstand infantry for long. Holles's men, brave as they undoubtedly were, would soon be swept away if they continued to resist.

Tainton found his own troop regrouping at the stables to the rear of the house. They had been involved in intermittent but bitter skirmishes with the Cavalier horsemen since the initial attack had been rebuffed by Quarles's cannon. They would be thankful to leave this place. A trooper appeared, carrying his commander's polished metal armour in a large hessian sack. Tainton beckoned to him, and the man scuttled over, hefting the jangling sack. 'God's teeth, man! That is not a bag of cutlery!'

Tainton's eye caught a glimmer of silver in the distance, like the crest of a giant wave. As he stared out at the tall hedgerow beyond the house, he realized that the silver wave was the massed shafts of Salusbury's dense pike battaile, dipping into the roiling cannon smoke, ramming home against the thinner ranks at Quarles's command.

'They've made it through the hedge,' he said.

Tainton waited until the gleaming Milanese armour was fastened to a sturdy but comfortable tension and then met his subordinate's eye. 'Fetch my horse, Bowery.'

Bowery sprinted away towards the stables. Men were killing and screaming, weeping and bleeding and dying in the fields hugging the flanks of the road. Tainton watched as a young lad, one of Salusbury's drummers, was flung back, spitted on the end of a pike. Blood flowed freely from his mouth while urine dripped from his hose and down his boots.

A musket-ball splintered the brickwork somewhere behind Tainton. Shots at this range might not be accurate, but his experience of fighting Stryker's sharpshooters had taught him not to assume too much. He hurriedly put on his helmet.

Ducking behind the nearby colonnades, he slipped into the familiar pre-action ritual, strapping on gauntlet and cross-belts, checking his carbine's firing mechanism and sliding the long sword in and out of its scabbard a number of times to ensure that it would not stick when the time came. All the while he watched the battle, counting men and gauging strategy. The men of Holles's Regiment of Foot were offering staunch resistance, but their fire was becoming increasingly sporadic as more and more of the enemy made it through the gap between the hedges and into the open ground in front of Wynn's house. It was not a rout yet, for Holles's lads were retiring in good order, but the regiment of London apprentices were simply too few, and more of them fell back towards the house with every passing moment.

More smoke-wreathed pikes came into view on the far side of the hedge. Tainton took a few paces away from the building so that the structure did not obstruct his view, and counted two more companies behind the first few. This was a very large force. More, perhaps, than the entire Parliamentarian army between here and the capital could handle.

He had seen enough. His horse was ready now, and he leapt into the saddle, turning to the remainder of his troop. 'We'll not abandon them, lads! By God we will not!'

The Parliamentarian defenders kept their fire rapid and their courage strong until the last of the vast Royalist vanguard squeezed through the gap between the hedgerows and fanned out in the clearing to face the remains of Holles's regiment.

Lieutenant Colonel James Quarles was still on the right flank of his beleaguered force. He bellowed orders at the ranks of musketeers who fired, reloaded, fired, reloaded and fired in a professional rhythm that made him proud. To his left a pair of men fell together, a ball ripping through the first's forehead and out the back of his skull, before punching through the face of the man behind.

'Enough,' Quarles whispered. His men were being battered by the greatest of hammers and their duty was done.

'Beg pardon, sir?' a nearby lieutenant called.

'I said, enough,' Quarles said, louder now. 'We cannot hold our shape any longer. Not against this many muskets.' He glanced across the thinning line of redcoats and filled his lungs. 'Retreat! Retreat! To the bridge!'

Despite the dank, oppressive air of Sir Richard Wynn's cellar, Sergeant Malachi Bain was in hog's heaven.

'M-miss me?' he said as he reached floor level, a trio of wary musketeers at his back. The soldiers had been guarding the cellar, and were on the verge of abandoning their posts at hearing the commotion outside, when Bain had reappeared.

Bain stepped forward confidently, muskets levelled behind him, poised to blow holes in the prisoners' chests. Clutching the big halberd he had liberated from Quarles's stores, he lowered the shaft so that the blade hovered in line with Stryker's throat.

'Back so soon?' Stryker said calmly. He glanced up at the open hatch. 'And there I was thinking you'd turned your tail as well as your coat.'

Bain sneered. 'I ain't runnin' away. Not yet, leastwise.' The big man glanced at the others. 'D-do you know,' he said, nodding towards Stryker, 'I take c-credit for that? I always figured him for an ugly bastard, that's for certain,

318

but me and the captain made it sure. Didn't we, Mister Stryker?'

Stryker stepped forward. 'Yes. You held me down. You watched while your master lit a fuse and you laughed as the powder took half my face.'

'And now I've come to finish what I started all them years ago.' Bain shook his head confidently. 'M-Makepeace and the spy are on their way f-from here even n-now. I'll see to you and meet 'im at the b-bridge.'

Forrester stepped forward. 'But we are not yours to kill, Sergeant. Tainton is our gaoler.'

'That p-pious bugger's got his 'ands full fightin' the Welshies. He's forgotten all about you.' A grin that might have sat well on Lucifer himself spread slowly across Bain's blunt chin. 'But I ain't. So I'm going to make an end of y-you. 'Cept this time I'll 'ave s-some sport while I'm at it.' Bain's eyes, darting and beady, swivelled to where Lisette was standing. 'Hoped you were dead, missy.'

'Sorry to disappoint,' Lisette said.

'Oh, I ain't d-disappointed, love. Not a bit. Now come 'ere. I wants a look at your sweet little c-cunny.'

Lisette spat at him, backing away, but she could not keep the fear from her expression.

'Leave her, Bain!' snarled Stryker as the sergeant took a step forward.

Bain let fly a coarse, pitiless laugh. 'Who'd have thought it, eh? The great Stryker dies defendin' a froggy slut. Still likes her d-does you?' He laughed again. 'Well, you'll not have so much as a lick now. She's all mine, sh.'

Stryker stepped forward, but Bain was fast for a man of his bullock-like physique, and his big fist lashed out to crunch into the Royalist's cheek. Stryker hit the ground, and when he was able to look up he could no longer see Bain. As he regained his bearings, he located the brawny sergeant at the foot of the staircase. Lisette was on his shoulder, pinned like a trussed lamb. The light streaming in from above illuminated their profiles, and it looked like an angel and a demon hovered on those steps.

Skellen took Stryker's hand, hauling him to his feet. The latter made to move toward Bain, but his progress was blocked by the red-coated musketeers who had stepped into the space between the sergeant and Stryker's men.

'Have you no honour?' Stryker bellowed, as Bain threw his prize to the cold stone of the floor, pinning her at the throat by his boot heel.

'Honour?' the demon said, pausing for a moment. 'You took me honour a decade ago.'

The men of Denzil Holles's Regiment of Foot had, finally, broken ranks and were streaming on to London Road.

The Royalists of Sir Thomas Salusbury's Welsh regiment gave chase, ably supported by their eager, but hitherto restrained, cavalry. The rout was not as easily executed as they might have wished, for a well-drilled troop of rebel horsemen, led from the front by a black-clad officer screaming oaths and psalms in equal measure, had kept many of them at bay, allowing a sizeable portion of the fleeing infantry to disappear into Brentford End and towards the bridge beyond. But this small victory was soon secured and the chasing pack recalled, the Royalist commanders keen to maintain discipline even in triumph. There was much fighting yet to come.

The vanguard reformed into its order of battle and continued its eastward advance. The ground around Sir Richard Wynn's house had been churned up horribly by thousands of feet and hooves, turning hard, frostbitten solidity into a sticky morass, and the men were happy to reach the relative comfort of the road to make good their pursuit. Some of the swarming Royalists diverted their attention to the house and its many outbuildings, but most were bullied by officers and sergeants back into their practised marching formations. Discipline was holding for the time being. They would advance on the bridge.

Below ground, Lisette Gaillard was struggling against Sergeant Malachi Bain's grinding boot heel. Bain opened his mouth, baring rows of broken yellow and brown stumps. It was a face of lust and anger and savagery and hunger and cruelty. A tear swelled at the corner of Lisette's eye and tumbled down her cheek.

The light streaming from above Bain shone against the tear, and he saw it gleam as it traced its way down her skin. His grin widened and his eyes darted down to drink in the swell of her chest and curve of her hips beneath the cloak. A guttural grunt escaped from him then, and he licked his lips slowly. 'There's a good girl.' His voice was thick. He glanced at one of the musketeers, a lanky man with oval eyes and a broken nose. 'Keep those bastards back, Corporal Matthews. Sh-shoot 'em if any move.' A flicker of hesitation crossed the redcoat's face, and Bain glowered. 'You w-wish to discuss the order?'

The musketeer shook his head quickly.

'That's why you helped Makepeace?' Stryker suddenly blurted, desperate to stall Bain. 'Why you helped him take my eye?'

'Eh?' The sergeant turned towards Stryker. 'My honour?' Bain repeated. 'Aye, me honour. Taken from me – stripped – by an upstart officer after Lutzen.'

Stryker frowned. He had no idea what Bain was talking about, but knew he had to distract him as long as possible. 'You were at Lutzen?'

'I was. A musketeer. A g-good one.'

Bain dropped to his knees, straddling Lisette just above her waist. 'Enough talk!' He glared down at the woman, her hair splayed out across the floor in a great golden fan. He dropped a hand to his belt and drew out a nasty-looking dirk, thin and long and sharp.

Rather than cowing her, the sight of the blade made Lisette thrash and struggle, scratch and curse, trying to push Bain's weight from her. But he thrust out his free hand and clamped thick fingers round her neck, slamming her back on to the stone floor. She spluttered, her tongue forced out slightly between blueing lips, as Bain loomed over her. Lisette could smell the man's breath as he leaned close. 'I'm going to f-f-f-fuck you n-now, f-froggy whore,' he hissed, the frenzy of the moment aggravating his stammer. 'And I ain't p-partial to a f-f-fuck while you're leaking bl-blood everywhere. So lay nice and still. Try anythin' and you'll 'ave it through your eyeball qu-quicker than you can b-blink.' His tongue darted out to lick hers. It was vile and she would have vomited if she'd been able to breathe. He licked her mouth again, a tendril of saliva hanging stubbornly between them. 'Very tasty.'

Bain turned his head to glance up to the redcoats, their brows furrowed in concern. 'Keep your eyes f-f-front, damn you.'

The musketeers averted their collective gaze. Bain's attention drifted beyond them, fixing his predatory stare on Stryker. 'You stay still too, Cap'n. I w-wants you to s-see this. You do as I say, she might live. You turn away or make any move—' He jerked his chin toward the dirk in his strong grip. 'G-got it?'

Stryker nodded. His eye swivelled to catch Forrester's for a moment. He was half tempted to charge the muskets down, but the match-cords were glowing ominously in the half-light, like three malevolent spirits, and they would lash down on to opened priming pans instantly if he made a move. He thought of the way Bain had earlier lost focus.

'I was at Lutzen, Sergeant!'

Bain looked up again. 'I know you f-f-fuckin' were!'

The ferocity of Bain's response startled Stryker. 'I don't remember you.'

The sergeant gritted his teeth. 'But do you remember the corporal what got a hundred pissin' lashes and broken back to the rank an' file? Do you remember *that*?'

A memory came to Stryker then. The memory of a defeated tertio of pike, and of one of the most brutal melees he had ever had the displeasure to be a part of. And Bain's words rang somehow true. There *had* been a corporal, a callow piece of spittle as he remembered, whom he had found hidden under a pile of bodies. Hidden and cowering. Stryker had passed him by, marched over him when the Swedish army had gone forward to secure their victory. But afterwards he had spotted that same

323

corporal lording it up in a tavern, telling tall tales of his great valour.

'That was you?'

Bain sneered. 'No it fuckin' wasn't.'

'Then who was it?'

'My *b-b-brother*.' Bain could barely force the words out. 'He was humiliated when you told the provosts he was yellow. Humiliated and h-hated.'

Stryker frowned. 'It was no more than he deserved.'

Malachi Bain's little black eyes glistened in the dim light. He still clutched the long dirk and he still had Lisette's body pinned between oak-bough thighs, but his mind was wandering. 'They beat him,' he said. 'His own company. Own mates. They b-beat him for the d-dishonour he'd brought the unit.' He refocussed, eyes burning bright with what seemed to Stryker to be a new depth of hatred. 'I found him next mornin', swinging from a tree, eyes p-pecked at by ravens. Took 'is own l-life. They stuck the bugger in a pit. Nameless. Honourless. It were you what done th-that.'

The knife Lisette Gaillard produced was tiny, no longer than her little finger, so small that she had been able to conceal it as a hair pin against her scalp. But the blade was nevertheless strong, and keenly sharp, and it drove into the fleshy underside of Malachi Bain's wrist with little resistance.

Bain brayed in stunned anguish, releasing the dirk so that it bounced on the smooth flagstones and skittered away. The three redcoats turned, instinctively looking for the source of the terrible sound.

Stryker pounced like an animal. In three paces he had closed the gap between himself and Corporal Matthews and his hand darted out like a viper's bite to grasp the barrel of the tall man's musket. Matthews was alert enough to pull the trigger, but by the time the smouldering match had sparked in the priming pan the barrel was pointed at the cellar's high ceiling. The pan flashed, coughing a billowing pall of smoke into the room.

In the unventilated chamber, the roiling, acrid cloud obscured everything and Stryker's men took advantage of it. To his left, Stryker caught a glimpse of Will Skellen, the sinewy sergeant surging forward to grapple with one of Matthews' men. Skellen was upon the musketeer before the man had turned. Stryker heard the long-arm clatter noisily to the stone slabs, its smouldering match jolting free of the serpent.

To his right, Forrester went for the third musketeer, but the guard was able to bring the musket to bear before Forrester could reach him. There was a second shot, unnaturally cacophonous in the subterranean dungeon.

Stryker was still locked in a hand-to-hand struggle with Corporal Matthews. He was shorter than Matthews but far stronger, and he used his muscular frame to force the Parliamentarian back towards the stairs. Matthews kicked out, but Stryker hardly felt the blow and thrust his head forward in a brutal move that smashed Matthews' nose. Matthews released his grip on the musket and Stryker drove his fist into the redcoat's stomach, doubling him over. Behind the two men there was a great flash and a scream, and the room seemed to glow orange. Matthews vomited and Stryker pressed his boot heel into the open mouth. Matthews was felled like an oak, crashing to the ground in a mass of flesh and steel.

Stryker vaulted the body and plunged into the gun

smoke, trying desperately to gain his bearings amid the chaos. Two shots had rung out in the small melee. Stryker saw Skellen battering his opponent with the remaining musket.

He saw too that Forrester had bested one of the musketeers with the Roundhead's own sword. The dead man's musket was lying at his side, a thin wisp of smoke drifting up from the muzzle. Forrester pulled a face. 'Silly bugger missed.'

In that instant, he saw Bain. Blood flowed freely from his wounded wrist, but he was standing, tall and belligerent, at the foot of the staircase. The bloody arm was hooked around Lisette Gaillard's throat, and he was dragging her backwards toward the first steps. Stryker noticed his other hand; it held a smoking pistol.

'Burton!' Forrester exclaimed, even as Stryker realized what had happened.

Stryker stooped to draw Matthews' unused sword, and levelled it at the turncoat. 'You're beaten, Bain.'

Bain screwed his face into a grimace. 'Not so f-fast. I've still got your froggy punk.' He scraped the pistol butt along Lisette's scalp. She winced and struggled, but he held her fast. 'This'll crack 'er bonce like a duck egg.'

Stryker glanced down at the prostrate Ensign Burton. Bain followed his gaze. 'Bugger came at me from nowhere. D-daft bastard.'

The last shot that had rung out in the brawl had come from Bain's pistol. Forrester looked up. 'Took it in his shoulder, sir. He's out cold.' A pistol ball was small, but at this range it might have come from one of the sakers outside. Burton would have been virtually touching the muzzle when its powder had ignited and the lead missile entered the top of his arm with crashing, devastating, irresistible force. The ball, Stryker knew all too well, would have smashed Burton's bone with agonizing ease, flattening as it went, tearing a wide terrible hole, before bursting out through the back of his shoulder to rest somewhere in the wall beyond.

A dark stain was creeping from somewhere beneath Burton's upper body, like an ever increasing shadow. As it grew, it spread into a lake, adding to the metallic stench of fresh blood that already choked the cellar.

The space fell silent. All eyes turned to Bain. He held Lisette in a firm hold.

'I'll st-still kill you,' Bain hissed to Stryker, as he backed away. 'I'll g-gut you like a trout. But for n-now I'll bid y-you farewell. We've a w-wagon to catch.'

Forrester moved over to stand with Stryker and Skellen. The latter held the unfired musket, and he passed it to his captain, though there was no chance that Stryker could fire it while Bain held Lisette.

Holding the girl close, Bain took the first couple of steps towards the stair, careful not to turn his back on the Royalists.

Bain was concentrating so intensely upon the three former captives that he did not notice the bloody spectre rising from a dark corner of the room, amid the swirling smoke. By the time he caught the sudden movement, Ensign Burton was only an arm's length away. The young man was ghostly pale, his torso drenched in his own blood, but he was wielding one of Sir Richard Wynn's glass amphorae in his good arm.

Bain was completely taken by surprise. As Burton hefted the heavy flask above his head, the sergeant lashed out with his pistol. The solid wooden butt obliterated the glass with an ear-splitting crash, drenching the gigantic man and his small captive in dark liquid. In moments the small room was filled with a sharp stench that seared nostrils and stung at the eyes.

In his shock, Bain allowed Lisette to wriggle free and she broke away, dashing across the room toward Stryker. Snarling with fury, Bain turned to bolt up the staircase, but Stryker called to him, 'Sergeant! Catch!'

Stryker had scooped up the smouldering piece of cord that had skidded away from the unfired musket – dropped in the face of Skellen's assault – as soon as he'd noticed Burton lift the amphora. The match sailed toward Bain, twisting and rolling in the smoke-veiled air, and all Bain could do was watch. His small eyes followed its progress towards the steps, and widened with each turn the burning cord made, triumph turning to trepidation, turning to terror.

All was still as the match landed on the step at Bain's feet. For a second, nothing happened. Then the spark found the alcohol, and small, flickering flames emerged across the cold stone.

A fraction of a second later they raced across the step, surging, roaring, consuming. Before Bain could respond, orange tongues were engulfing his boots and his breeches.

He screamed. The flames enveloped the vast body, blazing at his alcohol-soaked clothes, melting the skin of his face, frying his eyeballs and mouth. He flailed. He bellowed. He cursed Stryker's name.

The people gathered below the steps staggered back as the sergeant writhed, swathed in a raging inferno. Bain slumped to his knees. And then he rocked forwards, toppling off the staircase and crashing on his blackened face against the stone floor. As the stench of charred flesh filled the cellar, Malachi Bain finally fell silent.

CHAPTER 18

Captain Roger Tainton was in retreat. His troop had joined the desperate skirmish at Sir Richard Wynn's house, the first of Parliament's defensive positions along the road to London, and had harried the advancing Royalists with skill and valour.

Tainton had agreed with Lieutenant Colonel Quarles's bellowed order to break ranks. They had retreated in good order for as long as was possible, forcing the myriad enemy infantrymen to fight tooth and nail for every inch of ground. It had been an impressively pugnacious strategy from Quarles, and necessary in order to give the men at the bridge time to build up the barricade. The bridge was crucial, worth the lives of some of Holles's redcoats, for it was the only route over the River Brent for miles and the Royalists would have to cross it. That bridge would form a narrow pass, where the defenders could pour their stinging fire, at least for a time. And time was what they needed, for messengers had already been despatched to London, alerting Robert Devereux, Earl of Essex, to muster his field army. If the Royalists could be delayed, even for a few hours, that might be enough.

Tainton was cantering at the head of his troop. They were well clear of the slow-moving enemy column, and he would not be seen to panic. The houses of Brentford End came into his sights quickly. It surprised him that civilians still seemed to be abroad here, for he had thought they would have scurried across the river and into the new town like rats from a sinking ship, but many remained. He presumed they were either supporters of the king or misguided individuals who believed they might successfully defend their property from the inevitable orgy of plunder. He shook his head at their lamentable ignorance.

The three settlements that formed Brentford hugged the north bank of the Thames. The River Brent, a tributary of the great river, spurred away northward, separating Brentford End and New Brentford. As Tainton's troop rode beyond the last of Brentford End's buildings, the narrow stone bridge came into view. On the far side of the river, the east bank, Holles's redcoats were massing, making muskets ready and passing dozens of objects – barrels and stakes mostly – to the men on the crossing, in order for them to bolster the rapidly growing barricade.

Quarles was on the bridge, overseeing the barricade's construction, and he hailed the horsemen. 'Captain Tainton!'

Tainton raised a hand. 'Sir.'

'Bad business back there, eh? Glad you survived.'

'May we cross, Colonel?'

Stryker and Lisette emerged coughing into a large room at the rear of Sir Richard Wynn's house. Forrester was behind them, and he turned to haul Sergeant Skellen into the light. Across the latter's shoulders was Ensign Burton. The lad had slipped back into unconsciousness, blacking out as the pain of lifting the amphora overwhelmed him.

'Check in there!' a voice cried from out in the corridor on to which the room's door opened.

'Hold up your hands!' Stryker told the still spluttering group. They did as they were told.

The door's painted timbers cracked as it was kicked savagely open, and a group of musketeers burst through, immediately aiming their weapons at Stryker and his companions.

To his surprise, Stryker saw that these men were not wearing the red uniforms of Denzil Holles. 'King's! King's!' he shouted urgently, desperate for the soldiers not to shoot on sight.

His Royalist cry, coupled with the group's raised palms, caused the musketeers to hesitate. 'Who are you?' the heavily accented soldier snapped.

'Captain Stryker, Mowbray's Foot. We've been held prisoner down there.' He pointed to the open hatch.

The musketeers were Welshmen, part of Salusbury's regiment, and they had continued to doubt the allegiance of their new captives until Stryker produced the prince's letter. The text meant nothing to the soldiers, but they could see the imprint of Rupert's seal right enough.

'Leave 'im 'ere, sir,' the lead musketeer, Gareth Howell, had said on laying eyes upon Burton's shattered shoulder. 'They're settin' this place up for the chirurgeons.'

Sure enough, as they paced through the main entrance hall of Sir Richard Wynn's large home, they could see that the area was already filling with the battle's wounded.

Skellen laid the ensign down gently, careful not to damage the wound further. Burton's eyelids flickered tremulously at the unwelcome movement, but he did not regain consciousness.

Stryker took a handful of the nearest chirurgeon's shirt collar. 'See that he is well cared for, sir.'

The chirurgeon's brow rose and his mouth opened. When he met Stryker's single eye, his mouth shut. He nodded mutely.

As the group made their way out into the afternoon sunlight, Stryker turned to Howell. 'Have you taken any other prisoners?'

'We have, sir,' the musketeer confirmed. 'Many.'

'A red-haired man? He wears a ring of gold in each ear.'

The Welshman shook his head. 'None by that description, sir.'

'A crippled man, then?' Stryker persisted. 'He has no use of his legs. Plump and pale-faced.'

'Not that I've seen, Captain.'

Forrester thumped a fist against his ample thigh. 'Some rise by sin, and some by virtue fall.' He glanced at Stryker. 'Makepeace and us, don't you think?'

'Forget them!' Lisette snapped. She turned to Musketeer Howell. 'What of a horseman? He is blond, like me, and wears black armour.'

The Welshman stopped in his tracks. 'Not took as prisoner, ma'am. But I seen such a man out in the fight. Couldn't say as to his 'air colour, but he's the only feller I seen with blackened plate. Rides a big bay thing.'

'That's him!' Lisette exclaimed. She turned to Stryker, clutching his shoulder. 'That is him!'

Stryker shook his head. 'But he's not been taken, Lisette. He's out there still.'

'So I will find him!'

'Are you mad?' Stryker snarled, more aggressively than he had intended. 'You cannot hunt the man on a battlefield!'

'Where is that bastard Makepeace?' replied Lisette calmly. Stryker did not answer. 'Precisely. He is somewhere out there, too. With your spy, I should not wonder. Will you let him go?' When Stryker remained silent, she brandished a determined smile. 'Then we both hunt, Captain.'

'Where the blazes have you been?' Lord John Saxby barked from his highly polished saddle. 'And who the devil is that?'

Stryker and his three remaining companions had joined the Royalist force as they advanced through Brentford End, collecting up discarded weapons as they went. Stryker was thankful for meeting Howell and his men, for their presence ensured the dishevelled party would not be taken for enemy deserters or spies.

The huge infantry column was pacing rhythmically along the high road, small bands of musketeers breaking away to search the buildings at their flanks, scouring the windows for hidden snipers. At the rear of the last tertio, Stryker spotted a group of mounted staff officers. Among them, proud and resplendent atop his expensive animal, was Saxby.

'We've been out for a stroll, sir,' Stryker said. 'Weather

was lovely.' Saxby guffawed. Stryker grinned back. 'And this is Lisette Gaillard, sir.'

Saxby's jaw dropped. 'Dear God.' He squinted down at her, disbelieving. 'Dear God. It *is*. I thought you were—'

'Dead, my lord?' Lisette replied.

Saxby nodded slowly. 'Aye.' He looked at Stryker. 'Drowned.'

'Lisette is here on the queen's business,' Stryker said.

Saxby's stare lingered on the woman for a long moment. 'I dare say she is.' The colonel was clearly taken aback.

'May we join you, Colonel?'

Saxby tore his gaze away from the diminutive Frenchwoman. 'Join us? Ain't you tired, Captain? With all due respect, man, the earl don't need more bodies. We're taking care of this bit of business splendidly!'

Stryker grimaced apologetically. 'My mission is . . . incomplete, sir.'

Saxby frowned in consternation. 'Moxcroft evaded you?'

'A turncoat betrayed us.'

Saxby chewed the inside of his mouth, staring off into the distance.

'Sir?' Stryker prompted.

'Sorry, Captain,' the colonel said, jolted back to the man at his horse's flank. 'The prince will not be pleased. Still, nothing you can do about it now, I suppose.'

'On the contrary, sir,' Stryker said, urgency lacing his voice. 'The traitor is here. Somewhere in Brentford. And he has Moxcroft with him.'

Saxby shook his head. 'Go to the doctors, Stryker, there's a good man. Have your wounds seen to.'

There was a moment's silence.

'That's not going to answer, is it?' asked the colonel quietly.

More silence.

'Damn it, man,' snapped Saxby. He kicked up his horse. 'I give you leave to do as you will. Go and find your traitor, if you must. Just grant me one boon. Try not to perish in the attempt.'

Lisette Gaillard had been ordered to stay at the rear of the column by Lord John. The colonel was a member of the king and queen's inner circle, fully aware of Lisette's skills, but even that was not enough to convince him that a woman had a place in the front rank of battle. Lisette had spat her refusal, but Saxby was most insistent.

As Stryker conveyed her to the protection of the Royalist artillery train, he paused briefly, holding her shoulders in firm hands. 'You promise to remain here?'

She shook her head vigorously. 'Not for a moment.'

Stryker smiled. 'Then stay safe.' He paused, thinking. 'Back in the cellar, when you attacked Makepeace. You wept.'

Lisette looked at her boots. 'I remembered what he did to you, Stryker.' She raised her chin, meeting his eye, and held out a hand to his scarred face. 'It was the worst time of my life.'

'You did not have to tend my wounds, Lisette. I did not ask it of you.'

She glared. 'No, you great oaf! It was not the worst time because I had to care for you. But because I loved you. With all my being.' She stood on the tips of her toes. 'And that is why I cried. He made me remember that love.'

She kissed him, hard and intense, before turning away. She was gone before he could say a word.

Stryker, Skellen and Forrester moved to the head of the advancing force, eager to get to the bridge, for it was there that Bain had said Makepeace would be. Although this was far from certain, Stryker guessed that Makepeace would not wish to stay west of the River Brent, given the fact that the area had now entirely fallen to the Royalists.

Although the breeze was weak, it managed to carry the beat of drums like a whisper across the rank and file. It was not music that the drummers played, but coded messages. They contained orders for the men to follow. A young lad, his instrument dwarfing his torso amid the experienced drummers that marched with him, paused to vomit on the side of the road. The grizzled veteran at his side did not break his rhythm as he called words of encouragement to the youngster. He affected not to notice the wet patch on the boy's crotch.

As the force passed through Brentford End, frightened faces could be seen peering cautiously from windows and doors. The shops and houses that lined both sides of the road were scarred from battle, and yet more musket-balls thudded into their wooden frames when Holles's men were spotted seeking shelter within. Most doors, however, were shut and barred, and the Royalist companies passed them by. There would be plenty of time for plunder, of course, but later, once the enemy had been destroyed.

The Royalists made good progress through the westerly part of the town, receiving and giving fire as small pockets of retreating redcoats appeared before them, but for the most part their massively superior numbers ensured a safe passage until the Brent's glistening water could be clearly seen beyond the buildings. And then the bridge itself came into view. It was a stout, well-built affair of three stone arches. Across its crest was a makeshift barricade of wattle fencing, upturned tables, large barrels, sharpened stakes, earth-filled bushels and bales of rotten hay, behind which the remainder of Denzil Holles's Regiment of Foot lay in wait with primed muskets and charged pikes. This was evidently to be the next protracted stand the rebels would make.

Lord John Saxby galloped up and down the road, shouting and encouraging the infantry as he passed, whipping them into a bloodthirsty frenzy. 'Smash 'em here, boys! New Brentford lies on the far side o' that bridge! Then the old town! Kill the buggers dead, and it's on to London! We'll be sipping mulled ale in the Commons come Christmas!'

Captain Eli Rushworth Augustus Makepeace was already at the bridge. The going had been infuriatingly slow, for the road was sticky and the cart's wheels had slipped and skidded every few yards, but eventually Makepeace and Sir Randolph Moxcroft had reached the comparative safety of the barricade. They paid little heed to the panicking residents of Brentford End, who scuttled back and forth on all sides, collecting their worldly goods before escaping into the fields to the north. The men bellowed at their offspring, women chivvied and scolded, children wailed, scrawny pet dogs scampered back and forth, energized by the excitement. With the vast force of angry Royalists coming from the west, the people's natural escape route to the east was the bridge, and that had been barricaded by Parliament's soldiers, while the swirling torrent of the Thames hugged the town's southern edge. Those cold, boggy enclosures to the north were the only remaining option, and they would lead them out into open country infested with brigands. Makepeace couldn't care less. He had a spy in his cart, the man whose knowledge might even change the course of the war.

'Where the deuce is that lumbering man-servant of yours?' Moxcroft snarled from the back of the cart.

'My sentiments exactly, Sir Randolph,' Makepeace said sourly. As he watched the road, he began to realize that the crowd of soldiers coming from Wynn's estate were no longer redcoats. There were different coloured uniforms now, and the troops were marching in tight formation. He turned to the spy. 'I'm afraid Bain'll have to look to himself. We must take our leave.'

'Parliament! God and Parliament!' Makepeace screamed when he reached the bridge. He did not wish to be skewered or shot, especially when triumph was so near. 'Parliament!'

Moxcroft, pushing up with his arms so that he could see over the side of the cart, enthusiastically repeated the call.

The men in the front rank, stood behind the screen of wattle and wood, seemed to hesitate, for the approaching man was the very image of an aristocrat. The pious, stoical soldiers of Holles's regiment were taught to despise such men, rich sinners who paraded their wealth like a badge of honour. Instinctively, one or two had even stepped forward, prepared to spit the frantically waving man on the end of their lances.

'Let him through!' Sergeant Major Timothy Neal ordered. His broad, imposing frame came into view. The front rank raised their pikes immediately, parting like the Red Sea, and Makepeace was allowed to draw the cart past and beyond that first barricade.

Leaving the cart, Makepeace pushed his way through the bodies, making directly for where Neal stood. He would have preferred to bring his request direct to Quarles, but the tall colonel was away on the east bank, organizing his men for the coming assault.

'I must leave,' Makepeace said, deciding upon the blunt approach. 'I have Sir Randolph Moxcroft in the cart. He has vital information for Parliament. He must be taken to London forthwith.'

Neal stared at him. 'You have a cart.'

'Aye, sir. Sir Randolph cannot walk.'

Neal ignored the captain's words, instead turning to one of his men. 'Get that man out of the cart, Pikeman McCarthy!'

McCarthy climbed into the vehicle and hoisted Moxcroft into the air, passing him down to a waiting comrade.

'The cart will do nicely at the barricade, Captain Makepeace. Your passenger can be taken to the east bank. But I require every able-bodied man here. Vital information or no.'

Makepeace's jaw dropped. Moxcroft's plaintive cries could be heard fading away into the distance as he was carried off between two burly pikemen.

'We are about to face a horde, sir,' Neal said upon seeing Makepeace's furious expression. 'We are out-gunned and outnumbered. I need every man. No parliamentary duty is greater than this. I will defend my judgement with steel, if I must.'

'Do not be so bloody short-sighted, Neal,' Makepeace hissed, balling his fists in exasperation. 'I am an officer and I will not be dictated to! The news I carry will see the war won.'

'Lieutenant Colonel Quarles has placed me in command of the bridge, Captain. I command here. And I say that we must have every pair of hands on this barricade. A barricade strengthened by the addition of your wagon. We must stall the enemy advance for as long as we are able. If we fail today, sir, there will be no Parliament. No one to whom Moxcroft may convey his blasted information.'

Makepeace opened his mouth to launch a retort, but the words caught in his throat as the shouts began. The Royalists had reached the west bank.

It was a large force, a thousand strong at least, with many more coming up behind. But Makepeace ignored the multitude of musketeers and pikemen that spilled from the buildings of Brentford End. He saw only the group of men at the foremost fringe of the Royalist attackers. The majority of the Royalist companies, formed in haste to answer the king's call at Nottingham, were without standard uniforms and their ranks were a miscellany of browns, russets and blacks, punctuated by smears of scarlet where sashes were worn around waists or diagonally over the torso. In their midst were three faces. On one side of the trio, the thin, leathery, weather-beaten features and implacable stare of Sergeant Skellen,

341

standing stark above the crowd. On the other, the chubby, ruddy cheeks and permanent half-smile of Lancelot Forrester.

And in the centre stood a man who might have been handsome once before a savage wound had mutilated his face and taken his left eye.

Bain had failed.

The first musketeer companies reached the western bank of the Brent and emptied their barrels at the men on the bridge. Most of the balls hit home in the barricade, though a handful of men were killed, only to be replaced by their comrades from the rearmost ranks.

Holles's musketeers returned the fire, though they were severely outgunned and their volley did little to dent the Royalist force.

Stryker and his companions were with a company from Sir Edward Fitton's regiment. One musket-ball had already flown past Stryker's temple and he'd flinched as the air sang in warning. The shot hit a man behind and to his left, taking him in the forehead, and he fell in a spray of scarlet mist.

More volleys were exchanged across the narrow expanse of water. It was a good place to defend, Stryker knew, because the king's men had to get across the bridge. They could fan out along the bank and expend their bullets into the red-coated ranks of the men barring the way into New Brentford, and eventually those men would fall away amid the hail of shot, but would it take long enough for Essex to muster a relief force from the capital? Stryker did not know, but he was sure it was long enough to cover Makepeace's escape.

He scanned the rows of defenders, those behind the protective works and those further back and along the eastern bank. Makepeace and Moxcroft would surely be long gone by now, racing like rats along the High Street that was New Brentford's main artery. If they had found transport for the spy, they might well be beyond the new town and into the old, pressing on towards Chiswick.

'Look for a cart,' he shouted to his companions. 'He'll have found transport for Moxcroft. He could hardly have carried him.'

Skellen cleared his throat. 'Don't know about a cart, sir.' He pointed a long, gnarled finger to a spot some way behind the ranks of defenders. 'But that feller's awful familiar.'

The two captains followed Skellen's gesture until their eyes fell upon a man slumped against an upturned barrel about fifty paces back from the edge of the east bank.

'Unless he's taking a nap,' Forrester said, 'I think that's our friend, Sir Randolph.'

Stryker slapped Skellen on the back. 'Good work, Sergeant! If Moxcroft is there, then so is Makepeace. Somehow the bastard's got snarled up in this fight!'

Forrester let out a bark of laughter. 'No doubt against his wishes.'

Stryker agreed. 'So keep looking!'

When Stryker first caught sight of Makepeace, he was just one man amongst so many other heads on that teeming bridge. But only one head was topped with a shock of flame-red hair that, even from this distance, he could see fell in great tendrils about the man's shoulders. Stryker began to load his musket.

The drums changed their rhythm, ordering the advance, and a great cry went up from Stryker's left. Several companies of infantry – pike and musket – surged forward. Fitton's men were to be held in reserve, but the three soldiers from Sir Edmund Mowbray's Regiment of Foot broke ranks, stalking briskly toward the barricade as they blew on smouldering match-cords. When they were glowing hot and ready to flare, Stryker, Forrester and Skellen began to run.

Stryker scanned the bridge. He slowed his stride and stared, trying desperately to identify the target for his single musket ball. He narrowed his eye, squinting through the battle smoke to discern his enemy from an array of other bodies.

Pain came in a stinging wave of fire that made his head feel like exploding and turned his vision to a dazzling blanket of white. He dropped to the ground, feeling the warmth of blood at his temple.

'Jesus,' Stryker hissed, still prostrate, his fingers sticky as they probed the wound. 'I've been shot.'

For all her skills, Lisette Gaillard was not a proficient sailor.

Slipping away from the rear of the Royalist column, Lisette had mounted a riderless horse, its owner lying dead on the cheerless field. She had watched the infantry advance, seen the way they swarmed up London Road into Brentford End, and knew she could not follow. Stryker had warned her that a barricade had been set at the bridge over the River Brent, and that the defenders would fall back on that bridge and consolidate their resistance there. Understanding that she would not make it through the fire-fight, she had kicked the horse southward, through

344

fields and a vast orchard, following the Brent all the way until it met the River Thames.

She dismounted at the water's edge, the sounds of battle ringing at her back. The riverbank was fiendishly slippery as she slid down it.

On her gallop through the fields hugging the Brent, Lisette had been vexed to note that there were no larger rivercraft. The town's Parliamentarian defenders had wisely removed any means by which the king's men might cross either the Brent or the Thames and outflank them. But during her time on the *Cormorant*, she had seen many small, oval-shaped vessels stored among the long reeds. They were coracles, Horace Crumb had informed her; fishing boats made of wicker, made river-worthy by a covering of boiled hide. Those defenders would not have known about the smaller coracles concealed at the river's edge. She knew that if she searched hard enough, she might just be in luck.

The vessel now carrying her rocked and pitched with the slapping water and Lisette's ungainly balance. She swore loudly at the necessity of using this cursed contraption, but she needed to be in the main town, since it was to there that Tainton's troop would ultimately be forced to retreat.

The coracle wobbled violently. '*Merde!*' Lisette snarled. '*Mer—*' Her second curse was never finished, for the coracle had jolted and then hissed its way onto a sandbank. Lisette peered over the side and, realizing that the sand reached nearly to the water's surface and that she was a mere ten paces from the eastern bank, stepped out of the coracle. She quickly splashed her way to shore and praised God as her feet found solid ground. Above her loomed the great spire of a church.

*

345

When Stryker regained consciousness, Skellen was at his side. The captain struggled to his feet.

Skellen grinned. 'You've been hit. Fortunately, it's no more 'n a scratch. Sort of. Ball bounced off your 'ead, sir.'

The first men to reach the bridge had been greeted by a full Roundhead volley. It snatched them back, plucking men from their feet in gouts of blood and screams of desperate agony, but the attack was near a thousand strong and the gaps left by the dead and maimed were filled long before the next rank of Holles's musketeers could bring their weapons to bear.

'God and King Charles!' was the Royalist cry as the barricade was reached. Pikes were thrust from beyond the tough wattle fences, and three men were spitted on the spiked poles before they could twist away. But there were always more, and the men of Holles's regiment were already falling back. There were just a few hundred of them, and they knew that further into the town another, stronger barricade was being erected. It was surely time to rely on its safety.

A tall officer with a square jaw and jet-black hair was on the eastern bank, barking orders at his panicking men. Stryker was on the bridge himself now, his vision restored, though his head smarted under a mass of congealed blood, and he recognized the enemy officer as Lieutenant Colonel Quarles. Immediately, his musket was raised and levelled, the serpent snapped down and the priming pan flashed. His vision was obscured by the acrid cloud of smoke that billowed around him, but he strode through it, regaining a good view of the far bank, and saw that Quarles was down. The ball had taken him in the chest. The men on the Royalist side saw Quarles fall and those that recognized him as the senior enemy officer whooped their joy.

The Royalists pressed on, slashing and hacking and battering the barricade and the men beyond. The first broke and its defenders fell back on to the second, where, caught between the fence and the Royalists, they offered only token resistance as fingers and faces were severed without pity. When the Royalists were at the last work, they tore down the fencing and the bales and kicked away the tables that had been commandeered from peoples' houses. A cart had been placed in the midst of that last obstruction, and the fleeing defenders set it alight to delay their swarming enemies. But the Royalists were victorious, and, hungry for blood and for plunder, they used their pikes to propel the flaming vehicle back on to the land and streamed past it with impunity.

All but a few of the muskets were spent by now, as the Royalists advanced with butt-ends presented like clubs, bludgeoning any redcoat foolhardy enough to remain at his post.

'Kill 'em! Kill 'em!' cried a familiar voice from Stryker's right, and he glanced around to see that Sergeant Skellen had joined him in the assault. He was pleased to see Forrester there too.

In just a few more strides they were across the bridge and the first houses of New Brentford were in sight. But between the Royalists and the houses were a half-dozen companies of pike, arrayed on the narrow swathe of common grassland that split the river and the first timber-framed gable ends.

So many Royalists had flooded on to the eastern bank

that the outcome of the fighting was no longer in question. The victory was theirs for the taking. The king's men piled forward like a pack of hungry wolves.

In their excitement they had lost all order, and the first men ran headlong on to the waiting pikes, to be spitted, disembowelled and left impaled for the carrion birds that already circled above. In an even fight this foolhardy charge might have proved the Royalists' undoing, but they still had the numbers. More and more of the king's men came after that first reckless wave, and they were soon inside the pikes' deadly points, cutting down the defenders with a feverish ferocity. The line broke. Holles's men had fought well, but now they cut and ran back into the town.

Stryker felt his feet sinking into the slippery mud. He would be happier when the attacking force reached the settlement and could regroup and advance along the firmer ground of the road. He glanced around, searching for Makepeace, but the man was nowhere to be seen.

'No sign, sir,' Skellen called out as he returned from the place where he had seen Moxcroft. Forrester had been searching the bodies, and he returned with similar news. There was no corpse dressed in purple silks.

'They're together, then,' Stryker said. 'And alive.'

He looked up, inspecting the houses that lined the road through New Brentford. Makepeace had to have escaped in that direction, along with all the other routed Parliamentarians.

The fighting was petering out. The men of Denzil Holles's Regiment of Foot, having defended Wynn's house and then the bridge with such gusto, had lost too much ground, too many men, and ultimately their nerve. It had been clear they would never win the day, but Quarles had asked them to delay the enemy advance for as long as possible by fighting on during an ordered and stubborn withdrawal. In that, they had been successful.

But Quarles was now dead, as were two of his captains, Bennett and Lacey, and the regiment was utterly shattered. They had fought bravely, as they had on the fair-meadow at Kineton, in the face of an irresistible tide. This time, however, their courage was not enough. The remaining officers called the final order to break ranks, and the men turned their backs upon the advancing Royalists. The slower men, or those carrying wounds, would look to secrete themselves within the houses and shops, hoping to hide out for however long it took for the Cavaliers to move on to London. Their faster comrades would not pay so much as a second glance at the buildings that huddled on both sides of the road. They knew there were more of Parliament's forces further east, where new town met old, and they would march or run until their legs failed in order to reach that place of safety.

In the sudden lull, as the victorious king's men crowed to the sky and began to give chase, the drums started again. The beat drifted over the heads of the Royalist force, pounding out the order to reform companies. The commanding officers were clearly aware that they had the advantage this day, but that discipline must be maintained.

A staff officer was encouraging the troops as they filed past. 'You've done well, lads! By God, you have! But they won't quit the town when we're but eight miles from London. There's more fighting to come!'

Stryker heard the drums and looked to his two

comrades. 'He can't have carried Moxcroft across the Thames, and I doubt he'll go north where he'll have no protection.'

Forrester nodded. 'I hear the rebels have blocked the road between new town and old. Our quarry will have headed for that barricade, where his allies are still strong.'

The idea of a slow march towards Old Brentford, allowing Makepeace to make good his escape, filled Stryker with despair. If he left the rank and file, charging off into the new town on his own, he would surely run into hidden snipers or, God forbid, the second barricade Forrester had mentioned.

Captain Roger Tainton was in New Brentford, the part of the town that sprawled to the east of the Brent. To his left, beyond the rows of buildings, was the River Thames. To his front was the River Brent. But he could not see that second waterway, for the road ahead was packed with Royalist soldiers.

Quarles had allowed Tainton to cross the bridge, and he had led his troops beyond the river and into the new town, ready for the inevitable time when the barricade would fall. Tainton had been impressed with the bullish nature of that barricade's defenders, for the redcoats lasted far longer than his expectations suggested, but eventually the work had toppled.

Now there were no more bridges to cross, no more man-made funnels into which the Parliamentarian forces could squeeze their aggressors, so it was up to Tainton's troop to harass the oncoming infantry column in that all important bid for time. Tainton prayed that their sacrifice was worth this extraordinary effort. He prayed the people of London were not sitting idly by, but stirring into action in preparation for the king's final assault.

He thought of the ruby. It still hung at his neck, and he lifted a hand to brush his blackened breastplate with gloved fingers. If he could just survive this day, he would be able to convey the jewel back to his masters at Parliament. It might just make up for losing Stryker and the other prisoners.

But all that was pushed to the back of the captain's mind. He still had work to do this day. Tainton twisted around in his saddle, catching as many of his men's eyes as possible. 'We charge on my mark! Do not engage, for they will present pike, but wheel back and form again! We must keep them at bay for as long as God allows!'

The men of Sir Edward Tainton's Regiment of Horse could not see their charges home, for the bristling tertios of pikemen would turn the enemy column into a gigantic hedgehog, spiked and deadly. But by the very act of compelling the enemy to present their pikes – the pikemen having to halt to brace the butt of the pole against their boot – Tainton's horsemen would slow the oncoming force down, and that delay would, at the very least, force more valuable time to tick by.

Tainton raised his sword. '*Charge!*'

The streets of New Brentford teemed with panicked men and women. Lisette had emerged from the grounds of St Lawrence's church and on to the part of London Road that formed the town's High Street, only to discover that the advancing Royalist column had not reached this part of town yet. But that, of course, did not stop the terrified citizens from hearing the volleys of approaching musketeers.

Lisette was beautiful. She knew it because wherever she went she would draw remarks; appreciative ones from leering men, or snide ones from jealous women. Yet today she felt as though she could run naked and screaming through Brentford's lanes and alleys and no one would pay heed. No one would hail her, no one would accost her. The king was coming, and with him, he brought death.

Crowds of refugees from the western fringe of the town were pushing and shoving their way past, desperate to get away from the fighting that had already consumed their homes. Lisette fought against the tide, guessing that Tainton's men would be engaged in the battle toward the town's western entrance. But this was a battlefield of the narrowest proportions; due to the surrounding houses and the fields beyond, the rivers Thames and Brent, and the rebel barricades, the front line was squeezed into a small area. Had this been a traditional battle, fought across a great plain or fair-meadow, Lisette could never have found her enemy. But here, where the London Road bisected Brentford, Tainton's whereabouts were easy to predict. She had heard Saxby inform Stryker that the rebels only had horsemen from two troops. One of which was commanded by Roger Tainton. Lisette understood that if she were to locate Parliamentary cavalry, then there would be a good possibility that with them would be Tainton. And the ruby.

Another volley of musketry crackled in the distance. She thought of Stryker, a pang of concern attacking her. She pushed it away.

Progress was painfully slow amid the human river. Lisette knew she must push beyond the town centre and out to where the battle was joined in earnest, but it was too far to be travelling at such a dawdling pace and in such sloppy mud.

'Damn it all! Get out of the way!'

Lisette looked to her right, where, fifty paces away, a man stood in his stirrups, bawling at the people filing past. He was also attempting to travel in the opposite direction to the mass of frightened civilians. His horse was big and sleek and strong.

Lisette moved as fast as she could towards the man on horseback, dragging her feet from the sucking mud with difficulty. '*Sir!*' she called up to him.

The chestnut mount reared, startled by her sudden cry, and the rider glared down at her.

'What the devil . . . madam?'

'I see you swim against the tide. You are going west?' Lisette demanded, placing a hand on the skittish mount's filth-specked bridle.

'What is that to you?' the rider barked, though he could not hide the sparkle that lit his eyes as the young woman brandished a gleaming smile.

Lisette reached up, resting her free hand on the rider's knee, squeezing gently. 'I should like to travel with you.'

Lisette's horseman was chirurgeon Ptolemy Banks.

He was not on any regimental staff – which vexed him, he told Lisette, for he missed out on the daily pay of four shillings – but had served many decades patching men up across the Continent. 'I retired here,' he had said as they threaded their way along High Street towards the western limits of New Brentford, 'for a quiet life, would you believe? No matter, the long and short of it is that the battle has come here, to my home, and I shall help fight the good fight any way I know how.'

For all Banks's initial reluctance, his assistance had not been difficult to secure, once he'd had a good look at Lisette. He had told her that he was on his way to tend the rebel wounded at the front. Lisette had pleaded that he let her accompany him, for the front was where she must go, too. She had important news for the defenders, she said. Vital news that could not be delayed. Chirurgeon Banks was a Parliamentarian to the core, and had quickly agreed on the grounds that he would not obstruct something that might aid the defenders. In reality, Lisette knew, his capit-ulation had more to do with the hand she had slowly snaked along his thigh.

'The man I need to find,' Lisette said as they cantered in and out of the oncoming traffic on their way past the last buildings, 'is commanding one of the cavalry troops. He wears black armour. Do you know him?'

'Forgive me, ma'am, but I do not,' Banks called over his shoulder. He offered her a greasy smile.

Lisette didn't dislike Banks. She might even forgive him his rebel sympathies at this very moment, because up ahead were perhaps two dozen horsemen. The road curved steadily here, and she could not see what was beyond the troop, but it was clear from their bloodied bodies and labouring animals that they were fresh from the fight. As Lisette watched, the troop halted, and she presumed they had reached a point on the road that was outside the musket range of the most advanced Royalist infantry. The troop checked their horses' hooves and took long draughts from water flasks. And in their midst was a man on a bay stallion, his head and torso encased in gleaming black.

Lisette leant forward, pushing her mouth to Banks's ear, ensuring the chirurgeon's obedience with her warm breath. 'May we stop, sir?'

'Why can we not rest here?' Sir Randolph Moxcroft said. The spy's arm was hooked around the narrow shoulder of Eli Makepeace as the latter dragged him through New Brentford.

Having rounded the bend, they were now on the part of High Street that straightened out as it began to climb toward Old Brentford. Makepeace groaned as he hauled Moxcroft's dead weight through the mud, the spy's toes lagging behind like a pair of anchors. 'No we cannot, Sir Randolph!' He glanced over his shoulder, checking for enemy soldiers. 'If we rest here, we'll be skewered in no time. The king's men were close to smashing the bridge blockade when we left. They'll surely be on this side of the river by now.'

Makepeace thought back to that deadly fight. When the enemy had engaged, he had been armed with nothing but his sword. It might as well have been a toothpick in the face of the horde they faced. The man at his right shoulder had been felled by a shot that had dashed his brains, spattering Makepeace from his wide-brimmed hat to his comfortable bucket-top boots. Realizing that the dead man's musket was still primed, its match keeping a feeble glow despite having been dropped to the bridge's stone surface, he had snatched it up and taken aim.

And there, just paces away on the opposing side of the barricade, stood Captain Stryker.

For the first time since the attack had crashed home, Makepeace felt his spirits lift. He squeezed the trigger steadily, forgetting all around him, and emptied the barrel. A great cough of smoke immediately obscured his vision, but at such close range there was no chance he could have missed.

As soon as the shot was away, Makepeace turned tail and raced back to where Neal's men had dumped Moxcroft. There was a risk that one of the redcoats might take umbrage at seeing him leave the ranks, but they were all far too busy fighting for their lives to spare a thought for him.

Makepeace decided to aim for the next barricade on the rising land between the new town and the larger Old Brentford, praying that the commander there would not enlist him as the obstinate Sergeant Major Neal had done. He had considered selecting an alternative route to London, but that would take them either north or south, and the idea of facing lawless countryside to the north did not appeal. Negotiating the Thames to the south with Moxcroft on his back was downright impossible.

They pressed on, grunting in the face of excruciatingly slow progress, cursing the soldiers that ran by without pausing to offer assistance. As Makepeace forged ahead, his efforts were finally rewarded when he caught his first glimpse of the blades that stood glinting above the bristling ranks of Lord Brooke's Regiment of Foot.

'There!' he gasped excitedly.

Moxcroft stared up to the crest of the slope, to where the barricade stood strong and proud. He glanced sideways at Makepeace. 'Then pick up the pace, Captain.'

Makepeace glared at him. 'I'm going as fast as I bloody can, Sir Randolph!'

As Moxcroft twisted his head to glance back down the incline, his eyes widened as he took in the sea of men that were appearing from the road's curve. 'So are they.'

CHAPTER 19

'Thank you, Ptolemy.'

'My pleasure,' Chirurgeon Banks said, blushing profusely as Lisette jumped down from the saddle. He winked at her. 'Anything for a beautiful woman.'

She left Banks at the large house the chirurgeon intended to use to treat casualties. He wished her Godspeed, and even risked a little pat on her bottom.

Now she was running down High Street, through New Brentford, Brooke's barricade at her back and the Royalist column gradually appearing from the road's curve at her front. She skirted units of retreating redcoats, the occasional walking wounded, and several galloping staff officers carrying messages. One such officer, a callow youth on a black mare, had responded to her hail, reining in beside her. 'You are lost, madam?' he called down, his face speckled with mud and sweat. 'I suggest you turn back. You'll find only trouble this way.'

Lisette took a breath. 'I have a message for Captain Tainton.' She pressed on before the officer could speak. 'I am sent from Lord Brooke.' She pointed to a building across the road with a swinging open door, its occupants long since evacuated in the face of the impending Royalist storm. She stepped toward the horseman, eyes burning with intensity. 'Captain Tainton must come to here immediately. Tell him it concerns Captain Stryker.'

The youth gaped at her.

Lisette glared. 'Do you think we have time to dither? I do not wish to report your incompetence to Lord Brooke!'

Her forcefulness seemed to shock him into action. 'I shall report to Captain Tainton, of course.' As the officer kicked at his mount, he suddenly pulled back on the reins, halting the horse. Doubt had twisted his face into a confused frown. 'Wait! Who are you?'

But Lisette was already gone.

'Well?' the familiar bark echoed around the abandoned building. 'I was told Lord Brooke had news of my prisoners.'

Lisette had waited several minutes before Tainton appeared. The building must have been the workshop of a boat-builder, for it still contained tools, wood shavings and a large vat of tar that – judging by the small wisps of steam wafting into the air – carried the last vestiges of warmth. The low-beamed, rectangular room had been mostly emptied – hastily, judging by the open door and discarded objects – and now stood cavernous and bare.

Captain Roger Tainton stalked in, his sword still in its scabbard and his helmet in his hand, and snapped at the hooded figure who stood in the centre of the room.

'Well?' he said again. 'This had better be of great import, sir. What do you want? Come, sir, the king's men are almost at the door!'

Lisette drew back her hood. 'You know what I want, Captain.'

*

The Royalist army surged through New Brentford. It was no more than a matter of a few hundred paces between the bridge and their current position, at the end of the road's curve, but to the attackers it represented a marker laid down, a Rubicon crossed. They were now on the east side of the Brent, choking this defiant town with their men and horses and weapons. Brentford was falling at the king's feet. In days the capital would surely follow and the rebels would be pushed into the Channel, where they would drown in the angry swell, choking on their treachery to the Crown.

They passed big brick houses, home to local gentry or merchants, and the smaller, ramshackle dwellings of the common folk. There were the premises of tanners, blacksmiths, bakers and coopers. They marched beneath the shadow of the great church, St Lawrence's, and felt God's blessing upon them.

Stryker and his men were back in step with a company of musketeers, and the captain let his eye dart left and right, examining the buildings for any sign of danger. At least, he noted with relief, the Parliamentarian cavalry under Vivers and Tainton had finally ceased the continual raids that had forced the column to move at such a sluggish pace. The Royalist cavalry should have been there to ward them off, but word had spread that they were delayed at Brentford End.

'Fuckin' cavalry!' Skellen had snarled. 'After plunder while we do the hard work.'

On rounding the bend beyond St Lawrence's, High Street began to slope upward on its way towards the old town. Stryker's gaze followed this gradual incline until it reached the brow of the rise. 'Look,' he said.

Forrester followed Stryker's stare. 'Sir?'

'Brooke's lads.'

It was another barricade. There were fences that stretched from one side of the street to the other, pushed flush against the flanking buildings so that the Royalist army could not simply walk round. It was an even more impressive and daunting sight than the work at the bridge. More sharpened pikes, more bales, more barrels. And more men. Lord Brooke's Regiment of Foot was out in force, distinctive in their purple uniforms. They were massed behind that barricade, pikes lofted high, ready for the fight. Their officers could be heard bellowing orders up and down the ranks, while the men themselves called challenges to the oncoming king's men.

'Company! Halt!' The shout reverberated along the great Royalist column, repeated by sergeants and captains as each unit's turn came to hold the advance. The drums reiterated the call to take heed. They were to advance in regimental order, keeping discipline at all times.

A mounted officer reined in nearby and Stryker hailed him. The man nodded towards the barricade, 'We're to go straight at 'em, sir.'

'Can we not work around the flanks?' Forrester asked.

The officer shook his head, his expression rueful. 'Would that were possible, sir. But there ain't enough room between the buildings on our right flank and the river beyond. It'd be a narrower pass to negotiate than the damned road.' He switched his gaze to the left flank. 'And over there they've stationed plenty o' musket and pike. It'd be a bugger picking our way through. Take too long. Besides, the earl wants to make an example of 'em.'

'A show of strength,' Stryker said.

'You have it, sir. Wear 'em down, so to speak. One

regiment at a time. Advance, discharge muskets, push the bastards back. Simple as that. And our cavalry will work round to their right flank. They'll take a longer route round, but it'll be easier than letting the infantry do it.'

'Who'll take the lead at the barricade, Lieutenant?' Stryker asked.

'Salusbury's boys need a rest, I dare say, so it'll be Earl Rivers' men.'

Stryker glanced back to the defensive works that lay in wait. 'It's a bloody big barricade. It's higher, deeper and manned with fresh troops. I'd say it'll be a deal of trouble digging them out.'

The rider grunted. 'Like a big-jawed tick. You're most likely right, sir. Well,' he continued, looking back down to the men on foot, 'I believe Gerrard will take up the challenge if Rivers fails, and Lord Molyneux is to be third. Not certain after that, truth be told.'

'Sir!' Skellen's coarse tone was urgent. 'To the right o' the work, sir.' He pointed up the sloping road and indicated a spot where the barricade came flush up against the buildings. 'A couple o' houses down. What d'you make of those?'

Stryker and Forrester followed the sergeant's lead towards a house near the slope's crest. It was unremarkable, save for the pair of figures that stood outside, staring down at the oncoming mass of Royalists.

'Less I'm mistaken,' Skellen said, 'one's holding t'other up.'

'You are surprised to see me?' Lisette said.

She and Tainton stood on the wide floor of the abandoned boat-builder's workshop, the sounds of battle emanating from beyond the building.

Tainton nodded. 'I confess, madam, I did not expect to see you again.'

They regarded each other silently. Tainton was heavily armed. His body was encased in the ostentatious black-enamelled armour, with its gilded rivets, his left arm safe within an iron gauntlet. The cross-belts that passed over his shoulders carried the long sword at his left hip and an exquisitely crafted, but empty, carbine at his right.

Lisette had snatched up a discarded sword from outside on the road, but she carried no firearms and had no other protection. Her blue eyes darted down to the cavalryman's scabbard. Tainton had let his right hand drop in a diagonal sweep, and his fingers were tickling the top of the iron hilt.

'Give me the strongbox, Captain,' Lisette said.

Tainton smiled. 'The box? You imagine I hefted that thing into battle?'

'The ruby then.'

'The ruby? That is all you seek?' He shook his head. 'Then you really are no more than a common thief.'

The Frenchwoman watched Tainton lift a hand to his collar. His fingers appeared presently, grasping a thick cord that looped about his neck. He lifted it over his head, his eyes narrowing as the leather pouch swung like a pendulum from his outstretched fingers.

'What do you mean?' Lisette asked uneasily.

Tainton gave a mirthless chuckle. 'The ruby is a fine piece. Worth a great deal. But nothing in God's grand scheme. Still, a common thief would not understand.'

Lisette watched the pouch swing enticingly. She did not understand his taunts, but that did not matter now. She levelled her blade. 'Give it to me.'

Tainton mirrored her move. 'You'll take it from my dead hand, Romish whore,' he hissed.

Lisette stood implacable. 'And you will have to kill *me* before you can take to your horse, sir.'

The advancing Royalist regiment marched quickly, for they were becoming easier targets for the defending musketeers with every step. A large house of red brick protected the final approach to the barricade, and the men braced themselves for the hail of shot that would soon come upon them. But it was not the crackle of musketry that greeted their assault. Instead, the air exploded in the thunder of an almighty winter storm, shaking the ground and rocking the houses and shops.

'Cannon!' a sergeant screamed, though his alert was unnecessary. Every man on the road knew what he'd heard.

The Roundheads had artillery. Two pieces, positioned either side of the barricade, black muzzles pointing ominously towards the oncoming column. The Royalist infantry scattered left and right, seeking shelter within the doorways of shops and homes. To their relief the heavy ball careened between them, missing limbs by extraordinary chance as it bounced and skittered along the mud, eventually burying itself in the wall of a fishmonger's.

The second gun had been poorly aimed and its shot had flown clear of the massed infantry. A great cry went up from the Royalist ranks. It started with the officers and spread down to the sergeants with their formidable halberds. They realized that the ordnance pieces had been impotent and it would take them far less time to reach the barricade than it would for the artillery teams behind it to reload the smoking iron monsters. The officers and non-commissioned officers cheered, the corporals shouted and urged, and the men surged forward in their tightly packed companies.

In open battle the attackers might have opted for steady rolling fire, the musketeers presenting by rank, each rank firing and then moving to the rear as they reloaded. But today the strategy was one of speed and shock. The Royalists advanced to within a hundred paces, so that their weapons would be devastating against the mass of bodies beyond the wattle fencing, and offered up their muskets in a single salvo. The late afternoon air was shattered once again as hundreds of priming pans flashed, sending their deadly missiles soaring into the Parliamentarian rank and file.

'*Charge! Charge! Charge!*' the officers cried, and the king's war-machine – created at Nottingham but hardened beneath a ridge called Edgehill – pitched forward suddenly, pikes levelled and muskets wielded as clubs.

The pikes crossed from both sides of the barricade, points passing in midair, ash shafts becoming entangled like the strands of a basket. In some places the Royalist pike blocks did not meet shoulder-to-shoulder, and musketeers, hammering at the barricade and its defenders, filled these gaps. It was a savage affair, but a near bloodless one, for once the push of pike had been joined the deadly points were often beyond their killing range, and it became a shoving match, a contest of strength and of will. Similarly, the musketeers' weapons, so murderous when loaded and primed, were no more than heavy clubs when they met the enemy in hand-to-hand combat. With the barricade between the opposing forces keeping the men at arm's length, the melee was reduced to little more than a street brawl, scarcely deadlier than the annual football match the townsfolk of Brentford had made a tradition.

The lack of fatalities did not detract from the sheer brutality. Men on both sides of the defences found themselves bludgeoned by musket stocks and jabbed by smoking metal barrels. Those in the push of pike were locked in a desperate tussle to force their enemy backward, trapped in the tight mass of bodies by their own unwieldy weapons. The men at the back surged on, digging the balls of their feet into the steadily loosening earth, seeking that vital degree of purchase, while those at the front were leaned precariously over the barricade, close enough to smell the foul breath of their enemy. They drew swords in that close, muggy, rancid fastness and stabbed across the fences and barrels at the opposing ranks. There was no room for powerful thrusts or wild swings, and the blades invariably struck ineffectually at their targets, scoring thin lines on breastplates or biting into wattle and wood as the barricade shielded groins and guts.

As the fight raged, its ebb and flow took on a subtle change. Men were tiring. The will to push had left the pike battailes and the musketeers' movements were becoming sluggish and ineffective. It was increasingly apparent that a stalemate had been reached.

The Royalist drums started up, announcing the order to disengage, and, like a great beast waking from slumber, the mass of men gradually began to shift into animation once again. The slow separation was punctuated by the odd swing of a musket or jab of a tuck, but men on both sides of the barricade were dog-tired and simply yearned for rest.

The Royalists withdrew, retreating westward down the gently sloping road. The occasional musket-ball whistled above their heads, but none found a deadly mark. The purple-coated men beyond the barricade jeered them. They crowed and cheered and offered challenges. They shouted their defiance and declared that the king's colours would advance no further this day. They were an ancient, insurmountable cliff-face, letting the waves of King Charles break upon them.

They didn't know the next wave was rolling in.

Sir Gilbert Gerrard's lads were sent forward to take up the Royalist initiative. They broke into a swift march as Rivers' exhausted bluecoats streamed down either side of the road to reform with the main force. They picked up the pace as they began to climb the slope, eventually reaching something near a full canter, for their officers were well aware of the threat posed by the brace of cannon. Those guns, poorly aimed in their first salvo, would be near ready to eviscerate the next wave of attackers.

Stryker was on the flank of the main Royalist column, itching to make an assault. He had no particular wish to fly headlong into the determined foe and their obdurate barricade, except that he now knew where Eli Makepeace and Sir Randolph Moxcroft were hiding. He had watched as Makepeace had hoisted the old spy across his shoulders and disappeared between two buildings adjacent to the barricade.

For the time being, though, he had little alternative but

to focus on the battle at hand. Stryker watched Gerrard's regiment storm forward, closing the gap between the opposing factions, and knew instinctively that their advance was far too slow. The guns would blaze within moments and the brave men of Sir Gilbert's unit would be shred like parchment.

Turning to Skellen, he indicated the artillery teams with a flick of his head, 'We need to shift those.'

Skellen followed his gaze, chewing the inside of his mouth as he considered. 'Fair few, sir. Four to each gun.'

Stryker nodded. Four artillerymen to each cannon presented a formidable obstacle. He was about to offer an alternative plan when Lancelot Forrester snorted. 'Three of us, old man. Hit our marks, they'll not stand.'

Forrester's confidence was persuasive. They had only three muskets between them, but if they could hit the lead crew members it might be enough to dissuade the rest from firing.

The three men split up, Skellen and Forrester staying on the right flank while Stryker went left. They broke away from the column and dashed along the road, careful to stay in the shadows cast by shops and houses.

As they moved they went through the familiar motions of loading and priming their muskets. By now they were well within range of the rebel saker crews. Those men were busy, frantically preparing their iron pieces to spit fire and brimstone down the slope, acutely aware of their importance to this day's fight.

The lead man in each gun crew was holding a long stick, on the end of which glowed a saltpetre-soaked match, its tip glowing ominously.

Sir Gilbert Gerrard's Regiment of Foot were advancing

at a pace, but as they slipped along the mud of the road's surface a sickening realization began to dawn. The big guns could be made to fire before they reached the barricade. They would be caught in hellish rain.

'*On!*' the officers screamed, for retreat was not an option. They ran on, instinctively keeping their heads low. Only when they were less than fifty paces away from the barricade did they realize they had beaten the fearful artillery. In a heartbeat the officers called the halt, and, though sporadic musketry was beginning to spit at them from the purple-coated defenders, they stood firm in order to present their massive volley.

The muskets sparked, pans and muzzles flaring bright in the grey afternoon, and several of Brooke's men went down. Gerrard's troops were on the move before the wounded had even fallen. In a moment they were at the barricade and the push of pike was joined with cheers and curses ripping the air as sure as the gunpowder had done moments before. The men of Sir Gilbert Gerrard's Regiment of Foot thanked God for His divine intervention. It was as if the very host of heaven had spiked the guns into silence.

Back in the main Royalist column, Stryker, Forrester and Skellen congratulated each other, their musket barrels still smoking.

After Gerrard's men had fought to exhaustion, the drums called them back. They disengaged, allowing Lord Molyneux's men to take up the assault. Soldiers poured forward, closing the distance between the Royalist column and the barricade in swift order. It was clear that Brooke's infantrymen were worn down, depleted, bleeding, tired. They had put up a staunch fight once again, letting the wattle and hay and wood blunt the blades of the fresh Royalists, but they knew that Molyneux's regiment would stand where Rivers' and Gerrard's had been. Ruthven would use his vast reserves to attack and rest in rotation for as long as it took, with the surety that eventually the great barricade would fail.

Not far away, an entirely different duel was taking place.

Roger Tainton and Lisette Gaillard cut, thrust and parried in the boat-builder's workshop. They cared nothing for the men screaming and dying out on the road, or for the great bursts of cannon fire that had shattered the building's windows around them. Each cared only for the person and the blade in front of them.

Both Englishman and Frenchwoman were skilled in hand-to-hand combat, and they appeared to be evenly matched. Tainton had strength on his side, while Lisette had guile, agility and experience. The cavalryman was protected by expensive armour, born in the forges of Milan, while his golden-haired adversary was clothed in simple doublet and breeches beneath her long cloak. But what she lacked in protection she gained in speed.

Lisette darted forward, as she had half a dozen times already, and jabbed her sword at Tainton's face. His helmeted head presented a clear vulnerability for Lisette to exploit, but he flicked his wrist up to bat the danger away and slashed a venomous backhand at Lisette's exposed throat, forcing her to duck and step backwards out of range. They circled again. Lisette lunged, Tainton fended her off. Tainton swept his tuck low and the Frenchwoman was made to bring her blade across to block the blow.

Every so often she risked a glance to the area behind Tainton. This was where he had dropped the pouch, taunting her into making a play for it, and each time he saw her eyes flick to where it lay he grinned broadly.

'You don't even know what we fight for, do you?' the cavalryman said. 'You've never seen it. Never understood. All you care for is the ruby, a trinket you have never so much as laid eyes upon.'

Lisette ignored him. She had been charged with retrieving the strongbox and its contents. That was all she needed to know.

She lunged for the side of Tainton's neck in a great arc. She was becoming more desperate with every passing moment. Tainton was a good fighter, a classically trained swordsman, and could wield a blade better than most men Lisette had ever fought.

Lisette punched her tuck high, aiming for Tainton's proud chin, and her black-clad opponent was forced to lift his own blade to block. They closed with one another, swords aloft, steel locked above their heads.

'You cannot best me, my dear,' Tainton sneered, their noses almost touching. 'You are good, I'll give you that, but nowhere good enough. The contents of the pouch will remain with me and will win this war!'

Tainton was by far the stronger, and he shoved Lisette away easily, but she came at him again, and again, and in their third sally, Lisette thought she might be finally achieving the ascendancy. But then a terrible, gut-wrenching crack split the air between them and Lisette's forearm jarred painfully, and she knew that the unthinkable had happened. Her blade had snapped, just above the hilt.

Tainton grinned venomously, and Lisette was close

enough to see the gleam of his brilliant teeth. Acting instinctively, she hawked as much phlegm into her dry mouth as was possible and spat the sticky spray into the cavalryman's face.

The spittle found Tainton's eyes and hung in gloopy tendrils from the end of his nose. It did not blind him, but it threw him long enough for Lisette Gaillard to jam the hilt of her shattered tuck into Tainton's proud face. The nose, straight and handsome, exploded and Tainton recoiled in a gush of blood and mucus and sinew. He did not release his sword, but the blow knocked his senses and sapped the strength from his legs. Lisette was searching the workshop for another weapon before he could even straighten.

As Tainton's vision began to clear he saw Lisette a few paces away, bent over, hands scrabbling in the thick layer of wood shavings. Hefting his sword, he staggered forward in preparation for a heavy, killing blow.

When Lisette Gaillard stood, she was wielding a mallet. It was short and stout, no match for the long blade of Roger Tainton, but his reflexes had been dulled by the strike to his nose and he did not expect her to rise from the wood shavings with such speed and ferocity. She launched into him, even as he brought his own sword down toward her head, but the mallet hit home before the sword had completed its arc.

It was not a killing blow. The mallet was certainly weighty, but it was ultimately a blunt instrument and had been wielded with little strength. Lisette had only intended to set Tainton back a few paces, to buy some time so that she could locate another, deadlier weapon. But the mallet caught Tainton in the centre of his chest, above his sternum. Already dazed, the impact sent him staggering back haphazardly, his sword clattering to the ground. As his arms flailed wildly, Tainton desperately sought to steady himself, but he was weighed down by the heavy armour and still shaken by the injury to his nose. It was only when the backs of his legs collided with something solid that his stumble was halted. He rocked back, his eyes wide as he toppled, his face a mask of sheer horror as he realized what was happening. And, with a quickly stifled cry and a glugging splash, he fell backwards into the vat of tar.

The regiments of Molyneux and Blagge had taken their respective turns to dash themselves against the Parliamentarian barricade. They were readily replaced by the men of Sir Thomas Lunsford and Sir Edward Fitton.

Fitton's lads had three extra bodies in their ranks, for Captains Stryker and Forrester were on the right flank, accompanied by Sergeant William Skellen. They had swords, dirks and muskets, match-cords smouldering, barrels loaded, pans primed.

As the barricade drew close, a man several paces to his left was chopped to the ground by a pair of musket-balls that shattered shoulder and thigh. Stryker knew very well that wounds which were not fatal in themselves could lay a path for a more agonizing death in a day or two, as the devastation caused by flying shot that flattened and pulverized became infected. He shuddered involuntarily.

Fifty paces, Stryker, Forrester, Skellen and all the other musketeers of the line hoisted their muskets, cushioning wooden stocks into the muscles of their shoulders. The order to fire came immediately and in an immense flash and a bitter, choking cloud of smoke that sent tears streaming from their eyes, they launched fire and lead upon the barricade.

The musketeers waited then, for out of the smoke their comrades in the pike blocks surged in vast units, bristling like gigantic hedgehogs.

Twenty paces; pikes were levelled from both sides of the divide, men cursed and snarled and pissed their breeches.

Five paces; the opposing tertios stabbed home, coming together in a throng of roars and cries, spittle and blood.

And then the musketeers joined the fray, swinging their guns, half-metal clubs, crushing arms and cheeks and skulls like eggshells. It was murderous work.

Stryker was at the wattle fencing, thrusting his reversed musket at faces, aiming to bludgeon and blind the men who dared stand in his way. He was a snarling, horrifying vision of death and violence. His long hair was loose now and framed a twisted face that sneered and grinned like a shark, teeth bared from behind lips that were bloody and split; a face from where a single eye, shimmering with quicksilver intensity, sought out prey and told its victims of a hundred ways they might die. Men quelled when Stryker's shadow was upon them. They backed away, but only to find themselves pinned by the men behind. So they stood and fought until Stryker hammered each man down with speed and brutal efficiency. The joy of battle had come to Captain Stryker once the fighting became a hand-to-hand affair. He was a musket, he was a sword, he was a saker. He was the fight and he revelled in it. It was as close to death as a man could reach, and yet it made him feel most alive.

Brooke's Roundheads were tired now, tired enough to allow their weapons to droop. The Royalists saw this and were reinvigorated, for they knew the defenders had had their fill of this murderous labour. With excited energy, they pushed on, tearing at the fences and kicking the bales. A drum-major turned the stacked barrels to kindling with the axe-edge of a halberd. A lieutenant bellowed encouragement as his men forged small inroads into the hitherto stout defences.

Suddenly, amid the anarchic melee, a cry went up from the purple-coated side, a terrified, panicked scream that sent heads turning.

'Cavalry! Cavalry!' the man was wailing, and as his comrades followed his petrified gaze, their eyes fell upon a vision of hell. Horsemen were weaving between the buildings to their right, the north side of High Street, and it was clear from their cries, their crimson sashes and their many standards that they were the king's cavalry. Rupert's men had ridden around the town and skirted beyond the barricade, surging down through Old Brentford from the north.

Lord Brooke's men were outflanked and outmanoeuvred.

And then, with a crack of splintering wood, the fences and thick-hewn spikes and all the furniture that had been taken by force from the homes of the townsfolk came crashing down. Like the locusts that had plagued biblical Egypt, exultant Royalist soldiers swarmed through the gaps in their dozens. The Roundheads ran for their lives. The barricade was breached.

*

Just below the great barricade, at the back of a house that had been barred and bolted shut by residents too stubborn to leave, Eli Makepeace and Sir Randolph Moxcroft had found a bolthole.

It was a little shed, a wooden structure to the rear of one of the big houses overlooking the road. Makepeace had tried to break into the building, but the thick oaken door had resisted the attentions of his boot heel with sturdy ease. Abandoning the premises, Makepeace and Moxcroft had looked over the adjacent property, anxious to conceal themselves before the victorious Cavaliers arrived. But that next building appeared just as strong, just as secure, and Makepeace knew that the gardens would have to suffice.

'What if the barricade falls?' Sir Randolph had asked as Makepeace dragged him round the side of the house.

'*When* it falls,' Makepeace corrected. 'They will not keep that lot at bay for long. They're just stalling for time. That's all this is about. If the rebels can prevent the king from reaching the outskirts of the capital by nightfall, he'll have to wait for dawn to press home the attack. And by then, Parliament will have heard the news of Brentford, they'll have embellished the gory detail and roused the Trained Bands and citizens to the cause. If every man jack of 'em 'll turn out to defend the city, they might just stand a chance.'

'So what happens to us?'

'We, Sir Randolph, are going to hide. God knows what's happened to Bain, but I do not suppose it's anything good, seeing as Stryker appears to have emerged from the cellar unscathed. So it is just the two of us. And without a ready means of transportation, we are trapped in this

God-forsaken town. So we'll hide until the king's men either flounder at the barricade, which I doubt, or until they knock it flat and march on to London. They'll leave a garrison behind, naturally, but we'll play at being good citizens of Brentford and we might just get away.'

Makepeace had come close to soiling his breeches when he'd first cast his eyes to the foot of the slope. He had known the Royalists would be streaming across the bridge and into New Brentford soon, but that did nothing to assuage his shock at seeing the massed ranks so close. As soon as the foremost enemy units rounded the bend at the foot of the sloping road, he realized that he and Moxcroft would be overrun. They were agonizingly close to the vast barricade at the top of the highway, where new town became old, but with the cripple on his back they were never likely to reach the safety of Lord Brooke's purple-coats in time. He had been tempted to dump his burden and sprint into the fields, or even jump headlong into the Thames, but then he remembered his master. He might evade Stryker this day, but the master – as sure as hell's fires burned hot – would track him down and inflict a far worse death.

So the turncoat and the spy had made for the houses to the right of the road, close to the protection offered by the barricade. When they first discovered the shed it had been filled with kindling, keeping it dry for winter's coldest months, but Makepeace scrabbled at the thick splints of oak until there was enough space for two men to lie. He had helped Moxcroft into position first, shifting the immobile legs into the necessary curve to allow his own body to squeeze in. And there they stayed.

*

Lisette Gaillard found Tainton's bay stallion outside the boat-builder's, tethered to a post. The horse did not appreciate this strange new mistress at first, but Lisette was an able rider and quickly managed to gain control. She trotted down the passageway between the workshop and a tannery, until she reached the yards at the rear of the buildings.

Once she was safely away from the immediate battle she jumped down from the saddle, feet squelching in the passageway's chilly mud, and fished a hand within the bag to withdraw the stone. It was everything she had imagined; big and gleaming, rich shards of deepest scarlet glowing against her palm. But Lisette had noted Tainton's goading words, his talk of the ruby being nothing compared with God's true plan. At first she had thought him simply pious, a Puritan heretic spouting the usual zealous diatribe, but something about his mocking had perturbed her.

She plunged her hand inside the bag again and pulled out the brooch and posy ring. They were exactly as Henrietta Maria had described; of good quality, finely crafted, the sort of item befitting the Queen of England, but nothing exceptional. Feeling in the pouch again, she laid fingers on a brittle square of parchment, folded tight and unassuming. She drew it from the bag and carefully opened the yellowing scrap to reveal the contents. What she read almost turned her knees to jelly, and she had to steady herself by gripping a nearby water trough. She read it again. And again.

'*Mon Dieu*,' she whispered. '*Mon Dieu*.'

Lisette leapt back on to the saddle. All she had to do was gallop down the slope to the place where the road curved, and take the spur left across the land around St Lawrence's church. Beyond the church was her coracle. If she could reach it, she would be able to get away from this place, to take the ruby and – her heart raced at the thought – the parchment away from enemy clutches.

But as she looked around her to check her path was clear, Lisette had an excellent view across the yards and gardens of the entire row of buildings. And she noticed something she knew Stryker would want to see.

And then she was galloping up High Street and towards the barricade. Even from several hundred paces away she could see the king's forces had made a breach, streaming between and beyond the various objects piled together to form the makeshift parapet. Lisette was not interested in the skirmish; she was only interested in Stryker. Even in the midst of the elation she felt at defeating Tainton and her relief at knowing her mission was so nearly complete, Lisette could not abandon the man to whom she owed so much.

The Parliamentarians were in utter disarray. Even the most optimistic of them had begun the day with a fear that the barricade would crumble in the face of the Royalist onslaught, but after withstanding the attentions of five different regiments they could not help but believe a miracle might now be possible. If they had kept the ordnance trained upon the men at the foot of the slope, then perhaps that miracle might have happened on this misty afternoon, but hidden sharpshooters in the doorway of a butcher's shop had gunned down their artillery crews, leaving the cannon empty and silent. The sixth unit to advance to push of pike had proved to be one too many stresses to bear for the beleaguered regiments of Denzil

Holles and Lord Brooke. Now those men – ranks splintered, discipline destroyed – would be forced to stand and fight against the king's vengeful multitude.

Stryker had battered his way beyond the barricade in those first moments after the breach was made. The noise was a cacophony. A crashing, thunderous cauldron of screams and snarls and drums and steel and explosions and weeping and vomiting.

The man he chose to fight first seemed to have whatever bravery he possessed sapped out of him. He lowered his weapon, perhaps with a vain thought of surrender, but Stryker was through him in a moment, shattering his face with the butt-end of his empty musket.

The next man was there immediately and he swept the proffered tuck aside contemptuously, the cheap weapon snapping on the musket's stock. With one hand Stryker reached for the Roundhead's collar and dragged him forward, splitting the man's nose with a vicious headbutt. The man staggered back, blinded by blood, and Stryker clubbed him aside. He felt the infantryman's arm break beneath the weight of the blow, but ignored the man's scream as he strode on.

And there, as the land sloped away from the tattered remnants of the barricade, stood the packed buildings of Old Brentford. Brooke's men were retreating along the road, and civilians were dashing between homes and businesses in panicked frenzy.

Stryker watched them, a pang of guilt stabbing at him as he saw their terror in the face of the Royalist advance. This was their town, these buildings their livelihoods, and they could do nothing but hide, wait out the carnage and pray to God for protection.

The cold stab of steel replaced the stab of guilt, and Stryker realized that a dirk had scraped against his ribs. He dropped the musket and swore as burning pain careered along his diaphragm. Cursing himself for the lapse in concentration, he swivelled around to see a purple-coated soldier wielding the offending weapon. The blow had been wild, inaccurate, for the soldier was already wounded and could barely stand. Stryker kicked him in the chest, where a musket-ball had evidently entered, and the man crumpled with a great shudder and a cough of blood.

Stryker looked around, scanning the chaos for a glimpse of his two comrades. As he searched the bodies – both prone and standing – his eye fell upon the rangy figure of Will Skellen. The sergeant was holding court, his halberd, the blade glistening now, sweeping back and forth in great horizontal arcs, cleaving as it went. The men coming against him were numerous, but the tall, lithe man from the south coast went at them with all the serenity of a farmer cutting wheat with his great scythe.

Ahead was Captain Forrester. The man, all florid face and sweaty jowls, was screaming at one of Brooke's men with livid ferocity. He parried a heavy blow from a long sword and whipped his own blade down the length of the opposing steel as the weapons clashed. The move, executed at the speed of a striking snake, sent his blade ricocheting off his enemy's guard and into the purplecoat's upper arm. With a shrill cry the Roundhead saw that his bicep was torn open, and as he stared in horror at the gaping wound, his fingers seemed to lose their feeling and he released the sword. It was over before the man could wrest his gaze from the split flesh, and Forrester moved with deceptive agility to face the next man who fancied his chances.

'Captain!' a warning cry snapped from somewhere behind Stryker. He turned to see a Parliamentarian pike-man lurching at him, mouth peeled back in a yellow-toothed leer, a short-handled axe raised high in his right hand.

Stryker saw the attack and just managed to lurch backwards as the axe plunged down from above his assailant's head. The cutting edge passed excruciatingly close to Stryker's face, for he felt the air part alongside his chin, but the blow missed. The Parliamentarian tried to bring his weapon up in a back-handed swipe, but Stryker stepped close and jammed his elbow into the man's throat. The attacker stumbled back, gargling pain and anger as spittle frothed at his lips.

Stryker strode on, turning back to see that a blue-coated corporal – one of Rivers' boys – was engaged in a desperate struggle. He had lost his tuck and was locked in an embrace with a big man in Holles's red uniform.

The big Roundhead collapsed suddenly, the air hissing from his lungs like a great pair of bellows. Stryker jerked the dirk free, twisting it so that the suction of the flesh would be broken, and nodded to the corporal. 'Thanks for the warning,' he said. 'Consider the debt repaid.'

The corporal grinned.

'Cap'n! Cap'n!' Skellen's voice chopped through Stryker's whirling thoughts. 'The houses! They went into one of those houses!'

Patrick Ruthven's black mount twitched nervously as he cantered through the town.

The order to send Rupert's cavalry into the fray had

signalled the final death knell for Lord Brooke's courageous regiment. They had cut and run in the face of the victorious Royalist infantry, but remained defiant in small pockets along London Road. The cavalry had ended that, for the few Parliamentarians who continued to fight were not able to withstand a mounted charge. Ruthven had ordered the town purged of rebels, and it had been done.

Now Ruthven, the Earl of Forth, commander of the king's army, would take the remainder of his twelve-thousand-strong force and make good his victory. They would stay on London Road and consolidate this crushing blow by sweeping through Chiswick and then Hammersmith and beyond until they were at the gates of London itself. He had a vision of offering the king his own horse, leading him in to cries of welcome from loyal subjects.

Brentford had made it possible.

'A good day's work, Marcus!' Ruthven called to the nearest staff officer.

The man twisted in his saddle to catch the earl's eye. He nodded sagely, 'Aye, right enough, my lord. God's mercies abound.'

Ruthven laughed. 'Lord love you, Marcus, but you're a pious wretch! At least you're on our side!'

One of Prince Rupert's aides galloped in from the fields beyond Old Brentford's eastern fringe.

'Compliments of His Royal Highness, my lord,' the messenger said breathlessly.

'Well? Spit it out, man!' the earl barked.

'Our cavalry has the field, my lord. Their right flank scattered into enclosures to the north. We circled around them. Cut them down in their scores, sir. The left flank routed. Most took their chances in the Thames.'

383

Ruthven nodded his satisfaction. Dozens – perhaps hundreds – would have died attempting to swim the deathly cold river. 'All is well, then.' He patted his horse's muscular neck, feeling comfort in the trusty beast's solid lines and raw strength. After a moment, he glanced up at the rider. 'We can advance on the city's gates before Essex musters his field army.' He raised his voice so all his staff officers could hear. 'That's the crux of the matter, gentlemen! Get to London before the rebels have time to turn out their full force.'

'And the Bands, sir,' a nearby major added.

'Aye,' Ruthven agreed. 'Skippon's Trained Bands add a fair few thousand to their tally. We must reach the city before they have time to organize a defence.'

The aide cleared his throat nervously. 'That is the second part of the message, my lord. Greencoats. Hampden's regiment. They're blocking the road.'

Ruthven's shoulders sagged. 'Then the day is not yet done,' he said quietly. 'Where?'

'Open fields outside the town, sir. Toward Turnham Green.'

CHAPTER 20

A portion of Ruthven's units – those paying the highest price at the barricades – were afforded respite. The earl would have to leave a force to garrison the newly conquered Brentford, and that posting would be their reward. The majority, however, were ordered to continue straight through the town. They were to hammer home the Royalist advantage, to get as near to London as possible before the dying light failed entirely.

Captain Stryker was back on High Street, standing amid the carnage of the destroyed barricade. All about him were bodies, mostly marked by their uniforms of red and purple, though some carried the blue or tawny of the Royalist ranks. He ignored them. The men he sought had not fought bravely for either side. He peeled away from what was left of the defensive work, and ran to the buildings on the right-hand side of the road.

With the Roundhead position shattered, he reached the houses unhindered and kicked the door of the first, smashing its hinges. As soon as he crossed the threshold he was set upon by a Parliamentarian corporal who had secreted himself in a dark corner. He beat the man senseless with his fists before striding into the first room. In moments Forrester and Skellen were at his back and he turned to them. 'Search every room! Every corner!'

The first enemy troops to come past the woodshed were Salusbury's men. Makepeace, balled in the foetal position with Moxcroft lying silently curled behind, could not see them, but the Welsh accents were unmistakable. Curled in the mildewed darkness, the scent of ripe wood swirling around him, Makepeace willed the Royalists to move on. He clamped his eyes shut, held his breath, kept the tightest check on his every muscle. They were close – agonizingly close – and he found himself wishing he had collected a discarded sword before taking up this position.

The soldiers had evidently abandoned the skirmish, for they seemed to be moving aimlessly. And then he smelled the haze of alcohol. It wafted, acidic and strong, into the shed, overpower-ing even the tang of mould and wood. The men were drunk. The odours of ale, wine and spirits mingled in the gathering dusk. Makepeace silently cursed. The Royalists, like any victorious army, were ransacking the town for drink and anything else lootable.

Eventually, after several terrible minutes had ticked past, the soldiers began to drift away, melting back into the tall shadows cast by Brentford's houses. Perhaps they were seeking further spoils, perhaps they were responding to the faint sound of beating drums echoing in from the east. 'Jesu,' Makepeace whispered.

'Come,' Moxcroft's voice came from behind him. 'Let us take our leave of this cursed place.'

'No,' Makepeace said. 'We should wait until dark.'

'But the damned Royalists are sacking the town,

Captain. They are cupshot already. We must get out while we can, before they regain control of this rabble and set a proper garrison.'

There was wisdom in those words. Makepeace relented. 'Fine, Sir Randolph. Have it your way. But we cannot simply stroll away. You are not as light as you may look.'

Makepeace wriggled free from the shed, turning to grasp the spy by his reedy wrists and haul him out. He stooped, grumbling as Moxcroft put his arm across his weary shoulders and cursing as he lunged upwards with aching knees so that they were both now standing.

'There,' Makepeace said. 'Let us be careful about this, Sir Randolph. We must find a mount.'

Moxcroft nodded. 'Aye, well there ought to be a multitude of riderless horses hereabouts, wouldn't you say?'

The shadows were now melding into one another, and the ground was becoming cloaked in the first shade of grey, heralding the night to come. In that burgeoning darkness the two fugitives did not see the horse appear from the gloom until its rider spoke. '*Bonsoir*, good sirs. You are lost?'

In a field to the east of Old Brentford, Colonel John Hampden was stalking across the front rank of his regiment like a prowling cat. He was clothed in a thick, wax-crusted buff-coat, breastplate and helmet, looking for all the world like a dismounted harquebusier, though his men were resplendent in the honourable green that coloured his family's livery.

'Enough!' he barked at the drummers that stood out in front of the massed blocks of pike and musket. The instruments fell silent immediately. Hampden kept walking, slowly, purposefully, glancing up from the long grass every couple of paces to make contact with the eyes of his nervous troops. 'Here!' he shouted again, though this time the word was meant for all ears. 'Here we stand! Here we fight!' He stopped, drew his sword and plunged it into the soil at his feet. 'Here is where the king will be turned back! He and his malignant advisors will remember this day, should they survive it, for ever more as the day they faced God's blessed greencoats and ran for the hills!'

The men cheered. Hampden's regiment were believers to a man. They were men of faith and of conviction and they loved their leader as they loved their God. He had led them here, to this cold Chiswick field, to face an army. And here they would show him their true mettle.

'Our brothers have bled for a righteous cause this day!' Hampden continued, zeal marking every word. 'We were too late to support them at Brentford, but by God we shall do our duty now! Hold them here! That is all I ask! Hold them here 'til nightfall and we'll have saved our great city!'

The men cheered again, more vigorously this time.

Hampden retrieved his sword, jerking it from the earth in one swift movement. Wiping its tip on the sleeve of his buff-coat, he replaced the ornate blade and stalked back to his waiting horse. An aide helped him into his saddle and he swung a bucket-booted leg over with consummate agility, finding his balance immediately. He looked down the line from his new vantage point. They were a good unit. A strong, God-fearing, superlatively trained regiment of true Parliamentarians. This was why he would meet the king's forces gladly. It was the chance to lead men like these and to throw off the yoke of a corrupt monarch.

The first Cavaliers came into view as they cleared the road's bend. Hampden's men were arrayed across that road, bisecting both fields on either side, and presented a deep wall of men and arms through which the king's army would have to wade if they were to reach London. Hampden himself squinted into the fading light, seeing the shadows of men moving from beyond the tree line. His brown eyes took on a glint of iron as he realized the task ahead. His men were arguably the best equipped, most highly drilled fighting force in this new rebel army, having been furnished with pike, tuck and musket with funds from his own, deep pockets, but they were untried. They had missed Kineton Fight, having been delayed while protecting the Roundhead artillery, and open battle would be a new experience for most of the men.

But they had seen the red and purple coats of the terrified, wounded souls that fled from the tatters of the Brentford barricades. They had parted the ranks to allow those retreating men through, listened to the stories of brutal cavalry charges, forced drownings and overwhelming odds. Every one of them knew this would be a hard and bitter fight. But fight they must, if they were to cover the retreat of Holles's and Brooke's regiments while delaying Ruthven's bloody progress.

More Royalist troops were filing on to the field now. There seemed to be no end to their numbers and they drew up into companies of musket and blocks of pike with startling speed. The plan, it seemed to Hampden, was simply to fill the killing ground with troops and brush his lone regiment aside.

'This will not do,' Hampden said quietly.

'Colonel?' a major replied.

Hampden glanced up from his thoughts, his voice louder this time, infused with a confidence he struggled to find. 'Charge the popish villains, Major!'

'Sir?' The major was startled.

'I said charge 'em! They may have the numbers, sir, but they are tired as pack-mules.' He looked back along the line and, drawing his sword, raised his voice so as many could hear him as possible. 'They are weary! D'you hear me, lads? They are thinking of nothing but rest and the plunder they might find back in poor Brentford. We'll give them something else to think about!' They cheered. 'They will taste our steel and our shot. We'll drive them from this place on the end of our blades! But we must move swiftly, my lads! Before they have the opportunity to find their ranks!'

A visible quiver ran along the rank and file as the words sank into nervous minds. They had come here to defend the road, to prevent the Earl of Forth from advancing any further towards London. But John Hampden was asking them to attack a swirling mass of Royalist soldiers that continued to grow with every moment. They gazed up at him and saw the man who had defied the king before and had lived to tell the tale. A man whose fervour was infectious and intoxicating and whose hazel eyes burned like coals.

Hampden's blade swept downwards, slicing the air in a broad, singing arc to call the charge. The soldiers began to advance, so fast and so frenzied that the men in the front rank could do nothing but surge forward, driven by the weight of their comrades behind. The greencoats became as one giant beast, like the leviathan of old, eating up the ground between them and the enemy in moments.

*

'Stryker's whore,' Makepeace hissed through gritted teeth.

Lisette dismounted. She had taken Tainton's sword as well as his horse, and she levelled it at the red-haired officer's chest. 'I wanted to kill you in the cellar, Captain Makepeace. There you had that witless oaf to protect you. Now, it seems, you do not.'

Moxcroft was leaning against Makepeace, his arm slung around the latter's shoulders to keep him upright. His disability might have made him vulnerable, yet his voice was as smooth as new-churned butter. 'Who the devil are you, madam? What could you possibly want with us?'

'I want nothing from you, sir,' Lisette replied. She glanced at Makepeace. 'It is *him* I want.'

'I will pay you,' Makepeace said hurriedly, eyeing the steady blade and detecting the seriousness in the Frenchwoman's tone. 'If you let us go, I will make you rich.'

Lisette stepped forward. 'Ah, but it is not riches I desire, Captain Makepeace. It is forgiveness.'

Moxcroft was clearly mystified. 'This is absurd!'

'Damn it, Sir Randolph,' Makepeace growled, 'still your infernal tongue!'

Lisette Gaillard was silent for a moment. And then she grinned, for now she understood. 'Sir Randolph Moxcroft! Of course! A pleasure, sir.'

Moxcroft did not reply.

'I have heard so much about you, Sir Randolph,' Lisette continued acidly. 'And now it appears I will be requiring your presence as well as that of the charming captain, here.'

Moxcroft took a steadying breath and managed a confident smile. 'You have heard of us? I do not think that likely. You are clearly weak in the head, madam. You rant of forgiveness. What can you possibly achieve by killing Makepeace and ourselves?'

'Not by killing you, sir. By making a gift of you.'

'A gift?' Moxcroft repeated incredulously. 'A gift for whom?'

'For a man named Stryker.'

With a great cry of fury, fear and determination, Makepeace shoved the spy forward and Moxcroft collided with Lisette, her sword glancing off his collarbone and impaling the flesh between neck and shoulder. Lisette could do nothing as Tainton's razor-sharp blade stuck fast and she rocked back, collapsing to the ground, pinned beneath the bleeding, screaming man.

Lisette heaved Sir Randolph's thrashing body from her own, savagely twisting the sword free, producing a fresh fountain of blood and more screaming. She tried to scramble to her feet, ready to spit Makepeace, but she found herself thrust back to the earth with savage force.

Makepeace may not have been armed, but he was fast. He kicked the blade from her grip as she lay there, and leaned over her, smashing a fist into her cheek.

Captain Stryker was despairing. Together with Forrester and Skellen, he had searched every building in the immediate vicinity of the barricade and found nothing.

'He must have gone,' Forrester said, his eyes red with exhaustion. 'Perhaps he joined Brooke's mob as they ran.'

Stryker rounded on him. 'He was carrying Moxcroft, Forry. For God's sake, man, he can't have run anywhere!'

'He can't be round the back, sir,' Skellen said. 'We've searched the gardens o' most of these places, and them Welshies were lookin' out for the bastards as well.'

Stryker grimaced. 'Those Welshies were more jugbitten than eagle-eyed, Sergeant. Perhaps we should check again.'

'*Stryker! Stryker!*'

The voice came to them in a shrieking wail from no more than fifty paces down the road. All three men recognized it immediately. They turned as one to see a diminutive woman running towards them, cloaked in black, with great strands of thick fair hair flowing about her shoulders like a golden hood.

'Stryker!' Lisette shouted again as she drew close. 'I had him! I bloody had that son of bitch!'

Stryker's heart began to beat faster. She had reached them now, and stood, bent over slightly, heaving great breaths into burning lungs.

'I had . . . your . . . your spy,' Lisette gasped.

'And Makepeace?'

'*Oui.*' She straightened, meeting that lone, grey eye. 'I am sorry, *mon amour*. They got away. Stole my horse.'

Stryker nodded. 'How long ago?'

'Moments only.' Lisette brightened slightly, reaching up to jab the flesh above Stryker's collarbone with a finger. 'Your spy. I stabbed him here. He bleeds a lot.' She pointed up the slope to the land beyond the barricade. 'They went that way. East. They're tracking the river.'

Colonel John Hampden wheeled his horse in a wide circle, veering away from the waiting pikes with not a moment to spare. He had gone in with the first charge, at the head of the small Roundhead force, his beloved greencoats, and stood tall in his stirrups for all to see. A musket-ball had ricocheted off the side of his helmet, and he thanked the Lord for the armour.

They had crashed into the head of the vast Royalist column while it was still shuffling into formation and the great phalanx of pole and firearms were not yet arrayed in battle order. The effect was devastating. For a brief moment Hampden felt a stab of doubt, wondering if his paltry force would not impact the packed ranks of the battle-hardened king's men, but the moment vanished in a torrent of newfound faith as the men in green roared psalms into the dusk. Their piety left him shamed but jubilant, and with renewed zeal he urged his mount forward at the head of the regiment.

It was a dirty fight. No push of pike here, no polished formations slipping with practised ease into the fashionable Dutch or Swedish orders of battle. It was a desperate charge meeting an equally desperate defence and the men of John Hampden's Regiment of Foot slashed small furrows, two or three ranks deep, into the larger force so that discipline was quickly lost by the Royalist vanguard. A ruck of bodies and blades ensued. Muskets were discharged in haste by both sides and now, barrels empty and smoking, they were upturned to be used as clubs. Pikes had also lost their usefulness, for the greencoats had already reached beyond their killing range and had drawn sword for this hot, stinking close-quarters work.

Men on both sides went down to musket butt, fist or blade and, as Hampden stood high in his stirrups to order his men to disengage, many small duels flared up and down the great skirmish line. A pair of young men were scrabbling on the rapidly freezing turf, rolling back and forth as if engaged in a childhood scrap. It was only when one fell still that the knife could be seen jutting from his guts. Two more men stumbled across the still warm corpse, locked in their own private struggle. Neither held weapons any longer and their bodies clung together in a snarling, hateful, spittle-showered bear-hug. The bigger of the two seemed to be winning the upper hand, his sheer brute strength wearing his opponent down with every passing moment, but then the smaller man jerked forward, sinking his teeth into the end of his enemy's nose, and the former favourite released his victim with a shrill cry of pain and outrage. The lower half of his face gleamed beneath a spreading sheet of red and his hands went instinctively to protect his torn appendage. But his opponent did not relent. He kicked the bleeding soldier in the crotch and then, as the reeling man doubled forward in agony, kicked him again in the face.

Hampden had seen enough. If they did not withdraw in good order now, they would be outflanked by the far larger force. Better to hit the Royalists in rapid bursts, bloody the Pope-loving bastards and regroup for another sally. 'Disengage! Hampden's; disengage!' He was already cantering back to where his regiment had been arrayed before their charge when he spotted the three drummers, who stood awaiting orders behind the colour-bearing ensigns. 'Sound an orderly retreat! Regroup on me!'

The drums beat out their colonel's orders and slowly – painfully slowly – the melee dissolved into two disparate groups as the men in green broke away from the Royalist force. Hampden watched as his regiment retreated in good order, and was elated to see that far fewer of his men had been left dead or wounded in amongst the enemy formation than he had feared.

'That's it, my lads!' he bellowed while his men filtered past him to reform in their original units. Many were without pikes or muskets now, having lost them in the frantic chaos of the skirmish, but Hampden felt a swell of pride as they drew blades and dirks, already preparing for the next inevitable charge. He harboured no wish to send these men to their deaths, but he knew that Essex and Skippon were already making hasty preparations for the defence of London, and they needed as much time as he and his men could provide.

Hampden waited. He gave his ranks time to regroup and check their weapons, to tend to superficial wounds and to take innumerable and well-earned lungfuls of air. He took a deep breath for himself, and then said the hardest words he'd ever spoken. 'We charge again, boys! They've tasted our steel and they're on the back foot! Join me and drive our victory home!'

Eli Rushworth Augustus Makepeace thought his very heart might burst through his chest as he galloped head-long through the fields east of Old Brentford. The River Thames was to his right, London Road to his left.

It had not been easy to prop the wounded, whimpering Sir Randolph Moxcroft on to the bay stallion, but the terrible urgency gave Makepeace a reserve of strength and he had somehow managed to lift the spy to the saddle. Moxcroft had flopped across it, legs on one side, head on the other, while Makepeace had shoved at his rump to get him properly centred. Sir Randolph, still bleeding profusely, was now bent, face first, across the horse's back.

As they got nearer the capital, the Thames began to sweep away southward in one of its many vast bends, and the ground began to become boggy. The horse, already labouring under the weight of two men, started to slow to an arduous canter, and Makepeace decided to veer left, towards the road.

The road itself was masked by a row of tall trees and he could not see beyond them, but he was careful not to spur too close to the broad highway, for cries and drumbeats and musketry emanated from that direction.

'What's that noise?' Moxcroft moaned. From his position he could see nothing but the blurred ground as it sped by.

'The king's men have found more rebels to kill,' Makepeace replied bluntly. He squinted as, through the tangled trunks, the shapes of men and horses became apparent in the adjacent field. 'We ride parallel with the road, and we are passing the next fight, it seems. Greencoats, by the looks of things. Hampden's perhaps. No matter.'

Let them fight it out, Makepeace thought. His purpose was on a higher plane. He would deliver Sir Randolph safely to Parliament and demand an audience with John Pym himself. He would be handsomely rewarded by his master, and feted by the new regime. He had done it. All the hardship and the danger had been worthwhile. It irked him that Stryker still lived, and that Bain had evidently fallen foul of the one-eyed bastard, but all that really mattered was that Eli Makepeace would become a hero of the rebel cause.

He was startled from the glorious images that danced across his mind by a splinter of bark. A musket-ball bounced off a tree trunk nearby. They were still some distance from the fighting, and yet it seemed that the shot had come from close by. With a sickening feeling in his guts, Makepeace twisted around.

Captain Stryker cursed viciously as his shot flew wide.

He had dashed up the road to Old Brentford upon hearing the news of the traitors' escape, and had come across a lone despatch rider.

'Are you carrying despatches now?' he had asked the bewildered junior officer.

'No, sir.'

'Excellent,' Stryker had replied, before reaching up to haul the lad from his saddle. 'I apologize,' he said, as he manhandled the struggling rider, 'but I am duty-bound to commandeer this horse. You shall have it returned.'

The young officer's hand twitched at his sword hilt for a moment, but he had heard stories of the deadly one-eyed captain and, on facing that cold grey gaze, did not wish to discover if the rumours were true. He removed his hand and kept silent.

Stryker had leapt up into the saddle and raked savagely at the horse's flanks, only glancing back to call over his shoulder, 'You have my word!'

He had left the road and struck out toward the Thames. Sure enough, he had spotted a large bay stallion up ahead. It had not been difficult to close the distance between them, for the leading horse carried two men – one of them slumped awkwardly across its back – but he wanted to end the chase quickly, and had taken aim while the range was still ambitious.

Now, as Makepeace spurred on, safe, Stryker was

furious at himself for risking that lone ball. He was no dragoon, and did not have the skill to discharge such a weapon from horseback. Now, for the sake of his own arrogance, his advantage was gone.

'Head toward the river,' Sir Randolph Moxcroft urged between yelps of anguish as he was buffeted by the galloping horse.

'You wish to swim?' Makepeace replied sarcastically.

'There may be a boat.'

'Has the loss of blood drained your wits, Sir Randolph?' Makepeace snarled. 'There'll be no boats. If the rebels have any sense, they'll have set 'em ablaze as soon as Ruthven's army appeared. No, we stay near the road, where the ground is firmest. It will be night soon and we'll lose him in the darkness.'

'Nightfall? He's gaining, Makepeace!' Moxcroft cried. 'We can see him out the corner of our eye!'

Makepeace thumped the spy's back, provoking an anguished cry. 'Then shut your fucking eyes, damn you!'

But his anger only concealed panic. Stryker was gaining. Makepeace knew he would have to act quickly. He leaned to his left, feeling the saddlebags for signs of a weapon. Nothing.

Then Makepeace leaned to the right. His fingers met hard, cold resistance. He almost shrieked with triumph as his hand felt the butt of a pistol. He yanked it from its leather holster, and, without warning, wheeled the horse around.

Moxcroft screamed, but Makepeace ignored him. As their Royalist pursuer drew ever closer, he rummaged in the saddlebag's other pockets for ammunition. As he had hoped, it was all there, and he rapidly loaded the flintlock short-arm.

Makepeace watched Stryker come close, feeling triumph course through his veins. He *would* deliver Moxcroft. He *would* defeat this most troublesome of enemies. He thought of his brother. And he saw himself riding up to the grand house on a fine stallion, befitting his newfound wealth and status.

'Hello Eli,' said Captain Stryker.

Makepeace fired.

Stryker had felt a rush of confidence as the horse carrying Makepeace and Moxcroft slewed to a halt. He watched Makepeace jump down from the saddle and kicked his horse on, eager to prevent the traitor from attempting an escape on foot.

And then there was no distance at all to cover, for he was but a few paces away. But he could not see Makepeace well, as the turncoat was concealed on the far side of the saddle.

At first his horse did not seem to react to the gunshot. Stryker peered into the dusk air, clouded now with acrid smoke, and wondered how on earth he had not been hit. But then his mount began to whinny, a high-pitched noise speaking of extreme distress, and its legs wobbled beneath its muscular bulk.

Beyond the smoke, Makepeace, pistol in hand, was grinning, and then the weapon was tossed aside and he was drawing an already bloodied blade. Stryker watched but could do nothing, for his horse was staggering, pitching forward. He saw a great gush of blood at the animal's neck and realized then that the pistol ball, aimed at him, had hit the horse instead.

Seconds later, the beast was on its knees, and, before it crashed sideways into the long grass, Stryker leapt from the saddle to roll clear of the heavy body.

When he looked up, he could see Makepeace's grinning face emerge from the grey dusk. He looked around, praying there would be a discarded musket lying close that might miraculously be primed and ready to fire. No such miracle was forthcoming.

Makepeace loomed over him. 'Lovely to see you again, *mon Capitaine*.'

The skirmish still raged in the adjacent field, Hampden's greencoats withdrawing to their side of the enclosure, taking a breath, and then charging again. But here, not more than three hundred paces from that anarchic scene, all was calm in the gathering dusk.

'You look well,' Makepeace said, letting his sword hover above Stryker's head. 'Considering I shot you back at the bridge. A remarkable recovery.'

'That was you?' Stryker whispered, an image of a smoke-wreathed assassin resolving in his mind. He remembered the musket shot and the searing pain as the ball clipped his temple. He also remembered that, from such close range, the shot had been a poor one. 'You need practice, Eli.'

Makepeace held up his blade, smiling thinly. 'Not with this.'

Colonel John Hampden was exhausted. He had sent his men into the fray for a fifth time and this, he conceded, must be the last.

The greencoats had done their duty. Two regiments of fine men had fallen by the wayside this day, obliterated by the king's swarm, and yet his, the third to stand before this irresistible force, had held their ground and kept their form.

Hampden turned to a bearded sergeant-major. 'It's damn near dark, George. Our duty was to cover the retreat of Holles and Brooke, while stalling the Cavaliers long enough for night to do our job for us.'

The sergeant-major nodded. 'Sir.'

'You hear that?' Hampden went on. 'Ruthven's orders.' The sound came from the dozen drummers standing at the opposite end of the murky field. From Royalist command. Hampden did not comprehend the exact orders issued forth from those tight, thunderous skins, for they sang out in code, but he understood their implication right enough.

He grinned. 'The buggers are retreating.' He turned to the dishevelled ranks at his command. 'They withdraw from the field, men! It's back to Brentford for the night!'

The men of John Hampden's Regiment of Foot gave their heartiest cheer of the day.

'Sound the order to disengage!' Hampden called to his nearest aide-de-camp. 'We'll remain at Turnham 'til dawn.'

In the grand house at the west end of New Brentford where the road curved toward the River Brent, Chirurgeon Ptolemy Banks was busy tending to the wounded.

The chirurgeon did not turn when the large door swung open, nor did he look round when a pair of burly pikemen staggered in under the weight of the man carried by shoulders and ankles between them.

'I may be Parliamentarian by persuasion,' Banks was

saying through gritted teeth as he pulled at a grimacing man's bare chest with a pair of pliers. 'But the Royalists have requested I take care of you men too, and I ain't the kind of spiteful bastard to deny a man treatment for political reasons. Besides, they'd have shot me if I'd refused.'

The man currently receiving Banks's ministrations was seated on a high-backed wooden chair, his hands gripping the seat below his rump, while another soldier stood stoically behind, holding firm hands at the patient's shoulders so that he could not move.

The patient screamed as Banks gave the pliers a sharp twist and jerked them free.

'There you go, son.' He held up the bloody pliers, which clasped the flattened remains of a musket-ball. 'Looked like the hole was clean in your shirt too, Corporal, so, God willing, you don't have any scraps of fabric to turn your blood bad.'

Banks turned to a small lad, his assistant for the day's action. 'Patch him up, Billy. Don't let it fester.'

Chirurgeon Banks placed his pliers in a little bowl of cloudy red water and picked his way across the wide sheet of linen on which his various tools were laid. 'Who's next?' he said. Just then, he noticed the newcomers. His jaw dropped.

One of the soldiers spoke, 'Found 'im up the road, sir.'

Banks looked at the wounded man, his own face tinged with horror. 'He lives?'

'Aye.'

The chirurgeon waved a scarlet stained hand at the floor. 'Lay him down, man, lay him down.' He went to stand over the still patient. 'His face is badly smashed, but I'll do my best.'

'It ain't the face so much,' the burly soldier said. 'Poor bugger's 'alf drowned.'

Banks knelt down, wiping fingers across the wounded man's brow. When they came away, they were smeared, dark and sticky. He gazed up at the men. 'Evidently not in the Thames.'

The soldier shook his head grimly. 'Found 'im beside a big old vat o' tar.'

Before abandoning his stricken horse, Stryker had thrust a hand into the saddlebag and grasped a small, metal object. It was a pricker, intended for clearing a musket's touch-hole when the weapon became clogged during action. It was sharp and solid, and Stryker had jammed it straight into Makepeace's foot.

The wound was not serious, but Makepeace had staggered back reacting to the unexpected pain, and that had given Stryker time to rise to his feet and draw his own blade.

As the skirmish in the adjacent field had ground to a standstill, Stryker and Makepeace had traded blows in a dozen bursts of snake-fast swordplay. Both heaved on their lungs, dragging air into their bodies as the strength ebbed away.

'I have to hand it to you, *mon Capitaine*,' Makepeace breezed as he regained his composure. 'You're certainly determined. Like an old Irish wolfhound my father once owned. I was hoping Bain had culled your little pack while you were languishing in Wynn's cellar. Decided to drink himself insensible, did he, instead?'

'He decided to die,' Stryker retorted.

'How foolish of him,' Makepeace said bluntly. He

slashed forward with his blade in a nimble move that had his enemy stumbling back rapidly. Stryker parried half a dozen blows and the exertion wrenched at the barely healed wounds that were scattered about his body in a network of pain. The glancing blow from Makepeace's musket-ball had torn the skin along his temple, while the duel was taking its toll on the old wound to his abdomen. It was beginning to pulse fresh gouts of blood, and Makepeace's brown eyes fixed gleefully on the circle of scarlet that bloomed on Stryker's shirt.

'Why are you here, Stryker?' the turncoat sneered. 'Look at yourself. You're bleeding like a gelded boar. You don't care about the Royalists. Leave now, man, and you'll hold your head up high. Turn your back and walk away. You don't need to pursue this any more. Hampden's done his work well. He's held your army too long and they'll be forced to wait out the night. Where do you think the survivors from Brentford have gone?' Stryker remained silent and Makepeace sniggered. 'London! They'll have scuttled all the way back to Devereux and squealed in his ear. And I'll wager you know what that means?'

Stryker's temple throbbed dully and was sickeningly painful. It was all he could do not to slip to his knees and close his eyes.

Makepeace went on with mocking relish. 'This place'll be sick with Parliament's soldiers by sun-up. You've lost, don't you see? If the king ever gets this close to London again, it'll be minus his head!'

Stryker met his gaze and spoke as steadily as he could. 'You have Moxcroft. I need you to give him up.' He glanced over Makepeace's shoulder to catch sight of the spy, still slumped horizontally across the bay's saddle. 'If you won't, it is my duty to take him from you.'

'You really are a gullible sap, Stryker. How many men have you ordered to their deaths for this mission? How much blood must be spilled for your misguided loyalties?'

Stryker gritted his teeth. He raced forward, sweeping his blade down in a heavy blow that took all Makepeace's strength to block. But block it he did, and in less than a heartbeat he had stepped to Stryker's side and forced an equally desperate parry from the long-haired captain that forced him to disengage lest he be outmanoeuvred.

Makepeace was fast, faster even than Stryker remembered, and he had to concentrate hard to keep his focus amid the pains that racked his torso, the sweat that oozed like acid into his eye and the burning in his lungs.

Makepeace looked him up and down. He grinned fiercely. 'You're getting sluggish,' he hissed. 'Old and blind. Not a handy combination, Stryker.'

'And why am I blind, Eli? She was barely more than a child.'

'Ah, but she *was* more than a child, *mon Capitaine*. Young, I grant you, but more than a girl.'

'You stopped to ask her age?'

'I could see she was old enough. And then I found out I was right. She did not resist my attentions, did she?'

'You bastard. When I found you she had no tears left. Nothing. You violated her. Broke her.'

'She grunted with pleasure, *mon Capitaine*. Grunted and moaned and begged for more, I well remember.'

Stryker remembered that day too. It was a week after the horrific and costly Battle of Lutzen, and the English

406

mercenaries who had fought for the victorious Swedes were still encamped around the German countryside. He remembered walking into the Saxony tavern on a bitter November evening, and, even now, could see that poor girl's face. Her chin and neck glistened with her vomit, and her cheeks were bruised and swollen from the fists.

He remembered seeing Bain propped on a stool in the corner of the room. The sergeant had been calmly smoking a long pipe, guarding the door while his officer had his fun. The girl was bent over a table, while Lieutenant Eli Makepeace, his breeches bunched around his heels, thrust violently at the girl's motionless form in front of him.

As Stryker entered, Bain had thrown his pipe down and had reached for the vicious halberd propped at his side, but Stryker's sword was drawn before the gigantic sergeant could fully rise to his feet. The blade's solid guard had smashed into Bain's temple, battering him into his chair and out of consciousness. And then Stryker had turned on Makepeace.

'I still have the scars,' Makepeace hissed.

'You deserved the beating, Eli.'

'Beating? I was barely alive when you left me. It was near a month before I could walk! Still, that month was spent wisely. Gave me time to plan my revenge.' The turncoat's grimace eased into a cruel smile 'And we repaid you a hundredfold.'

Stryker remembered the payment. How his ale had been drugged as he had celebrated the year's turning in a dingy taphouse, and how, in his sluggish state, he had been jumped by the vast Sergeant Bain, battered by fist and cudgel. He remembered waking to find himself bound and gagged at the rear of a small, disused stable, a trail of black powder fizzing across the earthen floor, manically tracing its way toward the stout keg at his side.

'I'll never understand how you survived,' Makepeace said. 'Should have blown you to kingdom come.'

Stryker could not remember with any precision. He knew he had rolled away, desperately wrenching his trussed body across the room as the fuse had run its course. All had become bright for a single, cacophonous moment, before the shroud of black descended.

He remembered waking amid a flood of searing pain in the chirurgeon's quarters in Leipzig, his body monstrous and damaged. And he remembered Lisette Gaillard and her tender ministrations.

'You should have swung for that, Eli,' said Stryker, his voice thick and distant.

'But there was not a scrap of evidence, *mon Capitaine*,' Makepeace replied. 'Of course, *you* knew it was Bain and I. We *wanted* you to know.'

Stryker forced himself to refocus, raising his sword slightly, tempting Makepeace to walk on to its point. 'I'll take Moxcroft and bury your corpse here, in amongst the trees, and no one will ever find you.'

Makepeace's face twitched. Stryker persevered. 'You'll be nothing. Another body rotting in the ground. No one will remember you. No one will mourn.'

Makepeace pounced forward, swinging the long sword in a vast arc that started behind his head and which he intended to finish in the top of Stryker's skull.

Stryker stepped to the side, allowing the blade to slice nothing but air. Makepeace stumbled forward with the weight of the blow, and only just managed to right himself as Stryker attacked. He struck at Makepeace in a series of

sharp, staccato blows that had the red-headed man stepping back, parrying furiously.

Makepeace danced to the side in an impressive turn
of speed, hoping to switch defence into attack, but Stryker
saw what he was about and blocked the Parliamentarian's
low thrust, which might easily have severed the artery
in his groin. They were close now and Stryker slammed
his free fist into Makepeace's mouth, smashing teeth as
the officer's head was snapped back. Makepeace did
not fall, but his face was now a gruesome mask of
blood.

He tried to speak, but pain seemed to grip him as he
opened his jaw.

Makepeace spat a globule of blood, mucus and tooth
that caught on the long blades of grass between them,
dangling in a gelatinous tendril.

Stepping forward, Stryker swung his blade in a
massive sideways blow that, though lacking finesse,
rocked Makepeace to his core as the Parliamentarian's
own steel took the force. Makepeace staggered backwards, his sword arm swinging low at his waist, and
Stryker advanced again. This time he reversed the swing
so that Makepeace had to move his blade across to affect
a back-handed parry. Makepeace was drooling blood
now and grunting with every action. The fight was leaving him, and his defence was weakening with every
movement.

Stryker came on again, delivering three crushing blows
to Makepeace's head in quick succession. The first forced
Makepeace to sink to one knee. The second battered the
sword from his numbed grip. The third cleaved deep into
Makepeace's forearm at the wrist, making him scream in

pain, anger and terror. It was a shrill, pitiful noise that cut across the sounds of the nearby armies like a banshee.

Stryker buried his boot in Makepeace's chest, sending the captain collapsing on to his back.

Makepeace whimpered, words of agony and desperation bubbling incoherently through his shattered mouth. But Stryker ignored his entreaties, tossing his sword to one side and drawing the long dirk from his belt. He moved to kneel beside the wounded man, blood and dew soaking his knee.

'I'll make it quick, Eli,' he said in low, hoarse tones.

Makepeace retched. A thick mass of vomit and blood and spittle and bile boiled up from his throat, turning his mouth into a macabre cauldron, and he twisted to the side to expel the foul liquid. When he turned back his brown gaze was calm as it met Stryker's cold, grey eye. He tried to speak, but his words were so indistinct and quiet that Stryker could barely hear them.

He leaned close, and then the words took form. Makepeace had whispered a name. A name that explained many things and destroyed so many illusions. Stryker momentarily lowered his weapon.

The blade was deep in Stryker's stomach before he felt it.

At first his body made no reaction, and he moved his own dirk toward Makepeace, but then his vision blurred, his guts lurched violently and the strength left his hands. The dirk fell from his grip as surely as if his hand had been severed, and he slumped back on to his haunches in shock. Only then did he notice the handle of the weapon Makepeace had wielded with such venom in his remaining good hand.

Eli Makepeace laughed. One hand was useless, the wrist clouded in steam as hot blood still pumped from it. His face was white, his mouth too damaged to smile.

His movements were painfully slow, as if he were fighting the great current of the Thames, but he managed to heave himself to his feet, gathering up Stryker's discarded sword as he moved.

Stryker tried to rise too, but a flame of agony shot in all directions from his belly to his head and feet and hands, pushing him back to the ground.

Makepeace loomed over him now. 'I hate to leave you,' he said, his voice hoarse, every word an effort, 'but I have a prior engagement, of which you are no doubt aware. Sir Randolph must find his way to London.' He held out the long blade so that its point trembled at Stryker's throat. '*Bon voyage, mon Capitaine.*'

Stryker awaited the killing blow.

But Makepeace's narrow, feral eyes had widened. The two men held each other's gaze for what seemed an eternity, neither speaking, neither moving. And then something began to appear from Makepeace's midriff. Amid his own pain and confusion Stryker did not realize what was happening until the bloody point of a halberd burst through the exquisite purple doublet to glint dark and wet in the evening light.

Makepeace's expression fell blank, his face sagging, the life seeping from him like sap from a tree. He dropped Stryker's sword and, with the pole-arm still protruding through his chest, slumped to his knees.

Behind him stood a dark figure, one who had now released its grip on the long halberd shaft. The shaft dropped to the blood-smeared grass, its weight pulling down on Makepeace's body so that he stayed kneeling, his upper body unnaturally contorted like a grisly marionette. The turncoat's blood pulsed across his torso like the blooming petals of a scarlet flower. His eyes stared blankly into the gathering gloom and his chest groaned in one last, great sigh.

He was gone.

'*Bon voyage, mon Capitaine,*' Lisette Gaillard said quietly.

EPILOGUE

'Liberated from Sir Richard Wynn's magnificent cellar,' General of Horse, Prince Rupert of the Rhine said, raising a crystal glass. He stared at the crimson wine that shone richly within, before glancing up to the man seated opposite. 'I believe you know the cellar in question?'

Captain Stryker, of Sir Edmund Mowbray's Regiment of Foot, caught the glint in the prince's eye and smiled ruefully. 'I spent a little time there, yes sir.'

Rupert sipped the dark liquid, swilling it theatrically, savouring the flavour. He swallowed it down and glanced around the faces assembled at the long, polished table. When he caught the eye of one man in particular, he dipped his head. 'My apologies, Captain Forrester, please continue.'

Lancelot Forrester, cheeks burning bright with the heat, the wine and the eminent company, grinned. 'So we're standing there,' he said, continuing the tale that had been interrupted by the servant's decanter, 'and the goddamned Trained Bands draw up, clear as day, noisy as a tree full of rooks.'

'And they're watching you?' Prince Rupert prompted enthusiastically, enjoying Forrester's flair for storytelling despite having seen the debacle at Turnham Green first-hand.

Forrester nodded. 'Watching and waiting. We look left and we look right and what do we see? Thousands of the rebellious buggers. Thousands!' he shook his head, still shocked by the memory. 'Not just troops, d'you see? Shop-keeps, apprentices, tanners, bakers, every man and his dog!'

Stryker's brow shot up in surprise. 'They didn't attack?'

'Damndest thing, old man,' Forrester continued. 'Must have been twenty-five thousand of 'em and they wouldn't fight. And we could hardly attack, given the struggle we had digging them out of Brentford. Didn't have the stom-ach for it, truth be told. Not neither side.'

A week had passed since Brentford.

Lisette Gaillard had led Stryker back to the Royalist lines. Helping him on to her horse, she had left the dirk in his belly for fear its removal might cause catastrophic bleeding, so he had been forced to sit astride the beast, rather than lie across it. Sir Randolph Moxcroft was still slumped, face-down, across Tainton's gleaming saddle, and the last thing Stryker remembered was looking across at the spy's terrified, pallid face as Lisette had taken that second horse's reins in her hand.

Lisette had commandeered her own horse in pursuit of Stryker. Unlike him, she had not checked whether the aide was carrying despatches, but merely dragged the hapless fellow into the mud, spouting a stream of threats in her native tongue. 'And then I followed you,' she explained. 'You were not hard to track in those wide fields. I just had to be careful not to run into the bloody greencoats.'

That first night was perilous, but the ministrations of the Royal Chirurgeon, ordered to the captain's bedside by Prince Rupert himself, had saved Stryker's life. He spent the first three days – buffeted in the chirurgeon's wagon as the army marched – in a feverish stupor. Occasionally he would respond to a voice he knew with a weak murmur, but efforts to rouse him from unconsciousness had proved fruitless.

Lucidity, when it came, did not spell immediate freedom from danger. For another three days the physicians clucked about him, keeping visitors – all but the fearsome yet charming *mademoiselle* Gaillard – away, valiantly attempting to minimize interference with his steady but fragile recovery. As a result, he did not hear about what had passed at Brentford and its aftermath until considerably later.

Stryker was not released from the chirurgeon's ministrations until the Royalist army reached Reading. Shortly after, he received a summons to dine with Patrick Ruthven, the Earl of Forth.

Stryker now found himself, still slightly shaky, seated opposite Prince Rupert at the great, mirror-like oak table that dominated Ruthven's commandeered quarters, sipping the finest wine and basking in the guttering glow of three-dozen fat candles. He was clothed in his new uniform, purchased with Ruthven's own coin. A blood-red sash with golden trim swathed his torso, from left shoulder to right hip, while his tawny doublet and breeches were of the finest quality. The collar and gorget around his neck complimented his angular – and newly shaven – chin, while his feet were comfortable in the soft leather riding boots that had been a gift from his patron, the prince.

Lisette was at his side, resplendent in a dress that flowed with white frills and winking pearls, and the assembled soldiers, chivalrous though they were, struggled to keep their eyes from her.

Stryker was pleased to see the well-recovered Ensign Burton at the table, the lad's arm still hooked in a tight sling, while the ebullient presence of Forrester made the evening one of good cheer. Sir Jacob Astley was there too, shaking his head in bewilderment, astonished by the story Forrester recounted.

'Forgive me, my lord,' Stryker said tentatively as he finished a mouthful of piping-hot mutton, 'but would it be disrespectful for me to say that Brentford was not the hammer-blow we had hoped?'

The room fell silent. Ruthven leaned forward, his lined face creasing under a heavy scowl. 'Aye, it would, Captain,' he growled. 'But it'd also be right, I'm sorry to say. Our progress through the town and those confounded barricades was slow, painfully slow. In the end, we ran out of time.'

Astley nodded. It had taken far too long to reach the eastern side of the River Brent, and that, coupled with Hampden's determined rearguard action towards Chiswick, had stolen the initiative from the king's forces.

'Those green-coated fellows charged our column five times in all,' Rupert said, not attempting to conceal his admiration for Hampden's men. 'Of course, that should never have set us back the way it did, but our lads were dog-tired. Hampden's were not. He played for time and his policy was successful.'

The armies had disengaged for the night, allowing the Earl of Essex, Parliament's commander-in-chief, to muster his army, ably bolstered by Major General Philip Skippon's London Trained Bands, and block the king's route to the capital.

'And you say the common folk came out, my lord?' Lisette suddenly asked of Ruthven.

'Aye, *mademoiselle*. So they did. Massed in their thousands in the fields about Turnham Green, they were. Shoulder to shoulder with the Roundhead regulars. A veritable sea of bodies. A sea too wide for our brave lads to cross.'

Lisette shook her head in wonderment. 'Such a sight. The common folk rise up against their king? It would be unthinkable in my country.'

Ruthven leant back in his chair. 'Our sacking of the town put their hackles up. They foresaw our lads making a mess of their homes and livelihoods, as they had at Brentford, and it set 'em against us.'

Stryker nodded. He had witnessed the looting of countless towns by victorious armies and was not surprised to hear of this reaction. The capital's citizens had come out in their masses to block the roads. The Royalist army found enemies all around the land at Turnham Green, while informants spoke of armed men at every ditch and hedge, every stable, every barn, every tavern along the road. They described armed ships on the Thames, extensive barricades in the great parks and cannon on every street corner.

'I'd have liked to have fought the traitors there and then,' Prince Rupert, head and shoulders above the assembled guests, chimed in. 'But my uncle was not willing to face such a horde.' He shook his head regretfully. The royal army had retreated from hard-won Brentford, recovering initially to Hounslow Heath and then to Kingston. 'Well, here we are. Reading provides food and shelter enough for now, but we'll be away to Oxford for winter.'

'May I make so bold,' Forrester addressed both prince and earl, 'as to ask why? After all our gains since Kineton Fight, why must we fall back so far as Oxford?'

Rupert pulled a face that suggested he had not agreed with King Charles's decision. 'It is a place my uncle feels to be loyal. It will become his capital until the next campaign season. We retire there for the coldest months, when it is too difficult for our armies to march, and we'll gather strength. When spring arrives, we will return to London with a greater force than Parliament thought possible.'

'Finish what we started at Brentford,' Sir Jacob Astley added in his gruff tone. The others nodded their agreement.

Stryker crammed another piece of the juicy mutton into his mouth and glanced around the room, letting his gaze idly take in bookcases, all packed with precious tomes, and the august figures staring down from fine portraits on the walls.

After Lisette had killed Makepeace and led a wounded soldier and a terrified traitor back to Brentford, she had eventually found Forrester and Skellen. The three of them had delivered Moxcroft to the cellar at Sir Richard Wynn's grand home.

And Sir Randolph Moxcroft, now taken from that impromptu gaol by the king's interrogators to face an uncertain fate, was the reason Stryker was here. Here in this town, here with this wound, with the woman he had thought long dead, and here in the Earl of Forth's private quarters, sipping wine with a prince.

Rupert suddenly thrust back his chair and stood, holding a full glass of the vintage wine aloft. 'Gentlemen,' he said loudly. 'We will pay our respects to Captain Stryker. He was sent at my personal behest to capture a notorious turncoat. You know he succeeded, and the trials he underwent in the process, for he and our new friends Forrester and Burton have enthralled us with their remarkable tale.' That brought a small cheer, Astley thumping the table enthusiastically, and Rupert was forced to raise his free hand for silence. He looked to Stryker, Forrester and Burton in turn. 'I thank you once again on behalf of His Majesty the King. Captain Stryker, you have exceeded your own impressive reputation.' He paused. 'These are turbulent times, gentlemen. We are beset with new enemies on all sides, it would appear.' He met Stryker's eye and his impish grin sparkled again. 'I feel certain we shall have further need of your special services.'

He raised his glass of wine aloft. 'A toast!' Rupert bellowed. 'To Captain Stryker!'

As night settled in, pitch-black and freezing, the assembled guests made their farewells. Stryker took his wide-brimmed hat, with its immaculate red, white and black feathers, and his newly honed sword from a waiting servant and stepped out into the cold, Forrester, Burton and Lisette at his flanks.

As the group paced down the steps of the earl's temporary billet, an austere town house, and reached the road below, the sound of approaching hoof-beats reached them from further along the darkly shadowed street.

Colonel Lord John Saxby drew up beside them, his mount's chest heaving frantically, and dismounted with a leap. 'I . . . I am here, Stryker. I was overseeing the garrison at Wokingham, but received a message to attend upon the prince forthwith.'

As he spoke, a dozen soldiers formed a circle around him and Stryker. Saxby peered with astonishment into the grim faces, and recognized one of them as Sergeant William Skellen.

'Surprised, sir?' Skellen said laconically.

Saxby turned to Stryker for explanation, but Stryker drew his blade in one quick motion that made the colonel jump. Before Saxby could open his mouth to remonstrate, the razorlike tip of the captain's sword was nestled at his throat.

Saxby froze, eyes darting left and right before finally resting on his friend's implacable stare. 'I . . . I say, Stryker,' he stumbled through his words, wincing each time his Adam's apple brushed against the blade's uncomfortable pressure. 'What the devil's happening?' He forced a thin smile. 'You jest with me, sir?'

'No jest, Colonel.'

'Captain Stryker tells me you've been playing the knave, John.'

Saxby did not turn, for fear of the blade nestled below his chin, but he immediately recognized the accent; perfect English, with the tuneful lilt of the Netherlands and a hint of Bohemian iron. 'There is some mistake here, Your Highness.'

Prince Rupert moved down from the steps to stand beside Stryker. 'Captain Stryker and I have been acquainted for many years, and I trust his word.'

Stryker applied pressure to the sword, making Saxby wince. 'And my word is that you are a spy, my lord. The man who almost ensured Moxcroft's safe passage to the enemy.'

'I . . . I do not know what you are saying, Stryker,' Saxby stammered. 'You have evidence of some kind?'

'Your own agent told me.'

Saxby turned his desperate gaze to the prince. 'You take the word of a mere captain over mine?'

Stryker jabbed the point of his blade into the skin beneath Saxby's chin, ensuring he regained the lord's attention. 'You were Blake's master. Forde's master. You sent Makepeace to Langrish, didn't you, Colonel?'

'Preposterous!' Saxby brayed, eyes darting rapidly in search of escape.

Stryker's face was implacable. 'Makepeace told me it was you, sir,' he said. 'He thought he had bested me, and would taunt me with the identity of his master.' Stryker glanced at Lisette. 'Only Makepeace died, and I survived.'

'Your evidence comes from a man now cold in the ground?'

Stryker ignored him. 'I admit, Colonel, it was hard to believe. But then I remembered you were present at the council at Banbury. One of a tiny elite who knew I was being sent to Hampshire and why.'

Saxby remained silent, but his shoulders sagged.

'Why, John?' Rupert asked, his voice taut with distress.

Saxby shook his head slowly, his eyes shining like hot coals in the dim street. 'The world changes. The old ways will be replaced. God means to lead this country in a new direction.' He glared from face to face in turn. 'England is destined to be a republic. Our corrupt monarchy must be destroyed.'

Stryker remembered the execution he had witnessed after Edgehill. 'Our pieces are in place. At the very heart of your army. That's what Captain Forde said.'

'His words were truer than we guessed,' Rupert replied. 'My God; and I thought he spoke of Blake.'

'Blake was nothing,' Saxby said. 'A pawn.' He grinned suddenly. 'I am not afraid. The Lord's hand guides this rebellion. It is blessed. My trial will merely allow me to spread the word of King Charles's corruption. The people will hear and join Parliament in their masses.'

'No,' Rupert said quietly. 'There will be no platform, Colonel.' He turned to Sergeant Skellen. 'Leave no trace.'

'I am surprised you did not ride for the coast the moment the battle was over,' Stryker said as they reached the far side of the road. He and Lisette were alone, pacing slowly along the street arm in arm.

'I could not see you take all the credit.' She frowned. 'What will happen now? In the war, I mean.'

Stryker thought for a moment then shrugged. 'It will continue. Brentford was a chance to end the conflict, but we let it slip through our fingers. Parliament will take heart from what happened at Turnham Green and they'll be yet more formidable as the new year turns.'

'More battles then? More killing?'

'Aye, I should say.'

'You will be in your element,' she said mockingly.

'As will you,' he retorted quickly.

Lisette laughed. '*Touché, monsieur.*'

Stryker stood still, leaning close, his voice low. 'What of the ruby? Will it really fetch such a price in Europe as to buy the king his vast army?'

Lisette shook her head. 'No.' Stryker stopped in his tracks. 'Do not misunderstand me, *mon amour*, it *is* a gem of extraordinary value.' She leaned close to, fishing in the neckline of her dress. In moments she had produced a small, wrinkled piece of parchment, which she unfolded with great care. 'But *this* is what I was sent for. I did not know it, and most of the rebels who guarded it did not know either. But the thief must have.'

Stryker frowned, considering the implication. 'Saxby?'

'Perhaps. But I would not wish him questioned,' she said, handing Stryker the parchment, 'for none must know of this. It is worth more than all the gems in Whitehall Palace.'

Stryker cast his grey eye across the parchment's brief lines of black text. He laughed suddenly. 'It is a love letter.'

Lisette nodded. 'From a king to a queen. Very romantic.'

Stryker read the letter again, and a third time. It was a letter in the hand of King Charles, expressing his undying devotion to Queen Henrietta Maria. He was about to hand the parchment back to Lisette, when his eye caught the very last line again, and he understood.

'I pray the Holy Mother will keep you safe and guide you always,' he read aloud.

Stryker stared at Lisette.

'Just a single line,' the Frenchwoman said. 'But in rebel hands—'

'In rebel hands,' Stryker said slowly, 'it would be devastating. The ultimate proof of the king's papist sympathies. He could try denying it. Say he was merely appealing to his wife's sensibilities.'

'But the damage would be done, *mon amour*. It is in his own hand. That would be enough.'

423

'My God,' Stryker whispered. 'No wonder they stole it. Little wonder the queen was so desperate to have it back.'

'And you see why I was sent to recover it? A rebel named Kesley told me they were keeping the ruby hidden until it could be removed from England. I believe the letter would have stayed, found its way to the printing presses. But they were keeping it safe, to use only in the direst time.'

Stryker nodded. 'A final gambit to use if the war turned against them.'

'You see why the queen could not trust an Englishman with this. Not when his religious beliefs appear to change with each tide.'

Stryker laughed, pushing the parchment back into Lisette's grasp. 'It will go to The Hague?'

Lisette nodded firmly. 'It will. The ship leaves at dawn. I would rather see it burnt to ash, but it is precious to my queen.'

Stryker felt a pang of sorrow. 'And you?'

She looked down, unable to meet his gaze, and when he lifted her chin so that the blue eyes stared straight at him, they were glistening with tears. 'I sail too.'

He smiled sadly. It was the answer he knew would come. 'I am to lose you again.'

'No,' Lisette shook her head. 'I must go to Queen Henrietta, for I am bound to her as you now are to Prince Rupert. I will do my duty. But I love you. As God is my witness.'

They walked, arms tightly interlinked, back to the men gathered at the steps below Ruthven's billet. 'Must you leave tonight?' Stryker asked.

She nodded. 'But I have one more thing to say.' She raised her voice so the others could hear. 'One more dark secret you must all know, lest my ship founder and the knowledge be lost forever.'

'*Mademoiselle* Gaillard?' asked Prince Rupert, his voice curious.

Lisette leaned forward, hooking her arms around Stryker's neck, pulling him close. And then they were kissing; long, warm, luxurious.

She released her arms, and was striding away before Stryker had even begun to regain his wits. The men stared after her. When she was thirty or so paces away, she turned back, her voice carrying down the road to them. 'Captain Stryker's name, good sirs. His Christian name. The name, gentlemen, is *Innocent*.'

And she was gone, vanished into the darkness.

'Innocent Stryker?' Prince Rupert said thoughtfully.

It was dark and it was cold, but the night was suddenly merry with the sound of raucous laughter.

ACKNOWLEDGEMENTS

This book would never have seen the light of day without the help and support of a number of people.

I am greatly indebted to my agent Rupert Heath, for his unswerving belief in the Stryker Chronicles from the very start, and to everyone at John Murray for their support and enthusiasm. Special thanks go to my editor Kate Parkin, for her invaluable advice and for steering me towards a smarter, leaner story.

I would also like to thank Malcolm Watkins of Heritage Matters for casting an expert eye over the manuscript, Simon Wright of the Sealed Knot for taking the time to answer some of my questions around regimental hierarchy and, as promised a decade ago, I must thank my friend Gus for telling me to get off my backside and write a 'proper' novel.

My poor parents have bravely waded through the reams of pretty terrible prose I've churned out over the years. For that, and for their pearls of wisdom, their dependability and their constant encouragement, I am truly grateful And last, but absolutely not least, much love and gratitude go to my wife Rebecca and my son Joshua, for just being there when I need them.

HISTORICAL NOTE

The period generally known as the English Civil War was, in reality, a conflict made up of three distinct wars, spanning the years 1642 to 1651, and encompassing the entire British Isles. This was arguably the most pivotal era in British history, a time that saw the death of feudalism, the birth of constitutional monarchy and the beginnings of a national standing army.

The events described in *Traitor's Blood* take place at the beginning of the First Civil War. On the evening of 22 October 1642, the armies of King Charles and the Earl of Essex blundered into one another. The following morning, the first major engagement of the English Civil War was fought below the ridge at Edgehill, Warwickshire. Often referred to as 'Kineton Fight', the battle was marked by incredible heroism, abject cowardice and levels of military expertise touching both ends of the spectrum. Edgehill ended in stalemate with both sides claiming victory, though King Charles perhaps took what advantage there was by securing the road to London.

Following the battle, and after taking Banbury and Oxford, the latter becoming Charles's headquarters for the remainder of the conflict, the Royalists advanced on

London along the Thames Valley. On 12 November a large detachment took advantage of a thick mist and attacked two Parliamentarian regiments quartered in Brentford – Holles's redcoats and Brooke's purplecoats – covering the approach to the city from the west.

I have alluded to a certain amount of confusion within Holles's ranks at the start of the fight, due to their belief that a truce had been signed. While there was not strictly a truce, the king had agreed to meet a Parliamentarian delegation for peace talks at Colnbrook. It seems he ordered the attack on Brentford – thereby positioning his army within easy striking distance of London – as a means to strengthen his position at the negotiating table.

I have described the battle as accurately as possible, with fighting concentrated first at the house of Sir Richard Wynn, and then at barricades erected at the bridge over the River Brent and along the road at the western end of Old Brentford. The fighting was hard, bloody and at close quarters throughout. John Gwyn, a soldier serving in Sir Thomas Salusbury's Welsh Regiment of Foot, described Royalist tactics: 'after once firing suddenly to advance up to push of pikes and the butt end of muskets'.

The second barricade proved extremely difficult for the Royalists to overcome. They sent regiments forward to attack in turn, and it was only after the sixth – that of Sir Edward Fitton – had engaged that it finally gave way. The Parliamentarians were routed, and then pursued by Rupert's cavalry who had ridden around the town to outflank them. In desperation, many took their chances swimming the Thames, and though reports of exact numbers differ wildly, perhaps as many as two hundred were drowned in the attempt.

The Royalists were eventually victorious and Brentford subjected to what became a notorious sacking, but their army was severely delayed by the dogged Parliamentarian resistance described in *Traitor's Blood*. To the east of the town they encountered the fresh troops of John Hampden's regiment. Though vastly outnumbered, Hampden's green-coats charged the exhausted Royalist army five times, keeping the larger force at bay until the light finally faded. This delay allowed the Parliamentary field army and London militia to muster on Turnham Green the following day, thereby halting the king's advance.

This would be the closest Charles would ever come to London during the course of the war. When, seven years after the events of *Traitor's Blood*, he eventually returned, it would be for trial and execution.

All the locations in the book are real, and can be visited today. The magnificent Tudor palace of Basing House came under Parliamentarian attack on three occasions during the First Civil War, and its fascinating, if rather haunting, remains are well worth seeing. I won't detail Basing's fortunes here, as I have a feeling Stryker may play a part in the forthcoming action, but the final story of this Royalist stronghold in the heart of rebel territory is one of excitement, violence and heroism that I look forward to telling.

Langrish House (now a hotel) was built early in the seventeenth century. While Sir Randolph Moxcroft is a fictional character, it is believed the house's true owners were probably of Parliamentarian persuasion, to which its series of subterranean vaults, carved out by Royalist prisoners after the battle of Cheriton in 1644, seem to testify.

Old Winchester Hill, to the north-west of Portsmouth, is now a nature reserve. It is, as I have described, crowned by an imposing Iron Age hill fort, but the events involving that fort are entirely fictional. There is certainly no evidence that it was used in any capacity during the war.

Captain Stryker did not fight at Edgehill, nor did he face Brentford's barricades, and there was no Forrester or Skellen, Makepeace or Lisette, but the wars have highlighted the lives of many similarly colourful and very real characters. Of these, perhaps the most fascinating is Prince Rupert of the Rhine. A giant, both physically and metaphorically, the king's nephew (just twenty-two years of age during the events of *Traitor's Blood*) was one of the most dazzling, reckless, loved and vilified figures of the entire period. His exploits – ranging from army general to naval admiral, inventor, and renowned tennis player – are too numerous to list here, but I heartily recommend Charles Spencer's biography *Prince Rupert: The Last Cavalier* (Phoenix, 2008) to anyone who might wish to learn more about Rupert's incredible life.

While I have attempted to make *Traitor's Blood* as true to history as possible, there will be the odd inaccuracy hidden among these pages. For this I apologise. All mistakes are, of course, my own.

And what now for Stryker and his men? The war is just beginning and there is much for them to do. There are many old enemies to be encountered, battles to be fought and new foes to meet as they march into the bloody turmoil of 1643.

Captain Stryker will return.

DEVIL'S CHARGE

MICHAEL ARNOLD

England stands divided: king against Parliament,
town against country, brother against brother.

For Captain Stryker, scarred hero of a dozen wars, the
rights and wrongs of the cause mean little. His loyalties
are to his own small band of comrades – and to Queen
Henrietta Maria's beautiful and most deadly agent,
Lisette Gaillard. So when Prince Rupert entrusts him
with a secret mission to discover what has happened to
Lisette and the man she was protecting – a man who
could hold the key to the Royalist victory – nothing,
not false imprisonment for murder, ambush, a doomed
siege or a lethal religious fanatic, will stand in his way.

Now read on . . .

www.michael-arnold.net

PROLOGUE

It was a good place for an ambush. The road was turned to swamp by a night-long deluge, making the going desperately slow, while at its flanks grew thick forests shrouded in a mist that made the great trunks seem like sentries guarding an otherworldly realm. Indeed, it was a very good place for an ambush.

Three men, waiting expectantly in the murky half-light beneath the bough of an ancient oak, glanced at one another. They had all heard the distant rumble of wheels, and hoof beats cut into the dawn. Finally the coach was here. Finally they could set about their work.

The tallest of the three, a middle-aged man of impressive stature and pallid, warty complexion, swallowed hard. He was not a man given to anxiety, but this assignment had burrowed its way beneath his skin like a tick.

He forced himself to study the bend in the road, anxious for the coach to appear, but was startled as one of the advancing horses whinnied from the depths of the gloom. He thumped his thigh viciously, angry at his own timidity, and glanced again at his companions. Like him they were prepared for the morning's work: black-clad, heavily armed and resolute.

'Ready?' he hissed, running gloved fingers quickly over the firing mechanism of his musket. 'Remember,' he added, neck sinews convulsing in violent spasm as he spoke, 'the Lord guides us. He sends our fire true and deadly. We do *His* work. We cannot fail.'

The others nodded, fingering their own weapons.

His confidence growing, the leader strode out from the shelter of the oak and approached the edge of the road. The ground sucked at his boots, though he was thankful the sleety rain had finally abated. As he took up a kneeling position, chilling damp immediately stabbing at his knee, he silently praised God for giving him the foresight to use firelocks instead of matchlocks. He cocked the weapon; there would be no tell-tale matchlight for his prey to spy in the darkness.

Two more sharp clicks nearby told him that his men had made their own weapons ready.

The leader stared back at the road, his body tense as he waited for the coach to appear. It was close now, and he knew the sound of bouncing wheels and pounding hooves would be thunderously loud, but he could hear only the rushing of blood in his own ears. And then, like a ghoulish apparition, the coach horses finally materialised from the darkness, their eyes floating like something conjured by witchcraft, nostrils flaring as they pumped gouts of swirling steam into the air around their heads. And there, careening along in the wake of the furious animals, was the prey.

'Now!' the tall man snarled, squeezing the firelock's well-oiled trigger. It eased back smoothly, as he knew it would, and the dawn was shattered by the scream of a dying horse.

The second and third muskets cracked into life, and their leaden balls whipped across the short range before the coach driver had time to react, slamming into the terrified animals, sending blood spraying into the grey air and across the sodden road. The horses stumbled, fell and rolled, and the coach clattered across their broken bodies, throwing the driver and the roof-stacked baggage skywards.

The vehicle itself seemed to take flight for an instant, gliding almost serenely above the bullet-riddled beasts, but then it crashed down in a symphony of splintered wood, sliced chains and shattered axles. The wheels came away as though the coach was no more than a child's toy, speeding madly into the undergrowth at the road's verge, and the carriage, now simply a large box, hit the ground, skidding across the mud, spinning once, twice, until it left the road and slammed into the trunk of a gnarled tree.

The tall man stood up, discarding his spent musket and reaching for the spare that was slung on his back. 'Tom!'

'Sir!' the response came from somewhere to the rear.

The leader did not look back, but called over his shoulder as he began to run towards the battered carriage, 'See to the driver! Micky!'

'Aye, Major!' the second man replied.

'With me!'

As he reached what was left of the vehicle, tall major cocked and levelled his second firelock, pointing it at the deeply scratched door. 'Out!' he called.

Nothing stirred. No voices called, nor figures emerged.

'Shall I?' Micky asked, eagerly.

The major nodded. 'Bring him out.'

Micky, a stocky man whose eye level did not even reach

437

his superior's shoulders, raised his musket and stepped forward carefully. He shoved the black barrel through the window of the coach and called again. Still no response. Micky leaned in, poking his head through the frame to inspect the dead passenger within.

The shot which followed almost immediately was more like an explosion within the confines of the coach. From several paces away, the major saw only the bright orange flash, followed by a black pall of smoke that billowed manically out of the windows, rising quickly to mingle with the bare branches of the surrounding oaks. And with the smoke came Micky's heavy torso, flung back with so much force it was as though God himself had slapped him.

The major looked in disbelief and horror as Micky came to rest in the sopping grass and rotten bracken, his face a mess of torn flesh and gushing blood. He raced forward, yanked open the battered door, wisps of dirty smoke still playing around him, and shoved his musket into the gloomy interior, pulling the trigger as he did so.

The ball thudded home, tearing a hole in one of the empty seats. Of the passenger there was no sign.

The major had made great efforts to cleanse his language since the true faith had cleansed his soul, but now he screamed his fury to the dawn in a stream of oaths. He cast down the empty firelock, twisting away to snatch up Micky's still-loaded weapon, and bolted into the dense forest after his quarry.

He kept his step artificially high to avoid tripping on the winter debris, praying aloud with each breathless moment, beseeching Christ to forgive his failure and show him the path his enemy had taken.

And there, some twenty paces ahead, lumbering like a terrified bullock between bent trunks and beneath the grabbing claws of branches, was the man he had come to kill. The fat, sweating, despicable, popish excuse for a man he had dreamt of dispatching for so long. But to his surprise, he saw a second person in the misty distance. A slighter, hooded figure, gripping a pistol in one hand. The other hand tore at the fat man's bulky arm, urging him on, forcing him deeper into the mist's protection.

The major wondered then at Tom's whereabouts, for he had but a single shot, and could not hope to take down both fugitives, but the report of a musket somewhere to his left told him that the young man was still busy making an end of the coach driver.

He would have to choose which of the two fleeing figures was to die. The thought rankled for, though the fat man was his intended target, he dearly wished to put a bullet in Micky's killer. He resolved to place duty before vengeance. He halted, levelled Micky's firelock and finding his target along its slim barrel, pulled the trigger.

For a moment the fugitives vanished in the cloud of smoke that belched from the musket. But the major knew his business and was confident of the shot. As the scene cleared, he thanked God for His provenance. Only the thinner figure was weaving its way further into the safety of the wood.

'Driver's a dead 'un, Major,' a voice broke into the tall man's thoughts.

The major turned, seeing Tom emerge from the trees to his left. 'Well done, lad.'

Tom frowned. 'You get him, sir?'

'I did. Praise the good Lord, I did.'

Tom squinted as he scanned the land before them. He saw the distant figure disappear into the depths of the forest, his form gradually swallowed by the mist. 'There were two?'

'Aye, there were. Romish coward had a bodyguard.'

'Shall I go after 'im?' Tom asked eagerly.

The major scratched a wart on his pointed chin. He shook his head. 'We shan't catch him now. Let him go. Our work today is done.' He turned away.

Tom stared after him. 'Today, sir?'

'Sir Samuel gave us two targets,' the major replied, not looking back. 'Lazarus is no more. Now we must locate the other. Fetch the horses, Corporal.'

CHAPTER 1

It was perhaps three hours after midnight, and the town was still and silent. The sky was crammed with thick, grey clouds, and the earth was ankle-deep in snow. The scant moonlight danced brightly on the sparkling white blanket, illuminating streets and rooftops with an ethereal glow.

And gliding like a wraith in that strange half light, shoulders hunched, eyes keenly attentive, was a tall, cloaked man. He moved swiftly along the outside of the town's ramshackle defences, tracing the path of the ancient walls, the legacy of a long-since fallen empire, rows of densely packed streets always on his left, fields and hills rising away to the right. He was wary of patrols, acutely aware of the fatal consequences capture would bring.

At length he came to a halt where the crumbling walls had been built up with new stone, topped with wooden stakes to form a makeshift palisade. This, he remembered, was where the road from the south-west pierced the town limits. He stared into the darkness for several moments, until he was able to discern the road from the fields at its flanks. There was a pile of rubble nearby, left over from the day's frantic rebuilding, and the man dropped down, and scrambling towards it on hands and knees. Here, in this place of relative concealment, he scrutinized the road, eyes straining to distinguish its path, until his gaze settled on a group of shapes some three hundred paces away. They resolved into walls, buildings, rooftops. A farm.

'There she is,' he whispered.

The man waited for a few moments, ensuring there were no movements on the exposed ground between his hiding place and the distant buildings, before breaking forward again. He ran beside the road, following it away from the town walls, praying silently – desperately – that he would not be seen. He reached the farm's outer wall, dropping with his back against it, chest heaving rhythmically, yearning for his nerves to calm. Footsteps crunched through the brittle snow nearby. They were shockingly close, the other side of the wall, and he held his breath sharply, gritting his teeth as icy air needled labouring lungs.

The steps seemed to be heading away from his position, but then, in a moment of utter terror, he heard voices to his right. They had circled round, and were now on his side of the wall. Like ghostly apparitions, their bodies gradually resolved from the night just a few paces away. There were half a dozen; soldiers all. Lord Stamford's men. They stood chatting, a couple leaning on the very wall he was crouched beside. He smelled the smoke from their pipes, heard their inane banter.

He did not move, praying the soldiers would fail to notice him in his shadowy place. He allowed air into his lungs again, for fear they would burst, but kept his breathing shallow, lest he send plumes of vapour into the air like a hideous beacon.

The soldiers did not spot him. He heard them speak of the large force camped a mile from the hastily bolstered walls of this newly garrisoned farmyard, but they were not expecting the enemy to be sneaking about on this side of their pickets.

The soldiers left, heading towards the farm's central cluster of buildings, and the ghostly figure was finally able to edge out of his protective shadows.

He reached the farm's first structure, flattening himself against its wattle-and-daub wall, and edging carefully to peer out beyond the gable end. Satisfied there were no more patrols, nor common folk abroad that might accidentally catch sight of him, the figure took his first steps into the dangerously exposed area between the farmhouse and its outbuildings.

A screech startled him before he had taken a dozen strides, and his stomach twisted violently, but no soldiers burst from secret hiding places, no priming pans flared, no halberds sliced at his head. As his pulse settled, and the prickling of skin began to fade, he realised with a gush of relief that the sound was not human. Perhaps a fox, perhaps not, but certainly not the alarm his anxious mind had conjured.

Pulling the long cloak tighter about his shoulders, the man set forth once again, this time at a run. His goal was up ahead, less than twenty paces away, and the sooner he reached it the sooner this damnable mission would be complete.

A stout barricade was the target. The farm sat adjacent to the south-west road and, on hearing of the enemy's return, Stamford's men had decided that it would make the most logical place of defence. They had erected a barrier of stakes, wagons and bushels, of old fences and of commandeered furniture and, as an attacking force spent their energy against its dense strength, the defenders would pour fire upon them from the walls and buildings of the farm complex.

He reached the makeshift barricade without obstruction and studied the tightly packed array of objects it comprised. Presently his eyes fixed upon a large cart, stacked full of mouldering hay. It was wedged at the very centre of the temporary defensive work. The vehicle had been destined for the town the previous evening as dusk had closed in. But the soldiers manning the ever-growing barricade had stepped into the road, unbridled the two scrawny oxen and ignored the driver's pleas.

'Please, sirs,' the old man, bent and withered by age, had spluttered through a wracking cough that sent large globules of spittle to rest on the settling snow. 'Please, sirs, have mercy! She's me livelihood: I'll perish without her to carry me wares.'

The sentries had been deaf to his appeal, stating in surly tones that the rickety vehicle would be used for the good of the town. He had grasped at their sleeves, begged them to relent, but they just thrust him aside.

The old man had wept. 'Jus' let me warm these old bones while the snow falls,' he had pleaded. 'Let me find shelter in the town, sirs.'

The sentries had growled and cursed their displeasure at the old fool's ramblings, for no pilgrims were to be granted freedom of the town while the great army threatened its very existence, but it was snowing hard and they

444

had no wish to stand and argue when they could be warming their hands at the farm's hearths.

'I swear I'll not see mornin' else,' the old man had whined, though the sergeant in command was already stalking back to the shelter of his billet, thinking of the plump whore waiting within.

'I want you gone by this time on the morrow,' he had barked over his shoulder at the cart's driver. 'Dusk on the morrow, you old palliard, hear me?'

The snowfall had faded since then, and the carter had found an inn. But after the tired oxen were led away by a spotty stable boy, the carter had not slept and had taken only small beer. Instead of resting, he sharpened the dirk hitherto concealed within a filthy boot, and rather than sheltering from the foul weather, he had waited for the dead of night and crept out into the snow once more.

The man was not old. Nor was he infirm, though it had pleased him to give that impression to the sentries. He was a man of war: a *petardier*. Now, as he crunched his way across the last few paces and climbed up into the cart, burrowing his way beneath the damp, snow-encrusted hay, nostrils overwhelmed by the ripe stench of purification, the petardier knew that the wheels of victory had been set in motion. He almost pitied the rebellious townsfolk. Almost.

— m —

Captain Innocent Stryker, of Sir Edmund Mowbray's Regiment of Foot, was not a pious man. Indeed, he was not sure he believed in any higher power than a loaded gun and a keen blade. But today he prayed. He prayed for a white flag. He yearned to see it flutter tentatively from the town's beleaguered walls, a grimy symbol of the citizens' submission. But, as he watched the black funnels of smoke thicken as they rose from the defenders' belching artillery to smudge the pale horizon, he knew that God would not answer his prayer.

One of Stryker's officers came to stand at his shoulder. A man whose fluff-covered upper lip was at odds with his confident bearing and weather-beaten skin. Andrew Burton might have still been in his teens, but he had seen more fighting than most men witnessed in a lifetime. His right arm was withered, propped close against his ribcage within a tight leather sling, the shoulder shattered months earlier by a pistol ball. 'Men are ready, sir,' Burton said, glancing back at the ranks. 'It's past noon. Will we advance, do you think?'

Stryker removed his hat, fiddling with the once bright feathers at its band, careful to have them in good order for the inevitable assault. Somehow it was important. 'Imminently, Lieutenant.'

Burton stared at the earthworks hedging the town. 'I had hoped we might pound them a while,' he said wistfully.

'Aye,' Stryker agreed. Royalist ordnance had softened the town's resolve during late morning, the damage becoming increasingly visible amid the low rooftops, but here, at the south-western entrance, the defences were left unscathed. 'It seems the prince will require an escalade.' He regarded the younger man with interest. 'Frightened?'

Burton's neck convulsed as he swallowed thickly. 'Aye, sir.'

'All is well then,' Stryker said. 'You'll not get yourself killed for misplaced bravery.'

'Sir?'

'The colonel did not promote you so that you could dash away your life against this damned town's barricades. Caution, Andrew. There'll be time enough for valour, lad, but you must choose your moment.'

Lieutenant Burton nodded solemnly, and paced back to the men at his command. Stryker frowned slightly. His protégé had proven himself more than once since joining Stryker on their suicidal mission to arrest Sir Randolph Moxcroft in the weeks after Kineton Fight, and had been rewarded for his bravery and rapidly increasing skill, but a streak of recklessness had also shown itself. Burton was now second in command of the company. Stryker needed a man with a level head as much as he needed one of stout heart.

The drums rolled.

They rumbled low and ominous across the snow-blanketed fields, lingering in echo as they climbed the white summits of hills beyond.

Stryker studied the nearest buildings. They were not within the town's dilapidated walls, but outside, straddling the road. It was, he had been told, a small farm known as The Barton. It was there that the defenders would stage their first attempt to repel the closing horde. By the look of the old Roman walls that surrounded the town, he imagined The Barton would be the most difficult obstacle. Once they were beyond it, the town would quickly fall. He wondered whether the inhabitants had had the good sense to bury their valuables and flee into those high, sheep-crowded crests. Somehow he doubted it.

'Capital of the Cotswolds,' Captain Lancelot Forrester

said as he came to stand at Stryker's side. All but Colonel Mowbray had dismounted for the day's action, the horses corralled at the rear by the dour Wagon-Master Yalden.

Stryker's thin lips twitched in amusement as he acknowledged Forrester. 'Not much to crow about, is it?'

'Perhaps not,' Forrester agreed, absently fingering the gold trim of his blood-red sash.

Stryker frowned. 'Should you not be with your lads?'

'They're neat, tidy and ready for the off, old boy, worry not!' Forrester exclaimed brightly. He had been with Stryker and Burton on that terrible mission the previous autumn, had shared those same dangers and carved his own swathe though the hellish barricades of New and Old Brentford. His reward had been the posting of his choice, and the death of Mowbray's fourth captain in a skirmish outside Banbury had provided a vacant position serving with his old comrade.

Stryker stared down the line of pike and musket to cast an appraising eye over his friend's new command. 'A good group, Forry. You've done well with them.'

'Kind of you to say,' Forrester said simply, though his big cherubic face became a little pink. He hastily rummaged in the snapsack slung at his shoulder, eventually plucking out a short, tooth-worn clay pipe.

Stryker's lone brow shot up. 'You lost the game, Forry.'

Forrester glanced at the pipe. 'I did, I did. And I had not forgotten the forfeit.'

'No sotweed for a month.'

Forrester propped the pipe stem in the corner of his mouth. 'The chirurgeon prescribed it for reasons of health.' He pulled a hurt expression. 'You would have me

448

give up tobacco, to the detriment of my lungs, for a little game of dice?'

Stryker laughed and turned back to point towards The Barton. Forrester followed his companion's gaze as he touched a smouldering length of match to the pipe bowl, eyes resting on the walls of stacked clods and stout barrels that formed the deep works. Those works were crowned by a palisade of sharpened stakes, behind which would doubtless be as many immovable objects as the townsfolk could gather. He remembered this method of defence from that terrible day west of London where the men of Holles and Brooke had proved so damnably difficult to shift.

'Bloody waste to dash them against those works,' Stryker said bluntly.

Forrester sighed, cheeriness eroding. 'I'd prayed we'd avoid a climb.'

'Prayed?' Stryker said, failing to keep the surprise from his tone. 'Hardly a religious man, are you?'

Forrester smiled weakly, pipe smoke wreathing his round face. 'No, I'm not. But when faced with imminent death, one's thoughts do turn to one's saviour.'

Stryker kept his tongue still, though he could not help but agree.

'The good news,' Forrester added, forcing brightness back into his voice, 'is that they're seriously under strength.'

Stryker knew that was true, and knew that he should have been elated by the news, but the prospect of witnessing the town's inevitable demise was not one he relished. Once the Royalist force had breached The Barton and the ancient walls beyond, they would give no quarter to those inside. He let out a heavy breath that obscured his face in roiling vapour. 'Why do they not surrender, damn them, and save us all a bloodbath?'

'Parliament heartland, Stryker. The good citizens are misguided souls, harbouring rebel sympathies. Every man-jack of 'em. The whole shire's rife with it.' Forrester chuckled blackly. 'Like French-Welcome in a bawdy house.'

Stryker turned to him. 'The townsfolk will fight?'

Forrester nodded slowly, ruddy cheeks bright. 'No bloody doubt about it. When they turned the prince away last month they declared they would die for the "true religion".' He blew out his cheeks at the thought of the day's almost inevitable bloodletting. 'They're ready for the slaughter, Stryker. Now Stamford's buggered off with most of his men to Sudeley Castle, and he's mired in snow and mud. They'll never make it back in time. So the town has what's left of his force bolstering the walls, while the streets'll be lined with pitchfork-wielding peasants.'

Stryker shook his head. 'God's teeth.'

Forrester shrugged. 'Worry not, Stryker, we'll be warming our arses by their hearths in short order.'

'It's not the assault that worries me most, Forry, but what follows.' He looked back to the settlement and the buildings huddled within, remembering well the horrors inflicted on so many similar towns and villages in Germany and the Low Countries. 'Bloody town.'

Cirencester had grown rich from its wool, and sat between Charles's new court at Oxford and his hotbed of support in Wales and Cornwall. It was a fat, juicy apple, crying out to be plucked. But if its wealth and geography made it a logical prize for the Royalist army, a forthright defiance of the king had made Cirencester a personal target for their commander, Prince Rupert. So he had brought a horde to its walls. Stryker knew the price to be paid for defying men like Rupert of the Rhine. By dusk, so would the folk of Cirencester.

'*Bloody, bloody* town.'

Cirencester was surrounded. Prince Rupert held a large division of horse, dragoons and foot, of which Mowbray's men formed only a fraction, before the town's south-west entrance. There were several units further out on the Stroud road and, Stryker knew, more bristling companies to the east. On the road leading south-west towards Bristol, Lord Wentworth had three companies of infantry, one of dragoons and one of light cavalry, while to the north-east, in the direction of Sudeley and Winchcombe, the Earl of Carnarvon led a similar number. It was a force to be reckoned with.

The Royalist artillery had pounded away with little reply as the assault troops moved into position, gnawing at the defences, reducing them from nothing more than a display of pitiful insolence. If the attackers were able to force their way inside the town, it would be short work, Stryker knew, for the remains of Stamford's troops would be spread pathetically thin manning the perimeter of the town, while patching up the myriad breaches in the fortifications.

'And all the while Robert the Devil intends to gallop straight through the main gate,' Forrester's well-educated tones startled Stryker from his thoughts.

'You read my mind,' Stryker said grimly, taking the pipe from Forrester and inhaling deeply. Carnarvon would lead an assault against Spitalgate to the north while,

451

according to the orders hammered out by Rupert's drummers, the prince would take his cavalry directly through The Barton and on into the town. The strategy baffled Stryker for, though entering Cirencester by the south-west road was the shortest route to the town's heart, a cavalry charge against the only heavily fortified point in the relatively weak perimeter seemed futile.

'You try and teach prudence to the youth of today,' Forrester went on, snatching back the tobacco-filled clay stem and twitching his head at Lieutenant Burton, 'and our good commander proves himself entirely devoid of the stuff.'

Stryker's laugh was more like a bark. 'Aye, the prince has a way about him. They won't expect him to make for the front door.'

'The surprise alone'll win him the day, I'd wager. He's mad, Stryker. Quite mad.'

'But you're glad he's on our side,' Stryker replied.

Forrester slapped his friend on the back. 'I thank God for it daily!'

'And I thank Him for the two of you, though I can't comprehend why, what with all your whining!'

Forrester's face turned cherry red with embarrassment as Prince Rupert of the Rhine reined in behind the officers. The young General of Horse seemed like a giant atop his great stallion, an impression only enhanced by his russetted armour and thick buff coat. The portly captain stared up at King Charles's nephew, snatching off his hat in rapid salute to reveal sandy hair that only made his cheeks appear more livid. He stuttered the beginnings of an apology, but the prince stopped him with a great bellow of laughter. 'At your ease, Captain Forrester! We will indeed make for the front door, as your one-eyed compatriot so eloquently put it.'

Stryker met the prince's gaze. Rupert seemed to be fidgeting in his saddle such was his unbridled excitement. 'May I ask as to your plans, General?'

Rupert offered another beaming grin, his neat white teeth bright beneath the sliding nasal bar of his Dutch-style pot helmet. 'Plans, Stryker? I plan to toast a great victory this evening. Find me after. We'll share a bottle, if the God-bothering stiffs ain't poured every drop o' drink in the Churn!'

'After, sir? We attack soon?'

'We do, we do. Carnarvon strikes to the north even now. We'll take the southern entrance while their heads are turned.'

Stryker frowned. 'Beg' pardon, General, but the southern defences are stout. Do you not require infantry to first clear that barricade? We . . .'

To Stryker's surprise, the young prince's eye twitched in conspiratorial wink. 'They say I use sorcery, Stryker.' He indicated the giant white poodle that stood, as ever, beside his horse. The dog had been a gift from Lord Arundell during the prince's time in an Austrian prison after the battle of Vlotho in 1638, and was now Rupert's constant shadow, even joining its master's often death-defying cavalry charges. 'They say Boye, here, is my familiar. Would you countenance such puritanical drivel?' Rupert laughed at the notion, though his sharp features hardened a fraction of a second later, his eyes darkening with a steely seriousness. 'Well today, Captain, I mean to show 'em some *real* magic! Look to the barricade!'

In moments the prince was gone, galloping away down the line, Boye in tow, to find his famed cavalry.

The drums sounded again.

Stryker turned to Forrester, noting the sheen of sweat that had already crept across his fellow captain's plump jowls despite the oppressive cold. 'That's our order to advance.'

Forrester upturned his pipe, letting the still-smoking contents litter the snow, and shook the proffered hand. 'God speed. I must see to my own lads. Once more unto the breach an' all that, what?' He stared back at The Barton, perhaps imagining the rows of muskets that must wait behind the piled wall. It seemed almost inevitable that those muskets would repel the cavalry charge with devastating ease, leaving the task of assault to his infantrymen. 'Rather wish there were a breach to assault.'

Stryker shrugged. 'Watch the barricade.'

Forrester shot him a wan smile. 'I'll watch it. By God I'll be watching nothing but.'

Stryker set his jaw, determination puckering the ragged tissue that covered his long-shattered eye socket. 'Fair you well, Forry.' He turned away. 'Sergeant!'

A tall man appeared from where he had been waiting patiently some distance behind the officers. His sinewy frame and weather-hewn face marked him as a seasoned winter campaigner. 'Sir!'

Stryker craned his neck up to look into the sergeant's face. 'Make them ready, Will. He'll send in his beloved horse first, but we'll sweep behind right enough.'

''Bout bleedin' time,' Sergeant William Skellen murmured.

'What was that?'

'Men'll have a grand old time, sir,' said Skellen, his

voice suddenly finding clarity in the crisp air. 'Armed and eager, Mister Stryker.'

Stryker jerked his head back towards the ranks of brown-coated infantry, pike files bristling, musketeers blowing on match-cords to prick bright holes in the gloomy day. 'Get on with it then, Sergeant.'

Skellen gave a curt nod and turned away.

'And Sergeant?'

Skellen looked back. 'Sir?'

'Try not to come back dead.'

The sergeant grinned ferociously, showing stumps of mottled amber. 'Never did yet, sir.'

The first cavalry units began to move. Of the four thousand men at Prince Rupert's disposal, the majority were harquebusiers, and they surged forward, raggedly at first, but soon forming into a great wave of armour and hooves as the charge gathered momentum.

Stryker watched the horsemen go, and he felt the land shake beneath his tall boots. He wished he could be in that great assault. But, as the elation of battle prickled along the nape of his neck and quickened his pulse, he bit it down savagely, forcing himself to focus on his own command. He knew them for hard, confident men, men who had followed him into the terrors below the ridge at Edgehill and had survived. Fifty-three musketeers, thirty-six pikemen, two commissioned officers, two sergeants, three corporals and two drummers: Stryker's company. Ninety-eight men that would take on the entire rebel army if he asked it of them.

'Ensign Chase!' Stryker bellowed at a stocky, full-bearded fellow standing at the front of the company.

'Hold that bloody colour high, man! Let 'em see who they face!'

Chase had not been Stryker's ensign long, but he knew his business well enough. With a powerful heave, he lofted the banner as high as he might, so that the square of red taffeta caught the breeze, its pair of white diamonds flickering taut and proud.

The dense swathe of horse was a hundred paces away now, charging inexorably towards the ominously robust barricade, and the Royalist infantry units to Stryker's flanks began to move. Colonel Mowbray was out in front, standing tall in bright stirrups, proudly urging his regiment to the fray. In turn, Stryker sucked air deep into his lungs and bellowed, 'Forward!'

The men of Sir Edmund Mowbray's Regiment of Foot took their first steps towards Cirencester.

'They have artillery, sir,' Burton, away to Stryker's left, chirped uncertainly.

Stryker snorted. 'They dragged their culverins over to pound Sudeley Castle. And their best crews, to boot. What they have left are half a dozen small pieces. Don't sound a deal more than drakes. It is not their guns you should fear, Lieutenant, but their bloody muskets poking at us from beyond that barricade.'

Burton's brow creased in consternation as he assessed the grim task ahead. 'Our horse will never break that.'

Stryker understood what he meant. It seemed as if the cavalry and infantry would take it in turn to hammer uselessly upon the thick barricade, only to be shot at by jeering defenders. And yet something in Rupert's nervous energy had infected him, made him dare to share in the young general's confidence.

'Have faith, Lieutenant.'

Burton briefly sketched a crucifix across his chest with his left arm, the right hanging uselessly in its strap. 'I do, sir. I do.'

Stryker grinned. 'Not in God, Burton. In Rupert.'

'Sir?' Burton seemed baffled.

'I believe the general has something hidden up one of those long sleeves of his.'

Burton said something in reply, but Stryker did not catch a single word for, in a single great, ear-splitting, earth-shuddering second, Cirencester vanished.

It was a matter of moments before the cavalry hit home. But they did not blunt their blades against the earthworks or hurl pathetic insults up at men safe behind the palisade. Instead, the horsemen whooped and cheered and screamed their thanks to God. They stood high in their stirrups and vanished into the red flame and black smoke that billowed about The Barton.

'Fuck me,' Sergeant Skellen said quietly from somewhere behind Stryker.

'A petard,' Stryker breathed. He was as astonished as every other man in the company.

'How the blazes did 'e get a petard in there?' Skellen replied.

'Magic,' Stryker replied softly, staring ahead. A mighty explosion had reduced the barricade to a jagged mass of gigantic splinters. And between those great, raw stakes streamed the exultant Royalist horsemen.

The company had slowed in the aftermath of the explosion, amazement breaking the usually measured stride, and Stryker blinked himself back to the duty at hand. He turned quickly, facing the stunned ranks as his tall boots kicked up the churned snow. 'Prince Rupert's in the town, lads! Do we join him inside?'

The men cheered, and the sergeants growled. Stryker drew his sword, a fine weapon of Spanish steel, with a swirling half-basket hilt to protect the hand, and a pommel decorated with a large, crimson garnet.

In less than a minute they were at the farm, following in the wake of the horsemen, searching for men to kill. But there were none. The defenders had fled with Rupert's exultant cavalrymen slashing at their backs. Those that remained were dead, blown to pieces by the initial explosion, and Stryker stepped over scorched limbs and splintered weapons as he led his company on.

Cirencester was a vision of hell. Bodies lay strewn in the streets, twisted and broken, blood freezing in pools beneath them, faces describing final, horrific moments. Some were clearly soldiers, the unfortunates Lord Stamford had left behind, but it was clear that many – rough-hewn clubs or kitchen utensils still clutched in stiffening fingers – were ordinary folk. Butchers and coopers and tanners and merchants. These were common men sucked into a war against their own kind. And not just men; to Stryker's right, emerging into view as he turned his head repeatedly to make full use of his one remaining eye, was the body of a woman. Stryker felt little sympathy, since the blood-gleaming scythe, held tight in a grotesquely curled hand, spoke plainly of her willingness to defy the Royalist attackers. But her waxen features and golden hair reminded him of Lisette. His stomach turned.

This lapse angered Stryker and he swore bitterly. 'On!' he snarled, and the company surged forwards, picking their way across the obstacles of rubble and flesh. It soon became clear there were no enemies to confront. Rupert's lightning charge had had the desired effect. The soldiers and townsfolk manning the initial defences had fallen back into the muddy streets that scored the town, narrow tributaries of the impressive Market Place at Cirencester's heart, a gigantic cobbled spider in a web of roads and alleys.

Hooves sounded, the ground vibrating beneath Stryker's feet, and from the direction of the town centre, a place still hidden from Stryker's view by Cirencester's close-cropped buildings, came the cavalrymen who had inflicted such damage in that opening assault. This time, though, those men were not yelling in victory, nor standing triumphantly in their stirrups.

A harquebusier came near. One gloved fist gripped a long cavalry sword, blood tracing its way in gleaming beads from tip to hilt, while the other snapped expertly at his mount's reins, jerking the beast's muscular neck round to regroup with his troop. Stryker hailed him, but the man paid no heed, absorbed as he was in the moment.

He knew the horseman would probably hear nothing above the rush of his own pulse, a rhythmic, persistent waterfall flowing hard within his skull, but Stryker wanted information. He reached up to take the horse's bridle in a cold hand. The animal responded by turning fractionally towards him, and the trooper's face instantly clouded.

'Damn your pox'n ballocks, you bliddy plodder,' the trooper snarled, his right arm instinctively lifting the long sword in furious reaction.

'Captain Stryker, Mowbray's,' Stryker barked quickly, hoping his action would not result in a cleaved scalp.

The trooper faltered, blade easing to his side. ''Pardon, Cap'n, sir.'

Stryker did not know whether it was his rank that had cooled the horseman's ire, or his name. Nor did he care. 'No matter. What news, man?'

The trooper stared down at him, chest heaving as he regained composure after what had evidently been a hot fight. 'Buggers are 'oled up good 'n proper, sir.'

'Holed up? They have barricades?'

The trooper snorted ruefully. 'Harrows, sir. Big buggers, stretched 'cross all the roads into the square. And plenty else. Bastards are on the thatches an' up the church tower. Shootin' at our fuckin' heads, sir!'

'Jesus,' Stryker whispered, releasing the bridle. Forrester's assessment of pitchfork-wielding peasants might have been accurate, but they were peasants ready and willing to fight. And fight hard. A harrow may have been more typically seen on a farm, but the heavy, spiked chains were lethal barriers for horses to negotiate.

'Mowbray's!' Another voice snapped sharp and crisp above the din of the milling Royalist infantry. 'Mowbray's, to me! Form up!'

Stryker saw it was his commanding officer, Sir Edmund. The armour-clad colonel had finally managed to negotiate the dense mass of men still pouring from the direction of The Barton and was now cantering his grey gelding to the head of his regiment. The silver-streaked auburn of his hair and beard shone bright above the dark-coated infantrymen, a beacon his men might follow. The colonel would never consider the fact that his appearance, and pale horse, would also draw the eye of a potential sniper.

'Cavalry are stalling, sir,' Stryker bellowed at Mowbray.

Sir Edmund caught the familiar voice and scanned the mass of men for sight of his second captain. 'Stalling? Why? We're goddamned through!'

'Chained harrows, sir.'

Mowbray paused as thoughts raced through his mind. He fixed Stryker with a hard stare. 'Take your boys, Captain." He pointed to where the cavalryman had come. 'Take 'em down that road and find those harrows. The general has cutters, but he'll need covering fire.'

The sharp reports of musket fire carried to Stryker's ears as he led the way. The road curved to the right and, as it finally began to straighten, the company saw the full horror of their task. Up ahead was Market Place, the vast parish church of St John looming beside it. It was here that the rebels would make their final stand. And it was here that they had draped their vicious harrows from one side of the street to the other.

Stryker saw Prince Rupert standing tall in silver stirrups, bellowing orders, desperate to break through the unexpected obstacles. If Mowbray was right and the prince's men had brought cutting tools, then they would probably make light work of the harrows, but how could they hope to get close enough to conduct the task?

Muskets coughed from the thatches all around Market Place, spitting deadly venom down towards the attackers The range was far enough that their bullets did not find a mark, but it kept the Royalists at bay.

'Musketeers!' Stryker ordered, and the men wielding

primed long-arms hastened to the front of the company. 'Get up to that bloody harrow and give fire. The horse'll deal with the chains if you cover their heads.'

The montero-capped musketeers surged forward, splitting to the left and right of the street, until they were up against the harrow. From there they aimed their weapons into the great open space that was Market Place, finding targets amongst the wooden barricades and up in the windows that looked out upon the town centre.

Prince Rupert surged forward, waving his own men on, for they knew their work would be unhindered as soon as Mowbray's infantrymen opened fire.

'Cut that bloody chain, God damn you! Cut that bloody chain!' Rupert thundered, eyes wild, sword-tip tracing manic circles above his head.

The musketeers gave fire. It was no ordered volley, but then this was not open battle. It was hard, vicious street fighting that required nothing more than guts and brutality.

Sure enough, the rebel fire seemed to ebb in the face of this new assault. Perhaps Mowbray's men had found their marks, or perhaps the enemy snipers possessed little skill and ancient weapons.

The harrow was cut. The chains fell. Rupert and his horsemen surged through like avenging angels. They fanned out, picking off the easiest prey first, leaving the bulk of the rebels at the centre of the open ground.

'A gift for us, is it?' Sergeant Skellen droned to Stryker's right.

Stryker ignored him. He ran forward, jumping the pile of cut chains that had been hitherto so formidable. He shouted at his men, and knew they were at his back as he burst through to sweep the final defenders aside. But those defenders did not know when they were beaten, and they strode out from behind their makeshift shields – wagons and barrels and table-tops and wooden chests – to meet the Royalists, and Stryker's men, bolstered now by Mowbray's other companies, slammed into them.

It might have been the fairmeadow below Edgehill, the barricades of Old Brentford, or the killing fields of Lutzen. It was always the same: always melee; always chaos. Pick a man, bring him down, move on. Cut, thrust, parry, slash. The natural rhythm of men groomed in warfare.

Skellen was there. Stryker could not see him in the mass of snarling faces and slashing weaponry, but he heard his guttural roar and knew the halberd would be scything a path through the enemy for others to follow.

A woman was on her knees, cradling a man's head in her blood-drenched hands, and Stryker stepped over her, deaf to her wails. A youngster came at him, no more than a boy, toting a thick table leg that had already seen action, judging by its scarred surface and bloody sheen. Stryker ducked the wild swipe, ducked the reverse swing and jammed the ornate hilt of his sword into the lad's mouth. He heard teeth smash, felt the wet spray of fresh blood course across his fingers, saw the boy fall to his knees. Stryker cursed, for a bloody hilt was no aid to effective swordsmanship. He kicked the boy in the face and moved quickly on.

Mowbray's men enjoyed massively superior numbers and already the defenders were beginning to thin. Many lay where they had fought, while others took flight into the surrounding alleys, only to be tracked down like foxes by Rupert's huntsmen.

'You men!' a shout came from somewhere to the rear, and Stryker turned to see Lancelot Forrester, red-faced and sweating like a roast hog, hailing a group of his men. 'Get up in that fucking church, Tobin! Clear out those blasted snipers!'

The day was won. Rupert's vast force had ultimately swamped Cirencester's courageous but outnumbered defenders and, from the moment The Barton's barricade had been blown, their victory was assured.

Some of the conquering soldiers were already looting. Stryker saw one of his own pikemen lay down his weapon and crouch beside one of Lord Stamford's fallen men. Ordinarily he would not frown upon the practice of emptying a vanquished enemy's pockets, but the fight had not finished, and he suddenly felt a surge of anger. He strode over and kicked the pikeman hard in the ribs, snarling a furious rebuke.

All around them Cirencester began to burn. Some of the houses had been subjected to grenadoes, the small incendiaries tossed through windows and doors where snipers were suspected. Other buildings were fired as a simple means of instilling terror into the townsfolk. Stryker stared at the fires, watching the burgeoning flames lap indiscriminately at thatches and beams.

The rebel came unseen from the direction of the church, darting from its shadows, across Market Place and barrelling into Stryker, sending them both to the hard cobbles. Stryker was first to recover, but found he was without his sword, for his grip on the slippery hilt had failed him. The blade went skittering away and he had no time to retrieve it, for his assailant was quickly on his feet, holding out a broad-bladed knife, teeth bared in a grimace of pure hatred.

The man was young, his body thin, his clothes those of a peasant, and fury had transformed him into a formidable opponent.

The man came at him in a series of arcing swipes and Stryker swayed out of the weapon's reach, stepping ever backwards. But luck was not on his side, and his heels met, perhaps inevitably, with a prone body. His balance gone, Stryker was sent tumbling backwards, clattering onto the ice-cold cobbles for the second time, and the townsman was upon him, stabbing down with all the force he could muster.

Stryker was not heavily muscled like some of his pikemen, but he was stronger than most. He fended off the wild young man, gripping at wrists and at the throat, scrabbling at eyes, anything to put the man off his killing stride, but one stab made it through his desperate defence. One blow, clean and hard, found the flesh of his left shoulder. He felt the blood pulse warm and steaming down his arm, and for a moment he thought he saw death approaching, but the youth, even in his second of triumph, had frozen. His eyes were locked on the wound he had inflicted, his hands were rooted at the blade's hilt, unable to draw it from his victim.

'Never seen blood before?' Stryker hissed, and launched upwards, pulverising the man's face with his forehead. The blow sent fresh pain streaking through Stryker's own skull, blurring his vision, but the weight suddenly lifted from him and he was able to scramble to his feet. When the mist cleared, he saw the youth was lying flat on his back, nose gushing crimson, eyelids fluttering feebly.

'Christ's robes, Stryker!' Forrester appeared at Stryker's side.

465

Stryker followed his friend's gaze, only to find a pair of iron shears protruding from the flesh of his shoulder. 'Not pitchforks, Forry,' he said quietly, jerking the unlikely weapon free with a wince and a fresh spout of blood, 'but you weren't far off.'

Read more . . .

Jack Hight

SIEGE

It will be Christendom's last stand . . .

The year is 1453. For more than a thousand years the mighty walls of Constantinople have protected the capital of the Eastern Roman Empire, the furthest outpost of Christianity. But now endless ranks of Turkish warriors cover the plains before them, their massive cannons trained on the ramparts. It is the most fearsome force the world has ever seen. No European army will help: the last crusaders were cut to pieces by the Turks on the plains of Kosovo. Constantinople is on its own. And treachery is in the air.

From the intrigues within the Emperor's household to the Sultan's harem and the savage fights on the battlements, *Siege* is a full-blooded historical adventure novel.

'This is an ambitious book, written on an ambitious scale, offering a fascinating picture of momentous events' *Daily Mail*

Order your copy now by calling Bookpoint on 01235 827716 or visit your local bookshop quoting ISBN 978-1-84854-296-9
www.johnmurray.co.uk

Read more . . .

James Jackson

REALM

England's hour of peril . . .

1588. In Lisbon the great Spanish Armada stands ready. In the Low Countries the forces of the Duke of Parma prepare for war. And in the shadows an even greater game is underway – a game of espionage and murder, treachery and deceit, played with the stiletto-blade, the poisoned chalice, the torturer's rack . . .

Faced with such deadly foes, legendary spymaster Sir Francis Walsingham sends young Christian Hardy to discover the truth. But as one by one his agents vanish, time is running out – for Hardy, for England, and for its sovereign Queen Elizabeth.

Order your copy now by calling Bookpoint on 01235 827716 or visit your local bookshop quoting ISBN 978-1-84854-003-3 www.johnmurray.co.uk